CW00536106

Nick Heddle

Simon: a Decline and Fall of the English Landed Gentry

Published by

An Imprint of Melrose Press Limited
St Thomas Place, Ely
Cambridgeshire
CB7 4GG, UK
www.melrosebooks.com

FIRST EDITION

Cover designed by Nick Heddle
FLANDRIN, Hippolyte, Jeune homme nu assis au bord de la mer.
(Nude Youth Sitting by the Sea). 1836
Paris, Musée du Louvre © RMN/© Daniel Arnaudet

ISBN: 978-1-906561-01-7

Printed and bound in Great Britain by:
CPI Antony Rowe, Chippenham, Wiltshire

For Michael, Simon and Guy

For Michael, Simon and Guy

Chapter 1

2001 – A Service Area beside the M1 Motorway

The temperature gauge on the dashboard had shot up into the red. Clearly the fan belt had snapped again. Dominic turned the old Land Rover off the M1 into the motorway service area to try to find a new one. But someone would have to stay behind because none of the doors would lock. Everything seemed to be going wrong at once. In the twenty–first century, Land Rovers didn't have fan belts any more. What hope was there of finding one to fit something which had come out of the factory in 1958?

I said I would stay behind to stop anyone stealing our belongings from the back. Dominic would go and talk to the people at the service station. Simon and Harry would go to the cafe for something to eat and bring me a takeaway later. We might have to wait for the AA if a new fan belt was not available. So I sat in the passenger's seat and looked out of the window. Somewhere in the car park a security alarm had gone off. Nobody took any notice whatever and just walked past. A young man came by. He put his foot up on the bumper of the Land Rover to tie his shoelace. He couldn't see me because of the sun on the windscreen. I watched, spellbound. His long hair rippled in the breeze. He wore a vest and shorts like Simon did so many years ago. Unlike most youngsters today, he was well–built and strong. I tried to imagine him naked, without a stitch of clothing, like Simon when he was a hunky 23–year–old. Suddenly my daydream was shattered. A child ran up carrying an ice cream shouting, 'Daddy, it's melting!' The young man grabbed the ice cream, licked it and led the infant away by the other hand.

The car park was full. We had been lucky to find the last space by the perimeter fence. That's where I saw it. Not far away, on the side of this fence, in the overgrown field, was an old tumbledown barn. I gazed at it. Somehow it seemed to be familiar. The roof had disappeared. The end wall had collapsed except for one part which still supported an ornate weather vane, rusty now and still pointing north. I reached for the binoculars and focussed them. There it was – Simon's family crest still emblazoned on top of the weather vane. Suddenly it all came back to me – the snowstorm which was so heavy it even brought down the roof of the west wing of his ancestral home.

So below us, under the concrete of the car park beside the M1 must lie the foundations of the estate, the home farm, the chapel and the baroque palace. I stared at the family crest in disbelief. Two griffins rampant over a Latin motto I had long since forgotten. This tumbledown barn had survived, like the last bastion of the English landed gentry, in defiance of the decades of neglect and the compulsory purchase order imposed by the Ministry of Transport back in 1958. The new M1 had simply cut a slice through the valley. The heritage of England had been worth nothing when compared with Britain's need for the London to Leeds motorway, the trendsetting M1. So under the concrete of this motorway service area also lay the hopes and aspirations of Simon's father, his grandfather and generations going back to King Henry VIII and the dissolution of the monasteries. Alas, poor England! Oh decline and fall! The words which Simon's brother Harry had muttered about the two of us came back to me like an echo from the past. Over forty years ago ...Yes, that really was over forty years ago when I was still living in Cumbria or Cumberland as it used to be called in those days...

1957

My life had become nothing more than an episode of 'The Archers'. I listened to it on the radio sometimes but my wife could not stand it. Now it was milking time once again. As I unhooked my brown coat from the back of the door I took another look at the picture postcard I had pinned there. It was from the Louvre in Paris and showed Flandrin's classic painting of a gorgeous, naked young man sitting by the seashore in 1836. I removed the drawing pin so I could have a closer look by the window at this painting. The rock this Adonis sat on appeared to be some height above the waves because the artist showed a rocky island jutting out of the sea in the distance. Did it predict his destiny? Was it there to represent the trials and tribulations of his adult life to come? The youth's head was perched on his knees while his strong arms hugged his beautiful legs. His curly black hair extended in the suggestion of sideburns around his ear. What was he thinking, I wondered? Was he resting after an exhausting night of passion in bed? Whose bed? Had it all been worth it? Perhaps he was in despair. I had often wondered. Was he about to dive off the rock into the depths below, to which his toes pointed jutting suggestively over the edge of the rock? I ran my finger along the picture on the postcard, imagining what it would be like to touch such a fabulous young man, instead of a wife who went frigid as soon as I even looked at her. But how could I have known that someone even more beautiful and erotic than this young man was about to walk into my life that very day and stay for the next forty years?

Every day for the last few years I got up to milk the cows at six o'clock. The lorry would be stopping at the end of the lane to collect the shiny metal churns by mid–morning. I was listening to the weather forecast on the radio over the doorway of the milking parlour. We could do with a spell of dry weather. The Lake District had had too much rain over the last twelve months. Now I had grown to like this daily routine. I never thought I would enjoy milking–time. But I was fond of the cows. At least they didn't argue as much as my wife indoors.

"Steady now Mildred!"

I stooped down to have a look at her udder. The ulcer was still there. The vet must come again. More expense to add to my woes. My father–in–law had just died in Manchester and my wife was going to stay with my mother–in–law until the funeral. But how could I possibly leave the cows? Another row... I would be on my own for a couple of weeks. I switched off the milking machine and undid the chain so Mildred could back out of the stall. She was the last, so I turned on the tap to wash the place down with the hose. My wife appeared at the door.

"I'm off," she said. "Your breakfast is getting cold on the table. I did call you."

"The weather forecast was on. I couldn't hear you."

"Men! ... I don't know why women bother sometimes..."

She turned to go and start the car. No kiss, no goodbye. That's what our marriage had become. She never did like the country – a town lass, my Elspeth. Marrying a farmer had been her biggest mistake. She hated the daily grind, the mud, the smells and all the rain. I suppose we could sell up but land prices were depressed in 1957. The farm would be difficult to sell. Our neighbours in the next farm had started to take in paying guests but I couldn't see Elspeth making beds, picking up cigarette ends and getting breakfast for even more people.

I heard the car go off down the lane and went back to the kitchen. The scrambled egg was stone cold so I scooped it up and put it on a tin over the hotplate on the Aga. The teapot was lukewarm so I tipped the contents down the sink and got out the Camp Coffee. Oh what a life! Then the postman banged on the window.

"Morning, George."

"More bills, sir," he laughed.

"Will the weather dry up today, do you think? What does your crystal ball say?"

"It hasn't worked for years... A bit like our telly."

"That hasn't gone phut again!"

"Last night – in the middle of 'Radio Newsreel.' I think all this bad news was too much for it."

I laughed. At least George was good for a giggle – anyway, more than Elspeth these days. The postman got back on his bicycle and went off down the lane. It was time to wind up the little grey 'Fergie'. This tractor had been my father's pride and joy. It was the first he ever owned but it looked sad and neglected now – everything was covered in mud. It was time to shift the muck from the end of the barn. I slipped the gearbox into reverse and backed it out of the garage.

I stopped by the hay barn to see how the owl was getting on. 'Wol', we called it, after the character in Winnie the Pooh. Only this owl had reared chicks and I could hear them cheeping in the nest on the wall up in the loft as I climbed up the ladder. The noise stopped for a while so I stood still and waited. There was a flutter and the adult bird stared at me through the cobwebs. I started to climb higher up the old wooden ladder and caught a splinter in my thumb. In the gloom I tried to pick it out but only managed to snap off the end of the splinter. This had happened before and I had ended up having it cut out at the cottage hospital.

"Damn!"

I stuck my thumb in my mouth and tried to suck the splinter out. It wasn't a good day at all.

"Hello!"

There was a noise in the yard outside. I climbed down the ladder again to find a backpacker standing outside in the rain. The yellow oilskin hid his face.

"The youth hostel's up there," I said, in a rather bad–tempered way, pointing up the lane with my throbbing thumb.

"Could I buy some milk?" he asked. "And do you have any bread?"

"The village store will be open at nine."

I walked over to him. He turned, pulled the hood away from his face,wiped the rain away from his eyes and smiled. I was stunned. The ache in my thumb suddenly faded away. Such male beauty was rare – worthy of an oil painting in the Louvre. The rain had made his long hair wet so it stuck around his face. One saw pictures of women models like this in fashion magazines but I'd never seen a young man like him before. His beauty was natural and honest, without the need for make–up or expensive haute couture.

"Nice weather for walking in the hills," he said, looking up at the grey clouds.

"You on holiday?"

"I thought it was time to get away from London."

"Is it raining there too?"

"No, the sun was shining when I left on Monday."

I laughed. He smiled and suddenly the sun seemed to appear for a moment. I was captivated already and my thumb had stopped throbbing.

"Look," I said. "Come in. I'm making a fresh pot of tea. I expect we've got some bread in the larder – it may not be all that fresh. Anyway, we'll see."

We walked across the yard to the house, where the young man started to undo his boots at the door. While he was bending down I looked him over. He was slim and muscular with curves in all the right places. But I'd always been straight and conventional. I'd resigned myself to the traditional attractions of women. I'd said yes at the altar to marriage with Elspeth...How could I be sexually attracted to someone like him already?

He was struggling with a knotted bootlace.

"Oh don't worry about that."

"I'll leave them here all the same," he said, taking off his oilskin cape and shaking it outside.

"Bring everything in to put around the stove," I suggested. "That's what I do. My wife always complains but she's gone off today so it doesn't matter."

He laughed. The telephone was ringing in the hall and I hurried out to answer it. The dairy was phoning to say the milk lorry would be late today so could we keep the churns out of the sun until noon. "What sun?" I asked. They'd be lucky. "Was there any news about our latest tuberculin test?" We had always prided ourselves on the TB–free status for our cows. They couldn't tell me about the lab test yet. I put down the phone. I'd been talking on the phone longer than I had expected. It wasn't a good idea to leave a complete stranger alone in the kitchen – not that there was much to steal in our house. I went back in the kitchen to find the backpacker leaning against the Aga waiting for the kettle to boil on the hotplate. Cups and saucers had been arranged on the table. He'd found everything somehow.

"The stove could do with more coal," I said. "Have a look in the scuttle, will you?"

"Why don't you get an electric kettle?"

"The wiring just wouldn't cope. We have enough trouble with the electrics already. My wife's hairdryer usually blows the fuse. The heavy–duty cable only goes as far as the milking parlour. We got a government grant for that but then the money ran out."

He smiled again. I was growing to like him already. He couldn't have been a lot younger than me. He took a look in the coal scuttle.

"It's empty ... Shall I go and get some more?"

"Well, it's outside in the old wash house. And take a look at that sheepdog out there, will you? She's about to have puppies."

He opened the back door.

"Ok, I'll do that... Look, the sun's just come out. "

He put his boots back on again and went out. I sat down at the table to open the letters. But I was not able to concentrate on the post. It was as if a beautiful angel had suddenly walked in. This young man had brought a vision of another world – a world of sublime beauty, classical proportions, sunshine and grace – everything that was missing in my life. I gazed at the letters. There was an invoice from the garage after they patched up the dent on the Land Rover and a circular from the Ministry of Agriculture, Fisheries and Food. I screwed that up and tossed it in the Aga. The young man soon reappeared with the coal scuttle. He'd rolled up his sleeves to reveal arms you'd see on a classical statue like one of those in the British Museum.

"You lift the lid, here," I said, grabbing the hot handle with the oven glove.

He poured the coal on the fire and I closed the lid again. I caught a whiff of 'Old Spice.' He smiled again. It was as if his whole face suddenly lit up. I was entranced.

"Are you a student?"

"I'm doing nuclear engineering ... It is a new course."

"What college is that? Or is it something to do with the government?"

"It is a degree course at London University."

We sat down at the table while the kettle started to heat up.

"So what do you want to do when you qualify as an engineer? ... I mean for a living. Research? Or are you going to make bigger atom bombs?"

I suddenly thought I might have said the wrong thing but he saw the joke and we both laughed as I pointed at the picture on the front of the 'Daily Mail', which lay unopened on the table. There was the photograph of an enormous mushroom cloud above the latest British atom bomb test.

"No idea. I haven't got that far yet. I'm more interested in peaceful applications for nuclear energy like making electricity. The future of electrical engineering is what interests me. I wanted to see Calder Hall nuclear power station for myself – you know the one the Queen opened up here in October last year. I think it will be the first of many and bigger nuclear power stations all over the world..."

"Is that a three–year course you're doing in London?"

He nodded and smiled again. I suddenly realised my life had always been missing something special that I'd never found until now. But how could I make him stay?

"Well," I said. "There's plenty of work up here. This house hasn't been rewired since 1935 when the power lines first arrived in the village. I can just remember it. The old oil lamps got put away in the cupboard. I grew up here, you see. Suddenly, you could walk in a room and switch on a light. Then we knew progress had really arrived. My mother went out and bought that radio set over there. Mr Churchill used to talk on it during the war... We will fight them on the beaches! My God, my father thought the Germans would be sailing on Lake Windermere by Christmas 1940."

We looked at one another. Our eye contact was already communicating on another more intimate plane than this casual conversation.

"Thank goodness it never came to that," he said. "Are your folk still around?"

"No, not now."

The kettle started to boil. He got up to make the tea. I couldn't take my eyes off him. He was still wearing his waterproof over–trousers. I wanted to see more – a lot more. He turned round.

"Do you mind if I use the loo?"

I smiled and pointed at the door opposite in the hallway. He went in but did not shut the door. I stared in amazement as he pulled down his waterproofs and pants and stood there with his back to me apparently not caring if I watched or not. His thighs were muscular, his buttocks beautifully rounded. His back tapered to a slender waist. I just stared. Tattooed in black letters above his buttocks were the letters AC / DC. He turned to the basin and washed his hands. I just stared at this Adonis. Here was Hippolyte Flandrin's nude male figure but even more sexy and curvaceous.

"I'm going to change out of these wet things," he said, taking off his jumper. The shirt he lifted off next. I leaned back on the kitchen table, now convinced this strip routine was for my benefit. He stooped down to pull off his socks and turned with his back to me again.

"Could you pass me my backpack? I'm going to change out of all these wet things. I'm soaked to the skin. "

I fetched his backpack from the porch outside while he returned to the kitchen. There was a big wasp crawling inside the glass. I tried to get rid of it but finally crushed it with a shoe. When I returned the young man was completely naked, now leaning back on the kitchen table where I had been moments before. I couldn't help staring. He was, quite simply, the most beautiful creature I had ever seen in my life. As I stared, he smiled back. A shaft of sunlight from the window fell across his body, emphasising his muscular torso. Here was a vision so intense that it felt like an epiphany of religious dimensions like James Joyce might have described in his 'Portrait of the Artist as a Young Man'. I was staring at a living work of art. What struck me in particular was his beautiful skin, hairless and entirely free of blemishes – not a mole nor a single spot of acne, as if painted in oils by the artist, omitting any distraction from this divine vision of virile masculine perfection. I wanted this moment to last forever but the sun disappeared behind a cloud and the revelation was gone. He smiled at me again as I put the pack down beside him. I still remember the smell of him – young, athletic, firm, muscular, male flesh. It was magical and I was entranced. As I got up he put one hand on my shoulder as if to steady me. I put a hand on his hip and felt an electric shock, like brushing against the electric fence I used to keep the cows out of the new pasture. Did he feel it too?...

"Please will you do something else for me?" he asked... "I mean as a special favour."

He looked at me seductively under his long eyelashes.

"Anything!"

"Will you give me a hug?...I need to feel wanted… I need a cuddle now, please."

It was the first time I'd ever put my arms around a naked young man. In turn he put his arms around me. I ran my hands down his back and he took a deep breath. But then, the most amazing thing occurred. He started to sob on my shoulder. I tried to look at his face. He clung to me much harder.

"No!...No! ...Please don't push me away! ...I need …!"

I put my arms around him again and remained silent. It was as if something mystical was happening between us – a kind of bonding ritual so ancient and intense that words were not possible. Were our hearts learning to beat in synchronism as we swayed gently to and fro on the edge of the table? We stayed like that for ages, just holding each other until his sobbing stopped. Slowly he got up from the table so I could clutch his buttocks. He sat in my hands and put his legs around me as well. Now he leaned back and then his face suddenly lit up in the most wonderful smile. It is such an amazing thing in life when a private fantasy suddenly comes true. Here was Hippolyte

Flandrin's naked young man, now come to life and sitting in my hands. How could I have known, then, how important he would become? I'd found my other half. That was the start of it all, so many years ago. Afterwards, we sat at the table holding hands, just staring at one another, but saying nothing at all. Was I about to wake up from some erotic dream?

Suddenly my thumb started hurting again. He had been sitting on it. The splinter would have to come out. I looked at it closely.

"Let me see that…" the young man said.

He took hold of my hand and gazed at my thumb closely.

"I've got a razor blade in my backpack. I could sterilise it and cut this out…."

Instead, he put my thumb in his mouth and seemed to rub his tongue gently around the splinter. After this morning's experience this became immensely erotic. I just stared at him. He took my thumb out of his mouth.

"Saliva is a good antibiotic…and it helps to soften the skin." I lay back in the chair unable to believe what was going on while he continued to massage my splinter with his tongue. Was this a prelude to penetrative sex? Gently he started to nibble my thumb with his teeth. I felt the splinter shift a bit. He took my thumb out of his mouth again, stared at it closely, and gripped the splinter between his fingernails. Out it came. As simple as that!

"There!"

He held it out for me to see. I looked at my thumb, which had started to bleed. He put it back in his mouth and sucked it again. If only Elspeth could have seen me now! With my other hand I ran grateful fingers through his beautiful hair. This was ecstasy. He smiled at me again – another of those unforgettable smiles in which his whole face lit up. Within only a couple of hours of her departure, I was in love already.

2001

Memories! I stared at the weather vane on top of the remains of the old barn at the other side of the fence around the motorway service area. 1957 seemed so very long ago. First the years, then the decades started to fly by. But I was so happy to spend them with Simon. My disastrous marriage to Elspeth now seemed like an old nightmare, fortunately fading with the years. I climbed back into the Land Rover. It was ancient although usually reliable but parts were starting to wear out, like the fan belt, the door locks and the exhaust system. So I sat and waited, staring out of the window. The security alarm from a car parked somewhere suddenly stopped. At last I could hear the distant roar of traffic on the motorway and the birds in the trees. There seemed to be so many more birds in the sky back in 1957. I remembered the rooks which circled the neighbouring churchyard, our owls in the barn where we had a hayloft and the seabirds which followed the plough. Life seemed to be so much simpler then, back in the good old days.

But were they really so good? I knew nothing other than a sham and barren marriage to my wife Elspeth and the sure knowledge that one day on the farm would be the same as the day before. That is, until Simon walked into my life.

1957

So Simon and I sat in the kitchen together. All I could do was stare at him. He stared back at me as if viewing the depths of my soul. Suddenly his unspoken thoughts seemed to be coming out into the open. It was obvious to him that I was sporting an enormous erection. I could hide it no longer.

"Do you think you could love someone like me?…." he asked eventually.

I continued to stare at him, not knowing what to say.

"…..Well, could you?"

"But we've only just met… What do you think?"

"Just give it time. But, I know…I could love you …yes, really…if you want me."

I had been thinking about sex and now he was talking about love. I was at a loss to know what to say next. My aching thumb reminded me of the tin of bandages in the bedroom. It was time to change the subject. So I asked him if he would like me to show him around the place while the tea was brewing. The stone farmhouse was small and old–fashioned but he admired the views from all the windows. We stood side by side in the dormer window and I put my hand on his shoulder. He put his arm around my waist. We were already behaving like a married couple. Gently he wrapped the plaster around my wounded finger and then he kissed it. I felt numb.

"Nice, these Agas," he said, returning to pour out the tea in the kitchen. "My folk have one too. Ours runs on gas."

He came back to the table and sat down while I watched and relaxed. He seemed to be part of the place already.

"What were you going to do today?" I asked, glancing out of the window as the rain started again and blew against the glass outside.

"I thought I might walk down into Coniston."

"Well, I need to go down there in the Land Rover later. I'll give you a lift. It'll save you getting wet again. Perhaps you could give me a hand with the sacks of feedstuff from the dealer."

"Ok."

He got up to pour more hot water in the teapot.

"Shall I get rid of this scrambled egg here? It seems somewhat dried up."

I laughed. He was poking at it suspiciously with a fork.

"My wife left that before she went off this morning. I just couldn't face it. Well, there are more eggs, bacon and sausages in the larder. Why don't you cook something fresh for both of us?"

"Ok."

"Look," I said. "I don't even know your name."

"Simon."

He smiled just as the telephone started to ring outside again. I got up, pointed at the larder and went out into the hall. It was the same woman from the dairy again. The milk lorry had broken down somewhere and was waiting for the garage to tow it away for repairs. The dairy would send another in due course but couldn't say what time it would arrive. But, she said, they'd just got our tuberculin test results and our cows were still all clear. I smiled. At least this was one bit of good news. I was still a bit concerned about that ulcer on Mildred's udder. But at least it wasn't tuberculosis.

"Good news, Simon," I said.

He looked up from the frying pan on the Aga. His shorts revealed the most beautiful pair of legs I'd ever seen on a man. They were shapely and muscular with a fine coat of fair hair. In a state of wild imagination I thought of snuggling next to them in bed. I wanted to hold him again – to feel his pulse race and to hear his heart pounding.

"What good news?"

"Oh...yes...Our TB test results are clear. That's a weight off my mind. Where's this fry–up, then?"

I sat down at the table and started tapping the knife on the plate. I just could not understand how anybody could casually walk into my life like this and change it so that it would never be the same again. I knew that already but I could not have known we would still be together over forty years later.

"Do you want fried bread as well?"

Simon put the plate down in front of me. This looked really good. He'd found tomatoes to fry from somewhere. There were fried mushrooms as well. Elspeth really hated them. He never found those in the larder.

"Where did you find these?" I asked, sitting down in Elspeth's place.

"My rucksack. I got them in Windermere yesterday. They needed eating up."

There was a flash of lightning outside the window and the electric light over our heads flickered, dimmed and went out.

"Well Simon, now you know why we don't have an electric kettle."

"Does this happen very often?"

I nodded.

"We're right at the end of the power cables. They stretch for miles over the hillside. One flash of lightning and that's it... as you see... So why can't you engineers do something about it? This is 1957 after all. What happened to the white heat of technology and all that sort of thing?"

"We do... to prevent ten million volts of electricity flowing down your domestic supply and through your radio set, over there." He laughed. "It must have triggered the emergency cut–out. Electrical engineers are only human when faced with an act of God like a lightning strike. Anyway, why blame me? It would be better to talk to the vicar in your local church over there, I think."

I laughed too. I hadn't shared a joke with Elspeth for as long as I could remember.

"Toast?"

We smiled at one another – one of those deep, erotic smiles with which we communicated so much that was still unsaid, back in those early days.

"How are you with a toasting fork?" I asked, pointing at the electric toaster on the shelf. "Well, that thing's not going to work now, is it? God has put the mockers on that for sure!"

I reached for my mother's old brass toasting fork, which still hung where she left it, hanging from a hook beside the fireplace, and passed it to Simon. Accidentally my hand brushed his arm. Again, I felt a more powerful electric shock as my arm retracted. Maybe I had knocked the wound where the splinter had been. It was just like grabbing hold of the electric fence we used in the field to stop the cows eating too much grass. I should have known. It was a milestone in my life... I had found my significant other as he became known forty years later.

"Huh!...What was that?"

Did he feel it too? He slid a slice of bread on the end of the toasting fork. We sat quietly for a while. Then we glanced at one another again. I could tell. He knew already. Would he get up and go or would he stay?

"So," I said, "Why Coniston in the rain? Why not wait until tomorrow? The sun might come out."

He passed me the toast on the end of the fork and placed another slice on the end for himself. This was fun. Elspeth just shoved bread in the toaster. But I was already starting to ask myself more fundamental questions. Had my marriage been a mistake?

"I'll go and have another look at the dog," he said. "She seems to be in a bad way. My mother used to breed pedigree poodles. I've seen this sort of thing before. The bitch stops eating and gets too weak to give birth properly. Once the puppies are born she may not have enough milk. Has the vet been yet?"

"Too expensive," I sighed.

"But you can't let her suffer like that. It's cruel."

"My father would have shot her with his shotgun, just to put her out of her misery. You can't be too sentimental down on the farm."

"Well, I'll try giving her some milk," he said, picking up the milk jug.

He got up and went back to the wash house. I got out some paperwork for the Inland Revenue, sat down with it in the easy chair by the stove and stared blankly into the air. Even my thumb had stopped throbbing. I seemed to be drifting away, suddenly relieved of all worries and stress now Elspeth had gone, and just drifted off to sleep. I still remember that dream. I was being led by the hand along a very long corridor. I couldn't see the face of the person I was following until we came to a doorway. That's when he turned. It was Simon. He pushed the door open. Beyond was an open field. The sun was shining. Buttercups and daisies with occasional red poppies made a carpet as far as the eye could see. I suddenly felt happy and free of some immense burden. Skylarks were singing above us. I knew I had never been so happy.

"Look at this, now!"

I woke up suddenly. It was getting dark. Simon came into the kitchen with a puppy under each arm. Old English sheepdogs – the real McCoy. He passed me one.

"She went into labour while you were asleep. It all happened so quickly... There were five...but one died. It must have been the runt. I tried the massage technique my mother used with the poodles but it didn't work..."

The puppy was licking my finger.

"It wants milk," I said. "How's the mother?"

"Cleaning them all."

"Well that's a good sign."

"Have you got a bottle anywhere – like the ones farmers use for orphan lambs?"

I got up out of the chair and followed him to the old wash house. The mother dog was now suckling three puppies. She looked exhausted. I stooped down over the pen and tickled her ear and she licked my finger. Simon put his hand on my shoulder. I felt another tingle.

"They look good, don't they," he said. "You should get a good price for these."

I turned to smile at him.

"Seems like you've played midwife before."

"Pedigree poodles have a difficult time. I've sat up all night before now just so mum could get some sleep. One time they all died and the mother dog too. I don't think I'll ever get over that. That's the sort of experience you learn from."

I just stared at Simon as he got down in the pen to return the puppies to suckle at their mother. Elspeth would never, never do anything like this, especially while I was asleep in the chair.

"She's short of milk," he said, stroking the mother dog's nose.

"I'll get the bottle. They'll have to make do with fresh cows' milk from the dairy."

I had expected to be alone for a couple of weeks after Elspeth left but now I lit the fire in the parlour. It provided the only light apart from one stub of a candle. The electricity had stayed off all day. Simon sat on the floor holding one of the puppies in his arm and was feeding it with cow's milk from the bottle. I threw another log of apple wood in the grate. A shower of sparks flew up the chimney. The puppy stirred for a moment and then settled back to suckle once more.

"I wish you'd been here at lambing time," I said. "You're a natural..."

He smiled.

"I've always liked animals."

I looked at him again. He did know how I felt. He was not just a quick fuck. He hadn't made some excuse and gone. He was here, right now, with me, smiling at me again with those come–to–bed eyes under such long eyelashes.

"Why choose engineering and atom power then? You would have made an ideal vet if you've got a way with animals."

" It seemed the right thing to do at the time. Years ago, our local gamekeeper took me to The Festival of Britain on the South Bank in London. I was really inspired by that tower they called the Skylon and the Dome of Discovery. I don't know… Perhaps I was just a bit naïve when I was 17. I wanted to become a scientist in the New Elizabethan Age. Maybe I really did believe that I would be the one to harness the power of the sun, for the good of mankind… Well, I was still a teenager!"

"My mum and dad took me to see that," I said. "Why did you go to London with a gamekeeper and not your parents?"

"Do you really want to know? Well, my father had taken Mama to the South of France to stay with friends. He never had time for me anyway. So handsome Hamish took me to London for a treat and…, What shall I say?"

"Tell me… But, only if you want to…"

"He was my first lover. Yes I do mean!…Have I shocked you?…But enough of that!… Then, last year, it was so exciting to watch the Queen on television when she started up the generator at Calder Hall, the first nuclear power station, to make cheap electricity for the people of Britain. But I suppose I've never really asked myself what do I want from life?... What would really make me happy?"

"Well, are you happy now, Simon?"

He lifted the puppy up to his face and let it lick his nose – the last thing Elspeth would have ever thought of doing. She had a thing about germs.

"Oh yes… I think we're happy now... Aren't we?..."
I got down off the chair to sit on the floor beside him to look at the puppy more closely.

"...I could love it out here," he added "like this... with someone special."

He turned to me and smiled. I was right. He did know.

"Really?"

Instinctively I put my arm around his shoulder. We sat like that for ages, saying nothing, while the puppy drank the bottle dry, just staring into the fire. I had never been so happy. By now Simon was leaning back with his head on my arm. It seemed the natural thing to do and I suddenly kissed him. He put his arm up to my face, leaned forward and kissed me in return. That had never happened before. He said nothing and just seemed to fall asleep while the puppy slept quietly in his arms and the empty bottle rolled down into his lap. I withdrew my arm as carefully as I could and went out to the wash house to have a look at the rest of the litter. They and their mother lay snuggled together, sound asleep. As I walked back out of the wash house, I took a look at the sky. A brilliant red sunset was spreading above the mountains in the west. I was looking at another epiphany – a divine revelation. It was an omen – a shepherd's delight…

"Stay here tonight," I said, returning with mugs of tea.

Simon sat up and put the puppy aside in front of the fire, looking around.

"On the settee? I'll put my sleeping bag down there."

"Or there's the spare bed upstairs. You could use that..."

"Yes, I will. But I haven't found the bathroom yet."

"What bathroom?..."

He stared at me.

"...We did apply for a rural development grant. It was turned down. Then the local council said no to any extension – we wouldn't get planning permission for it. So it's a tin bath in front of the stove there. Elspeth always goes to the hotel in town – she has friends there. They've got showers at the youth hostel – you could go and talk to them."

We said no more about it until the following day. I'd been putting off the mucking out while the weather was so wet.

However, the sun came out for a while again and he helped me by scraping the concrete with a spade while I drove the tractor. Elspeth would never have done this but with Simon around we did everything in half the time I usually took to do the job. But by the evening we were both in need of a wash. I got the old tin bath from the hook in the scullery. There was a tap on the side of the Aga to run off hot water and we always used a jug to fill the bath. Afterwards, the two of us could lift it out of the back door and tip it down the drain in the yard.

"I'll leave you to it," I said, making for the door to the parlour.

"You don't have to go... Please!"

"I thought you'd want some privacy."

"Stay and talk, huh?... Just for me. I'd like you to stay."

I sat down in the easy chair and turned on the radio for the news while Simon stripped off his clothes. Harold Macmillan had done this at 10 Downing Street, the Queen and the Duke went to open that and so on. Then I did sit up.

'…Reports of a serious fire in an atomic reactor at the Windscale plant in Cumberland have been denied by the government. Claims that milk from local farms would be dumped have been criticised as undue alarm, a scientist told the BBC this morning…'

I switched off the radio set and watched Simon instead.

"What was all that about, then?" he asked, taking off his shirt to reveal muscular shoulders and a trained physique.

"We'll ask the guy next door," I said. "He works for the Windscale fire brigade and he might know something about it. There have been incidents before. The local press play at scaremongering from time to time. What they forget is that Windscale has brought a lot of employment to the region. Farming has been shedding workers. One tractor now does the work of two horses and half a dozen men. Local young people can now go and get jobs at Windscale or Calder Hall instead."

"What do you think they get up to at Windscale?"

"A lot of hush–hush stuff. There was a meeting a while back at the village hall to convince us it was for medical use and stuff for industry . They also promised us cheap electricity from nuclear power – too cheap to meter, so they said – well, I thought, and pigs might fly. That didn't go down very well. Folk around here are too down–to–earth to believe in fairy tale stuff like free electricity. The meeting was not a great success. Too many people were afraid the new–fangled technology would all go bang one day. Like an atom bomb on our front door step."

"Perhaps it has!"

"Everyone thinks they are really refining uranium for atom bombs at Windscale. I don't know. What do you think, Simon? Do they teach you anything about such things at London University? What do you think of this low–cost electricity everyone is so hopeful about? And is it all going to be as cheap as they say? I think they've got problems they don't want any one to know about."

"Well, I don't know," he laughed. "Why ask me? I'm only learning the theories, not the day–to–day practice…"

Simon took off his pants and stepped into the bath. It was a long time since I had seen Elspeth naked. She was quite sniffy about it. Simon had no such inhibitions, however, and seemed quite happy for me to watch him again. He was quite, quite beautiful. I had already made up my mind I would ask him to stay here.

"Do you want me to scrub your back?" I asked.

He smiled and I got down to kneel by the bath. Being so near such a gorgeous naked young man was something new. I wanted him already. He handed me the flannel and I rubbed the soap over it. Then he turned his muscular back towards me as I gently rubbed his shoulders. This was so erotic. No electric shocks now. He leaned forward and I ran my finger down his spine. I'd never done that before, even to Elspeth. She would usually go frigid when I touched her now. Simon was quite different.

"You like this?"

"Mm..."

I reached around him to rub soap over his chest and dipped the flannel into the water again and touched his erect penis, which was sticking up above the water. It was long and uncut. Simon grabbed my hand and placed it firmly back on his erection.

"Love me please!" he whispered in my ear. "And I need someone to love."

I started to massage him. He threw his head back and moaned.

"Oh yes!"

He was like a volcano erupting. Here was a prize stud indeed. He stood up in the bath for me to wash his thighs. They were covered in thin downy hairs. I put the flannel aside and rubbed the soap up and down with my bare hand. I'd never touched another man like this before, only the post card of Flandrin's nude pinned up in the milking parlour outside. But this young man was even more beautiful. I had been completely unprepared for the real thing. He turned round in the bath to present his beautiful buttocks in front of my face. I couldn't resist it and kissed one. He waggled his shapely hips. I kissed the other one. He giggled. This was quite simply the most sensational thing that had ever happened in my life. There was a stream of soap running down his back. I rubbed it between his thighs. He parted his legs and sighed.

"Huh!...Don't stop!"

"Why don't you stay here for a while?" I asked, looking up at him. He stooped down and kissed me. I was in love already. Elspeth had got some competition for my affections, that is if she would care a damn. I had my doubts about that.

It was a glorious evening so we walked down to the pub and sat outside on benches in the garden. Simon was quiet and looked at the view. What was there to say? Why make casual conversation just for the sake of it? I'd never felt this way about anyone else before, even Elspeth. Now I knew. All of that had been a mistake.

"So," I suggested. "You're not going to settle down and get married, then?"

"You mean... like my parents think I should?..."

I laughed and we shared another glance.

"...I could only make a woman unhappy, surely you must have realised that. Well, you are one person I feel I can be honest with. My parents just don't want to know. They see their oldest son raising grandchildren they, and the Empire, could be proud of. What right do they have to expect all that? I told my mother straight... I don't want a wife, a mortgage, a house, two point one kids and a dog. She was quite upset. I didn't tell her what I really wanted, of course."

"And what's that, Simon?"

"Seriously?"

"Yes."

"Someone like you... I'm not joking...for the rest of my life."

I looked away. How could he have known? Rooks were circling in the trees. Their daily routine was repeating the same as before. But my life would never be the same again. I turned back to look at Simon. He stared at me with his come-to-bed eyes.

"How soon did you know?"

"I used to dream about all the wrong things... wet dreams about the paper boy, the gardener ... didn't you have those too?"

"Can't remember. I don't think so... Did your family really have a gardener?"

"The Palace has at least two full–time, ... and a housekeeper. The gamekeeper I told you about looked after my father's deer park. We used to eat roast venison on Sundays."

I was suddenly shocked.

"You live in a palace?"

"Well, that's its name – a sort of stately home. Couldn't you guess? We used to hold posh garden parties – Madeira wine and seedcake for Church charity occasions…"

"How divine!"

"Yes, the ladies of the church used to say how sweet I was, ruffle my hair and pass me jelly babies. I always bit their heads off. I was a rebel in disguise, waiting for my moment to come."

"And did it?..."

He smiled at me and we stared into each other's eyes again.

"Sleep with me tonight?...Please... Now I know, I need a real man to give me a good seeing to every night!"

I must have looked shocked for a moment.

"Will I do?"

"Yes, I will do anything for you...anything at all... So you know... I just desperately need to feel wanted."

This took me by surprise.

"Well," I said, "I'm not much experienced at this sort of thing. I don't want to be a disappointment to you..."

We got up from the bench and made our way back to the farmhouse. Things had happened so quickly. I just wasn't used to this sort of proposition. As I closed the back door and locked it, Simon came to put his arms around my shoulders and gave me a hug. I ran my hands down his back to clutch his pert buttocks inside his shorts.

"...I only want to make you happy," he said. "Will you let me try? If it doesn't work out, I'll go, I promise...and no hard feelings."

"But what if I'm not good enough?... I've never done this sort of thing before..."

"You'll do fine...Just do what comes naturally, ok... I'll teach you. You'll soon learn... How about right now? ..."

He took my hand and led me up the stairs into the bedroom. I felt as if I might be in a dream and would wake up at any moment. He pulled my jumper up over my head.

"Let me look at you this time. Take off all your clothes!..."
I didn't need to be told twice. He pushed me back onto the bed.

"Fantastic! But you work hard on the farm all day. Now I'm going to make you happy... Lie down and relax! ... Let me do everything... I'm going to give you a massage like you've never had before."

Soon I was lying naked on my back while Simon sat, naked, on top of me with his legs either side of my chest. I rubbed my hands firmly up and down his firm thighs. The muscles rippled and his penis rose up in front of my nose. He moved forward so I could take it in my mouth and massage the tip with my tongue. He groaned.

"Huh! ... Oh yes!"

Now that we were both completely naked, neither of us seemed to have any inhibitions left at all. I felt my penis rise hard up between his buttocks. Now he slid down onto it slowly and smiled with those come–to–bed eyes. It was the most sensational moment of my life.

"Fuck me! ...Come on now! ...That's it ... take me for a ride! ...Huh! ...Oh yes! ...Harder!"

I put my hands underneath his buttocks to hold them apart and lift him up so he could slide down my pole again and again.

"Oh yes! ...I'm going to come! ...Oh fuck!"

Suddenly we climaxed together. His sweet cum splattered my face. He gently wiped it out of my eyes and smiled at me again. Sex had never been like this before.

"What other positions are there?" I asked. "I want you to teach me everything..."

Simon lay on his back and took hold of his knees.

"This is another way we can still look at each other...Now if you kneel on the bed like that...But perhaps you need to rest a moment...Hey! What a fantastic stud you are! ...You don't need a rest do you?"

I'd never been so sexually aroused and penetrated him again.

"Wow!...Oh yes, that's it. You're a natural... Harder! ... Blow me away!"

We smiled at one another as I climaxed deep inside him once more. Then Simon quickly turned over to kneel in front of me with his knees apart. I put my hands around his hips and mounted him from behind.

"Hey! ... You super man ...What a super stud I've found! ... That's fantastic."

Having both climaxed at the same moment for a third time, we lay back on the pillows and smiled at one another for a few minutes.

"So which is your favourite position, then?" I asked, finally, thinking he would be exhausted by now.

"Like my very first time...bending over the end of the bed."

"Show me..."

Now standing behind him, I could look down on Simon's muscular back, tapering down to a slim waist. I was completely unprepared to find someone who would give himself to me so I could do whatever I wanted. My fantasies had suddenly become a reality. I leaned over to kiss him around the back of his neck and he started giggling.

"Hey, you super man! ... Make me happy again!"

I put my hands on his shoulders and penetrated him once more.

"Amazing! ... And I thought I would quickly wear you out... Huh!..."

I reached down to grab hold of his erection, which was still as hard as my own, and started to slide my hand around it.

"Oh yes! ...Harder! ...Can we do it together again? ...Huh! ...It's never been like this before! ...Oh yes! ... That's it... I'm going to come! ...Huh! ... Oh ... f u c k ! ... Huh! ...Wow!"

Finally, completely exhausted, we collapsed on top of one another while our hearts raced and we struggled for breath. Words were no longer needed. My life would never be the same again. This gorgeous young man had taken me to the gates of delirium.

2001

Well! I sat in the Land Rover remembering it all. Simon and I had been out in the country, a long way from London. Local people in the Lake District had too many problems of their own to be seriously concerned about two men living together. It was not like this in London during the 1950s, however. The newspapers had been full of scandals about court cases. I actually did not know that the penalty for sodomy in those days was still life imprisonment. Perhaps it was just as well I was not aware that I could already have been committed to six life sentences, presumably to run concurrently! Actually, I was so happy that I don't think I would have cared, anyway. But perhaps Simon and I were just lucky. Other men ended up in prison and publicly disgraced. It was ages before Simon felt able to tell me about his family's connections with Lord Montagu and the high–profile court case surrounding him some years before. Looking back now, I realise how those events had influenced his life and his decision to forsake the high life of the aristocracy into which he had been born. Instead, he had opted to share his life with me in the Lake District.

Like many men of my generation I had lived a lie. To please my parents, I had got married, taken over the family farm and everyone I knew was happy, except me. I'd hidden my real self away from the world, resorting to glimpses at hidden magazines such as 'Physique Pictorial' and photos of naked men like the postcard hidden in the milking shed. But Simon had changed all that. He brought into my life everything that had been missing and which I could no longer live without.

Other gay relationships of the 1950s, I learned later, were temporary, transient and often unhappy. Perhaps the scandal splashed all over the front pages of the tabloid press when Simon was 18 had made him more cautious and more determined to make his own way in the world on the farm out in the countryside with me. At the time I did not realise how incredibly lucky I was. Now, in 2001, my active sex life was just a memory. But I wouldn't have missed it for anything.

1957

It seemed so natural to sleep with a man like Simon. With Elspeth it had become an ordeal, a pretence, because it was the right thing to do. But she wasn't here. Without her the bed would have been empty. Now Simon was in it beside me – a gorgeous naked young man with his head laid on my shoulder and my arm curled around him. I knew this was right. I wanted this moment to last forever. This is what I had been missing. Outside the window the owl hooted again and the moon shone across the bed through the gap between the curtains. I slid my hand down Simon's back to the firm flesh of his buttocks. He was truly magnificent. Women the world over would give anything to get their hands on a lover like him. But here he was, with me. I pushed my fingers down between his thighs. Once again, his penis sprang up in my hand. This was fast becoming an automatic reaction even though he was half asleep. Did I feel guilty? No I did not. Within seconds his sweet semen covered my hand once more. I'd had dreams but so they had remained and I was quite unprepared for the real thing. Now here he was in my arms – my own dream Adonis. But in a few days he'd be gone, back to London and the University. Would they teach him about life and what it is to really love someone else, I wondered, or just about stuff in books and technology? But why would anyone like him want to live on a farm in the Lake District with the mud, the rain, all the smells and the daily grind which Elspeth hated so much? The moon disappeared behind a cloud and I fell asleep. Now dreaming once again, I was following Simon through the same doorway into the field carpeted with flowers. When I turned to look at him, Simon was completely naked. He lay down amongst the daisies and stretched out his arms. I could remember no more. Memories!

••••••••

It was morning. I rolled over, expecting to find Simon but he wasn't there. Then I heard his footsteps on the stairs. The door opened. Breakfast appeared on a tray beside me. I sat up. There were yellow and white flowers from the orchard in an egg cup.

"I've seen to the dogs," he said. "We've overslept. Your cows are all queuing up outside the parlour wanting to be milked.

I think they're wondering where you've got to. They were all looking at me as if I was the guilty one, leading you astray."

I looked at the alarm clock. It was 6.30 already but the cows could wait for a while longer.

"Come back to bed," I said. "Make me happy again."

He took off the dressing gown and hung it on the back of the door. For a moment he paused to look back over his shoulder and smiled at me again. This Adonis really loved being admired. Then he got in beside me, proudly sporting his enormous erection once more. I grabbed hold of it so I could look straight into his blue eyes. He seemed to have no inhibitions whatever but, now, neither did I. We smiled at one another.

"I think I love you," I muttered.

"Sh! Sh!... I know!"

Together we ate everything on the tray. Not a crumb was left. Why couldn't life always be like this? I kissed him again and he laughed when we heard a lot of mooing outside in the yard.

"What price peace for the wicked?" he giggled.

"The poor things are complaining. Maybe they think I have led you astray."

"I'll come and help you."

"Have you milked cows before?"

"We've got the latest milking machine fitted in the new parlour beside the dairy on the Home Farm outside the deer park... I worked there during the last summer vacation. Well, it was a useful experience... I've learned how to handle cows, you see... but not women."

"Sorry, I shouldn't have asked."

We turned on the radio and I retuned it to the Light Programme. Our milking parlour usually had to make do with the Home Service and the weather forecast, but Simon had brought something new into the place. He was whistling to Frank Sinatra while we lined six cows up in the stalls. Never, not once, had Elspeth ever done this with me. Milking the cows would never be the same again. Even after only two days, I knew I wanted him with me for the rest of my life. But how?

The telephone was ringing. Above the noise of the milking machine was the noise from a big bell we had fitted on the back of the house facing the yard. It was the local branch of the Ministry of Ag. and Fish. Radioactive isotopes had been found in samples of the milk collected from our farm the day before. The tanker from the dairy would not collect it today. Until further notice we must dispose of all cows' milk by pouring it down the drain. This was a precautionary measure until the full effects of the fire at Windscale had been assessed. In the meantime, scientists would be arriving today to survey all our pasture with Geiger counters. We must co–operate and give them free access. There was no cause for alarm. Radiation levels were below current safety standards I was told. It would be appreciated if we did not make alarmist calls to the newspapers. A full statement would be issued at a press conference in due course. They were thanking us for our full co–operation. The Ministry would compensate us for our losses. Somewhat stunned I put down the phone and returned to the milking parlour. I pressed the emergency stop button to get rid of the noise. I'd never done that before.

"Why did you do that?" Simon asked, replacing the chain behind another cow.

"Leave it! There's not much point now."

"What does that mean?"

"The milk is radioactive. That was the Ministry on the phone. Smoke from the fire at the nuclear plant has polluted our pasture. The cows eat it so their milk is unfit for human consumption. They say we've got to throw it down the drain. "

Simon laughed.

"I'm disappointed... I was hoping you'd turned off the machinery because it was time for me to get another good seeing to!"

He looked at me under his long eyelashes and I put my arms around him again.

"Simon...Really! ... No... I need a cup of tea."

"What about the cows?"

"We've had power cuts at milking time before. They're used to it. Simon, please go and make us a cup of tea. We'll need to decide where to dump all this unfit milk. The drain is going to stink when it all goes off..."

He laughed.

"...I don't mean it's going to go bang... Well, you know what I mean. It can't be that radioactive, can it?"

••••••••

We took off our boots and sat down in front of the stove.

"What is this nuclear power all about then?" I asked. "I know hundreds were killed at Hiroshima and Nagasaki...twelve years ago, back in 1945..."

"No, there were hundreds of thousands and still more are dying today from the long–term effects of radiation..."

"Like we've now got on our fields..."

This was the first time I'd used the words 'we' and 'our'. He smiled at me.

"But much lower levels than in Japan... I hope!"

"That's what the Ministry said - 'below current safety standards...' Well, if that's the case, why are we throwing good milk down the drain? And what do the scientists expect to find with their Geiger counters?"

"What Geiger counters?"

"They're coming here today to survey the farm... That's what I was told. What was it that caught fire at Windscale?"

"How do I know?"

"But I know who will. He was at the fire. He lives next door – that fireman I told you about. I'll phone him now."

I found his number in the phone book. Yes, he had been at the fire in a reactor. It had been chaos. They'd been asked not to talk to the press. I told him our milk had to be thrown away. He promised to call in later to tell us all about it.

"By the way," I said to Simon after putting the phone down again. "There is time for you to get a good seeing to. Come here!"

"What ...here in the kitchen?"

Simon came to stand in front of me. I reached forward to undo his belt and pushed his shorts down to his knees. At once his penis sprang up in my hand.

"Why aren't you wearing any pants?"

"I didn't want to keep you waiting!"

I took hold of him around the waist and turned him away from me.

"Right!"

I pushed him over the kitchen table and cupped his pert round buttocks in my hands to massage them and help him to relax.

"Huh!... Oh yes!"

"Is this what you wanted then?"

He waggled his bottom and looked back at me over his shoulder.

"Where's the Vaseline?"

"It's empty...We'll have to buy some more... What about that margarine?"

"Will that work?"

"Well, try it. There isn't anything else."

Simon started giggling as I slid gently inside him. He spread his legs further apart and looked seductively at me back over his shoulder.

"Oh yes!...Huh!...That's it!... Harder!...Let's do this in every room in the house!"

"What happens when we've run out of rooms?"

"We'll start in the farm buildings outside... Huh!... Hey, you super man!... I'm going to come again!... Huh!... That's it!... Wow!"

"The farm buildings?... Are you sure?" I laughed as we climaxed together..."What... all of them?"

I collapsed on top of him and started kissing the back of his neck while he laughed. Never in my wildest dreams had I guessed that sex could be anything like this. It seemed a bizarre contrast to the horrors of the radioactive rain falling outside the door, but for a moment I just didn't care.

••••••••

Fred looked tired when he arrived. We sat him down in the kitchen while Simon made some coffee. Already it seemed the natural thing for him to do.

"You look all in," I said to Fred, who was clearly exhausted.

"We never had any training for this sort of thing. The Windscale people didn't know what to do. The atomic pile looked a bit like a 'Meccano' set. We could see everything red–hot inside. The smoke was acrid and metallic. We had to push the fuel rods out with scaffold poles. The scientists told us everything had overheated by accident. Our fire chief just did his best – but he's in hospital now. See this?"

Fred turned to show us the red burns on one side of his face.

"I haven't been feeling too well. The scientists gave us these iodine tablets to take every four hours..."

He tipped a bottle on the table and put one in his mouth.

"They told us to say nothing to the press. It was all hush–hush... Hush–hush my foot! We live here. Some folk live downwind of that plant. What about them?"

I didn't tell him Simon was studying to be an atomic scientist. Fred pointed at the side of his face again.

"I've only been burnt like this once before by flames when I got trapped in that warehouse years ago, but the flames from that atomic pile were going straight up. They never got near my face so why have I got burnt like this? My respirator didn't seem to fit properly... I don't know. Maybe it was a faulty one. My lungs are sore. Now I don't feel too good. I think I'll go home to lie down."

I could see Simon looking uncomfortable. Fred drank up his coffee and went away.

"How could I tell him?" Simon said, sitting down and turning the old 'Daily Mail' over to hide the photo of the latest mushroom cloud on the front page.

"What was that, then?"

"Radiation burns... that's what he's suffering from. How could I tell him?.. I've seen them once before when one of our technicians spilled a test tube in the lab. And they've given him iodine tablets! Well, I suppose they're better than nothing."

"So will he get better?"

"It depends on how much radiation he has been exposed to. I don't know. People at Hiroshima and Nagasaki are still dying. I told you."

"Oh. So what about us living here? Are we safe?"

Simon held up his hands.

"What time are the men coming with the Geiger counters?"

"Could you ask them what they think? After all, Simon, you speak their language. I don't... "

"Well, I can ask."

It was not until the following day that a small bus turned up with a team of technicians. We looked out of the window upstairs to see if they put on the protective clothing or helmets Simon had told me about but they didn't. They just wore white lab coats and tramped in teams around the fields. He said they might be looking for radioactive hot spots where it might be necessary to cart off the topsoil for analysis.

Simon did try going out to talk to them but they were obviously under a vow of silence as well. Their supervisor did knock at the door to thank me for our co–operation but he would only say we would get a letter in due course. In the meantime, all cows' milk would have to be thrown away under the directions of the Ministry. After that Simon walked around the sites where they had been to see if they'd caused any damage. I took him into the barn again to look at the owl nesting in the loft. He leaned back against the ladder.

"I need another good seeing to!" he said. "Please!"

"What, now?"

"Yes... I've never been fucked in a barn before."

"Ok."

I wedged the door shut from the inside. We climbed the ladder up into the hayloft above where Simon immediately stripped off all his clothes. The soft light filtering through the cobwebs from the skylight above gave everything a magical feel. His flesh felt warm and firm. I held him close to me and ran my hands up and down his back. Then I clutched his pert buttocks and squeezed them. He licked my ear.

"I want to stay with you," he said. "Here on the farm."

I cupped his round buttocks in my hand and lifted him into the air.

"You're serious, aren't you?"

"Fuck me hard!"

I put him down and he knelt in the hay to unbuckle my belt. Then for the first time in my life someone gave me a blowjob. Now he had much more than my thumb in his mouth. I was on the point of climax. He stopped, bent over the pile of hay bales with his legs apart and I penetrated him just in time. I put my hand down under his tummy and took hold of his pulsing erection. Within seconds we came together at exactly the same moment. Suddenly, fucking Simon had become the most fantastic experience of my life. I wanted to do it again and again.

2001

We'd been driving back from London when the fan belt broke. Years ago, back in the fifties, London had seemed like a den of vice, full of over–enthusiastic policemen planting agents provocateurs in the public toilets around Soho. Now, in the twenty–first century, the newspapers told us, the Metropolitan Police had recruited openly gay constables to act as liaison officers with the gay community. How times had changed! I had just been shopping at 'Prowler' in Soho to buy a couple of gay porn DVDs for Simon's birthday. But I could still remember feeling guilty about buying my first gay porn magazine in the early seventies. It was black and white, poorly duplicated and expensive. I also remembered the time when 'Gays–the–Word' bookshop was raided by the Porn Squad and everyone became afraid of a new crackdown by the authorities. But, from 1957, I had no real need of escapist pornography. I lived and slept every night with the real thing – far more erotic and much more exciting than mere pictures in exclusive magazines like 'Physique Pictorial'. Simon was the real thing – gorgeous, energetic and an amazing partner, in and out of bed. I had found someone who personified everything Elspeth, my wife, had never been. Simon had brought me out of my closet. With him I was now able to be myself – uninhibited, liberated and an active gay man – fortunately far away from the horrors of London. My only concern was about getting too much sex. Would I be able to rise to each new occasion? Would I be able to keep him satisfied?

1957

So I was lying in the soft hay looking up through the dust towards the light. Simon now lay face down on my chest, staring into my eyes. Never, not once had I ever done this with anyone before. I put my arms around him.

"Simon... I love you," I whispered.

"I know... I really love you too. Now I know why I was born... to be here with you."

"But we're not getting things done."

He got up off my chest, stood up and brushed hay off his skin. I stared up at him.

"You are truly beautiful," I said. "I don't know what I've done to deserve this... or you..."

"Fuck me again," he said, now lying back on the bales holding his knees with his hands. "Fuck me so I'll never forget! ... I want to be your wildest dream ... Let me be your fantasy... your ultimate hunky farm hand... This time I want to watch your face when you climax inside me... That milking machine of yours makes me feel so randy with those noises. It goes... Suck fuck... clunk... suck fuck... Clunk... suck fuck... and so on, for hours on end... It just drives me wild! ... Like sitting in a train... Anyway, I told you... Well, it must be something wrong with my brain!"

"There's nothing wrong with your brain that a good seeing to won't cure...!"

....

We climbed down the ladder and I took the prop away from the door. I gave it to Simon and he leant it against the wooden pillar which supported the hayloft above. That's when we found it. One of the technicians had obviously gone in there to relieve himself, put his Geiger counter aside but gone off again and forgotten it. Simon picked it up.

"Do you know how to use that?"

He switched it on. I heard the occasional clicking sound. He walked outside where it had been raining. The clicking sound got faster.

"The rain was contaminated. This farm must have been downwind of Windscale. Other farms may not have been affected so much."

I took a look at the scale on the dial. It meant nothing to me. He switched off the apparatus.

"Are we safe here?"

"Yes… The levels are low but the cows concentrate it in their milk... That's what the fuss is all about. They're taking the right precautions."

I felt relieved.

"But we would do well to have a bath and wash off anything suspicious."

We replaced the Geiger counter in the barn as we'd found it and went back to the house.

....

It was a glorious evening so we walked down to the pub and sat outside on benches in the garden. Simon was quiet and looked at the view. I couldn't take my eyes off him. He was still wearing the shorts he'd worn on the first day. They would look silly on 99 per cent of the population but Simon had the legs for them. What was there to say? Why make casual conversation just for the sake of it? I'd never felt this way about anyone else before, even Elspeth. Now I knew for certain. All of that had been a mistake. Simon turned to me and smiled again. Fortunately we were quite alone out here. So we could talk.

"I will stay, if you want."

"Yes please... I do want... It might even be legal one day," I said, pointing at the headline on the newspaper which happened to be lying on the next table. There was an article about the Wolfenden Report, just published, which recommended the decriminalisation of private homosexual acts between consenting males over the age of 21.

"Will the government pass that or reject it? What do you think?"

Simon shrugged his shoulders and turned back to look at the view again. I don't think he really cared, either. He was so happy now.

"It's lovely out here isn't it! People stuck in London don't know what they're missing..."

I picked up the paper and turned to another page. I hadn't read one for days.

"...But at least the grass isn't contaminated with radioactivity."

"Look at this now," I said, changing the subject. "The Russians have launched what they call another Sputnik into orbit. It says here that it circles the earth every hour and a quarter. Jodrell Bank radio telescope is tracking it. ... President Eisenhower is getting worried about Russian superiority in space... America is said to be slipping behind..."

Simon laughed.

"The space race they're already calling it in London. But are we going to be any happier for it?... That's what I wonder. Are the people going to be any better for it? Anyway... what about ordinary folk like you and me...?"

I put down the newspaper to look at him.

"You are not just ordinary!"

"Neither are you."

"Please stay... as long as you want. When do you need to be back in London?"

"Next week."

I looked around to check that we were still alone outside. I still felt nervous that people might overhear us.

"Well, I'm going to miss you, Simon. You could come back to stay any time. Come and help me with the farm if you want a holiday job. I'll pay."

"Yes, I will... but maybe I won't need the money. We'll see. Do you think two men can be happy living together like it says in the Wolfenden Report?... I mean partners... in and out of bed..."

"What do you think?"

"I could be really happy to live up here on the farm with you... but, I'm forgetting. You're married. "

I sighed and said nothing. Simon got up and moved round to sit beside me on the bench. He rubbed his thigh against mine and I put my hand on it under the table.

"Why did you get married to...?"

"Elspeth... I don't really know... security... respectability. My mother wanted grandchildren, just like yours... Oh, I don't know. I needed someone to help me look after the farm."

"And does she?"

"No, she hates it."

"Why didn't you try to find a man to help you with the farm?"

"I never thought I'd find the right one... "

"Perhaps you have now. Listen…I want to become the right man for you."

We both turned to watch the rooks in the trees around the churchyard across the road. The tombstones were now casting long shadows across the grass. Everything looked so peaceful, so picturesque, so terribly English. Under the table I pushed my finger inside Simon's shorts where his penis was already semi–erect. He nearly choked on the last drops of his beer.

"Huh! ... Careful!"

He turned to me with the most beautiful smile.

"Will you sleep with me again tonight?"

"Yes, if you want me to."

"You must know the answer to that!"

He pushed my hand away and got up with the empty pint glasses.

"Same again?"

I nodded and watched him as he went to the back door of the pub. I felt stunned. I was in love – the very last thing I expected at a time like this – no faking, no pretence, no attempt to conform. At last I was being myself. I turned back to watch the rooks in the trees. What did they know about love? What was it that compelled them to build nests in the spring? Simon put down the mugs of beer on the table and sat down again.

"I really love you," I muttered, almost on the point of tears. "I never thought..."

"I know...we should stay together. I could go on looking for years and never find anyone as fantastic as you. And you really are, you know!"

He put a hand on my arm. There it was again – a shock like grasping the electric fence out in the field. I placed my other hand on his, waiting for the electricity to discharge through him. So we just sat there for a while.

"Let's go back to bed," he whispered, pushing the beer aside.

"Don't you want that?"

"I don't want brewer's droop!"

We laughed and got up from the table. Never before had I walked away from a full pint of beer. I pushed open the metal gate of the churchyard and held it for Simon to go through. The sun was setting on the horizon – the ending of a perfect day. My wife had gone away and I had found myself. As we passed the porch of the church, I grabbed Simon. The church door was unlocked. I pushed him inside and closed it quietly behind us. There was silence inside. We were alone in the dark with the smell of rising damp and dry rot in the roof. I put my arms around him, drew him towards me and hugged him. We just stood like that for what seemed an age, saying nothing but breathing deeply.

"I got married here," I whispered. "It was all a mistake. It was pouring with rain. I could feel this place putting a curse on my life. Elspeth had a cold and kept sneezing. It was so cold, I was shivering. There was hardly any heating at all. I should have said No, I will not take this woman to be my wedded wife..."

"And why didn't you?"

"I hadn't got the courage...It's as simple as that...I wish I'd met someone like you..."

"Kiss me," he muttered.

"What? ... Here?... And now?"

I looked around in the musty gloom. Above us were the banners and flags of local regiments left over from the war

– fading and covered in dust. All those brave men had died. Now I was alive. I looked up at the shaft of sunlight from a high window catching the dust in the air. In this gloomy and musty church I had another epiphany – another life–changing revelation. Was this the first moment I resolved to live my life to the full and grasp every new opportunity? But I could not believe what Simon seemed to be suggesting. It still seemed to me to be wrong for two men to make love in our ancient village church. As a child I had sat here listening to sermons about sin, God's wrath and the terrible day of judgement. Now I turned back to Simon with a smile.

"Where?... On the altar steps?"

Simon paused a moment and seemed to listen to the noise of the deathwatch beetle in the roof above us. We looked at one another.

"On second thoughts," he whispered, "my father, His Lordship, would have me excommunicated! It would be too spooky. Can't you hear the ancestors stirring in their tombs and vaults?"

I gazed at all the memorials and stone figures around the church. In the gloom they seemed to me to represent everything that was wrong with old England. Had they blighted my marriage to Elspeth? How could I have got married here in such a dismal place? The spooks were not going to ruin my second chance to find happiness with Simon. He represented the exciting Elizabethan age of self–expression, confidence and the challenging spirit of a new scientific Britain in the fifties. I pushed him back outside into the porch and shut the door quietly behind us. Now the deathwatch beetle up in the roof was the only living thing left in that dismal place. The flowers in the vase were obviously dead. I was glad to be back outside.

"Take me back to bed," he whispered in my ear. "I need a really good seeing to. I want to get fucked until I can't take it any more."

••••••••

We lay in bed, side by side, too aroused to sleep. It was midnight. My thigh lay over his and I was running my fingers through his hair with one hand while still clutching an empty wine glass in the other. I'd found a bottle of my father's old tawny port down in the cellar.

"What would your father say, Simon? Does he know about you?"

"Can't you guess?... Well, I'll tell you anyway. I used to sing in the cathedral choir. I was the lead soprano. Butter wouldn't melt in my mouth... You could get a divorce."

"But you'd be cited as the cause of it all... in court."

"Yes, I hadn't thought of that."

"Your father might read about it in 'The News of the World' on Sunday morning after the morning service... Sex Shock! – Lord's son in flagrante delicto with farmer on altar steps – divorce court told."

"That would ruffle a few feathers... If I quit London University and come here to live with you, do you think we might be happy together?"

"I don't know, Simon... Would you really? But would you be happy living on a farm in the Lake District in the middle of winter? It gets pretty bleak up here at times, you know. We got cut off last year with all the snow. The snow plough actually got stuck in a drift... and the electricity cables were down for a week."

"But I might actually be happy living here with you... I haven't been happy at all. I hate big cities like London. "

Simon was lying naked on the bed as I knelt beside him. He stared at me. I reached out to tweak a nipple to make him giggle.

"Haven't you found anyone in London?"

"I did but it didn't work out..."

He put out his hands to embrace me.

"...Anyway, I need a real man!"

"Aren't there any left in London?"

"Nobody like you!"

I turned him over on to his front and stared at the tattoo again.

"AC/DC... what does this mean?... Well, I know the milking machine works on the mains ... 240 volts alternating current. The Land Rover has a battery... 12 volts direct current. But what does it mean tattooed on you?"

Simon sat up, put his arms around his knees and seemed to rock to and fro while he stared at me with those come–to–bed eyes.

"I told the tattooist to do something which said I was attracted to everyone... no matter which sex. I just like beautiful people. He said how much do I want to spend? I said not much. You are looking at the result."

"The economy version..."

"Something like that..."

"Thinking about it," I added. "That's what might have been wrong with Elspeth and me. So we never hit it off after our marriage."

"How do you mean?"

"Well, perhaps she was AC... alternating and I was DC... direct... Only I didn't know it until you came along."

"I'm glad."

I turned to look at Simon, who was staring at me again.

"Are you attracted to women?" I asked him.

"No... not any more. That was years ago. It seemed the right thing to do but I didn't know my own mind in those days…"

"Don't you even like Marilyn Monroe?"

"Your cow?"

I couldn't resist slapping him on the bottom.

"Ouch!"

"No… the film star!"

"Joe di Maggio – the baseball player, Marilyn Monroe's husband. I could go for him...and you!"

"But Joe di Maggio isn't here. Is that what you're saying?"

"This is getting silly."

"Have you always been passive in bed?"

"What does that mean?"

"Well, young hunks like you who go out cutting down trees before breakfast, running the four–minute mile like Roger Bannister and then conquering the world in the name of the British Empire... "

"You mustn't say that. It's the Commonwealth now!"

"Well, whatever you call it when England makes a profit from exploiting the red bits of the globe..."

"That's not my fault!"

"Well, aren't you all supposed to be red–blooded..."

"Some of us are different, that's all... Something my father, His Lordship, cannot come to terms with. I am the terrible stain on the family escutcheon."

We laughed at one another but I wanted to know more.

"You're the heir... Your brother is the spare... What about him?"

"Harry?"

"Is he going to continue the family line?"

"You mean to produce grandsons the Empire, sorry, the British Commonwealth can be proud of... How do I know? I've left all of that behind. I don't want to know about it any more. I'm yours now. I want to make a new life of my own here with you, far away from all that!"

"Don't you have any ambitions?"

"Yes, to make you happy. I love you. I like to watch you while you give me a good seeing to when I'm lying on my back with my legs around your shoulders. Let's do it again and see if we can climax together again. That was fantastic."

"Yes, I guess I don't know how lucky I really am."

Simon waggled his shapely hips.

"Come on, super man, fuck me again... please! Make me so worn out I can't think about all that sort of crap any more."

But later that night I was awoken by strange sounds from the kitchen downstairs.

At first I thought I must be dreaming. There was the familiar sound of my wife's washing machine and the electric iron going thump, thump on the ironing board. I put on my dressing gown and went downstairs. Simon was washing and ironing my shirts. I went in the kitchen and sat down by the Aga.

"You don't have to, really."

"I want to....Now go back to bed. You'll be up again in a few hours."

"I'd rather be with you."

"Then I'll give you something worth looking at."

He took off the dressing gown he was wearing and carried on ironing in the nude.

So we smiled at one another for ten minutes and I left him hanging the shirts on hangers to take upstairs. I got back into bed, finally convinced Simon was more than just a gigolo who would be here today and gone tomorrow. I needed to stop worrying. I'd found a gorgeous live–in boyfriend to look after me.

The Motorway Service Area – 2001

Well! I stared through the windscreen remembering it all, looking back over forty years. Simon had been the most amazing lover any gay man could possibly imagine. Not like the weedy youngsters today living on junk food, riding round in cars all the time and getting fat. I watched two obese kids returning from the motorway takeaway munching beefburgers. They dropped the packaging right in front of the Land Rover. Should I get out to challenge them and order them to pick it up? I sat there, while they walked on, thinking about Simon again. His body was muscular and hard. He had a six–pack stomach before the term was invented. His thighs were like tree branches. Only his pert buttocks were soft and sensual. How I loved to cup them in my hands and hold them apart as I slid my erection in between them. Age 23 he just could not get enough. How lucky I was in those early days. One day we went out on the train and he told me the noise of the wheels on the rails made him feel so randy – just like the milking machine. I listened as we stared at one another. He said the carriage wheels made the same noise over and over – fuck–a–fuck, fuck–fuck and sometimes suck–a suck, fuck–fuck! Fortunately, this was a corridor train that was nearly empty. We went to the loo and did it in there while he was bending over the sink. Now, at the end of the carriage, directly above the wheels, I could hear what Simon meant. So I fucked him in time with the rhythm. It seemed to give him a bigger climax than ever before. I remember we even had to wash his spunk off the words 'British Railways' along the edge of the mirror. It was so much fun in those early days when everything was still illegal. Memories are made of things like that!

Chapter Two

1957

We were starting to cope with the world's first nuclear disaster around the Lake District. It should have been a portent. Worse was to come in future decades but we didn't know that then, of course. Somehow I didn't care. I'd found love with a 23–year–old gorgeous hunk – the stuff of gay dreams. I was still wondering if I was going to wake up and find Simon was only a dream, or was it delirium? But for us the threat of atomic radiation had suddenly become a shocking reality. When we went back to the barn later, the Geiger counter was still there. I couldn't understand why nobody had come to collect it. How could the scientists just leave it behind?

"What if we just borrow it?" Simon asked. "Could we drive down to the beach beside the Windscale plant? I have a feeling that contaminated water from the firemen's hoses was just allowed into the drains. That's what Fred suggested – down the drain and out on to the beach to be washed away into the Irish Sea. Well, where else would it go? Don't tell me they've collected it all up for indefinite storage. Can we take the Land Rover?"

Within an hour we were down on the beach overshadowed by the atomic plant, which was surrounded by barbed wire and high fences with warning notices. I looked up at one chimney. It had a large bulge at the top.

"What's that for?"

"Cockcroft's folly, they call it. That's a large filter to collect any radioactive isotopes from the exhaust gases in case of an accident. It is supposed to prevent any contamination."

"Then why didn't it work the other day?"

"I don't know. Maybe the radioactive smoke from the fire just proved to be too much for it. Who knows?"

The coastline was desolate. We were walking not far from the railway line between Windscale and Selafield. Simon was looking for the waste water pipe running down to the beach from the nuclear plant. We found it. As the tide was out, we were able to walk round the front of it. There was a nasty metallic smell about and there were blackened bits of rubbish lying on the pebbles.

"Surely the scientists would have cleaned up properly after the fire," I said. "How could they just wash everything down the drain?"

I looked out to sea. Grey clouds were blowing in from the west. Suddenly I felt a wave of déjà vu. They looked just like the grey clouds in the background of Flandrin's oil painting of the naked young man. Only the distant island was missing from the scene. The clouds in the distance allowed a shaft of sunlight to glitter across the breaking waves. Seagulls swooped overhead. I felt elated, as if by another epiphany of divine revelation like the mystics in tales of old. Now here was my destiny – to be with Simon. Somehow, Flandrin's painting of a male nude had foretold my future today. I wanted to tell him just how I felt and turned back away from the sea just as he stooped down to switch on the Geiger counter. Suddenly the shocking reality of the present atomic age dawned on me. Mankind was no longer content with innocent studies of beauty and art but sought the power of the atom instead. My daydream was shattered. The alarming clicking sound was faster than before. Simon pointed the instrument into the end of the drainpipe but the clicking increased only slightly. So we followed the line of the rubbish along the seashore. Suddenly the Geiger counter seemed to go crazy. We watched while the needle on the dial shot up to the end of the scale.

"We ought to get out of here," he muttered.

"What is it?"

"I think it's found a bit of something seriously radioactive... plutonium maybe!"

"How could they dump that on the beach?"

"I don't know."

We walked on further. The needle on the dial of the Geiger counter started to fall back.

"We won't walk back the way we've come," he said. "I suggest we go over my boots and your shoes with the Geiger counter before we get back in the Land Rover, just in case. We don't want to risk treading radioactive material like that on the floor and then into the house."

So we sat down on an old tree trunk lying by the high water mark. I took my boots off and held them out for Simon to check. He was right to check everything but my boots were ok. But he had picked up something on the beach. The heel of Simon's right–hand boot was showing something decidedly suspicious. The Geiger counter was going crazy again.

"There's nothing to wash that off," he said. "Best to throw it in the sea. That's the safest place. You and I should start drinking lots of water or eating edible seaweed with plenty of iodine in it. I'm not joking – just like those tablets your neighbour, the fireman is taking. Iodine is to help the body to avoid absorbing anything nasty. That, whatever it is, should never be dumped on a beach where children play or seabirds might pick it up. Frankly, I'm disgusted. I know you think I'm depraved – wanting sex all the time... but this irresponsible dumping of radioactive waste really is obscene... This could threaten human life... and it has the support of the British Government to make nuclear weapons to kill even more people... For God's sake, take me away from here! I feel sick."

He filled both his boots with pebbles to weight them so they would sink and hurled them as far out in the sea as he could throw them.

"What do we do now?" I asked. "Shouldn't we notify some authority or phone the local paper?"

"I expect it's all hush–hush and covered by the Official Secrets Act. We'll probably find that nobody wants to know. A D–Notice may have been issued so the papers won't touch this story."

"But the beach back there should be cordoned off, just like that time my father found a wartime mine down here. At least the bomb squad took it seriously and came to blow it up. Supposing some local kiddies come down here to play and pick that up and take it home to put on the window ledge in their bedroom. How would they know it's going to give them radiation sickness?"

"That might be enough to kill them over a period of time!"

"I think we've got to do something."

"An anonymous letter is best, just warning the Windscale people about what we've found on the beach. It's up to them to come down here with Geiger counters and do a proper survey. They'll need protective clothing, facemasks and all that. How long were we walking around that waste water pipe?"

"Twenty minutes at most..."

"And we found at least one bit of something very nasty. There are probably others. You and I are not going to be popular if we go waltzing into the local paper and say look what we've just found down on the seashore!... Is it weapons–grade plutonium?"

We walked back to the Land Rover in silence while Simon plodded along in his socks.

"Well," he said eventually, "if I hadn't found it myself I would have said it was impossible to mislay radioactive material as dangerous as that down on the beach. If your friend, the fireman, was getting close to anything like that when he was pushing fuel rods out of the fire in the reactor, no wonder he's got radiation burns... but maybe he wasn't... Fuel rods are made of uranium, not plutonium... So, perhaps there have been other incidents before which we don't know about... yet."

On the way back to the farm, we called at the village store and bought one dozen bottles of tonic water. We drank one bottle each, there and then.

"It's worth me going over the Land Rover with the Geiger counter, our clothing, your shoes and ourselves with the Geiger counter again, just to be sure," Simon said.

So he did all this to satisfy ourselves that nothing radioactive had been missed. We still didn't know how long the batteries on the device would last. We had no way of recharging those on the farm. Besides, the scientists might be returning soon to collect the device. Simon replaced it in the barn exactly as we had found it. I still couldn't understand how anybody could mislay a Geiger counter like that. It was probably worth hundreds of pounds. But if scientists at Windscale could mislay a bit of highly radioactive stuff and let it sit down on the beach by the sea, I suppose anything was possible.

One of the first things we both did when we got in was to have another bath in front of the stove. I insisted he was first. I was starting to worry about that bit of radioactive material we had found on his boot. Had the radiation affected his foot? Well, if it had, only time would tell. In the meantime I scrubbed his back with a scrubbing brush and then Simon held up both his feet so I could scrub those too. Suddenly I found myself caring. We looked at one another. After days of rampant sex, our relationship was entering a new, more honourable and respectable phase.

"I don't want to be a nuclear scientist," he said suddenly. "This has been a wake–up call."

"What do you mean?"

"I've decided I do know what I want from life and it isn't nuclear engineering. I reckon I've been exposed to enough hazardous radiation for a year or two."

"I don't understand you. You worked so hard doing A–Levels to get to university and now you seem to be saying you don't want any of it."

"I'd rather be happy than earn a lot of money but end up glowing in the dark!"

"So what would make you happy?... "

"I've told you... By Staying here... with you!"

I didn't know quite what to say to this. Simon got up to step out of the bath. I put a towel around him and hugged him for a while.

"I need another good seeing to!" he said.

"Now? "

"Yes… I want to feel you right inside me... throbbing!"

He knelt down and gave me another blowjob.

"There may not be much left," I said casually.

"Shagged out?"

He looked up at me with those come–to–bed eyes.

"Is that what they say in London?"

"Well, try anyway."

He stood up and I pulled the towel away from his waist. For a while he just stood in front of me while I looked at him. His pert buttocks were completely hairless. The fine down on his legs began around his thighs. The muscles around his shoulders rippled as he flexed his arms. I put my arms on his hips and turned him round to face me. We smiled at one another again. It was the look of love which would last for forty years.

"You really are so beautiful, Simon!" I said. "Like something from Greece or Rome made of stone in the British Museum..."

His penis rose up as I grasped it in my hand. I knelt down

and took it in my mouth. This was the first time I ever gave him a blowjob. It was a compromise.

"You know, the popular press likes to rage about homosexuals corrupting the moral well–being of the English nation... but, today in 1957, press reporters should borrow a Geiger counter and walk along the beach by the Windscale plant to find real obscenity... There, registering on the meter for everyone to see they will find the true threat to the health of this nation... And it has the official backing of HM Government which my father is part of in the House of Lords ... It makes me so angry... I refuse to become part of that ridiculous institution. They persuade the public that nuclear power is for the good of the people – with the promise of electricity too cheap to meter. Only, I think there is a hidden agenda – to develop a bigger hydrogen bomb to kill millions more people."

"But if you did take your seat in the House of Lords, Simon, you might change things for the better... to get Windscale either cleaned up or closed down. Their Lordships might listen to a scientist like you if you told them what we have just found down on the beach!"

"Now you sound too much like my father..."

"Calm down Simon... Try to relax!"

"And, if you please, the Government now has the audacity to dispute the Wolfenden Report... It may never be implemented! ... You and I may never become legal ... We may always remain outsiders, undesirables, breakers of the law..."

"You must try to relax, Simon. You'll make yourself ill!"

"Yes... I need you much more than all that! 'The carriage awaits, My Lord...Now will you wear your best ermine and gown for Parliament today, My Lord' ...Now do you understand? ...You are more important to me than you can possibly imagine. You treat me as a real person – part of the real world. You love me for what I am and not what I represent... When I stand completely naked in front of you, you immediately get a hard–on. I don't need to pretend to be posh or honourable or respectable. With you I can be myself. I don't need to wear fancy clothes or march in a procession to impress you like my father does. You make me feel needed when I strip naked so that you can fuck me – I am human. I am loved. I make you happy. When you and I climax sexually at the same moment I am at my best. I know this is my finest hour!..."

I was starting to laugh. Simon hadn't spoken like this before so I grabbed his crotch to make him smile.

"...Yes, I know... I'm being boring already and sound too much like my father... Let's do it again, please. Make me forget! ...Where did you put that new tube of Vaseline?"

"I may not be up to it."

"We'll try a new position. You sit on that chair to relax. I'll do everything… I'm going to sit astride you… like this. Then I can kiss you while you fuck me…"

I liked this new variation. I leaned back while he lowered himself gently down on my erection. Now we could look into one another's eyes and kiss at the same time.

"Huh!… This is what it's all about!… …F u c k!"

I put my hands under his buttocks to hold them apart. Simon threw back his head.

"Oh yes!… Huh!… That's fantastic!… The best yet… Huh!… Oh fuck!… Look out!… …I'm going to shoot… Fuck!… Yes!… I love you!"

Simon's hot cum spurted all over my face. But I was in ecstasy. He gently wiped my eyes with a tissue.

"We must do it this way again, " I suggested.

"It's the best so far. How was it for you?"

"Fantastic…Those stuffed shirts who rant and rave against the Wolfenden Report don't know what they're missing…"

"You mean, in the Members Club of the House of Lords?"

"Surely… you are not suggesting… that… Honourable Members might try it for themselves? …A Parliamentary Committee investigation?"

"No, a working party… of real men! They shouldn't knock it 'til they try it for themselves."

I thought this was so funny that I creased up in hysterics. Simon could have this effect on me at times. He waited for me to calm down.

"We ought to dump that water so you can have a bath now."

"One day we must get a bigger bath so we can both fit in it together."

Still with a towel around his waist, Simon helped me to lift the bath through the door so we could empty it in the yard. The telephone started to ring again. It was the radiological protection department, who were wondering if we'd discovered a missing bit of scientific equipment they thought might have been left in our barn. I told them to come and get it. When I went back into the kitchen, Simon had got my bath ready.

Well, I thought, if Elspeth could see me now! I was very glad she couldn't. I lay in the bath being washed by a gorgeous hunk of a young man who clearly loved me much more than she did now. We started to talk about the future. Could I get a divorce? Wouldn't he really be happier to return to London University and switch to another degree course? What would his professor or his parents have to say if he quit? Didn't he want to get married and have a family of his own, one day? Wouldn't farming be too boring for him, up here in the Lake District, lashed by rain in the autumn, frozen in snow drifts in the winter? As we chatted, while he erotically washed me all over, I was falling deeper in love. Somehow I seem to have been waiting since the day I was born for this moment.

"Look, Simon," I said. "My wife will be coming home soon after my father–in–law's funeral. You really need to be back in London to get on with your studies. I'm going to miss you, sure ... but, of course, you could come back here in the holidays..."

"I'm going outside."

He disappeared into the yard. I sat thinking. Presently I heard the sound of wood being chopped up. We'd run out of firewood to light the fires when they went out. I took a look out of the door. Simon was stripped to the waist and splitting up the branches of the old apple tree, which had come down in the storm. So handsome, so athletic, so beautiful... he was everything I had ever dreamed of. How could I say no? But we both had to be realistic. I felt quite certain Elspeth wouldn't like him at all. They could never live under the same roof. Why was life so complicated? I just leaned in the doorway watching him. He seemed to be working off his frustration. Wood chips were flying in all directions as he reduced the apple tree to a pile of logs. I grabbed my old camera, which still hung on the coat hook beside me. Yes! There was some film left in it. I poked the lens through the door and looked in the viewfinder but he was just too far away so I rushed outside with it and shouted at Simon to carry on chopping. So he started posing with the chopper and, as I got closer, pulled his shorts down to reveal one shapely buttock while looking seductively back over his shoulder. This was fun. He stuck out his tongue at me. But after a few exposures the film ran out so I just stood and watched him. There was a lot of strength in those broad shoulders, which tapered down to a slim waist. The muscles in his arms rippled erotically. I walked over to him and reached out for the axe. He smiled at me. This time no words were spoken. I pushed him in the direction of my mother's summerhouse and opened the door.

"You need a good seeing to," I muttered, holding him close to me and running my fingers through his hair.

"You guessed..."

I started to undo the belt around his shorts and pushed them down.

"What... no pants?"

Simon smiled and kissed me but said nothing. Suddenly we were interrupted by the blast of a horn from the yard. We both looked out of the dusty glass. A lorry was about to deliver a load of feedstuff for the cattle.

"Damn," Simon muttered.

"Later!" I promised.

Simon pulled up his shorts and we hurried outside again to show the delivery driver where the sacks had to go.

....

As the lorry went off again I went inside to fetch a bottle of beer we could both share. But by now I was no longer in the mood for sex.

"The last few days have been fantastic," I said pouring beer into the glasses I had set down on the wall. "Yes, I do love you. It would be fantastic if you came here to run the farm with me, but life isn't like that, is it?"

"Why not?"

"Because it isn't…" I added on a more sober note while Simon looked sadly at me.

We sat down side by side on the low wall and I put one arm around his shoulder.

"...Ok, we love one another. These things happen but that doesn't mean they can go on for ever."

"You could get a divorce... I'll even pay your legal expenses..."

I said nothing but drank the beer instead.

"...I don't care if I'm named as the guilty party in court. Ok, I seduced you. I admit it ... but it is love, not just sex! ... Believe me, I'm not capable of faking anything like this!"

"Perhaps we both need some time to think things over. You must go back to London and get on with your degree course..."

"Why? I told you I don't want to be a nuclear physicist. Not any more! Not after Windscale! ... I'm happy here with you!"

"Perhaps you'll meet someone else next week..."

"You mean a girlfriend to keep my parents happy... so I can settle down and become respectable, living in Surbiton or Tunbridge Wells ... Can you see me as a sober and respectable pillar of Middle England?"

I poured out the last of the beer.

"You know I don't mean that at all!"

"Look, you and I could go through the rest of our lives never meeting any one else to relate to as we do."

"We've only known one another for a few days. How can you be so sure? How old are you?"

"Twenty–three."

"Well, I'm nearly thirty."

"You look younger but you're in such good shape! I go for older men!"

"So there must have been others!"

"Nobody like you..."

"We'll see."

"What does that mean?"

"I need some time to think... You must go back to London while I deal with Elspeth. I couldn't cope with the two of you under one roof... Look, let's make the most of the time we have left. I'll take you out. Where shall we go?"

"Let's go and make love in the hayloft over the barn again. I've always dreamed about sex in the barn. I want to go back to London totally exhausted. Let's have sex in every position – even some we haven't tried before."

"You mean there are more?"

"Well, I can think of one or two…"

"Ok, if that's what you want...You've asked for it!"

"Yes, back to bed. That's all I want. I want to go back to London totally exhausted. I want to have sex with you in every position. I want to get fucked until I can't take any more. I want us to make one another really happy... so you'll never forget."

We decided to spend our last day together in Windermere

so Simon could get a main line train back to London. There was an old steam launch taking passengers to a landing stage further up the lake so we went for a trip on that. Neither of us said very much. The reality of our parting was now beginning to hit us both. He was right. I would never forget our last session in bed. I was happy but exhausted – literally shagged out. The steam launch chugged along. There weren't many passengers. I looked over the side at the passing scenery. Would we ever see each other again? Was that it? Was it all over now? Should I resign myself to reconciliation with my wife and forget about Simon? No, that's something I would never be able to do. I turned to look at him sitting right beside me – the most beautiful thing that had ever happened in my life. Right now I felt more love for this guy than I had ever felt for anyone or anything at all. But this wouldn't do. We would just part with happy memories, that's all. Like two Atlantic passengers on board the Queen Mary who find each other on the way back from New York, fall head over heels in love, only to say goodbye at Southampton, never to see one another again. But I suddenly felt so grateful. He'd taken me to the gates of delirium where I'd never been before. This gorgeous young man had awakened something dormant inside me. In silence I put one hand on his bare knee. He'd worn those shorts all the time since that first morning. We smiled at one another as the steamer drew up at the Windermere jetty for the last time. The train would be leaving in fifteen minutes. We walked back to the Land Rover to collect his backpack.

The train was already at the platform. Neither of us spoke. I felt dreadful. I opened a carriage door and turned to Simon. Suddenly he got down on his knees.

"For the last time, I beg you... please don't send me away!"

I was glad there were so few passengers in case anyone should wonder what was going on. I looked up and down the platform. An old lady was lifting a suitcase into the next carriage but fortunately she was facing the other way. I turned back to Simon. I'd never seen him so upset before.

"But we've been through all this...You've paid for the train ticket to London."

I helped him to get up. He looked on the point of tears. I couldn't look as he climbed in through the door and opened the window to lean out. As I turned away he shouted at me above all the noise.

"You really are the most wonderful thing that's ever happened in my life. Do you know that?"

As the train gathered speed he smiled and blew a kiss. I waved back, caring nothing about what people might think. Two tearful lovers parting, that's all. I sat down on the seat behind me and watched the smoke and steam from the engine, which disappeared down the line out of sight. I felt empty and drained of all emotion. My life would never be the same again. Every waking moment of every day I would be wondering what if? Perhaps we would meet up again in the future? Who could say?

2001 A motorway service area on the M1

Why do we get more sentimental as the years go by? I reached for a Kleenex to wipe the tears out of my eyes and fished the old snapshot out of my wallet. After fifty years the little print was tatty and going brown at the edges. There was Simon in 1957, aged 23, holding the chopper in one hand and baring his left buttock by pulling down his shorts with the other. I think this picture was my most treasured possession and I still carried it everywhere. I tucked it back into the wallet and looked around the car park. Where on earth had everyone got to? Even Simon must have run out of things to say to his brother Harry in the canteen. And where was Dominic? Fan belts could not be impossible to find in the service station. But the Land Rover was old. I looked out of the side window. The handsome young man with the little girl who called him Daddy was coming back. No ice cream to worry about now. The girl was being carried by a young woman. Daddy was carrying a large bag of belongings with a drop–dead gorgeous young man who wore a pair of very brief shorts and nothing else except flip–flops. They put the bag down on the tarmac in front of the Land Rover. I carefully slid the side window open to try to hear what was going on.

"That's it, then," muttered the woman to the little girl who turned to Daddy.

"Same place, same time in a month?" Daddy replied.

"I'm not quite sure what the divorce court had in mind," the woman added.

Daddy now turned to his daughter, who seemed to be getting upset.

"You'll look after Mummy for me, won't you, Poppet?"

"Want to stay with you!" she muttered.

Daddy turned to the young man standing beside him and exchanged a glance.

"Well, we just haven't got enough room in the flat, Poppet. But Alphonse and I will be moving soon. You might have your own room there one day. Best if you stay with Mummy for now."

There was some noise from an aircraft overhead and I couldn't hear what took place next. Slowly the noise died away. I moved closer to the window and slid it open a bit more, hoping nobody noticed. The little girl was now in tears and being comforted by her mother.

"Say bye–bye to Daddy now."

She carried the little girl off to a car further down the line and got in. Daddy unlocked the passenger door of the diesel four–by–four opposite and helped his boyfriend to lift the luggage over the seat. Then he patted the pretty young man on the bottom and hopped over into the driver's seat. Well! Talk about gay liberation and in a public car park, too. I was shocked! I saw them kiss several times and drive off, sitting side by side. How different everything had to be back in 1957! But I was just showing my age. I had become one of the grey voters of conservative middle England. I looked at myself in the mirror and smiled. Had 'gay liberation' now just gone too far?

1957

I cannot describe the utter despair and loneliness I felt over those few weeks we were apart. That I had told Simon to go back to London was something I could not come to terms with. Even the cows looked at me with mournful eyes. They may not have brains like ours but I still think they knew what had happened. Besides, he wasn't in the milking shed any more. We weren't listening to the Light Programme on the radio. Simon wasn't whistling to Frank Sinatra. Somehow the monthly milk yield seemed to go down. I could only sleep for a couple of hours at night before waking to find the bed empty beside me. I found some comfort in sleeping with his towel under the pillow. I awoke expecting to hear his footsteps on the stairs. This just could not go on.

I went back later to the chemist in Coniston to collect the black and white snaps I'd shot in Windermere on that last day. One showed Simon standing at the back of the steam launch with the view across the lake behind him. Another print was from a negative I had exposed accidentally as I put the camera back in the bag. It showed Simon's shorts and his muscular thighs at an angle, but that did not matter to me. I put both of them in my wallet, safely out of the way.

It was a few days later the telephone rang again. Somehow I thought it might be him but it was Elspeth to say her mother was poorly. She would stay on longer to take care of her. Nothing about me, or if I was all right, running everything on my own. I should have told her there and then. I still thought I owed it to her to be honest. As I put down the phone I should have told her I wanted a divorce. I wanted to be free of the millstone of marriage. I wanted to be free to choose differently next time. But what would I have said? I've met someone new. That would have been the truth. I've been fucking with a backpacker who called at the farm for milk and bread? She would have been shocked. Would she really assume it was a female backpacker? How could I tell my wife the marriage at the parish church had been a sham? Now I knew it for certain. I could only really love another man. Simon had been right all along. I should never have sent him away. He and I were made for one another. I decided to write to him at the address in London he had given me and tell him everything. Should I say my life would be worthless without him? Would I confess I should never have made him go? Should I worry him by adding I could get no sleep and that I desperately needed to see him again? ... But it just sounded too silly, too effeminate and uninspiring. I never wrote that letter.

I happened to mention to George the postman that I could do with the services of a fortune–teller. He immediately recommended someone in Windermere. He even had her telephone number but added I shouldn't laugh. Her name really was Claire Voyante. She was infallible apparently and had actually foreseen the railway disaster at Welwyn Garden City in January. But when she telephoned British Railways to warn them exactly what she had seen in her crystal, nobody believed her. Then, when the Aberdeen express train to King's Cross ran into the Baldock train and overturned on the 7th, she was actually suspected of sabotage but later released for lack of evidence. George seemed to know all about it. I was fascinated and went for a consultation the following day.

Her room was dark, just as I had imagined. A cloth with magic symbols shrouded the light. I joked to her that it looked like something from 'Blithe Spirit', which had recently been performed in our church hall. But Madame sneered at this and said Noel Coward had brought her honourable profession into disrepute. I sat and waited while she gazed into her crystal.

"I see a really handsome young man," she said eventually. "He is sitting on a bed with his arms around his knees, rocking to and fro. He is looking at the rain on the window... London, I think. Well, I used to live there. I should know gloom like that..."

She polished her crystal with the cloth she carried in her hand.

"This young man has no clothes on... and he's been crying... Does that mean anything to you?... This crystal is old, like me. It doesn't see so clearly all the time, nowadays..."

I told her the crystal was probably being accurate today.

"You're not going to believe this," she added. "I'm not sure I should tell you..."

"Please... anything... I've got to know the truth!"

"Well, he's sitting on something... I mean ... intimately... If you know what one does with a rubber dildo... He seems to be getting some comfort... Now I see... He wants to be with you!... Oh, the crystal's gone dark... It blacks out sometimes when we get to the really juicy revelations... I think it's being a bit old–fashioned, today – silly old thing! ... It's Victorian, you see ... Life today gets a bit too much for it... We'll try again in a minute or two... Pass me my bottle of gin, will you? That usually does the trick! "

I passed her the bottle of 'Gordon's'. After taking a couple of swigs, Madame proceeded to breathe alcoholic fumes upon the crystal and then rubbed it energetically once more.

"Ah yes," she muttered, staring intensely into it again. "I see two people now. This young man is waving and so is a mature woman. They are both waving at you ... one to say goodbye... the other… this handsome young man... is trying to say hello... to you I think... Yes, I'm sure of it...You'll be hearing from both of these people very soon... Is that what you wanted to hear?"

I told her it was exactly what I had hoped but she continued to stare into the crystal.

"There is more, Sir," she added. "For a small consideration I can see everything."

"How much?"

"Another seven shillings and six pence, please... but you'll like this. I can see ten… twenty... thirty... forty... even fifty years into the future... This doesn't happen very often... It's so exciting, isn't it! I won't be around then, of course… But you will!"

I passed over another seven and six, which she placed on the table beside the crystal.

"What do you see now, Madame? What does the crystal foretell? This young man you can see…Will he get married, settle down and have a family?"

"Oh, yes... he will get married one day... I'm sure of it..."

My heart sank. I did not know what to say.

"You and this handsome young man... the one who I saw naked just now... The two of you will still be together well into the next millennium… Good Lord... That's 2007..."

Now I was completely confused. How could Simon get married and yet the two of us be together so far into the future? Perhaps he would leave his wife and come back to me. Yes, I thought, that must be it. Madame took another swig of gin, breathed on the crystal and polished it once more with her cloth and stared into it again.

"...I don't believe this! You and this beautiful young man are sitting together in a registry office ...here in England... Yes... Yes... I don't believe it! ... You are getting married ... In the eyes of English law...You are actually getting married! ...I'm sorry, Sir... This crystal isn't what it used to be. There's a crack in the base... I'll give you your seven and six back again. It's obviously made a mistake!"

"Keep it, Madame, please. You've made me very happy."

"That's kind of you, Sir. Business is not so good these days..."

She turned back to the crystal and rubbed it again.

"Damn, it's gone cloudy again. There must be a disturbance in the ether… I blame radiation from all these atom bomb tests… They just contaminate my communication with the spirit world and that's bad for business… Now I can't see anything at all…"

She turned to me and smiled.

"But perhaps this thing's Victorian morality has been outraged. I don't think it likes what it sees sometimes. We must wait a moment for it to cool off."

She took another swig from the gin bottle and then breathed on the crystal once again.

"Ah, the clouds are clearing. Now I see a different decade…

What's this… a mushroom cloud?… An atomic explosion I think, like Japan in 1945…No, no, wrong decade. I'm confused now…"

Madame rubbed the crystal again and then stared intensely deep into it.

"There's more," she added after a few moments, taking another swig of gin and glancing at me. "I see a disaster in the future... something to do with atomic radiation... like 1945 in Japan, I think. …But it's not going to be World War Three... Tell me... Have you had problems with atomic radiation recently?"

I told her about the Windscale disaster and our cows' milk going down the drain.

"I'm looking into the future about thirty years from now… 1986 to be precise. ...Something somewhere ...I mean very big… will go bang! ...An experiment will go wrong... It will be mankind's biggest peacetime atomic disaster... More radiation than Nagasaki and Hiroshima several times over... Kids born dead or deformed with two heads. It's too depressing! ... I pity the poor people living in the town nearby ... Russia, I think... Chernobyl near Kiev, or somewhere like that... But it hasn't even been built yet... Dreadful place!... What Communism does for the people!... But you want to know about your future with this beautiful young man ... Well... the two of you will sail through life as if you were blessed... If that is what you wanted to hear... Well, bon voyage! ... I've already foreseen my death, dearie. You don't want to know! ... I won't even be around in ten years' time... But listen to this..."

She turned back to the crystal again and stared into it.

"1967 will be a year of celebration and parties for men of your kind... I mean you and your handsome boyfriend… the one I saw just now...You have shared your bed with him, haven't you... Don't worry, the police are no friends of mine – which is just as well in your case... I mean intimacy and rampant sex… so often… on a scale which even I am surprised at... Good Lord... again, and again... and again... There's a new sex position I've never seen before... You both seem to be enjoying that one! …"

Madame rubbed the crystal vigorously with her cloth and then turned to me with a serious expression.

"How I wish there was a recording machine attached to this thing. I could sell this stuff on the black market in Soho! ...I mean to the men in grey raincoats."

I frowned at her.

"... I was once a prostitute working on the streets of London... Sorry... It was only a joke, Sir! ...I've seen a few things in my life… but…"

She turned back to have another look.

"... Gosh, isn't he beautiful – like a Greek god! He could earn a fortune in Soho ... None of us girls had stamina anything like that... Twice a day was my limit..."

Madame smiled knowingly at me again and then stared into the crystal.

"...I don't believe it ...You seem to be at it like rabbits in every room and all the farm buildings? No wonder he wants to come back! ... What a lucky boy... because this is real love and not just casual sex!"

Now she took a whole mouthful of gin and polished the crystal energetically while casting a knowing glance at me.

"I'm not sure that this poor old thing can cope with all this pornography. Before you know it, the glass will shatter… Perhaps it will exert the ultimate censorship…like camera lenses focussed on ugly people… only he is so beautiful..."

She seemed at a loss for words and then looked at me accusingly.

"… But why, oh why, did you send him away, the other day at Windermere Railway Station when he was kneeling on the platform in front of you? …True love was staring you in the face but you sent him away… after… yes, after so much sexual excitement. …Did it just get too much then, dearie?"

She turned away from me and gazed more intensely into her crystal, clearly unable to believe what she was seeing. I was on the point of tears.

"Tut–tut... outdoors too... You ought to be more careful, you know... at least until 1967 when Parliament will change the law... I think that really is all for today... I'm worn out, just thinking about it! ... I really must rest now! ... Could you see yourself out?"

I left her a special tip of a ten shilling note.

"Most kind, Sir... Most kind...You and your handsome young man are lucky to have found one another. I wish I could meet him one day. I don't see love and devotion like that in my crystal every day... And true love it is, believe me. Most people go through life never finding anything like that! ... I didn't!"

Some days later came another phone call from Elspeth. She wanted to stay with her mother. She'd never been happy on the farm. She wanted to have a life of her own now and to get a job so that she could be independent of me. I listened and said nothing. Somehow Elspeth had saved me the trouble of saying all these things for myself. I agreed to see our solicitor and make arrangements for a separation as soon as possible. I put down the telephone and breathed a sigh of relief. It was over. Now I was free! I locked up the farm, got in the Land Rover and drove back to Windermere. I wanted to revisit the jetty and the railway station once again – just to make sure they were really there – that I had not dreamed everything. They were the very last contact I had had with Simon.

••••••••

It was pouring with rain. The steam launch was letting off the last passengers at the jetty. I hopped on, just to sit where Simon and I had been that last day. I found the seat. It was wet but I sat there all the same, remembering the moment the camera had clicked its shutter as I put it back in the bag. I got the snap out of my wallet and looked at it as the rain splattered everything. I should never have sent him packing. He had never wanted to go back to London. I should have listened. But how could I know Elspeth would not be coming back? How could I have known then what I knew now – that I didn't want to live without him. It was as simple as that.

I got up from the seat to go inside the cabin of the launch and dry off a bit. Soon we were returning to the jetty at Windermere. I'd been daydreaming. Forty minutes had just gone by like that! I got out of the boat and walked up to the railway station. Something was drawing me there. I needed to sit on that seat too. Maybe another train would be leaving and I could watch the smoke and steam from the engine just as I had done that last day. I could blow it a kiss and wave, just for old time's sake. So I sat down in the same place and watched. The last passengers were climbing into the carriages. The guard blew his whistle and smoke belched from the front of the train. It drew out. I didn't wave or blow a kiss. Why not? I sat and watched the rear of the train go out of sight. The plume of steam from the engine disappeared around the back of a building in the distance to reappear again briefly just as another plume of steam came into sight. This must be the last train. I sat and watched it get closer. Why didn't I just get up and go home out of the rain? What was keeping me here? The engine appeared at the far end of the platform, belching smoke as it finally came to a halt. I couldn't see through the steam. Doors were slamming. A figure was coming towards me. She was leading a small dog behind her. Behind her came a clergyman with a large suitcase. With the other hand he held out his ticket for the man collecting them at the barrier. I looked back through the steam. Another figure with a backpack was appearing. I got up and started to run towards him but stopped short. It was just wishful thinking. No, this was not Simon, just somebody who looked like him. I sat down on the seat again. This couldn't go on. I'd have to find him.

When I returned to the farm I sat down and wrote Simon a letter to explain everything and to invite him up here for Christmas. I was now trying to sound confident, masculine and more matter–of–fact. But half way through I got cold feet. What if he didn't want me any more? What if he had found new interest in his studies and wanted to be a nuclear physicist after all? Perhaps he had found someone else... I was determined to squash these thoughts and finished the letter, posting it in the box at the crossroads just as the postie turned up in his van to empty it. The next few days I spent waiting for George to turn up on his bicycle with Simon's reply. I should have insisted that he gave me a telephone number where I could contact him quickly in London.

The telephone rang one evening after I'd come in from the milking parlour. It was Simon at last.

"Listen, I'm at Windermere Station."

"What ...now?"

"Shall I get a taxi or can you collect me in the Land Rover?"

"How are you?"

"I've quit the course. I'm through! I told you how I felt about nuclear physics now…"

There was a long pause. I feared the phone line might have been cut off.

"Simon… Simon!… Are you still there?"

"Do you still want me now? I've got nowhere to go."

He sounded on the point of tears.

"Stay there and don't move!"

"I'm not going anywhere. Believe me... not now! Besides, I've completely run out of cash. If you'd been out, I would have been sleeping on a park bench somewhere... I got your letter... Listen – I love you... and I'm so desperate. You know about the sound of the wheels of the train... and the effect it has on me..."

"We should never have said goodbye. Simon... I should have listened to you."

I don't suppose that old Land Rover had ever been driven faster down to Windermere. In the rear–view mirror I could see a cloud of blue smoke I was leaving behind. Simon was sitting on a bench outside the entrance of the station. He got up as I drew to a halt. I leaned across and opened the door for him to clamber in. He chucked the backpack and his suitcase in the back.

"What's that?" I asked, looking at a wooden box with a handle on the top.

"My record player... It's been the only thing to keep me sane in London... I've just bought 'Chet Baker Sings' on a long–playing disc. You'll like it. He's very romantic. The other old 78s were too heavy to bring. I've sent them home by British Road Services. We might collect them some time."

Then he leaned across to kiss me.

"I've also bought the 'Good Housekeeping Cookery Book'. I found it in Foyle's…"

I looked down at his legs.

"Where are your sexy shorts? I've never seen you in long trousers before."

Simon undid his belt and swiftly pushed his trousers down to his knees. I tried to keep my eyes on the road ahead.

"God!" he muttered. "I'm so randy! Take me home! We need to make up for lost time! ... I want you to fuck me so hard I nearly pass out!"

"I hope nobody can see in the windows. What if that policeman over there were to stop us?"

"I don't care. You'd better take me home quickly."

I put my foot down on the accelerator as we passed the de–restricted sign. I put my hand on his bare knee and squeezed it. Simon grabbed my hand and placed it on his groin but the Land Rover swerved and I quickly replaced my hand on the steering wheel. I turned to smile at him.

"Yes, I'm going to kiss you all over... while you have a bath in front of the fire... and then I'm going to fuck you like you've never been fucked before!"

"Yes! ... Is that a promise? I've thought of a new position we've never used before but you'll have to be careful you don't split me in half."

I put my foot hard down to the floor and we sped off down the road leaving another cloud of blue smoke. Very soon we were in the farmhouse behind locked doors. I put my arms around Simon and we just held one another for what seemed ages, then I led him up the stairs.

"I'm going to need some emotional support tomorrow," I warned him. "Elspeth is coming here to collect her stuff which is still left in the wardrobe."

"Have you told her about me yet?"

"No, why should I?"

"So what do you want me to do then – make a pot of tea?"

"I don't think I could face her on my own."

"Will there be a shouting match?"

I shrugged my shoulders and looked at Simon.

"Well," he sighed, "whatever happens, I know I have done the right thing. I was sitting in my tiny room in London, staring at the rain through the window. All I wanted to do was to come straight back here. I didn't want to talk to anyone or do anything else. That's when I knew..."

"What was that?"

"I didn't want to go on living without you. My home is here. My future lies here on the farm... Do you want me then?... I'm talking about for good!"

I reached forward to undo his shirt and pulled it over his head. Simon was about to say something. I stopped him with a kiss. He got down on his knees and looked up at me.

"Please, please... never send me away again... Promise? In return I will do anything for you. You can do whatever you want to me, any time, any place. I will never say no. I will help you with the farm like I did before and never need to be paid... How about that for a deal? All I need is a really good fucking every night."

I started to laugh at him.

"Sometimes you even wanted it two or three times a day."

I reached down and pulled him up to his feet again and kissed him full on the mouth.

"Let's just make one another happy," I added, now undoing the buckle on his leather belt. "Plenty of time for questions later."

He seemed slimmer than I remembered.

"I haven't been eating," he added. "Nothing at all."

I pushed his jeans down to find he wasn't wearing any underwear but said nothing. His penis rose up in my hand. He put his arms around my shoulders and I lifted him up off the floor with my other hand cupped under his pert buttocks, just like that first day. Together we toppled on to the bed.

"Will you promise me you'll never send me away again?"

"I promise. You can stay here as long as you like. Elspeth and I are getting a legal separation."

"Because of me?"

"No, she wants to go her own way. It seems she's made her own decision. I haven't told her about you yet."

He was pulling his vest over his head and I gave him a hand.

"I've been dreaming about this moment," he said, jumping off the bed and rummaging in the rucksack. "I found this in Soho... I've been making do with this..."

He passed me a rubber dildo. I stared at it in disbelief.

"...What's wrong with that? You've seen one of those before, surely."

I told Simon all about my visit to Madame Claire Voyante and what she'd seen in her crystal.

"She'd like to meet you, you know. We could ask her what she makes of your family – the future of the Palace, the family title and the estate..."

"Perhaps it is just better not to know, don't you think? Well, I'll think about it..."

Simon put the rubber dildo under the bed.

"...After you, this thing was a bit of a disappointment but it was better than nothing ... Fuck me! ... Now I need the real thing! ... I need to forget all that gloom and misery in London!"

He lay back on the pillow with his legs in the air and wrapped them around my shoulders. We gazed at each other and smiled. I hadn't felt so happy for ages. My beautiful boyfriend had just come home, for good, it would appear. I stretched forward to kiss him. Simon put his hands around my face to hold me closer.

"Now fuck me you super man… Fuck me to make up for all

that lost time."

I squeezed some Vaseline onto my finger and inserted it between his buttocks. Simon shuffled closer and moved his legs apart. We stared at one another – one of those long, lingering and sexually charged moments. Then I grabbed his erect penis while I slid mine inside him. He closed his eyes and lay back on the pillow.

"That's it... Oh, you super man, I love you!... Huh!... Fuck me harder!... Show me what I've been missing in London! ... Huh!... I'm going to come!...Huh!..."

Suddenly his swollen penis exploded in my hand and a jet of cum shot high up in the air splattering both of us. Simon stared at me again.

"Now will you promise never to send me away again?"

"Yes, I promise."

"I really couldn't go through so much misery again."

"I think we could still be together in fifty years' time..."

"Fifty years?"

"That's what Madame Claire Voyante said. But we've got to deal with Elspeth first. Listen... I will need you so much tomorrow. In fact I know I need you to be around for the rest of my life. Could you cope with that idea, now? I mean here on the farm with me. Believe me, Simon, I've learnt the hard way... I can't live without you any more..."

This was the moment Simon got up off the bed to kneel down in front of me as I sat on the edge with my feet on the floor.

"I want you to know... and you must always remember this..."

Tears filled his eyes. He took my hands.

"...I want you to know that you are everything to me... I've given up my degree and my studies in nuclear engineering just to be with you..."

I gazed in disbelief at the gorgeous naked hunk in front of me. He leaned forward to kiss my hand and looked up into my face again – one of those long, lingering glances in which he seemed to see into the very depth of my being.

"...I hope the fortune–teller was right and that we will still be together in ten, twenty, thirty years from now. For you, I am giving up everything – my birthright to a place amongst the landed gentry, the promise of my seat in the House of Lords, any other honours, graces and all that sort of crap... I am giving up now, this instant, to be with you. God, …I mean the God my father, His Lordship, believes in, that is if there really is a God, which I doubt, shall be my witness. Anyway I am telling you that I love you and I give myself to you from now on… I have missed you so much! Now please… fuck me again and if I wear you out, I'll leave you to have a lie–in tomorrow. I'll look after the cows and bring you breakfast in bed… That's all I want from life because I can't live without you any more… I've learned that the hard way…"

At this point Simon dissolved into floods of tears and I got down on the floor to hold him. It was just like that first day – the day of the power cut which seemed such a long time ago. There were no more words to say. We just held on to one another and swayed gently together.

•••••••

Elspeth arrived the next day about noon. Simon and I came to the door together when we heard the car pull up in the yard. I wanted to show her what I had now. She didn't ask about Simon but said she was in a hurry and dashed up the stairs with an empty suitcase. Within a quarter of an hour she had disappeared out of my life again. There was no row, only stony silence between us. As her car vanished down the lane, Simon put his arm around my shoulder and we went back inside.

"I'm so glad you were here," I said. "I couldn't have coped without you... not any more."

"Do you think she guessed who I was?"

"What does it really matter?"

"Well if I'd been something pretty in a pink frock, maybe it would have been handbags at dawn..."

He looked at me with his come–to–bed eyes.

"...I suppose I could have worn a Scottish kilt."

"You'd look really pretty in one of those... But, frankly, I don't think Elspeth could be bothered. Maybe she's just through with men."

"Are you through with women?"

"If you will stay with me."

"Well, it's up to you to make it worth my while," he laughed. "Let's go back upstairs. We haven't tried out that new position yet."

2001

Memories! I smiled as I looked out of the side window of the Land Rover at the Motorway Service Area. Simon and I had been sleeping together ever since. Was it really over forty years? I took another look at the barn over the other side of the fence. For the life of me I couldn't remember if I'd ever fucked him in there, so many years ago. Yes, there it was – Simon's family crest on the weather vane. I had not imagined it. Life! How could I know he would drop in for breakfast but stay over forty years? He'd been studying nuclear physics but somehow the Windscale fire had killed his enthusiasm for all that. The Windscale fire and love – two landmarks in Simon's life which had changed everything forever. How could we have known that the Windscale fire was the first. It had been a warning of disasters to come... later there was Three Mile Island in the USA and then the big one, a real melt–down at Chernobyl in the USSR in 1986, just as the fortune–teller had predicted. Once again radioactive rain blew across the Lake District.

I remembered what the locals said at the village pub. Nobody living near Windscale liked nuclear power after that second disaster. If only the government had spent those millions by building a barrage around Morecambe Bay to generate hydroelectric power. And for forty years we had our own hydroelectric plant on the farm and proved it would work. Simon saw to that but it was something he and I built together. It cemented our relationship all those years ago.

1957

Well! Simon's new cookery book changed my life. From that moment on I had never been better looked after and started to put on the weight I'd lost after my wife walked out. In those days we still had a village shop, a post office and a butcher. Simon soon got to know all of them. If there was any gossip about us, I never heard it. After all, in the late fifties, there were still lots of farm labourers. A neighbour of ours still used horses although he was one of the last. It was not unusual for farm hands to live on the premises. Local people accepted Simon as just another farm hand. But if they'd known he was my lover, would anyone have really minded out in the country? As time went on I discovered nobody had ever really liked Elspeth. They thought of her as an outsider from the city who never really belonged in the country.

For a while I forwarded any letters which came for her and explained to the postman that she had gone home to look after her mother in Manchester.

We had just finished clearing up after the morning milking when George the postman dropped by with more bills. I laughed. He had met Simon before but George leaned his bicycle against the door and suddenly started to tell him the story of Brady's Mill. The ruins of this mill were shrouded in stinging nettles and overgrown trees, beside the stream under the bridge, by the ledge where we left the milk churns every day at the end of the lane.

"Brady, he owned the mill, you see, Simon, as well as worked it and lived in it. He bought it from Joe, the old miller, who was there before and grew too poorly to lift the sacks any more. Anyhow, Joe had been teetotal. Not a drop of liquor ever passed his lips all those years. But Brady, he liked a drop... well more than a drop. He bought the booze cheap from God knows where and stacked it inside the mill. Then Joe died and they do say how he returned from the grave to haunt that mill to try to prevent Brady getting drunk on his liquor. Wild bangings and clatterings there were in the middle of the night..."

"When was that then... what year would that have been?"

"Oh before the First War... about 1900. Finally, old Brady did get drunk and in his drunken stupor, the ghost of Old Joe appeared to challenge him. ...Well, that's how the story goes. Brady threw a lighted candle at the spectre and set fire to the place. It burned down with Brady in it and has lain in ruins down there ever since. Local mothers used to tell their children the grisly tale so as to teach the poor kids about the evils of booze... That's how my mother told it to me."

"And did it work?" Simon was laughing. "Did it keep you on the straight and narrow, away from taverns, public houses, inns and such dens of iniquity?"

"No!..."

We all burst out laughing.

"...But it were a darn good tale, weren't it!"

George got back on his bicycle, still chuckling to himself, and disappeared down the lane again. Simon and I went inside for some coffee.

"It wasn't like that at all," I said, holding my mug out for Simon to drain the coffee pot. "I reckon George has dined out on that story for years. It gets better as time goes on."

"So what's left of the mill now?... It was a water–powered mill, I take it."

We left the coffee to get cold on the kitchen table and took the milk churns on the trolley down the lane to leave for the lorry to collect them later again. Simon and I then squeezed through a gap in the hedge in order to look at the ruins down beside the stream.

"Well," I said. "For one reason or another, it did burn down. Under all this rubble are the water wheel and the millstones as well. Over the years, villagers have come down here to cart off the stones from the walls to build or to extend their own houses, so one day, maybe, the remains of the wheel and the stones will come to light."

I showed Simon where the millstream now lay covered in undergrowth, leading up the hill, back up to the tarn lake which had acted as a mill pond. He was fascinated. He couldn't understand how I had omitted to tell him all this before. Finally, having climbed halfway up the valley, we found ourselves sitting by the remains of the sluice, which channelled water into the upper end of the old millstream.

So we sat side by side looking down to the farm, where smoke from the Aga was curling up into the mist.

"Thank you," he said. "This is how my life was meant to be... I know... Here with you... Let's wander over to that shepherd's hut... I want to get fucked in all the outbuildings as well..."

"What, all of them?"

He got up and put out a hand to help me up. I put a hand on his shoulder and we walked over to the hut. It was empty inside. There was nothing for Simon to lie on. I pulled down his shorts. He kicked them off and leaned forwards with his hands against the wall either side of the aperture where a window used to be. I cupped both his buttocks in my hands and pushed them aside. He moved his legs apart.

"Fuck me!" he muttered. "I need it now ...like never before!"

He squeezed through the window aperture so his head and arms went through outside. His bare buttocks now bent over the window ledge inside, his feet hardly touched the ground.

"How's this?" I said loudly while I felt his body tense and then relax.

Outside the hut I could hear some sheep nearby. One bleated

loudly. Simon bleated back at it and started laughing.

"Bah!... Yes, mate," he said. "It happens to us too!"

"What's that?" I asked, now about to climax.

"This sheep outside is staring at me," Simon muttered. "It's so funny. I think it knows what you're doing to me... Now, at last, I feel I'm at one with nature!"

....

We sat side by side again outside watching the birds circle in the sky.

"Are you ok?" I asked.

"That was just amazing... It's never been like that before!"

"I wasn't too rough with you...?"

"You must do it again, outdoors... just like that... yes, soon!"

"Well it was different... Funny about the sheep."

"I swear it knew what was going on!"

"Were you communing with nature?"

"Well, I've told you. I needed a real man ... Now I know I did the right thing to quit the university course in London..."

"Do I really make you happy...?"

"I wouldn't be anywhere else, with anyone else," he said. "My life is here... with you. Do you know?... I think we'll still be together in forty years' time..."

"I hope so... I love you."

He took hold of my hand and kissed it. Instinctively I looked around but we were miles from civilisation and there was nobody else about, except the sheep and they were only interested in the next patch of green grass. So we sat silently, leaning against one another, staring down across the view beyond. I felt really relaxed and blissfully happy and put my hand up to hold Simon's head. He instinctively kissed it again. So we just sat there, listening to the wind in the crags, the occasional bird in the sky above and the bleating of the sheep.

"Tell me more about Brady and the mill," Simon said eventually.

"George got it all wrong... The story I was told sounded more like some newfangled opera by Benjamin Britten. Old Brady had an apprentice to help him to run the mill but somehow the boy fell in the works and got crushed to death as it went round. So

Brady took a new apprentice. He was a handsome young soldier from the Crimea who wanted to learn a trade after the war ended. What George didn't tell you is that he fell in love with the miller's wife and Brady discovered them in the sack loft together. In the fight that followed, an oil lamp was upset and the mill caught fire. The apprentice escaped with Brady's wife but the miller was burned in the flames and died as the mill collapsed around him. Well, that's what I heard!..."

Simon was laughing.

"...Some say the apprentice and Brady's wife still live happily together somewhere after over fifty years. I think everyone you talk to has heard a different story!"

We walked down the valley again, retracing the old millstream right back to the site of the mill at the bottom of our lane. By now it was nearly lunchtime, so I took Simon to the pub for a pint. There we happened to meet the local butcher, who had now retired but still lived next door to the pub. I told him how we had spent the morning retracing the remains of Brady's Mill. Simon was already expecting a third version of the story.

"Well now, son," the butcher said. "I knew Brady because he used to buy his meat from my father's shop. He wasn't nearly as bad as they say, either. But he did like his tipple. The chapel crowd were over there in that old tin shack. They'd all signed the pledge and saw themselves shouldered with God's holy task to persuade Brady to give up his demon booze and come to chapel on Sundays... Well, that's what I was told. The mill apprentice – that handsome young soldier fresh back from the Crimea – he was chapel, too, you see. He tried to convince Brady to forsake the demon booze. There was a fight inside the mill and it all caught fire... You probably know the rest."

"So, what was the truth about Brady and his mill?" Simon asked while the butcher returned to the bar to talk to the barman.

"Who knows? ... Does it really matter?"

Under the table I put my hand on Simon's bare knee and squeezed it. He moved up closer to me. I moved my hand up inside his shorts to touch his penis. This time he did not protest but smiled as if it was my right to do this. I looked around to check that nobody was watching and stroked it to make him hard.

"Isn't it nice," Simon whispered. "They're already treating us like a couple... part of the local community... It's not like this in London... Now do you understand?"

"It's because of you," I added. "You are so beautiful. Everyone loves you."

"It can't really be such a sin, can it... like it says in the Bible?"

"I've given up worrying about all that, Simon. I think it takes a disastrous marriage to teach some of us..."

"But you know Harry and I had to go to church services every Sunday... thou shalt not do this! ... thou shalt not do that! ... from the time we could walk."

"Why worry about things like that now if we really love one another?... Did you really miss me so much in London?"

"I can't tell you!...But all the time my mind was wrestling with this sin thing... My whole body needed you... My mind would only be at peace again if I could be with you... But according to the Christian do's and don'ts with which Harry and I had been indoctrinated, what I craved for was sin of the naughtiest kind. Yes, just like this. Don't stop. I'm going to come."

"But you came back all the same... But maybe religious doctrine might be... well... a bit like the story of Brady's Mill... different interpretations and records of the same historical event... just as you might find different historical accounts and interpretations of the creation of the world in various religions. Who is to say which one is right?"

Suddenly his penis ejaculated and I withdrew my hand. So we sat quietly for a while and finished our drinks. He turned to me with another beautiful smile.

"I sometimes felt I was being punished by God... I had found you but you sent me away, back to London..."

"But I told you I had to deal with Elspeth."

Suddenly Simon looked on the point of tears. I had no idea, until then, that he had found life in London so difficult. I rubbed his thigh under the table.

"You just don't know what it's like to be brought up in a religious household."

"How do you mean?"

"Well, I went to church twice on Sundays to be told about sin and all that sort of thing… How God would expect me to find a wife and start a family… But all I ever wanted was another man… just like you. Of course, the Bible tells us that is a sin… Beware Sodom and Gomorrah…"

"It is only a sin if you believe it to be so."

"Yes, it was either to become myself or suicide. I could see no alternative."

My mind flashed back to the oil painting of the youth sitting on his rock by the sea. I had never shown it to Simon.

"You are not the first to think that, surely."

"I've got to give up this religion thing. I can't go through life haunted by guilt. That's why I need you so much… You accept me as I really am. I do not need to pretend when we are together. I could never survive in the closet... When I feel you inside me... I know I am fulfilling my destiny."

"Your destiny?"

"To love a man just like you, not a woman..."

"I'm very lucky, Simon. You know that, don't you."

"My destiny is to be an outcast, almost in the biblical sense... To find myself away from the world of London... society... and those conventions of the British establishment my parents represent... the House of Lords... sacred traditions of the church... and all that... I only feel safe up here in the Lake District, with you."

"Sh!"

The butcher came back to tell us that the barman had yet another version to tell about the history of the old mill, so when we took our pint glasses back for a refill, I asked him what it was.

"Well now. I sometimes used to pop in there to watch the mill working inside and to buy a bag of flour for my mother. Those millstones used to get hot going round and round all day. Brady had to control the speed of the mill with a kind of brake or by winding the sluice up and down to prevent the stones overheating and spoiling the flour with black bits, well that is what he told me! But he got drunk one day, see, and during a thunderstorm the water level in the millstream rose higher and made the water wheel go too fast. The millstones overheated and the whole thing caught fire... all due to confusion of the mind caused by liquor, if you believe that lot in the gospel mission ... devil's work they called it! ...Another pint, gentlemen?"

We laughed again and went back to sit outside.

"Now I'm getting confused," Simon said.

"Well, I did warn you... The truth is as varied as there are people to tell you how it really was! ... like creation, according to different religions, I think."

"But I'm thinking this... If there was enough energy to cause those millstones to overheat and catch fire, we must be talking about many kilowatts of heat... in electrical terms. Why not use the water from the mill pond to generate electricity like Scottish Hydro do on a bigger scale – I mean, in our case, enough electricity for a farmhouse and maybe to run a milking machine as well? We might not need to pay electricity bills any more. What do you say to that idea?"

So the two of us went to have another look at the lie of the land from the other side of the valley. Eventually we sat on the stone wall by the road and looked down towards the farm. I pointed where the original mill had stood.

"But I showed you, Simon. The mill wheel is buried under all that rubble under those trees... And the mill building would have to be rebuilt... because the villagers have gone off with any building materials worth having..."

"What if we pipe the water to increase the pressure and use a water turbine or a Pelton wheel...?"

"What's that, then?"

"It's a more modern version of a water wheel, which extracts more energy from the flow... especially at high pressure... It's just more efficient."

"How do you know all this?"

"Physics... I got a distinction in my first year exams."

"But you've given all that up... at the university."

"For you ...yes! ...I have no regrets."

We climbed over the nearest gate and strolled down the slope towards another barn built of stone. Simon pushed open the door. There was a smell of musty hay inside.

"I want to make love," he said. "Did you note that?...I said love not just a fuck..."

He pushed the door closed behind us. I put my arms around him and we kissed.

"Thank you for everything," I said, pulling him down onto the hay.

"I gave up engineering and found you... This is what life's all about... I realised that before I quit London. Real life is more important than abstract science... This is love..."

Simon kissed me tenderly.

"I could fake scientific results in a laboratory but I can't fake love for a woman... That's what my father intended. Before I met you, I'd almost given up hope."

"I think real love is the most powerful force in life... and, for me, that's you, Simon."

I held him tight to kiss again. He moved my hand away from his shoulder.

"Well, now is as good a time as any... to give you something of England's heritage."

"Heritage?"

Simon undid the neck of his shirt and lifted off a neck chain to hand it to me.

"Have a close look at the pendant there..."

I held it close to my eye in the stream of light filtering through a gap in the roof.

"It's what is left of our family seal... Henry the Eighth presented that to my ancestors when my family were given lands confiscated from a monastery… You know they were dissolved by Henry when he established the Church of England... after 1532."

"I remember..."

"My grandfather gave that to me before he died because I am next in line to the title... Yes... and the seat in the House of Lords which goes with it."

I was shocked and suddenly felt dizzy.

"You don't mean...?"

"Yes... I do mean... but I don't want any of it... So now I'm giving it to you... As a mark of my love... I'm appointing you keeper of our family seal... Look – there's not much left of the cross of St George, two griffins rampant and the Latin motto. They've been worn away over the last four hundred years."

"I can't take this!"

"You must take it. Otherwise I'm throwing it in Lake Coniston... or Lake Windermere. I haven't decided which."

"Well... I'll look after it in case you change your mind."

"Now how about a long, slow fuck? We haven't done it in here yet."

•••••••

When we returned to the pub later, another old character appeared beside us and sat down at the bench opposite. We both looked up.

"Well now, son," he said, chuckling already. "I know what really happened to Brady's Mill... Don't listen to the others. They've got it all wrong."

Simon and I shared a glance and tried to hide a smile.

"... It was like this, see. That young soldier from the Crimea – the one they all talk about. Well, he was an amateur chemist. He decided to use the mill to grind his own gunpowder so he put all the ingredients into the millstone while Brady wasn't looking and bang! ...Well, that's what I heard..."

I told him Simon had an idea to get the mill working again to generate electricity but he swore all the machinery had blown up with the gunpowder and we were wasting our time. Anyway, he added, Old Joe, the first miller had put a curse on the place. That's why nobody would go near it, even today!

He got up again and went back inside the pub, leaving Simon and me in fits of laughter. I think by now anybody could have seen that the two of us were in love. But nobody seemed to bother. Maybe they all realised I'd never been really happy with Elspeth. Some of them had actually been at my wedding. Did they all know it had been only a sham?

"So why not?" Simon asked, seriously.

"Why not what?"

"Generate our own electricity, using the lake as a source of water and that gradient up the valley to add enough power to run a turbine. I reckon it could be ten or even twenty kilowatts of power we are not using, simply going to waste."

"But think of the cost, Simon... clearing out the old millstream, rebuilding the mill, connecting up the generator... that is, after we have bought it. I don't think it's viable."

"Well, I'll think about it, anyway."

In spite of my reservations about Simon's idea, it seemed to me that I had finally found myself at last. My marriage and my attempt to play the usual role for a respectable young man in the fifties had failed. Through Simon, and only thanks to him, had I found my real self. I seemed to have found everything missing in my life in him. He was my other half. His energy, enthusiasm, imagination and technical skills had made up for my failings.

I would never ever have thought of harnessing the potential power in the old millstream to generate our own electricity. He had already become a partner, in every sense of the word, both in and out of bed. Perhaps we were entering the third stage of a lasting relationship. The initial excitement of rampant sex had been followed by the caring stage. Now we were starting to plan things together. This might be the creative stage. If I'd been any other man, I might have conceived children with a woman. But Simon and I were planning to create our own hydroelectric plant instead.

We found ourselves in the village pub again to continue our discussion about laying a pipeline for the water to our hydroelectric scheme. However, the locals were gossiping about the latest scandal in the national press. A famous actor had been accused of cottaging at a men's toilet in Soho. The landlord swore it would be the end of his career. Served him right, he added. He'd never liked him on television anyway. So Simon and I took our pints and retreated to the solitude of the garden. Neither of us wanted anything to do with this debate.

"I almost got caught in a public lavatory near the University," Simon said. "That was the other reason I came walking up here in the Lake District."

"So it wasn't just coming to see Calder Hall nuclear power station…"

"No. I used to get so desperate that I started to hang around outside the men's loo where I'd heard you could often find someone. Only he turned out to be one of those agents provocateurs planted by the Metropolitan Police. But I could run faster than the policemen and I lost them."

"I'm so glad."

"So I got fed up with London and escaped at the earliest opportunity and found you here, far away in the countryside."

"The best day of my life. Well, I didn't know it then. But it was."

"I think I need another pint. Same again?"

"No, let's go home and make love. I need more sex now."

It was around about this time that my old Land Rover let us down for the first time in a rather dramatic fashion. The fabric hood that made up the soft–top was fitted over metal rails to hold up the roof. This fabric had seen better days and had started to rot along the seams. We were sheltering inside during a sudden squall, which had descended on us from the mountains high above. So we sat nibbling a ploughman's lunch, which Simon had prepared earlier, hoping to get back to work when the rain stopped. Instead it got worse and we were rocked from side to side by the buffeting wind. While he looked though the windscreen at the torrents of rain, Simon had a sudden inspiration.

"Wouldn't it be exciting to have sex now... with this storm going on outside."

"But are you serious?" I objected. "Why not wait until we're indoors...?"

"Please!... It would be a new experience! Oh go on...Fuck me now!"

He looked at me through those come–to–bed eyelashes just as the rain turned to hail outside. It was clattering on the aluminium bodywork around us.

"... Well, what else is there to do?"

Another squall was clearly about to descend on us and we'd finished all the food.

"Are you quite sure?"

"Yes, I want a good seeing to. It might warm us up a bit."

I couldn't anticipate any problems. We were parked miles away from the public footpath and by now there was so much mist on the inside of the windows that nobody could possibly see what was going on inside. Simon was already wriggling out of his clothes, in spite of the chill. Just watching him do this was always enough to get me excited. So we clambered over the seats into the back of the Land Rover. He bent forward over the seats and I mounted him from the rear. Within moments we were hard at it when there was another mighty gust of wind outside, accompanied by a ripping sound from the fabric roof. Within seconds, the whole thing was ripped away, leaving us both exposed to the elements. If anyone had been standing nearby, it would have been a sight for sore eyes. We both watched in horror as the remains of the soft–top disappeared over the rocks into the gully below, along with most of Simon's clothing. There was only one old coat lying on the floor, which the sheepdog slept on. He grabbed it to wrap around himself while I started the engine and drove as fast as we could down the track to the farm. We were both blue with the cold by the time we reached the kitchen to warm up in front of the Aga. This also provided the hot water for Simon to thaw out in a hot bath. It was a while before either of us felt able to laugh about such an emergency. But eventually we did. I think that experience finally welded the two of us together as a couple. It proved to me that two men can be happy together, both in and out of bed, in spite of the worst that nature could throw at us. Would a conventional heterosexual marriage have survived such a challenge so well, I wondered?

But we started to ask much more fundamental questions in 1957. Why was the government arguing about the Wolfenden Report? After the two world wars I could accept there was a serious shortage of eligible young men capable of raising families. Far too many had died. The woman's role up to 1945 had often been to work as a land girl or in a munitions factory. When the men returned to civilian life they needed many of the jobs previously held by women. But why did the government not want relationships of two men living together? Did it still boil down to the need for post–war babies to make into soldiers the Empire can be proud of? Or was it just to appease hard line supporters of the Old Testament in the Church of England? Why would Simon and I always have to be looking over our shoulders for potential blackmailers or informers? Everyone we talked to in the village just seemed to accept us and even to like us. We never went round kissing in public or holding hands in Lovers' Lane but it must have been obvious to anyone who knew about love. And love it was, deeper than any emotion I had ever felt before.

We made the appropriate application for planning permission so as not to make enemies on the local council. In the end, they just did not seem to want to know. Nothing would go across their land but there would be no grant of money to help with expenses. As the pipe was green and would mostly lie in the bed of the old millstream, they saw no objection. Still, Simon had to find a water turbine and the generator to go with it. We bought the Exchange and Mart at the village store. Water turbines and alternators for ten kilowatts were obviously hard to find. There was nothing. So Simon phoned Scottish Hydro to ask for their advice. They recommended an engineering firm in Glasgow so he phoned them too. We were in luck. They would soon be reconditioning a small second–hand unit. Were we interested? I told him to say yes and could they quote a price? But he would need to go up there to see it first and to work out how to connect it to all the many pipes we had sitting on trailers round the back of the barn. Our next debate was about where to site the turbine and the generating equipment. How would we dispose of all that water which would come hurtling down from the lake through a twelve–inch–bore pipe?

Simon eventually agreed to visit Madame Claire Voyante in Windermere and I made another appointment. I told her on the phone that I was bringing the handsome young man she had seen naked in her crystal and how everything had turned out to be true. I congratulated her on her accuracy in predicting my immediate future. So, one wet and windy afternoon I found myself once again seated at her table while she polished her crystal and gazed into it. I glanced at Simon, who was feeling nervous today.

"Good God!" she exclaimed excitedly. "I'm looking backwards in history first of all. My Lord... No, no I see now, the title offends you... I'm sorry, Sir."

Simon cast a nervous glance at me.

"Well, I didn't tell her anything," I whispered in his ear.

We waited while Madame took a slurp from the gin bottle again and breathed on the crystal before wiping it slowly while looking Simon up and down admiringly.

"So handsome… You have clearly spent many hours in the gymnasium."

He glanced at me again.

"Not for ages, actually, Madame."

"Well then you must have inherited your good looks…"

She polished the crystal again with her cloth and gazed into it intensely.

"…Then, young man, it comes from your ancient and noble English lineage… Natural beauty like yours was much admired in 1533... You know about Henry the Eighth, of course, and his gift of lands to your ancestor Sir Cecil..."

"You told her!" Simon muttered at me.

"No, Sir," Madame assured him, patting him on the knee. "My crystal shows me everything... I'm looking backwards today over four hundred years... You and your brother... Is his name Harold?… after Sir Cecil's son? "

"My brother's name is Harry... Named after Harold's great grandson..."

"Oh, yes. I see it now... 1645... Did you know what happened to the original Harry, your revered ancestor, in the English Civil

War?…"

Simon looked at me in disbelief and then stared at Madame again.

"…Well, he was threatened by Oliver Cromwell's men, who tried to use your ancestral home as a stable for their horses... Your ancestor supported the royalists..."

"Yes, I know, Madame. Grandfather told me all about it."

"You know about the treasure then?…"

Madame now gazed closer at the crystal.

"…I can see your ancestor Harry burying a lead–lined box of treasure beneath the hearthstone in the inglenook fireplace... He's nearly too late to hide the evidence... He's brushing ashes from the fire to hide everything... before Oliver Cromwell's troops come bursting in... Did you know about that?"

"No, Madame... What's in this box of treasure, then?"

"It's lead–lined to a quarter–inch depth, Sir... The crystal cannot view anything through that. The rays can't get through... Is it still there where he left it?"

Simon started laughing.

"This was no laughing matter, Sir. He died within a month... Tortured to death in an attempt to extract secrets about the royalists... Very nasty! ...You don't want to know!…"

Simon stared at me in disbelief while Madame gazed deep into her crystal.

" ...Well, anyway, he is being hung and drawn. Are the human entrails really that long? ...But he's still alive... Tell me, young man, has anyone seen his ghost recently?... Perhaps, accompanied by loud screams down in the cellar by the light of a full moon..."

"I've never heard anything, Madame... but I've heard stories... Anyway, I think any self–respecting ghost might be more frightened of me... a raging poof out at night in search of another quick fuck with the gamekeeper... That might be enough to frighten any God–fearing ghost, don't you think?"

Madame now made tut–tut noises while staring in horror at the crystal.

"Well, I warn you, young man, Sir Geraint, another ancestor of yours, was burned at the stake in the local market square. I'm watching it in my crystal now. His enemies accused him of raping a stable boy and unnatural practices with other male servants. 'Faggot, go to Hell!' – the villagers are all shouting at him while they throw more bundles on the fire. Let that be a warning…"

I couldn't help laughing at Simon, who put his fingers in his ears, but Madame shifted uneasily in her chair and turned back to her crystal once more.

"Clearly you have inherited your stamina from ancestors like him, young man ...Oh no ! ...They didn't set fire to... Yuk! ...His entrails are smouldering... Your ancestor, poor man..."

Madame now covered the crystal with her cloth and turned away in disgust. "...Not a glorious chapter of English history!" She turned to Simon again and smiled at him.

"Have you heard of another ancestor of yours... Sir Eustace, who lived at the Palace about one hundred years later?..."

He turned to me again, clearly unable to believe what he was hearing.

"...Well, you used to sleep in the four–poster bed he had made for himself and his child bride... Was it later called the King's Bed?… The big one with side curtains to keep out the draught and the coat of arms on the canopy..."

Simon's bottom jaw dropped.

"No, Madame. It was called the Queen's Bed... after Queen Victoria stayed there one night following a railway disaster. Anyway that's what I was told."

Madame polished the crystal again and stared into it, clearly relishing what she could see there.

"You lost your virginity in it... under it? ...over it? ...when you were only seventeen years old and home from school in the holidays. You were so pretty! No wonder the gamekeeper wanted to give you a good seeing to when you had a gorgeous arse like that... But you really were a slut, leading him on so, poor man! ...I'm so sorry Sir. I get carried away at times! ...I blame General Gordon and his liking for distilled liquor..."

Simon laughed and turned red.

"...Do you know what were the last words on Hamish's lips when he died in that God–forsaken bomb crater in Korea back in 1952?"

"Tell me, I have no idea, Madame."

"He died saying 'Simon, Simon come and help me' over and over. You were the only one he'd ever loved, you see."

Simon swallowed hard, turned to me and then looked back at the crystal.

"Please tell me more about my revered ancestors,

Madame..."

She took a longer swig of gin.

"Well Sir Eustace is still angry... He's on the other side... looking at me now. Very angry he is! ...Well, young man, I warn you... He's never forgiven you for sullying the family escutcheon on... or over his beloved's bed... but he has no excuse. His child bride was only thirteen years old... disgusting I call it... She died in childbirth... too young, you see, giving birth to twins... Only one survived... until scarlet fever carried him off too."

"No, I never knew that!"

Simon turned back to me, shaking his head.

"I take it you probably will not be continuing the family line," Madame continued. "What about your brother Harry? Is he the marrying kind? ...Will he get married and produce a future heir?"

"Yes, I think so... What does your crystal foretell, then, Madame?"

"That'll be another seven and sixpence, Sir."

I put a ten shilling note down on the table in front of her.

"Keep the change, Madame."

"Thank you, Sir... Most kind! But I warn you. Predicting the future can be a dangerous business. You must have heard about the Welwyn Garden City train crash which I predicted in January. I saw it clearly in my crystal but when I reported all this to British Railways and the disaster occurred exactly as I said it would on the telephone, they wanted to have me arrested for sabotage."

She turned to Simon again.

"So, young man, what would you do now? Tell me. You are intelligent. I need to know because, yesterday, I saw another train crash happening in thick fog near Lewisham in South London. A steel railway bridge will collapse on to a steam train that is crashing into an electric train full of passengers. The toll of deaths and serious injuries… Oh dear, Simon… It is the date and the time I can never see in my crystal, you see. I only know it will be before Christmas because I saw fresh sheets of gift–wrapping paper lying in the wreckage of one carriage beside a brand new teddy bear. Today is the 3rd December so it will be soon, but when? Well, think about it… If I knew the date and the exact time in advance of a horse race, I would be as rich as the Queen Mother."

Simon tried to smile at her.

"But the Queen Mother probably owns the horse anyway, Madame."

"Now you are being dismissive like that dreadful man at British Railways. It is no laughing matter, young man. I tell you this will be one of the very worst railway catastrophes in English history. So… would you telephone Southern Region right now to warn them? They will want to know the date, the time and the exact location. And what happens when the police arrive to arrest me again after it happens exactly as I've just told you?"

He thought for a moment.

"I really don't know what I would do, Madame. Sorry… But perhaps it won't be foggy after all. You know what the English weather is like. The sun may come out so the engine driver can see the danger signal…"

Madame sighed, took another large swig of Gordons and turned back to the crystal. She made more tut–tut noises, breathed on it and wiped it again with the cloth. Simon turned to me with a worried expression. I don't think he really believed what she was saying.

"The future is more difficult to predict," she muttered, prodding him. "So much depends on you, you know... I can't see any future for the Palace... That is the name of your ancestral home, isn't it?"

She polished her crystal once more and took another look.

"...I can only see concrete mixers, men with pick axes, demolition and the intervention of a powerful government department... Something to do with motor cars... hundreds of them... racing up and down and very soon, too... It looks like one of those German autobahns... What's the new British word now? ... 'motorway'? ...The M1 it will be called... The scene of carnage, death and destruction for decades to come... Do you want to hear any more, then? ...Sorry, Sir, I can only tell you what I see in this thing."

Simon turned to me in disbelief.

"Are you saying there is no future for my family... Madame?"

"I can only tell you what I see, Sir... Sorry! Sometimes it can be better not to see into the future – certainly where railways are concerned, anyway. And that is why I sometimes turn back to the past... However, your future together with him, young man..."

She pointed and smiled at me.

"...Now that will be happy... You must have heard what I saw in my crystal the other day... in fifty years' time... in 2007... You two will get married or the equivalent in an English registry office... Yes, I swear it! ...If I hadn't seen it here in my crystal, I would have said it was impossible ...But the law will change, Sir, starting in 1967 ...in ten years' time... Parliament will lift the threat of prosecution...That same institution which Oliver Cromwell had so much faith in until he dissolved it. Was that 1653? ...Yes, one day Parliament will come to its senses and acknowledge real love between two men..."

Madame turned to me now.

"...You've told him all about all of that, of course..."

I nodded.

"...Well, I can see there are no secrets between you two... All I can say is good luck in your long lives together... fifty years! ...2007 will be a happy year for both of you... I've seen it!... I will be long gone, of course..."

Simon and I started laughing at one another.

"You'll look down on us from your cloud up there, Madame," Simon added.

"Oh, no, Sir," Madame insisted. "Floating on clouds in Heaven with the great and the good... So, so boring! ...I don't think so! ...I'll be down there ...helping to stoke up the fires of Hell! ...I want to meet that snooty spokeswoman from British Railways who assured me it was impossible to predict railway accidents. I told her where to go!... And I'd like to get my hands on that old sinner, England's only dictator, Oliver Cromwell... I've got a few ideas... My crystal has just given me a new one!"

CHAPTER THREE

1958

I soon wished that I'd asked Madame about the possibility of success for our hydroelectric scheme but if she'd given thumbs–down, I don't think it would have made much of a difference. She might not have known anything about such technical matters anyway, but for Simon it was simple. Working all these things out together, making plans together, talking about money together, discussing engineering problems together brought Simon and me into a closer relationship than I had ever felt with Elspeth. I realised now that I had never actually loved her. Granted I had said yes at the altar but that was to please everyone else in the parish church. Maybe I thought I was doing my bit for England. I just did not know, in those early days, what I really wanted. Maybe I really did think that love would grow with time when children arrived, but of course they didn't. Elspeth and I had never slept together for more than an hour or two. But Simon and I could spend all night, and all day in bed, if it wasn't for the mooing of the cows queuing up outside the milking parlour. Once George, our postman, nearly caught us naked in the kitchen together when we were having a bath by the stove in the morning. I grabbed my dressing gown and stood just outside the back door. George seemed to be on the point of hysterics this morning.

"It says here 'For the personal attention of His Lordship'... Funny people you know, mate. Would that be from the Department of Agriculture, Fisheries and Food, then? Or perhaps the Inland

Revenue winding you up..."

I pulled the door closed behind me so Simon wouldn't hear while he grabbed a towel.

"This is for you to keep under your cap," I whispered. "Simon is next in line to an honourable title, only he tries to keep quiet about it, you see... An estrangement with the family. Best not to ask... George."

"Very good, Guv."

"Not a word... please. "

"My lips are sealed... but Simon... a Lordship? Should I now say 'Morning Your Lordship' and tip my cap?"

I stared at him in horror.

"Don't you dare!... George... If you do, there'll be nothing in your Christmas box!"

"Point taken, Guv."

He got back on his bicycle and went off chuckling to himself. That's when the phone rang and I went back indoors. I didn't have time to introduce myself.

"Who's that?" insisted a dominant woman's voice at the end of the telephone line.

"Is that you, Flossy?" I asked, thinking it was the girl at the dairy again.

"No, this is most certainly not Flossy. I am Her Ladyship, Simon's mother. Now put my son on the telephone immediately."

I handed the receiver to Simon and went to warm up in front of the Aga but listened intently to the conversation outside in the hall.

"Now be reasonable, Mama," Simon interrupted briefly.

He paused while his mother gave him an earful. I could hear her stentorian tones from the kitchen.

"... No, Mama... I've left home now, Mama!..."

There were several verbal exchanges without any hint of warmth or love.

"...No, Mama, it is not my job to ride the leading horse with the hounds... I don't care, Mama!... No, I'm not coming home... I'm not interested in meeting your friend's daughter. Mama... Just listen to me... I don't care if she was on the front cover of 'Country Life'... No, Mama... I think that's my business, now I'm nearly 24, don't you?... Excuse me?... No, I don't think it is time for me to find a wife with a large dowry..."

Now I could hear Simon's mother making demands that he should return to assume his duties on the estate, but to no avail.

"... I'm sorry, no! ...Perhaps you should talk to my brother, Harry."

Simon's mother had begun to lose her temper at the other end of the line. I got the impression that Simon had heard all this before. Now he tried to be more dominant in handling the conversation.

"...I never asked to be born into the aristocracy, Mama... No, I do not believe it is my duty to take over from my father. I have made my decision, Mama... No I will not come back on the train. What's the use of telling the chauffeur to drive the car to the station?... You are not listening to me!..."

Unfortunately his mother dropped her voice so I couldn't hear what she was saying but clearly her entreaty had fallen on deaf ears.

"...Goodbye, Mama... Mama!... No, I don't intend to be rude... No, I will not speak to my father... Goodbye, Mama."

Simon put down the phone and came to stand beside me in the kitchen.

"Please don't ask what that was about," he insisted.

"I heard most of it, anyway."

"My mother still thinks I'm 13 – to be ordered about. You heard me say to her – I've left home now, Mama... Please don't let us talk about it. If she phones again, you must tell her that I've gone out."

We followed some of the debates over the Wolfenden Report, often over the radio in the milking parlour on the Home Service. Critics seemed to foresee Britain breaking down into Sodom and Gomorrah to be lashed by the wrath of God. Others spoke passionately about the need to uphold traditional family values. They claimed that England's moral stability might be undermined by deviants and undesirables trying to pervert the course of English justice. Some mothers were said to be concerned about their sons in a world where consenting adults could be free from prosecution. Was their need for grandchildren so strong? Perhaps it was – just as my parents had looked forward to bonny bouncing babies after my marriage with Elspeth. Stalwarts of the Armed Services were particularly keen to argue that there should be no consenting adults in the Army, the Navy or the Air Force. Morale in the event of an attack from Russia could be seriously undermined, we were warned. Battle readiness for World War Three must take priority at all times. I switched off the radio after more depressing news.

"What do you think, Simon?" I asked as the last cow went out through the door. "Is there going to be another world war?"

"Well, if there is, it will be nuclear. Plutonium from the local Windscale atomic plant has made sure of that!"

"Maybe we won't know anything about it up here in the Lakes. There will be a giant flash over Blackpool and we'll all be melted or burnt to cinders."

Simon started laughing as he swept the floor.

"But perhaps there will be time for one last glorious fuck after the three minute warning. ...The last time ever for you and me! ...A bit like having sex as the 'Titanic' goes down in that new film 'A Night to Remember'... We must go and see it when it comes up here after the movie opens in London!"

"You don't mean that sex is shown on the screen!"

"How do I know? I haven't seen it yet!"

"But Kenneth More is supposed to be in it ...The film will be about stiff upper lip and British grit... No sex surely!...None of that disgusting hanky–panky in 1912!"

Simon stopped sweeping with the broom.

"But if you knew the end had come... Supposing you and I were on the 'Titanic' and the last lifeboat full of women had just cast off... What would we do?"

"Sing 'Nearer My God to Thee' with the orchestra?"

"No, I'd drag you to the nearest cabin for one last time... a final fucking to end all fucking as the sea water lapped around our feet!"

"Simon... honestly... if the cows were still here they'd be really shocked! I'm sure they listen to us."

"Well ...how about it? We've never done it in here to the rhythm of the milking machine!"

"Right!" I said turning off the water at the hose we used to wash down the floor of the milking parlour. "Get those jeans off right now! There's a first time for everything!"

Simon took his boots off, dropped his waterproofs and bent over the steel framework nearby. I reached round to undo his belt and pushed the tatty denim cut–offs down to his knees. Then I cupped his round buttocks in my hands and massaged them again.

"Ok, Simon, you sexy boy... This is sea water lapping down here on the floor..."

I was splashing in a puddle under my feet when we were surprised by a deafening sonic boom from a jet aircraft above the farm, which rattled the windows.

"Listen… The ship's bulkheads are going..."

"No," Simon giggled. "Icy cold sea water has just exploded a boiler... Fuck me quickly before it's too late!"

We listened as the noisy plane zoomed down the valley into the distance.

"The final distress rocket has just gone up, Simon. No more flares left ... Are you ready?"

"Yes, fuck me quickly! ...Huh! ...Oh yes!…"

Now we could hear the milking machine, which was still switched on for cleaning. It went suck... clunk... fuck...suck... clunk...fuck ... behind us – something like an old ship's engine. But perhaps it was just my imagination running wild.

"Listen! One steam pump is still trying to empty sea water from the last watertight compartment."

"We can't stay afloat much longer now!…"

I withdrew from Simon briefly so that I could go and kick an empty milk churn to make a loud clanging sound.

"Now where are you going? … Come back here!… I need you to fuck me before it's too late!"

I kicked the milk churn once more.

"Simon, are you listening? That's the last ring on the ship's bell before we both sink beneath the waves…"

"Come back here at once!"

He waggled his hips and I could not resist slapping his buttocks playfully.

"Ouch! …Why did you do that?…It's not my fault we hit the iceberg!"

So I slapped him harder once more.

"No, you lost the telegram with the latest ice warning, stupid boy!"

Simon turned round to laugh at me over his shoulder and waggled his hips.

"Oh yes!" he muttered as I penetrated him again. "Harder!... That's it! ...I love you! ...Huh! ...The best yet! ...Now fuck the 'Titanic'! ...Oh yes! ...This is absolutely fantastic! …I am going to come!"

....

Eventually the day came for Simon to go up to Glasgow by train from Windermere Station. I took him there in the Land Rover just as before in less happy times. He was going to stay at the same time with friends who lived outside Glasgow. In his backpack was a sample 12–inch coupling ring we had removed from one steel tube to show the Glasgow manufacturers what their generating equipment would need to attach to.

For the first time in a year I was alone again – just me and the cows. It was strange to be working in the milking parlour without him. The cows seemed aware he was missing and looked at me disapprovingly. He was particularly fond of Marilyn, a Jersey cow – so–called because of her extra–long eyelashes and tendency to wobble her rear end as she walked around the field, just like Miss Monroe did in her movies.

Simon phoned from Scotland. We would need a control valve to adjust the water flowing through the turbine and to control the speed of the alternator that would, in turn, determine the electricity voltage and frequency. I was determined to think of something to give him when he returned. He wasn't one for jewellery or fancy clothes. While I was at the post office I saw a poster about the new Premium Bonds, which had been launched in an effort to raise extra money for the Treasury in 1957. So I sent off an application form for fifty pounds' worth in Simon's name. It seemed the right thing to do. On a lucky day we would both benefit from that investment.

He phoned me from Glasgow to say which train he would be on.

"It's been raining up here," he said. "Like that time I went back to university in London. I sit around all the time thinking about you and how it was in the milking parlour the other day. It makes me so randy... We must do that again soon to the rhythm of the milking machine. I've never come so much as that before."

There was a crackling noise and a click on the telephone line.

"Sh! Sh!" I insisted. "What was that noise? Somebody might be tapping our line! Perhaps the police are investigating deviant sex in Scotland. Maybe the long–distance operator at the exchange is listening in."

"Well," Simon giggled. "We'd better give them something juicy to listen to... I like to fuck! ....Fuck! ...Fuck! ... Have you got that ... MI5, Special Branch or whoever you are?"

There was another suspicious click. The line seemed to go dead for a moment. I tapped the mouthpiece.

"Simon! Are you still there?"

"You know me. I'm not going anywhere."

"...Honestly! Have you been drinking?"

"Just got back from the boozer with Jock and Colleen."

I arrived at Windermere Station to collect Simon late that Friday afternoon. I sat on the same seat as before, staring into the distance for the telltale steam and smoke. It was going to be late. Still, I was happier than on the previous occasion. British Railways had done it again! Forty minutes turned into an hour. I asked at the ticket office. As usual, the staff would not commit themselves. So I moved the Land Rover from the front of the station into a side street, out of the way. Delay increases the anticipation, so they say, and on this occasion it did. By the time Simon stepped down from the train with his backpack, I'd got through a whole packet of chewing gum.

"Derailment at the Scottish border somewhere," he said, laughing.

We made our way through the cloud of steam around the engine.

"Oh God, have I missed you, " I muttered, unlocking the side door of the Land Rover.

"I've got something special to show you... a surprise. I found it in Glasgow. I thought we might go to the young farmers' dance this year."

"That sounds interesting, whatever it is."

I told him the first thing we were going to do when we got in was to spend an hour in bed because I was desperate. The surprise would just have to wait but after that dreadful train journey he wanted a bath first. So, once again, I found myself kneeling by the bath in front of the stove while Simon stepped into it. I'd been saving myself for this moment for nearly a week. Here was the naked body with which I was already so familiar but had craved to touch again. – Simon's broad shoulders, his slim waist, his beautiful face... everything I had grown to love so much. Afterwards he stood up in the bath so I could admire him while I dried him with the towel.

"Please... please will you promise me you won't go off again?" I said as I put my hands out to hold him again.

"I promise!... I couldn't go through the last few days ever again! If it wasn't for Jock and Colleen I would have thrown myself in the Clyde."

"Oh!"

Still with the towel wrapped around his waist, Simon dashed up the stairs, making me promise to stay where I was while he located the surprise he'd brought back from Glasgow.

"Close your eyes!" he shouted from the landing. I sat by the stove quietly as I was bidden. Fabric brushed past my nose. I opened my eyes to find him standing right in front of me wearing the most magnificent highland dress, complete with kilt, buckle shoes, sporran and waistcoat.

"It was in the window of a pawnbroker's going for a song. What do you think? I couldn't resist it – not a famous tartan, unfortunately, but we can't have everything."

I was almost speechless. He looked truly magnificent. I lifted the kilt. He was wearing nothing underneath. Here was male beauty indeed!

"Well, I've got something for you," I said, now reaching into the bureau.

He took the Premium Bonds. We kissed. Nothing had changed.

"Let's hope the Electronic Random Number Indicator remembers our numbers. When are the generator and the water turbine arriving?"

"By road next month. By the way, I've paid them." Simon insisted, "This is my present for you... for having me on the farm... in more ways than one! Now we've got to work out any locations where I still haven't been fucked."

I didn't know what to say. Simon was giggling at his own joke. I grabbed hold of him, lifted the kilt and slapped him playfully.

"Granny left me some money... well, it's gone now, what with the kilt and the hydroelectric plant... Now we only have to get the equipment to work, when it arrives. I went to see another installation outside Edinburgh, which the company has supplied new. It was much bigger than ours but I got a better idea of what we're putting together. It was actually at a woollen mill where the millrace has been diverted through a turbine. I even went back to see it switched on for the first time. We ought to invite the local paper to photograph the Lord Mayor throwing the switch just like they did. His Worship christened it with Highland Malt so I've brought you some of that as well..."

He handed me a half–sized bottle. The new Chancellor had just made it even more expensive. Why not use it for christening the hydroelectric plant?

Now I was lying on top of Simon, staring down into his eyes.

"Listen, it's time for me to tell you what I've decided while you've been away."

He smiled at me.

"So do you like my poofy Scottish outfit?"

"You know I do... But listen... Oh it's so difficult now we're face to face..."

"Difficult to say what?"

"That you've changed my whole life... That you are the most beautiful thing I have ever seen in my life... That there has never ever been anyone in my life like you... I don't know what I've done to deserve all this... Well, all that sort of thing... And back in '57 I nearly sent you packing to the youth hostel... Just imagine what I might have missed..."

"What we would both have missed..."

"Did you always want this? ... I mean with someone like me?…"

Simon smiled, said nothing but kissed me instead.

"Come to bed now!" I insisted. "Your kilt will get creased and that sporran is sticking me in the... Well, where sporrans aren't supposed to go!"

We laughed. He got up and I watched him strip off and hang up his new outfit in the wardrobe.

"...Now you look your best... with nothing on! Why wear a kilt when you've got a truly magnificent figure like yours?"

He smiled again and said nothing but jumped onto the bed beside me. We stared at one another for a few minutes. Then I started to rub my hands up and down his thighs. They were more muscular now. His shoulders were broader but his slim waist seemed to stay the same, just like his smile and those come–to–bed eyes.

"Lie down!" I muttered. "I think I'm going to kiss you all over!"

2001

Life seemed to be so much more exciting back in the old days. I was starting to get bored, sitting by myself in the car park of the motorway service area. Had they just forgotten all about me? Where was my drink and something to eat from the takeaway? How time can drag when we get old!

I picked up the newspaper, which was lying on the seat of the Land Rover. More mayhem, death and destruction on the front page. I started to read the account of the latest murder in Central London. But half way down the column I lost interest and stared out of the window. Years ago there just didn't seem to be the time to do all the things I needed to. After Simon arrived in my life, of course, there were so many distractions. We seemed to spend so much time having sex! But, maybe, the tasks we set ourselves in our youth are just too demanding. It often happens in life that what we consider to be a simple job turns out, in the end, to last far longer after much more effort. So it happened when we began to excavate the site of the old water mill. Under a millstone we discovered a grave. There were two skeletons, side by side. They looked in such good condition that they might have been buried yesterday. Had we stumbled on the evidence of some dreadful local murder? Simon phoned the police at once. It was like a plot from 'Dixon of Dock Green' on the television.

1958

A detective turned up in a black Wolseley . It was quite clear these were ancient remains, he said, and we should not have bothered them. The bones must have been there for hundreds of years. The local museum might be interested so I phoned them too. They sent an amateur archaeologist who arrived on her bicycle and looked the spitting image of Margaret Rutherford – an actress I had seen at the cinema. It was she who found the rings. On one finger of each hand of both skeletons were matching gold rings. She thought that was rather odd. Another thing she noted was that both the skeletons seemed to have been young males. So we kept the rings. She didn't think they were particularly valuable and nobody would mind. After such an eventful day we retreated to the pub once again where news of our discovery had arrived at lunchtime.

Already there were various explanations for the skeletons. One said Old Joe inherited his mill from the family of Stewarts who had come down from Scotland. The barman said these skeletons were of brothers of another branch of the Stewarts who had arrived one day to lay claim their inheritance but got bumped off in an effort to silence them. Another regular of the pub said his great aunt had told him a tale of dastardly deeds by another Stewart who killed his wife and her lover. The archaeologist was wrong, he said. The skeletons were of a young man and a young woman. Was she with child, he asked? I told him we had found no evidence. But there was another story going round which did attract our attention. The butcher we had spoken to before had a story that one Stewart had a son who was destined to inherit the mill. However, instead of taking a wife, this young man found himself a male lover. The outraged father discovered them together, killed them to avoid a stain on the family escutcheon and buried them as we found them hundreds of years later.

Simon and I went to sit outside the pub away from all the gossip, where we decided that papa Stewart, splendid in his ancestral regalia, had relented at the last minute and placed his son and heir in the arms of his handsome lover before replacing the turf. Anyway we decided to stick to that explanation and also to move the skeletons away from the building works and rebury them in a marked grave close to the farmhouse. It seemed the right thing to do. So we clinked glasses and made a toast to the young male lovers who had blazed a trail for us to follow so many years before.

"Look at this then," Simon said, glancing at the local paper, which was lying open on the garden table.

"What's that?"

"'Brief Encounter' is on at the cinema – that film I told you was shot at the railway station down the A6 in Carnforth. I showed you... remember?"

"Celia Johnson's naughty extra–marital affair with Trevor Howard?"

"Yes that one... only it might not seem quite so shocking today... Well, it was the end of the war. I think you'd like it!"

So we went that same evening. Simon, bless him, thought I would enjoy it. I thought the music – he told me it was Rachmaninov – was just too over the top. And when Celia Johnson's faithful husband thanked her for coming back to him,

I disgraced myself by bursting out laughing. So we left quickly by the side door.

"Sorry," I said as we got back in the Land Rover.

"It doesn't matter."

"Well, if the stuffy husband had an affair with a gorgeous young man like you...then I wouldn't have laughed... As for those stiff upper–lip attitudes ...and the clipped English accents ... Where exactly do people talk like that?"

"It doesn't matter. They're showing 'Wizard of Oz' again soon. That may be more your cup of tea."

Simon tactfully changed the subject and we drove home chatting about our hydroelectric scheme.

The bones we'd found under the millstone were now reinterred with some dignity and marked with a wooden cross fashioned from branches collected around the mill. So we continued with the foundations for the hydroelectric plant. This arrived in a crate a couple of weeks later on the back of a lorry. Freshly repainted in bright blue, we found we could just lift this turbine if we unbolted it from the generator. The next task seemed much more daunting – to lay up to half a mile of foot–wide steel tubing along the track of the old millstream up to the sluice by the tarn lake. In the end we had to pay two lads from the village to give us a hand with the most difficult sections where trees had to be cut down and foliage pushed aside. They were friendly and glad of some extra work. One lad, called Bob, was incredibly cute, blond with beautiful blue eyes but his mate was less handsome. After one particularly difficult day when we had to uproot an old tree which had grown across the track of the millstream, the four of us retreated to the pub. Still in our working clothes we sat out in the garden. One lad went off to the loo leaving the other with Simon and me.

"I'm envious of you two," he said. "You are so happy together. Well, everyone knows, don't they? Maybe you've got a relationship so many other people have never found. Perhaps that's why they get married instead...and end up regretting it."

The other lad returned, sat down with us, and his mate turned to him.

"I've just said, Bob, how I envy these two and the relationship they have... a kind of marriage but between two men..."

I was quite amazed by this discussion and didn't quite know how to respond. It was clear he and Bob had been talking about us. But instead of getting annoyed, I was flattered.

"...Well," Bob added, "we've tried but it didn't work out. He wants to find a girl friend, settle down and get married."

The other lad put down his empty glass on the bench and smiled at us.

"I'm straight, you see. I'm the old–fashioned sort... I guess I need a woman to look after me and to get me up in the morning. He was no good. He just let me sleep all day."

They laughed at one another. I turned to Bob.

"You're not straight, I take it."

"I need to find myself a man... but he doesn't want me! I could love this one so much!..."

Bob pointed at his mate and then turned towards Simon.

"...Anyway, we agreed to stay friends and that's all. But now my landlady has found out about me and she's trying blackmail."

I was shocked but I had to know more about it.

"You have to pay her to keep her quiet?"

The two lads burst out laughing.

"No," Bob said, while his mate continued giggling. "I have to sleep with her..."

"She thinks all he needs is a good woman to put him back on the straight and narrow. Listen, Bob, here, is 20. She's nearly 50..."

They dissolved into giggles again. I couldn't believe it.

"...Man! It's gross! ...If he threatens to leave her, she says she'll report him to the police."

"And she's his landlady?" I asked, turning to Simon.

"Yes," Bob continued, pointing at his mate again. "When I have sex with her, I have to imagine I'm really rogering him!..."

All four of us rocked with laughter.

"...Well, I ask you, what do I do now?"

Simon exchanged a glance with me and I nodded.

"Bob, come and stay here with us," he suggested. "That is, if you want to…"

Bob's eyes lit up.

"Can I?…Perhaps until I've heard from the Army."

"This idiot wants to join the forces," his mate laughed. "Bob fancies himself going out to the Suez Canal and recapturing it from President Nasser and the Egyptians…in the glorious name of Queen and Country."

I couldn't help smiling. The Suez Crisis had ended only a few months before when Anthony Eden resigned from Number Ten.

"You could send us some cut–price petrol while you're out there," I suggested. "I used up all my ration coupons ...you know, during the rationing."

"Yer, right...but seriously, could I stay with you here on the farm?"

Simon turned to him.

"That's ok with me... Move in tomorrow. I'll fetch your stuff in the Land Rover."

Bob's fortunes started to change a few days later when we took him to an agricultural auction where we were selling some sheep. The bidders were grouped in a circle around the auction ring where Bob sat with us. It was here he caught the eye of a young man who seemed to be ignoring the action but just sat staring at him. During the lunch hour this young man happened to come into the pub where we were having a pie and a pint. He immediately brought his pint to stand with us. Bob offered him a cigarette and it was while he held up his lighter for the young man to light it, Simon nudged me on the arm. For one moment the two of them stared into one another's eyes. It was that same wonderful look of love which Simon and I had exchanged that first day we spent together. They sat down side by side in the corner of the bar while Simon and I returned to the auction. A couple of hours later they both came to find us at the close of the day's sales.

"This is Bazz," Bob said. "Let's all go and get a cup of tea somewhere."

We all shook hands and I suggested a cafe I knew where we could all sit outside. We walked in couples down a narrow side street. Simon looked at me with a worried expression.

"Is he a plant by the police, do you think?"

"Whatever do you mean?"

"Like the ones in London... an agent provocateur?"

Suddenly I knew where I'd seen him before. Bazz was the son of another sheep farmer my father had known years ago. He'd actually gone to agricultural college to train as a shepherd for a year and was probably better qualified than any of us.

"I know the family," I whispered as we went through the doorway to the cafe. "He's a shepherd on his dad's farm out

Keswick way. He's handsome, isn't he? You worry too much, Simon."

We went out into the garden with our cups of tea and sat down by the ornamental fish pond.

"So how was agricultural college, then?" I asked Bazz.

"How did you know about that?" he asked.

"I knew your dad years ago."

He and Bob sat down close together on the bench seat opposite. Simon nudged my arm again. Bazz smiled at Bob, looked around to see if anyone was looking and put his hand on Bob's knee for a moment.

"He's told me all about you," Bazz continued.

"Only nice things, I hope," Simon added.

"Can I bring Bazz back to the farm for dinner?" Bob asked. "I'll cook. He can peel the spuds."

His friend smiled at both of us.

"Your night off," I said to Simon.

"What's on the menu, then?" he asked Bob. "Shepherd's pie?"

"Yes, but we've got a special favour to ask."

Bob winked at Bazz, who smiled at him.

"And what's that?" I said.

"I've been telling him about your tin bath in front of the Aga and how romantic it would be if the two of us could have a bath together tonight..."

"But it's only big enough for one," Simon said, laughing.

"I think we could both fit into it. Anyway, we could try," Bazz insisted, nudging Bob on the arm. "We don't mind if you want to stay and watch. You could make us a cup of tea."

I liked this idea. It sounded like fun. The two of them were so pretty to look at.

Why should we refuse? So we paid for the teas and the four of us went back to the farm. Fortunately, there was plenty of hot water from the Aga. Simon and I sat back to admire what we would now call a porn video. But it was live in our kitchen, in real time and in front of our own eyes. I switched off the electric light and lit candles to make it more romantic. With the front of the firebox open, their bodies looked fantastic in the warm glow of the flames. Bazz was eye–poppingly beautiful now he was naked. Bob was more muscular but very gentle and clearly already deeply in love. Secretly I wondered if Bob had mentioned his application to join the British Army but what incentive was there for them to stay together? If the recommendations in the Wolfenden Report were implemented, loving relationships like theirs could have a future. But, for the time being, Bob and Bazz would have little to look forward to, unless they could find a remote retreat like our farm.

2001

So I sat there gazing out of the side window of the Land Rover just remembering it all. Bob came to stay with us for a month or so. He stayed in the spare room next to ours until he heard the result of his interview about joining the British Army. Now he was living on site, the three of us were able to complete the pipeline more quickly. In 2001, 'Brief Encounter' had just been on the television again for the umpteenth time but we'd watched it for old time's sake. It was important to us both because it was the very first film Simon and I had ever watched together. Common experiences like that are the making of a relationship to last a lifetime. We did go to see 'A Night to Remember' about the 'Titanic' but it was a pretty stiff upper lip affair to please middle England. I was right all along... Memories!... Fucking Simon in the milking parlour with water around our feet had been much more exciting!

But now I had other things on my mind. I couldn't understand why it was taking Dominic so long to buy a spare fan belt at the garage. Then I noticed two young men climb over the perimeter fence of the motorway service area. I don't think they thought anyone was watching but, from my high viewpoint in the passenger's seat of the Land Rover, I could see them through a gap in the fence. They started kissing one another. I was amazed. It was broad daylight. They seemed to have no inhibitions at all. How different from the late 1950s when everything was so daring and risqué. I watched as one pulled off the other's shirt to smother his chest with more kisses. I began to wonder what they might do next. Was I shocked? After all, they were doing no more than Simon and I had done behind locked doors for more than three decades. That's when they got up, moved away and I lost sight of them.

Talking of Simon, I had no idea where he had got to. Surely it couldn't take over an hour to eat a cheeseburger with his brother.

Still, they hadn't seen one another for a while. Why should I begrudge them an extra hour together? They were probably comparing notes about gay life in the twenty–first century, news about friends they might have in common and where the best gay nightclubs were these days. Simon seemed to be less interested in mechanical things nowadays. He left Dominic to deal with the Land Rover and the broken fan belt. Back in the fifties he would have been the first to get out the box spanners and lift up the bonnet. Perhaps there were more pressing things on his mind now. Maybe he just needed to talk to his brother about us.

Sex was less important now. The two of us had relaxed into a kind of happy relationship of two people where sex hardly featured at all. Was it like that for Dominic and Harry I wondered? But they were younger. I silently counted the years. They were only a few years younger than us. Perhaps it was the same for them. I turned to follow the petrol tanker, which had just pulled up at the filling station. The driver got out to connect his hose to the delivery terminal. Clearly it was about to offload more fuel into the underground tanks. It brought me back to Simon's problems with his pipeline for the hydroelectricity at the farm. Watching the tanker driver connecting the hose, I drifted into another daydream of the old days.

1958

It was hot that summer. Simon stripped off and went round the farm wearing only his ripped denim cut–offs. That made him feel randy and we always ended up having sex. But it was less wild now. Besides, our labours were becoming more exhausting. Building our own hydroelectric generator threw up so many problems. Securing the far end of the pipeline with the outlet from the sluice caused a few headaches. I would have given up but with Simon's technical skills we managed it in the end. The sluice gate had not been shifted for decades and was rusted up. The control gear had to be removed and soaked for days in oil to make it work but Simon would not be beaten. More than anything, this project cemented our relationship. The popular press was keen to follow the debate about the Wolfenden Report with speculation around the issue of homosexuality. Gay men were said to be weak, effeminate and lacking 'backbone'. London police were said to be doing society a favour by prosecuting illegal activities in men's toilets and hounding politicians and members of the aristocracy trapped in 'stings'. My experience with Simon was that he was in no way effeminate and in no way mirrored the image of the weak, decadent and vulnerable homosexual youth projected by the tabloid press. He differed from the very model of a young Englishman, beloved of every proud mum and dad, only in the way he enjoyed sex with me. But my parents were dead now. I no longer felt obliged to live up to the narrow and conservative standards by which they had both lived. It was Simon who liberated me from my closet. I felt as if I had been born again.

Bob continued to live with us and Bazz often came over for dinner. Several times they slept together in the spare bed. But the day of Bob's departure to join the Army drew nearer. By now he was regretting his decision because it was quite clear to both of us that they were deeply in love. A week or so before Bob's final deadline, he told us that Bazz wanted the two of them to formalise their union. Would we have any objections? Bob had made some suggestions, especially since his sister was about to marry her fiance in our parish church. Why should she be the only one to get married this month? I looked at Simon.

"What do you think then?"

"Why not?" he asked, smiling at me. " What harm would it do?"

Bob looked lovingly at Bazz.

"Well," Bob muttered. "If I don't come back from Northern Ireland..."

It was the first time he'd told any of us where his regiment might be sent.

"Oh God," sighed Bazz.

His friend turned to Simon, who was looking worried.

"Well, I'd just like to feel that I'd made a commitment with Bob... just like his sister and her partner in the wedding ceremony. Only we could never have our banns read in the church on a Sunday. We are not permitted to marry one another... So we're going to do it for ourselves. We'd like both of you to be our witnesses...And would you two please give us both away?"

I glanced at Simon but was already holding hands with Bob and Bazz.

"We'd be delighted." I insisted. "Just so long as there are no photos, no rings, no certificate... or anything which might end up in the wrong hands."

"We'll make a day of it," Simon added. "I'll buy champagne and we'll have a feast. Then you can both stay the night upstairs… to consummate…"

"No, no…" Bob protested. "It's going to be far more radical than that. Tell them, Bazz."

Bazz smiled at each of us in turn.

"I read about a native ceremony held in an African tribe… you know, one of those which Christian missionaries tried to stamp out when the British occupied Africa in the name of King and Empire… Anyway our ceremony is going to be based on that. It will have nothing whatever to do with the Christian Church … No words from the book of common prayer or anything like that. No, we will fuck one another while you are watching. In Africa, the whole tribe used to gather to watch the sexual coupling of a native girl with a native boy…to prove that the relationship was going to work, and to invite the tribal elders to give their blessing to the union. Besides, the boy and girl might not actually know how to fuck. The tribal elders were also there to give advice about arousal, sexual pleasure and satisfaction to encourage a happy and fulfilled life together…anyway, things like that, apart from making healthy babies to assure the future of the tribe."

Bob and Bazz hugged each other and kissed. I didn't know quite what to think of this idea. I'd never heard anything like it. I glanced at Simon but I could see he already liked the prospect of watching these two attractive young men have sex. Anyway, I said we'd think about it and everyone went to bed.

But I couldn't get any sleep that night. I lay awake thinking about our lives together. We were completing some ambitious civil engineering and solving difficulties as we went along. It amused me to wonder how far I would have got with Elspeth. How long before she downed tools and went back to mother? Simon was a tower of strength, literally. I had to prevent him trying to shift the sections of steel tube by himself. If he strained his back too much we would get nowhere. Finally however, with Bob's help, the very last section of pipe was laid and bolted together at the concrete foundations by the stream. That night it was too dark to do any more so Simon decided to take us all to the cinema again. They were now showing 'The Wizard of Oz'. I'd seen this during the war with my parents, of course, but it was a revelation to see it with Simon.

The cinema was almost empty. We were sitting by ourselves in the back row holding hands in the dark. Bob had his knee over Bazz's leg. At one point Simon groped my groin but I pushed him away in case the usherette came along with her torch. After a while Bob and Bazz disappeared to the gents' toilet to leave us in peace. I loved this movie. I whispered to Simon that the wicked witch reminded me of Elspeth. I loved the way she tossed fireballs at Dorothy and zoomed around on her broomstick. Simon commented that it was just like the one we had in the milking parlour. Perhaps Elspeth had used that when I wasn't looking. I was quite glad the cinema was empty because we were giggling so much. When they eventually returned from the loo, Bazz and Bob pretended to be outraged about the two of us making so much noise. Eventually we all went home in the Land Rover singing 'We're off to see the wizard'.

The complexities of installing a hydroelectric scheme were driving us both a little bit mad and we were getting rather nervous about the first practical test the next day. If it didn't work, all our expense and hard work might still be in vain. I suggested that Elspeth might have spooked it. Simon said she might have started weaving evil spells in Manchester. Perhaps, even now, she was spying on us in her crystal ball like the one the wicked witch used in the film. It was at that very moment the old Land Rover backfired and had us worried for a moment. Later in life we be both became devoted friends of Dorothy and watched 'The Wizard of Oz' again and again on our video!

The following day was Sunday so we let Bazz and Bob sleep in late. Even though the wooden hut had not been built yet, Simon and I decided to try everything out first. The turbine was bolted in place and attached to the alternator. I wanted to see if it would light up a lamp bulb after so much effort, just to put my mind at rest. Simon walked up the valley to open the higher sluice gate, while I waited at the lower end to see what would happen. There was a loud hissing sound as all the air trapped in the pipeline was pushed out by hundreds of gallons of water, which now came thundering down from the lake. It was like bleeding a hot water radiator valve. Finally water spurted out and I clamped the valve shut with a spanner. Simon finally appeared, breathless, having run back down the valley. He wired a 100–watt bulb across the terminals of the generator and we crossed our fingers.

"You do it," he said to me, pointing at the control valve. I opened it half a turn. There was a rushing sound. Some water spurted out of the end of the pipe from the turbine.

"Wait!" he said and dashed back up to the farmhouse.

He returned with the small bottle of Scotch and two glasses. I opened the control valve again, very gingerly. The flywheel between the turbine and the generator started to revolve slowly. The 100–watt bulb started to glow. I felt triumphant and opened the valve further. The bulb got brighter and Simon grabbed my arm and we went to sit down on the low stone wall. Behind us, water from the turbine was trickling back into the stream. I was amazed how little water it took to light up one lamp bulb. But would it run the milking machine?

"I love you. I don't know what else to say," I said, now holding the glowing electric lamp bulb in my hand. "I wish my father could have seen this. He would never have believed it. Free electricity from the old millstream!"

"How much have we spent on construction to date?...Two thousand? "

"Who knows... Does that really matter? Why bring that subject up now?"

"Go and get the electric fire," he said. "Let's see if it will heat up all three bars on that."

I walked up back to the house with the empty glasses and what was left of the bottle of Scotch. The electric fire had belonged to my mother. We didn't use it much because electricity had always been so expensive. That was the moment it struck me. We were now making it for ourselves. Simon and I were embracing modernity – in the promised age of cheap electricity. We didn't need nuclear power stations, uranium, plutonium or whatever they produced in secrecy at Windscale. I could hardly believe it and carried mother's old electric fire triumphantly back to Simon. He had now stopped the turbine and removed the wires to the 100–watt bulb. Time for the real test! Could we light up a three–kilowatt electric fire? That was more like the power we would need to run the milking machine. Simon undid the plug and wired the cable up to the terminals on top of the alternator. He insisted I should open the control valve again which I did slowly at first. Much more water was now needed before we could see the first element in the fire glowing red. He switched on the second bar. That too started to glow. Water was gushing out of our pipe into the stream and the machinery was whirring round noisily. Now I was really glad it wouldn't be sited by the back door of the house. I nodded at him. He threw the last switch. Yes – there it was – three kilowatts and the water control valve was only open by a few turns. We would be able to run the milking parlour with our own homemade power. 'Norweb'– The North Western Electricity Board – could take their costly meter, all the ugly poles and their cables away.

So it was a successful trial run. The machinery would have to be dismantled again until we had put up our own electricity supply cables to the farm and built the shed to keep the alternator safe and out of the rain. Simon made me laugh by adding that would be about the only new location left for us to have a fuck – locked inside our own power station, accompanied by the stimulating sound of rushing water generating kilowatts of electricity.

I walked back up the valley along the pipeline to check for leaks. We found one where a seal was faulty between two sections of pipe. Water was spurting out sideways. We'd have to deal with that later. So he shut the sluice at the tarn lake and we returned to the mill in order to clear up.

"Well," I said. "What a triumph... Are you happy now that it actually works?"

"What would you have done if it didn't work?"

"But it does... a bit like us!"

"And, most important of all, this is something we have done together."

I looked up at the bridge where the lane crossed over the stream. Elspeth's car drew up and she got out to look down at us.

"Look out for the fireballs!" Simon suggested. "She's been spying on us in her crystal ball... I know it!"

"Oh damn," I muttered. "Trust her to turn up and spoil everything. She could have phoned first."

"She must have come for her broomstick!"

But I wasn't in the mood for jokes any more.

"What the hell is all that?" Elspeth shouted down from the bridge.

I turned to Simon, not knowing what to say.

"What does she want now?" he muttered. "Did you know she was coming?"

We waited for her to park the car and scramble down to the pipeline.

"What is all this contraption, then?" she asked, looking back up the valley where the pipeline disappeared through the trees.

"We're generating our own electric power now," I said. "It was really Simon's idea but we've done all this since you were here last."

"Clever stuff!"

"Shall we show her? What have you done with that 100–watt bulb?"

"But I shut the sluice gate at the top."

"Perhaps there's just enough water left in the pipeline."

"We'll try it."

We walked over to the machinery. Elspeth seemed to be genuinely interested for once. I was amazed. She gasped when Simon reconnected the wires to the alternator and I turned the water control valve again to make it light up.

"Well," she said, triumphantly, "Now I know what you two have been up to... And I thought you two were still trying to make babies! ...But I've come to collect the last of my stuff. I need my mother's china tea set from the cupboard and my hairdryer. I forgot that last time. That's the lot. Have you got a cardboard box for all the china, Simon, or have you smashed it already, throwing it at my ex–husband? He can be rather infuriating at times... By the way, pretty boy, didn't they tell you in biology lessons at school, you can't make babies that way? ...No matter how hard you try!"

"Bitch!" I muttered aside to Simon.

"I heard that!" she said, turning away from me. "Well, Simon, where's this cardboard box then?"

I'd had enough and walked away. He led her up to the house while I sat on the wall by the stream, determined not to be tempted to say something else I might regret. Eventually she reappeared in her car over the bridge, blew her horn at me, stuck two fingers up from her car window and went off again leaving a cloud of dust behind her. That's when Simon turned up with a bottle of cider and two glasses.

"Did you see that?" I shouted. "Now you know how she treated me!"

"Calm down. She's gone now! Forget it!"

"I must apologise for what my ex–wife said to you. She has

no right! How I hate her."

"Now, now!"

Simon was laughing at me.

"The Wicked Witch has got back on her broomstick and gone home."

"It's all very well for you! You didn't have to live with that woman and her moods all those years."

"I will never understand how the two of you ever got married...!"

I was about to reply but Simon put his finger to his lips and passed me a glass of cider.

"...Forget it! Just be thankful the court awarded a divorce so quickly. You're free. The millstone of marriage is grinding no more – a bit like this one here! You've laid it to rest ...Do you get it? ...It was a joke!"

Simon kicked the stone we had replaced after discovering the grave underneath.

"Seems like you've helped me sort out two old millstones at the same time, Simon!"

"Let's hope the Wolfenden Report helps people like us to avoid the pitfalls of marriage, entered into for the wrong reason, with the wrong person, just because it's what middle England expects and claims it is respectable."

"She should never have said that bit about you and I making babies. Bitch!"

"Calm down! She's gone now. You don't have to deal with her any more. If she phones or darkens our doorstep again, I'll deal with her."

"Would you really?"

"Yes...You might not want me if you get all upset. I need you too much."

"Come," I insisted, grabbing Simon by the arm. "There's something I must do and I want you to hear everything..."

He turned back to the turbine and the generator.

"What about...?"

"No, leave those. They can wait...but this can't."

He followed me across the grass to the old parish church. I held the door open and waved him inside. Fortunately, we were quite alone, except for the deathwatch beetle up in the roof.

"Come over here," I said, going to the altar. "There is something I want you to hear. Kneel down!"

He was about to protest.

"Just do it!"

I knelt down beside him. I looked up at the altar and the crucifix.

"Lord," I whispered. "If you really exist... and I have always had my doubts... I want you to know my marriage here at this altar to Elspeth was a complete sham. In the sight of God, I declare that Simon is now my real partner and my true love..."

He was staring at me with his mouth open and I grabbed his hand and held it up in the air.

"...This young man here is everything to me. I promise to honour and to care for him, for as long as we both shall live. So help me God..."

I kissed his hand. This was something else we'd just done together.

"...If you really are looking down at us now, I know the Church of England does not see fit to bless such unions yet. But Simon's father believes in your Church and I am sure he would never condone reforms advocated by Wolfenden..."

I looked aside at Simon.

"... Would your father vote in favour of it in the House of Lords?..."

Simon shook his head and frowned. I turned back to the crucifix.

"...Well, maybe one day. In the meantime I want this day to be something Simon will remember with pride for the rest of his life. Perhaps his father will be proud of him one day... Amen."

I turned to smile at him.

"Thank you," Simon whispered.

"Does that put your mind at rest?"

He nodded and we closed the door of the church quietly behind us.

2001

Looking back now, in the twenty–first century, I think that was the day my life changed forever. I had finally severed my marriage with Elspeth. It had begun in that dreadful parish church. But maybe I knew deep down that my heart just was not in it. She and I had recited empty words without commitment or conviction. Now they were just another sad memory. But Simon had given me the courage to put everything right. Just as Frank Sinatra sang on our radio in the milking shed, 'I did it my way'. I had done it again in my own way at the very same altar when I had just committed myself to Simon. I had made my peace with God, if a God really existed. But, like Simon, I was beginning to question religion and whether it would have any place in my life from now on. No doubt we would have found ourselves in trouble if anyone had been listening to our do–it–yourself gay marriage but, except on Sundays, few people ever went there. As Madame Claire Voyante had predicted, our luck continued to hold out. We were the lucky ones. Our only witnesses were the silent statues of nobility and the deathwatch beetles up in the rafters. Today in 2001, issues of homosexuality were threatening to tear the Church of England apart. Gay clergy were being opposed by hardliners, particularly overseas where a more traditional approach prevailed. But, back in the 1950s, church and state were more concerned about campaigns to promote nuclear disarmament than gay rights.

Now, in 2001, our crumbling and under-funded parish church only held services occasionally and the local vicar was responsible for other parishes as well. There was even talk of deconsecrating the building and selling it for redevelopment. The power of the church was in decline and so was the rest of the village. The village shop had closed and, with it, the post office had now disappeared. The whole terrace had become expensive second homes for wealthy people from the midlands who had no need for local services. Local people could not afford to pay these fancy prices and many moved away. But these holiday homes usually remained empty for much of the year. Now, even the village pub was under threat. The recent foot–and–mouth epidemic of 2001 was threatening to lead to the closure of what was left of the rural economy in our part of the Lake District. I could only feel rose–tinted nostalgia for village life as I remembered it years ago. But how could we have just stood by and done nothing to save it? Only my loving relationship with Simon had survived for forty–four years.

CHAPTER 4

1958

The final stage of our hydroelectric scheme involved the construction of the shed over the water turbine and alternator beside the millstream. But we economised by buying an old garage from a man we met at the local pub. It had one asset that, at the time, saved us from our closest brush with the law. This was the self–locking Yale lock on the door, but, of course, when we dismantled and shifted this old garage to its new site we didn't know that then. Without this self–locking door, both Simon and I could so easily have landed up in prison because it was this garage which Simon calculated was the very last venue on the farm where the two of us had not yet had sex.

I was more concerned about the safety issues of such a venue. The alternator was capable of producing eight kilowatts of power, which was enough to electrocute both of us in one go. It involved a large flywheel weighing about a hundredweight that was spinning at about one thousand revolutions per minute. Water at high pressure to turn it was rushing through the turbine in vast quantities too large for us to measure. The idea of engaging in rampant sex within a foot or two of such a dangerous contraption filled me with misgivings. Simon just laughed and said I was worrying too much. However, he did construct a steel cage around the apparatus to protect our naked bodies to put my mind at rest. I had visions of the heavy flywheel breaking free from its bearings and slicing though flesh and bone at the very moment we reached sexual climax together! However, I did make him see the potential danger if his ejaculation should happen to short out two hundred and forty volts across the terminals on top of the alternator! So we covered them over with gaffer tape to make this event less of an electrifying experience. But at the time I could not have anticipated that our greatest threat would turn out to involve the long arm of the law.

The reconstruction of this second–hand garage was not complete until after dark and it was getting very cold – too cold for rampant sex, I told Simon. Why not delay everything until daylight? But Simon insisted it was now or never and nothing I could do would change his mind. So my mother's old three–bar electric fire was reconnected to keep us warm, with the 100–watt bulb for lighting as before. Fortunately, the self–locking Yale lock on the garage door kept us secure while we both stripped off inside.

"Right, Simon," I shouted while he bent over the safety cage around the flywheel. "The ship's lights must be kept burning as long as possible before the 'Titanic' slips beneath the waves! Captain's orders."

At this distance we were being deafened by the noise of the water rushing from the turbine into the millstream outside. Simon closed his eyes.

"Listen to all that water through the crack left by the iceberg! The boiler room will be completely flooded soon."

He waggled his bottom and looked back over his shoulder at me. I slapped him hard.

"Ouch! And what was that for?"

"If you hadn't forgotten to give the binoculars to the lookouts in the crow's nest, they might have seen the iceberg sooner."

"That's not my fault."

I started to massage him while we listened to turbulence in the water, which made the speed of our turbine drop momentarily.

"Listen! Pressure is dropping. The cold sea water must have swamped another boiler… Fire's gone out."

"You better hurry up then… Now fuck me quickly!…"

I mounted him from behind.

"…Huh! …Oh yes!… Harder!"

But I withdrew from him again. I loved to tease him like this and slapped him again.

"Ouch! Now what was that for?"

"You left one pair of binoculars on the quayside at

Southampton."

There was a noise outside but we were now both too excited and I slid inside him again.

"Ship's bulkheads are going. We can't stay afloat much longer now!"

"Huh!...Oh yes...I'm just about to come!..."

But there was another noise outside and then we heard banging on the door of the garage. I froze. Someone rattled the doorknob.

"Huh!...What was that?"

We tried to listen above the roar of the machinery. There was another knock.

"Who's that?" I shouted.

"Constable McRae..."

He was our village bobby.

"Oh God!...What does he want?" Simon muttered.

The door handle rattled once more.

"May I come in?"

Simon got up, looking shocked.

"Quick, get my clothes! This is it, just like London."

"Someone must have tipped him off," I whispered in his ear. "Now, who would have done that?"

"Your wife? She's mad enough..."

The door handle rattled again.

"Just one minute, Constable! We're busy. Hang on a moment."

We both scrambled to put on our clothes, which lay in a pile on the floor. I found myself trying to get into Simon's shirt. Fortunately the din from the equipment hid our panic.

"Grab the screwdriver!" I muttered to Simon after he'd pulled up his jeans. "Pretend to adjust something."

I looked around quickly to see if we'd missed anything and undid the Yale lock on the inside of the door.

"Good evening, Constable...Can I help you?"

"Just passing," he said. "Saw the light on. Just thought I'd look in to see what you were up to. The locals told me all about it at the pub."

"Told him about what at the pub?" Simon muttered, behind me.

"Well, Constable," I continued, "We're still adjusting the flow rate... The water pressure, you know... Simon's nearly fixed it...

A few teething troubles…"

I looked behind me quickly to see if Simon was ready but noticed his underpants still lying on the floor. I pointed at them frantically and he grabbed them to appear to get a better grip on the handle of the screwdriver. Finally I opened the door to let Constable McRae inside. I was afraid of being arrested but he seemed only interested in the hydroelectric scheme and I breathed a sigh of relief.

"You tell him how it works, Simon."

He got up and quickly stuffed the underpants in his pocket.

"Well, Constable…water comes down the hill from the lake through this pipe here…and spins the flywheel…as you can see for yourself."

He pointed at it and our constable got down to look. Simon took a nervous glance at me and I winked at him that everything was all right. He got down again to show how the nozzle might be adjusted with the screwdriver.

"Fascinating!" the constable said excitedly. "What's the electric fire for then? That's costing a pretty penny. We're only allowed a one–bar electric fire behind the desk back at the station."

"This electricity is free, Constable," I insisted. "This machine is making it…as you see."

I could see Simon grasping for inspiration.

"Erm… electrical resistance, Constable… The electric fire… erm... is to stop the generator burning out while we adjust it… We need to measure the voltage, you see."

He pointed at a meter on the wall.

"Really? How interesting…"

For a moment I was afraid the policeman wouldn't believe us. He turned to me with a sceptical look in his eye.

"So is that electric fire working on the electric power from the dynamo then?"

Simon smiled.

"It's an alternator, not a dynamo. A lot more power than the lights on your policeman's bicycle, Constable."

Constable McRae got up again.

"Yes, of course…alternating current like the mains."

I took another sigh of relief that we were not about to be bundled into a police car and bound in handcuffs. Instead, Constable McRae turned to me again.

"Fascinating! And you've done all this yourselves?..."

"With Simon's ingenuity and some help from two lads in the village."

"To keep the juvenile delinquents off the streets, what? I thought it had been a bit quiet lately..."

He smiled at us both and walked back towards the door.

"...Oh, sorry to interrupt all the good work. Just thought I'd look in as I was passing on my way back to the station... Late shift, tonight... Sheep rustlers about in the hills, you know."

I held the door open for him and watched him pick up his bicycle.

"...Good night, then."

He went off up the lane and I heard Simon take a sigh of relief.

"That was a bit too close for comfort!" I muttered. "Are you ok?"

He sat down on the cage over the flywheel, mopping his brow with his greasy underpants.

"Now you know what life was like in London. Do you think he guessed what we were up to in here?"

"Didn't sound like it to me! He's ok, that man. A Christmas box for the police station this year, I think... Goodwill gesture, don't you know...?"

"Don't you mean life insurance?" Simon suggested. "Now, before we were so rudely interrupted...!"

"No way!" I protested, backing away from him. "I'm really not in the mood!...Constable McRae has spoiled all the fun..."

He started laughing at me.

"No, really"...I insisted. "It's too late for any more hanky–panky!"

He shrugged his shoulders.

"Tomorrow then... Now I desperately need a drink. Let's walk down to the pub again."

We disconnected everything, turned off the water supply and locked up.

So we found ourselves once again standing by the bar waiting for the landlord to come to us.

"They tell me it worked, then," he said, pulling our pints. "The mill has risen like the phoenix to generate hydro–power."

"Thanks to Simon's ingenuity," I said. "Yes, we lit up a three–bar electric fire today."

"Really... You don't say. Your father would have liked to see that, I'm sure."

"They tell me all is not well at Windscale," Simon whispered. "There may be a government enquiry after the you–know–what... which nobody is supposed to know anything about and the newspapers aren't reporting."

The landlord looked around, winked at us and changed the subject.

"So you really will be making low–cost electricity. We could all do with some of that round here. Pity it's only for one electric fire. Now if the government were to block off Morecambe Bay with a barrage to generate hydro–power like they're doing in the Low Countries, I think people would be happier, don't you? I don't like this atom power any more than you do. But nobody seems to ask us, do they? The Prime Minister, Harold Macmillan, would do better to listen to the people. I ask you. How does a toffee–nosed twit like that really know what the people of Britain want today?"

"He did build a lot of council houses," I suggested. "Three hundred thousand of them."

"Yes, I suppose so and he'll be telling us all again how we've never had it so good...Well, I shouldn't say any more but this is a free house, after all."

The pub was almost empty and we found a quiet corner by the log fire. I looked at Simon, who still appeared to be worried, while our Landlord polished the glasses behind the bar. I put a hand on his knee as I sat down.

"Are you ok now?"

"A close shave…like the gents in Soho," Simon whispered. "But, listen, if we had been carted off to gaol, it would have been worth it…I really love you, you know that, don't you? The last year has been… Nobody else has come so close."

"Not even Hamish, the gamekeeper?"

"No, not even him…"

I stared into the crackling logs. They were from apple trees and wind in the chimney blew the fragrant smoke out of the stone hearth from time to time. The beer was helping both of us to calm down. I held out my glass.

"To hydroelectric power… and the white heat of technology."

"Yes," Simon smiled at last, "It works, doesn't it?…I love you so much."

"Sh!... Sh!"

The landlord came to throw another log on the fire. Another gust of wind sent smoke out into the bar. He got down to sweep up the dust around the hearth.

"The wind of change, perhaps?" I suggested.

Simon frowned at me, shook his head and turned away with a sigh. Our landlord looked puzzled for a moment and then remembered where he'd heard it before.

"Oh, yes, very good... Harold Macmillan... But I still don't like him."

Simon got up and went to the loo, shaking his head. Then our landlord got up and sat down beside me.

"Nice lad, your Simon. Clever too, but listen. You'll have to be more careful. People might talk. I've seen you two out in the garden. It's not my business what goes on under the table but, if anyone reported it, I might be closed down for running a disorderly house..."

I must have looked shocked.

"...You know, I had a boyfriend too once, out in the desert when I was in the Eighth Army fighting the Germans with Montgomery back in '42. Well, there were no women, except natives. Lots of us found comfort that way – gorgeous bloke and beautiful bubble butt he had... But this young corporal stepped on a landmine ...Boom! ...And that was the end of that. Well, I tell you. I wish he could be here with me now to help to run this place. You haven't heard yet. The wife and I are getting a divorce. She's fed up with the pub... That's life, I suppose... Anyway, perhaps you two could move further down the garden when you are together – out of sight, out of mind... We always did it behind a sand dune... Hope you didn't mind..."

Simon returned from the gents and the landlord disappeared behind the bar again.

"He knows," I muttered.

"Knows what?"

"About you and I and what goes on under the table in the garden outside..."

Simon looked worried.

"...He just wants us to move further down the garden and to be more careful next time, that's all. Nice bloke..."

Simon sat down beside me and put a hand on my knee

briefly.

"Now do you see why I moved away from London to live up here?"

Just then the landlord reappeared holding some photos. He held up one for us to look at. It showed a handsome young man sitting by the running board of a British Army lorry on the sand. He wore rolled up trousers and a vest. The landlord pointed at it.

"I only have a few photos of him. That was in the desert just before he died. Look, this one here was taken by a mate back at the camp. My wife hated these pictures. I hid them where she couldn't find them."

The second photo showed this handsome young man naked, standing beside our landlord, who was in full British Army uniform with his arm around his shoulder. It was quite bizarre.

"We might have been court–martialled if the authorities had found this one but they didn't…And here he is in his identity photograph – the official one. They're all I have left, apart from memories. I wish he was here now. He would have been 35 years old… What date is it?…Yes, today, if he hadn't stepped on a landmine."

"What was his name?" I asked.

"Tommy."

Our landlord smiled and looked at Simon.

"Oh dear, civilian life has been such a terrible disap–pointment… We, I mean the ones who survived, came back home in '45 expecting great things. What did we get? National shortages, more food rationing, Stafford Cripps and austerity budgets. But out in the desert with Monty we did great things – fighting, like Englishmen do best – against a common cause against Rommel and the Reich. We all felt like Henry the Fifth at Agincourt – on campaign for England and St George. Well, I tell you, I wouldn't have missed it for anything. But I do miss Tommy. I wish he was here right now…"

He sniffed and stuffed the pictures back in his pocket when there was a ring on the bell from the lounge bar. He tried to smile, raised his hand at us and went off to pull another pint while I drank the last of my beer.

"Same again?" Simon asked me.

"No, I'm taking you home to bed. You must be ready for more now. "

But he sat back, thinking, and seemed to relax, just staring into the fire.

"Wasn't that a sad story. Clearly, he really loved Tommy and they might still be happy today if it wasn't illegal in England today. Tommy gave his life for what? …We won the war but we haven't won the peace."

"Come on!" I insisted, turning around at the door. "Bed!" Simon put his empty glass down on the table and came to whisper in my ear.

"Yes, Sir! … I do love it when you're like this."

Finally, on the day before Bob was due to join his Army training course, we held the ceremony for his union with Bazz. They'd written out everything that they wanted Simon and me to say. Part of the ceremony even involved the burning of these handwritten notes, in case they should end up in the wrong hands. Letters and other written evidence had already proved to be the downfall of other gay couples in the 1950s. Nobody wanted any of this to be quoted on the front page of 'The News of the World'. The celebration of the union of Bob with Bazz was planned to take part after the main course of the dinner and before the sherry trifle was served. That was Simon's suggestion and everyone agreed. I spent a while making sure I could read what Bob had written for me to say. So I took Bob's hand while he stood next to his partner.

"Bob," I said, "This ceremony is to commemorate your union with Bazz who loves you. Do you love him too?"

"Yes, I really do. I swear it. "

"Do you wish to give him sexual satisfaction and to be his lover, even though you may be far apart when you go off to join the British Army tomorrow?"

"I do."

"Are you aware that the full penalty of the law of England for what you are about to undertake might be life imprisonment?"

Bob swallowed hard.

"I am fully aware of this ridiculous legislation but I really love Bazz and cannot love anyone else. I am sure of that."

I turned to smile at them both.

"Then I give Bazz to you for the purpose of companionship and sexual gratification. Now take his hand and kiss it."

Bob put Bazz's fingers to his lips and nibbled them. Bazz started giggling and that set Simon off.

"Boys... boys!" I insisted "... Some decorum please!"

"Just you wait!" Bob muttered aside to Bazz. "I'm going to give you something to think about in a minute..."

"Yes please! "

"Now, now!" I frowned. "This is supposed to be a serious occasion."

I suddenly remembered the doom and gloom of my own marriage to Elspeth in the parish church while Simon took Bazz's hand and they looked at one another. This was a joyful occasion. Finally Bazz stopped giggling.

"Bazz," Simon said in his best Sunday morning sermon voice. "This is Bob... He loves you. Do you love him too?"

"Yes."

"Well, he wants to fuck you and sexually satisfy you, to be your mate and your partner... Is that what you want, too?"

"Yes."

"Then take his hand and kiss it."

Bazz got down on one knee and Bob held out his hand, which Bazz proceeded to smother with kisses.

"You may now undress one another."

The undressing had been planned to be a formal exchange of clothing, shirt for shirt, sock for sock and so on but Bazz started giggling again and Bob tickled him. I sat down beside Simon to watch while the undressing turned into a riot of ripping and tearing. Buttons flew in all directions. Bob was now sitting on top of Bazz, who was in hysterics while they tore one another's clothes off. Finally they were both completely naked and almost helpless with laughter. This was a wedding ceremony to remember! How different from my formal union with Elspeth in the gloomy parish church some years before.

"Now," I said to Bazz, remembering the pencilled notes, "are you ready to be fucked by Bob to consummate your union publicly, in front of those present?"

"Oh yes please!"

I nodded at Simon to prompt him.

"Now Bob." Simon cleared his throat. "Will you fuck Bazz in order to consummate your union, publicly, and in front of those present?"

"You try and stop me!"

Bazz went to the kitchen table and bent over it looking back over his shoulder at his partner who, judging from the size of his erection, had every intention of ramming it straight into him. Then the most amazing thing happened. Simon got up and grabbed Bob by the arm to take him aside and started to whisper in his ear. Together they went over to the kitchen table and Simon got down to show Bob where Bazz's erotic zones were. Then, just as I had done with Simon, Bob started to massage Bazz's buttocks, rubbing his thumbs deeper and deeper in between them. Bazz lifted his head up off the table to groan appreciatively while Simon continued the instruction. Bob reached around his partner's waist to grasp his penis and began to massage that. Bazz looked around and smiled, parting his legs so that Bob could rub around his groin. Clearly Simon was showing Bob how to give greater satisfaction to his partner. I realised these were all the techniques I had used instinctively the year before to arouse Simon. I felt flattered. Simon was now teaching my own techniques to Bob. By now Bazz was groaning in ecstasy and had closed his eyes.

"Now kiss his buttocks!... Slowly now!... Make it last longer.... Use your tongue in those erotic zones I showed you to help him to relax. Make him wait a bit longer for it."

Bob got down to do just what I had done so long ago while Simon had his first bath. We could have written the first guide to gay sex. I had no idea he could remember everything I had done without thinking. It was the greatest tribute anyone has ever paid to me.

"Now ask Bazz if he wants you to use more Vaseline. That may not be enough. Better let Bazz put it on you. Then it will be what he wants. Also, it helps him to arouse you... Make it better for both of you now. That way you'll always come back for more but only with each other. Your relationship is going to survive longer that way. God knows, the British Army may do everything it can to prevent it. You do know that, don't you!"

Simon was right. I still remembered how HM Forces had conspired in the Montagu case a few years before to persuade vulnerable young men to turn Queen's evidence.

"Now Bazz, get up." Simon was clearly in expert control. "Put your arms around Bob while he lubricates you from behind and you can kiss each other...Yes, like that. He can hold your buttocks apart while he inserts the cream inside you with a third finger while you are kissing."

He passed Bob the Vaseline again. I sat speechless while I watched Simon educate the next generation in the skills of making love. He was right, too. The final union of Bob and Bazz had become a tender and moving event. Bob had already changed from a thoughtless ramrod into a caring and considerate partner for Bazz, just by Simon teaching him some basic skills about loving relationships. I was also starting to realise why Simon always said I'd been the best. But I had acted instinctively. It was immensely moving but I had a funny feeling that it was doomed not to last. The following day Bob tied up his kit bag, said goodbye to his lover and went off to join the British Army. A tearful Bazz got on his moped and went home to look after his sheep.

....

The night of the young farmers' dance arrived. I was in two minds about whether we should go in case it should cause gossip. We decided that it was best to stay apart and sit at opposite ends of the hall, just in case. It had never occurred to me that Simon had purchased a kilt because he could actually do Scottish dancing. I should have asked before. So what happened that evening was a complete surprise. There was one other dancer in highland regalia. Cathy was a bit younger than Simon and made a beeline for him from the word go. I had seen her in this outfit in previous years but she never seemed to have a partner, until now, that is. Simon did look magnificent. When he walked in, everyone turned their heads. I felt jealous already. Why couldn't Simon and I dance together in public? One day perhaps. For the time being I would have to sit on the sideline and watch.

I joined in the usual line dances and jigs, which the young farmers' club organised every year. I used to bring Elspeth to dance with her but I rather think it was beneath her dignity to dance in public with shepherds and cowmen. But Simon had no such inhibitions. He went up to talk to the leader of the band and asked them for a Scottish reel. All the other dancers seemed to be exhausted and retreated to the bar. I watched while Simon approached Cathy and bowed. She smiled. He took her hand and led her into the middle of the dance floor. Well! The bar was soon empty again when all heads turned to watch. There was instant magic between them. At 24 Simon was still very athletic.

I knew he had played tennis at the University and was talking about joining a local team in the Lake District. We all watched, spellbound at such twirling and whirling! He and Cathy were natural partners. Simon was no limp–wristed fairy portrayed by the popular press. As the band played the final chords, the applause was deafening. So they struck the opening bars of another highland reel. It was like watching 'Come Dancing' on television. I thought they were doing exhibition quality in the star turn. Finally they got tired and Simon took his partner to the bar while a buzz of conversation broke out around the hall. All I could do was stand and watch.

"They'll all be talking about the great romance," I said to Simon as we drove back to the farm in the Land Rover.

"Cathy is married," he said. "We might dance again some time."

"So, what about her husband?"

"Well, he's not a dancer. She says he just stays in to watch the telly."

"She wants us to be partners for a north–west regional dancing competition. What do you think about that?"

"Great idea. Tell her you'll do it! Just so long as I can come along to watch."

"Ok."

We parked the Land Rover in the yard and went inside. When the door was shut, I grabbed Simon. While we kissed, I reached down to lift his kilt with one hand and clutched his bottom with the other.

"Take these off!" I said, pulling at the elastic of his pants. "Real Scotsmen aren't supposed to wear anything under the kilt."

"Well they do if they're dancing and when it gets cold, believe me."

I led him into the kitchen, where the Aga had kept the place warm while we'd been out.

While he made coffee, he reminded me how he'd learned to dance the Highland way. His father's young gamekeeper came from Scotland and formed a close friendship with Simon when he was a teenager. The two of them started dancing together in secret and a love affair developed. They would dance in the woods at night or in the barn when nobody was around, accompanied by a portable wind–up gramophone. Once, he said, when everyone else was away, they even danced in the ballroom at the Palace accompanied by the bagpipes on an old scratched record. They'd got drunk and ended up dancing together in the nude. Fortunately his parents never knew about it but he had told his brother what was going on to prevent him getting too inquisitive. This revelation about Simon's past conjured up a colourful picture in my mind, like something out of 'Lady Chatterley's Lover', which the papers said might soon be published by Penguin as a paperback. However, Simon was reluctant to tell me very much about his home background. I'd learned most of all from the fortune–teller, Madame Claire Voyante. He seemed to find it all rather embarrassing but I was soon to discover a lot more for myself.

"So," I said, "Have you ever been fucked when wearing a Scottish kilt?"

"Actually, Hamish, the gamekeeper did it years ago!"

"Well, come here! Now it's going to happen again!"

I lifted up his kilt and pushed him across the kitchen table.

"Wait a minute! We've done this here before."

"Where then?"

"The coal shed outside has always been too full of coal. Now it's empty."

"But I thought you said the hydroelectric power house was the very last place."

"I forgot about the coal shed. Let's do it out there before the coal man comes tomorrow! Then I can tick that off on my list."

"You've got a list?"

"I have."

"You slut! ... But I love you all the same."

I slapped him hard and Simon started giggling.

2001

I looked out of the windscreen of the Land Rover across the car park. Here was England today, I thought. But, I asked myself, back in the fifties could we have foreseen all this? Cars, lorries, traffic jams, car parks and gridlock were now the order of the day. Well, we wanted progress! Some of us even applauded Harold Macmillan and his drive to build three hundred thousand new council houses when he was Minister of Housing. They even sprang up around our village. Then in 1957, as Prime Minister, he convinced us 'You've never had it so good' and won the general election with that same slogan in 1959. The first section of this M1 motorway had opened that very same year. But now look at it! Yes, I chuckled, looking at myself in the mirror, I really was in danger of becoming a grumpy old man – just like the character in the television comedy who shouted 'I don't believe it!' Memories! I looked in my wallet for another snap of Simon wearing his kilt. There he was, standing beside Bob and Bazz on our completed pipeline. The picture was fading and dog–eared now. Perhaps we could find the negative somewhere and get it reprinted. This was the only photograph we had of the two young lovers. I sighed. Gay love and tragedy so often went hand in hand back in the fifties but neither Simon nor I could see the tragedy coming. Madame Claire Voyante should have warned us.

1958

It was about a month after Bob had gone off to join the British Army. I was on my way to the market where he and Bazz had first met. Simon was out in the fields with the tractor. I was driving down the lane in the Land Rover, where I met Bazz on his moped. We stopped to chat.

"I really miss Bob," he said.

"Have you written to him?"

"Yes, but he said I must never do that."

"Why on earth is that then?"

"There's a flap on about homosexuals in the Army. Letters are being opened and read by officers. Lockers are being broken open..."

"Why can't he talk to you over the phone from a call box?"

"Bob can't get past the gatehouse without a pass signed by the officer."

Suddenly Bazz burst into tears. I told him to leave his moped in the barn and to get in the passenger seat beside me so we could talk about it.

"I really love him," Bazz insisted. "Why did he have to join the bloody Army?"

"He applied long before he met you," I insisted. "You know that."

"But if he really loved me he wouldn't have gone."

"It's not quite so easy to opt out..."

"But we're married. You married us together. We really loved one another..."

I switched off the engine and turned towards Bazz.

"When does he get leave from the army training camp?"

"Not until Christmas."

"Can't you wait 'til then?"

"No."

I didn't know what to say next but restarted the engine and we drove off to the market. Bazz remained quiet and stared out of the window.

"How are the sheep?" I asked, changing the subject.

"They're all still out on the hills."

"Will you bring them down for the winter?"

"I suppose so."

"Well, what about them? They will need you to look after them."

"But I want to look after Bob, not the sheep. Anyway, he hates the Army. He says the silly regulations and early parades are just a waste of time – all that boot polish and square bashing in the rain... The hut he lives in has one old coal stove which smokes if the wind blows. They're only allowed two blankets. Bob has to put his coat over the bed to keep warm. But I want to keep him warm at night. You've got Simon. It is all right for you. You are always together. Have you ever tried living apart?"

"Yes, but we both nearly went mad. I couldn't go through that again."

"There you are then."

"Bob could go AWOL."

"Yes, someone I met tried that but ended up in the military prison."

"Couldn't you move to get work at a farm near Bob's camp? Then, when he gets leave or a day off, you could be together."

"No, the Military Police would find out. Bob says they're good at that. We would be raided in the middle of the night. He's already getting paranoid about my letters. I mustn't use the words love or care, I miss you, or anything like that, in case the letter is opened and I give the game away."

With that Bazz burst into tears again so I took him with me to the market for a day out. He did cheer up but didn't want to go back to his father's farm in Keswick. So I invited him to stay for the night if he would agree to cook dinner for everyone. I told him Simon deserved another night off.

"Ok, I'll do that but on one condition… I need someone to give me a good fucking. I'm so desperate."

I had no idea how to reply to this proposition. I said I'd take Simon down to the pub to talk things over first. So we went outside in the garden again while the sun went down over the mountains. As we both sat at a wooden bench, as far out of earshot as possible, Simon stared at me.

"Now what has Bazz said?"

"He says he needs a good fucking, that's what. I said I'd have to talk to you about it."

"I could lend him my dildo. He could do it himself."

I thought for a moment and then looked at Simon.

"Have you ever fucked someone like Bazz?"

"What does that mean?"

"You might enjoy it…"

"I can't believe I'm hearing this."

"Well, have you ever fucked someone else?"

"After all this time you know I'm passive."

We sat quietly listening to the noise of the rooks going to roost in the trees. I really hadn't intended to upset him. Simon got up to visit the toilet, leaving me to sit quietly for a moment. We never had rows like Elspeth and I had done, only silences. I had no idea what to say next when he returned and sat down right beside me now. Under the table I put my hand on his bare knee.

"You'd like me to fuck Bazz then…"

"Only if you'd like to. Now is your opportunity…well, to broaden your experiences."

Simon picked up my glass of beer to sniff it.

"What have they put in this stuff you're drinking?" he asked.

"It's the same as yours!"

"Well, won't you mind and get jealous…if I have sex with someone else? You must know, since we've been together, you've been the only one…"

I ran my hand up his thigh inside his shorts again.

"…Huh! …I've told you before. Don't do that when I'm drinking!"

We glanced at each other and started laughing. Somehow the awkward moment had passed. So we emptied our glasses and went back to the farmhouse to eat Bazz's shepherd's pie. We told him he would have to make do with a rubber dildo for the night and wait patiently until Bob returned on Christmas leave from the Army. Simon told him that, speaking from his own experiences, delay increases the anticipation. I thought this was rather unkind, in the circumstances, but left it at that. Were we being tactless?

....

The telephone rang one evening. Simon answered it to discover his father announcing his planned visit to friends in a house overlooking Lake Windermere. He wished to bring Simon's mother over to the farm one afternoon to visit their son.

"How do I address your father?" I asked.

"Best to call him My Lord or Your Lordship. That way he can't be offended. My father is a stickler for tradition. Imagine what he'd have to say if he knew his son and heir was such a slut – That's what you said!"

I ignored this.

"So would it be best if I just went out for the day so you could deal with all this on your own?"

"No! ... I can't face him alone. I'll need you for support... Please!"

"What about your mother – do I call her My Lady or Your Ladyship?"

"It's probably best... at first... If she likes you, she may drop the formalities."

"Won't it be rather a shock, visiting a smelly dairy farm? Don't we have to put down a red carpet up to the front door, or something?"

"Don't you dare! I want them both to see the farm as it really is... somewhere I am so happy. That's what really matters."

I thought for a moment.

"Won't they try to persuade you to go back to university?"

"Probably..."

"How are you going to cope with that, then?"

"With difficulty. That's why I need you here... Well, you

wanted me to be around when Elspeth was here. Now I need you."

The black Rover saloon arrived one Sunday afternoon. The driver got out to hold the rear door open. He seemed to be wearing a uniform. Simon went over to the car and opened the other rear door. I wasn't really prepared for such a state visit. His parents followed him over to the door of the house where I was waiting. I had forgotten to ask Simon if I should bow but just held out a hand. His father shook it rather stiffly and went inside. His mother smiled at me and offered me her gloved hand. Simon led them both into the parlour, where we had arranged some fresh flowers and cake with fruit scones from the village bakery. I pulled out a chair at the table for Simon's mother. His father went to stand in front of the fireplace. It was clear he intended to preside over the proceedings as befitted a member of the landed gentry.

"What about the driver?" I whispered to Simon. "Should we not ask him in too?"

He shook his head at me and frowned.

"Now then, young man," His Lordship began, placing his cup of tea on the mantle shelf and turning to Simon, "Don't you think this nonsense has gone on long enough? You should go back where you belong at the University."

"No, father! ...This is not nonsense!"

I passed the plate of scones to Her Ladyship. She took one and placed it on her plate but said nothing. I got the impression she'd heard these discussions before.

"Listen to me, my boy," His Lordship continued. "If you are one day going to take my seat in the House of Lords, you need a decent education. How can you expect to govern the country if you are ignorant about what's going on?"

I was shocked. I had quite forgotten that so much was at stake. From the time he gave me the family seal he had kept quiet about it.

"No, father. You know I don't want any of that!"

His father puffed out his chest and glanced at his wife for support.

"But it is your duty, my boy."

"No, father ... I will not!"

The old man looked rather shocked and did not seem to know what to say next. I approached him with the plate of scones but he waved it aside. Her Ladyship finally put her oar in.

"Now, Simon," she said quietly, placing her plate on the table beside her. "You must be reasonable. One day you will inherit the estate... the Palace, three farms, the deer park and all the family responsibilities... How are you going to make it pay if you haven't got a profession to support it?... We really can't have the public paying for entry each day at the gate only to tread mud on the carpet and demand access to the toilet. It is enough for them to come round once a year in coach parties. You must finish your degree. It's what your father has always wanted. Well, you wouldn't go and join your family's regiment in the Army – not that British Army pay is anything to go by and I should know!"

"No, mother, I'm telling you I don't want any of it."

"So what's going to become of everything when... we can't look after it any more?"

"I don't know, mother. What about the National Trust?"

"Socialist nonsense!" muttered His Lordship. "Is this your last word?"

"Yes, father! Why can't my brother Harry look after it?"

"We'll see about that!"

Her Ladyship took a bite out of her fruit scone. I decided it was time to defuse the situation and switched on the electric light. "Do you see this, My Lord?"

"What of it?"

"Thanks to Simon, we are generating our own electricity from the old millstream. You must see it, Sir. Simon should take you and Her Ladyship down to see the hydroelectric plant."

Simon's father seemed fascinated.

"We could do with something like this on the estate. Show me!"

I helped Her Ladyship out of her chair and we followed Simon outside, down to the site of the old mill. But she took this opportunity to have a quiet word with me and paused for a while on the path.

"You seem to have my son's confidence… I wish I could say the same…"

I said nothing.

"…Has he spoken with you about any of this?"

"We have talked in confidence, My Lady…"

"Well, I'm his mother… Perhaps I was too distant… Some mothers are you know. How does that duet from the new musical play, 'Salad Days' go? ...We don't understand our children... There's a line I remember... They've flouted or destroyed all we learned from Freud... How poignant that seems to me now... Talking of Sigmund Freud, repressed sexuality and all that, you don't think he's one of those, do you?...I mean the subject of the Wolfenden Report. It ran in my family years ago, you know. My elder brother – 'the one we don't mention'– he ended up disgraced and in prison... Surely, Simon isn't one of those, I mean queer?"

"Perhaps you should talk to him yourself, Ma'am."

"We knew Lord Montagu, you know. My husband donated a vintage car for his motor museum. What an unfortunate business. It was sensationalised all over the papers for weeks – about him and his lover. I even found my personal maid had kept a scrapbook of all the sensational bits – the juicy revelations which came out in court. She had to go, of course. But why has my son moved in with you? You are not related. This is not a religious retreat or a centre for psychiatric care... I can't understand it, really, I can't. Any other young man would give anything to be in his fortunate position – handsome, athletic, intelligent, gifted even, of a noble family with expectations... Why doesn't he want to get married to a young lady with money? I have friends in the USA with eligible daughters and fortunes in the bank... Now, I ask you, why doesn't he want to meet any of them?..."

She coughed and tried to smile at me.

"...Well, I grant you one or two lack beauty or poise – things like that fade with the years, anyway... But a bank account full of lovely, silver American Dollars can make up for everything!..."

I had no idea how to respond. She turned to stare at me.

"...Well? You can tell me. I'm his mother! And another thing – why has he quit the university?"

"I really think you should talk to Simon yourself."

She realised I would not share any of his confidences and looked down to the site of the old mill in front of us. Silently I was beginning to change my opinion of my boyfriend's mother. She even tried to smile at me.

"Well, let's have a look at this hydroelectric scheme, anyway."

"Do you see, My Lady?" I said, taking her hand on the rough path. "Years ago, corn was ground here to make flour using water power in the millstream from the lake higher up the valley. Your son, Simon, had the brilliant idea of installing modern machinery to use the water power to drive a turbine which generates our electricity."

"He did this himself, you say? Extraordinary! Now why can't he come back home and do such things for us on the estate?"

I had to prevent her slipping as we clambered through the gap in the wall to climb down to the hydroelectric plant where Simon was already explaining everything to his father.

"Well, I'm damned!" His Lordship exclaimed, turning to his wife. "The power costs nothing, my dear. Now why can't our eldest son return to the family seat and use his ingenuity to sort out some of our problems?"

"No, father! You must count me out."

Her Ladyship put one hand on her son's arm.

"You could have the gamekeeper's cottage for yourself and your wife–to–be. That would give you the privacy you never had at the palace, I know."

"No, mother! I will never get married. I have told you so many times... You must depend on my brother for grandchildren."

She sniffed.

"Well, I'm sure it isn't so much to ask! Your father has always expected you would continue the family line."

"He has no right, mother."

"But what is to become of everything after we have gone?"

"I am not coming back, mother."

"So are you happy here?"

Simon smiled at me.

"I have never been so happy. I am here to stay. You must ask my brother to assume all my responsibilities. I want nothing to do with any of them or my seat in the House of Lords."

His father stepped forward.

"Is that your last word, my boy?"

Simon just turned and started to walk back towards the farm. His Lordship took the arm of his wife and I followed them in silence. As we approached the Rover saloon, the driver got out to hold open the rear door and Simon's parents both climbed inside. I stood beside Simon in the porch as we watched the car drive off in silence. Finally he shut the door and we went back to the kitchen.

"Why?" I insisted, holding Simon's hand as we leaned against the rail around the front of the Aga. "You must say something! I don't understand!"

"Don't you? What don't you understand?"

"Well, everything," I sighed

"I'm happy here with you... Trust me! ...You really are everything I've ever really wanted... You have fulfilled all my wildest dreams... You know that, don't you? ... I can't live with any of that silly pomp and circumstance...'Good morning, My Lord'...'Will you need the car today, My Lord?'..."

Simon turned round to take the kettle off the hotplate.

"Your mother and I had a little chat when you marched off with your father. She told me about her friends in the USA – the ones with eligible daughters…lined up for your consideration."

"I left home to escape Mummy's little chats. Now she's started on you. I tell you, she looks at photos of those American girls but all she sees are US Dollars. They all want an English husband with a title and invitations to the next garden party at Buckingham Palace."

"But maybe you have misjudged her. Perhaps she cares."

Simon put his fingers in his ears.

"I don't want to hear it! I might be sick."

"Why don't you talk to her?"

"I thought you were on my side."

"But..."

Simon held up his hand to prevent my objection.

"You must learn to trust me... Perhaps there are some things it is better not to know. Take me back to bed, please..."

He grabbed my hand and led me to the stairs.

"…Make me happy again and forget about the last hour."

"Ok, if that is what you want, Your Lordship."

He turned back to me on the stairs and looked shocked.

"Never, ever, call me that again!"

"Sorry, it just slipped out."

"Well, it mustn't... Promise me you will never call me that ever again!"

"Ok, if that is what you want."

"I do want..."

He grabbed my hand and pulled me up to the top of the stairs.

•••••••

Simon lay naked face down on the bed while I lay with my feet dangling over the side, my head resting on his thigh.

"It's all or nothing, you see," he sighed, leaning his head on one arm to look at me. "I could never accept all that and have this – I mean you – as well. If I returned to the Palace as my father wanted, I would have to play the game their way... marriage to a debutante or some Gorgon's daughter from the USA... Then rearing children the Empire can be proud of... to inherit everything after I am gone."

I turned my head to kiss his buttock and patted the other one gently. He suddenly sat up, staring directly at me.

"You're not going to gang up with them, are you?... Now, you must promise me..."

"I'm on your side."

"Do you swear it?...I'm serious... contra mundum."

"What does that mean?"

"Latin... it means... you and I against the world..."

I ignored this. He must have guessed I never studied Latin at school.

"... Surely you must know by now, I don't want you to go away from here."

He relaxed, lay down again, and put his arms around me.

"I need you...Don't you understand? ...Only you."

"Well you seemed to be so cold with them. They are the only mum and dad you'll ever have... They won't be around forever. Mine weren't... One day..."

"What I couldn't take were all the assumptions. They never asked me what I wanted. Simon will inherit all this one day. Simon will ride to hounds. He will take over the estate of 1,200 acres. Simon will get married to Cynthia Tweedsmuir or one of the Carnegie girls. His union will produce a male heir. Simon will join my old army regiment. He will go to university. He will assume my seat in the House of Lords. But now they have discovered I have a mind of my own and I say no, no, no... I'm going to make a life of my own here where I am happy, thank you very much."

"Didn't you ever love your parents at all?"

"How could I when they were always so icy cold and frigid?

Do you know? My father has never once hugged me or shown me any sign of love. At most he would shake my hand as if I was the estate manager or a new tenant farmer...and then it was only reluctantly...brrr, so cold. Like that! ... Not like you."

Simon put his arms around me to hold me tight and kissed me again.

"That's why I needed someone like you so much!"

"What about Mama? She didn't seem quite so stiff and reserved today."

"Harry and I both had a nanny. We were both shut in the nursery, out of the way... until we were sent off to public school to make real men out of us... as far away as possible. That's the way of it in the English upper classes... The wretched kids are seen, occasionally, but not heard and seldom loved. I should know."

"But you must have felt something for your parents... That's only natural..."

"At first but I went off them. Now I don't love them at all. No, you are right."

"Why?"

"Because I love you. That's why I quit university, remember, or have you forgotten already?"

"Don't let's argue about that."

"Fuck me... please! Make me feel loved! I want sex on my own terms... with you."

Simon lay back with his legs up in the air. He started giggling and became almost hysterical. It must have been a reaction to the stress of the afternoon. I slapped him playfully on the bottom.

"Ouch!... Well, I ask you... How long would it be before I brought the stain of dishonour upon the family escutcheon? How could I possibly talk about the feckless working classes and the immoral state of the nation in my maiden speech to the House of Lords?... Make me happy, please!... Let's not talk about it any more today. Fuck me so hard I'm too shagged out to think about all that any more. And when we're finished up here, we'll go down to the old garage over the hydroelectric plant, lock ourselves inside and do it again in there, like I said, now everything is finished. I don't think the local copper will be back in a hurry."

"Ok. ...If that is what you want!"

"I do want!"

"Where's the Vaseline got to now?"

2001

Well! I sometimes wondered if I would be able to keep him satisfied. There was a time I became ill with something or other, I couldn't remember what. All I could do was lie in bed asleep. But that was when Simon had to take over the farm for a while. But I need not have worried. He'd inherited an instinctive ability to look after the land and the animals. At home on the family estate his father would have been proud of him. But I was so grateful he was here with me. Somehow he coped, looking after me, getting up to milk the cows at six every morning, dealing with the deliveries of feedstuff for the animals. He even went to the market on his own to sell some calves and got a good price for them.

Suddenly I was roused from my daydreams and jerked back to reality in the twenty–first century. Simon reappeared with my takeaway.

"Where the hell have you been?" I asked, somewhat annoyed.

"We were talking, that's all..."

I opened the plastic packaging to find the cheeseburger.

"...The people in the garage are rushed off their feet. Someone's gone home sick. They've sent out for a fan belt which might do."

"Oh... How long do you think it will be? I need to go to the loo."

"I'll wait for you. A coach load of language students has just arrived. They're queuing in the cafeteria. We've been talent spotting. Dominic thinks they're from Poland. They all look so healthy and fit. None of them are fat and overweight like British youngsters today... "

I looked at Simon.

"You used to be like that. You could demolish an apple tree and chop it up into firewood in one morning, back in '57. I'd like to see some British youngsters do that today."

"But I enjoyed it... Besides, I would do anything for you."

"Was I that good at sex?"

"Why do you think I gave up everything – my university course and so on and came back to the farm?"

"Was I that good in bed?"

"You're worrying too much. You were just amazing! You could fuck for England!"

"You mean in the Olympics?" I laughed. " A bronze medal? Was that all?"

"I mean Gold! Time after time!"

Simon hadn't lost his sense of humour. We both dissolved into fits of giggles.

Rather stiffly I got down out of the Land Rover. He was right. There were handsome young foreigners everywhere. I wanted to ask them what they thought of England today? Had it lived up to their expectations? What did they make of British people their age – obese and Americanised? How different everything was back in the fifties! But I was showing my age again. I still thought that television had been the start of it all, when, some people complained, the rot started to set into British society. Back then we had 'The Lucy Show' and American movies which brought new ways of life, new ideals and new things to live for – fast food like the burgers and chips Simon had just bought for me. Was I just becoming old and bitter now? How lucky I was to have a second chance at happiness after my failed marriage to Elspeth. I remembered Simon as he was then – slim, muscular, incredibly strong and always desperate for sex.

Chapter 5

1958

After the first stage of rampant sex came the caring stage, followed by the creative stage of my relationship with Simon. My birthday in that autumn of 1958 began the final stage of our life–long companionship. I'd been suffering from backache for some time, partly because of the hard, unsprung driver's seat in our old Land Rover. It was welded to the floor and just could not be adjusted. Similarly, the hard metal seat on the old Ferguson tractor in the barn was dreadfully uncomfortable and provided no back support whatever. So I was lying in bed groaning, beset with aches and pains in my lumbar region. Simon put a cup of tea down on the bedside table beside me with a birthday card.

"Happy Birthday!... I couldn't find a card with a sexy bloke on. They don't sell those at the village post office. You'll have to make do with this teddy bear instead."

I looked up. Simon was taking off his dressing gown and getting back into bed. I put my hand out to touch his warm skin.

"You're the only teddy I want now..."

Simon ignored this and looked concerned when I winced.

"How are you feeling today, then?"

I tried to turn over but couldn't. It felt as if I'd slipped a disc in my back.

"Ouch!"

He gently pushed me back down on the pillow again.

"I insist...You must have a rest in bed this morning."

I tried to sit up, when there was loud mooing from the yard

outside.

"What about the cows?" I asked

"You're not well enough... I'll do the milking by myself."

"Do you think you could manage it?"

I put a hand out to grasp his knee and squeezed it. Simon put his hand on mine and passed me the tube of massage cream we'd found at the chemist in Coniston.

"Lie back and relax. I'll give you a massage..."

He helped me to remove my pyjama jacket and lie face down on the bedspread. Then I could feel his fingers gently pressing the tense muscles in my back. I groaned but said nothing.

"...You must let me do everything today. Trust me!..."

This would be the very first time Simon would be alone in the milking shed. Slowly and tenderly he worked his fingers around my spine, gently manipulating the muscles and helping them to relax. I groaned again and felt the aches and pains fade away. This was ecstasy.

"What would I do without you?" I muttered.

"Listen! Your birthday present is arriving today."

"What's that then?"

"You'll find out soon enough. Now lie back and try to get some sleep. Leave everything to me... You must learn to trust me after all this time..."

Now I moaned in frustration. Sometimes my boyfriend enjoyed being secretive and obtuse.

"...I'll milk the cows then I'll bring you breakfast in bed. By then, the van will be here. But they might be early. You may hear men working up on the roof by the chimney up there."

He pointed at the ceiling of the bedroom.

"What on earth will they be doing, then?"

"It's a secret... Now lie back and stop worrying!... Don't get out of bed. Don't come downstairs!"

"But!..."

Simon got off the bed and started to get dressed.

" ...Be quiet...or you won't get any breakfast later!...Go back to sleep now! Take one of these strong painkillers I got for you. They'll help you to rest..."

"Yes, Simon!" I muttered through clenched teeth.

"Like I told you! ...You've just been overdoing everything. And that dreadful old car seat really will have to go. I'm going downstairs now. Bang on the floor if you need the loo or anything."

I turned over slowly and soon dozed off to sleep. But it seemed only a short while before I was awoken by the noise of clattering outside the window. From the shadow on the curtains, it seemed somebody was climbing up a ladder on to the roof above the bed. I tried to sit up but the backache had returned and I needed to relax once more. I heard voices outside. Men were dragging something up the ladder on a rope. After another painkiller, I gave up trying to make out exactly what was going on and dozed off to sleep. When I awoke later, there seemed to be music coming from the sitting room downstairs. I listened carefully. It didn't seem to be the tinny sound from my mother's old radio set. Then there were voices outside the window again. "A little to the left...That's it, mate!" someone shouted from the path outside. "Now I'll go and try the other channel..."

There was a scraping noise from the brickwork of the chimney. I had no idea what on earth was going on. Slowly I put a foot down on the floor by the bed. The back pain was getting better now I'd had the medicine. I managed to sit up. Then I noticed the moment when Simon switched off the hum from the milking machine not far away outside. From the sound of distant mooing, I could tell that the cows had returned to the pasture. Now this new, louder sound of music downstairs intrigued me. It seemed to be more realistic with more bass, as if from a more modern loudspeaker. This noise didn't sound like Simon's portable gramophone. It certainly wasn't 'Chet Baker Sings' on his long–playing record. I stood up painfully and tottered slowly to the window to hold back the curtains. Outside the window, the ladder was being removed. What on earth was going on? As I turned back to the bed I heard something completely new. Through the floorboards from the room below came a new voice I didn't recognise–

"This is BBC Television from Alexandra Palace... There will now be a musical interlude provided by Frank Chacksfield and his Orchestra. Normal service will be resumed as soon as possible..."

As I got back into bed, I couldn't believe it. My boyfriend had bought me a television set for my birthday! Clearly, the noise above my head and the ladder outside meant a television aerial had just been clamped to the chimney of the cottage. Then I heard the noise of a lorry start up outside and drive off down the lane.

The bedroom door opened. Breakfast appeared on a tray beside me. I blinked at the bright sunlight from the landing.

"How do you feel now?" Simon asked.

"Help me to sit up again..." I groaned. "Can I have another painkiller yet?"

He opened the bottle and passed me a tablet.

"Please come back to bed," I sighed. "I need another massage."

"Your breakfast will get cold."

"It will keep," I insisted. "Take your things off... please... I want to look at the most beautiful boyfriend in the world..."

He smiled and quickly took off all his clothes to stand naked by the bed. I put my hand out. He moved closer. I ran my hand up between his thighs. He groaned. I watched his penis stand erect. He smiled at me again.

"But you must eat your breakfast...I insist!"

I turned over slowly. He helped me to sit up again.

"Come back to bed!" I sighed, rubbing his thigh.

"You eat some and I'll eat some, how about that?"

Now Simon put the tray down between us and knelt down on the bed. He passed me a fork.

"I've even cut it up for you...you poor, bedridden old soul, you..."

He giggled when I tried to tickle him.

"Just you wait, you gorgeous, sexy boy!"

"I'm not a boy. You know I'm twenty–four..."

I looked at the tray. There was the very same breakfast he had cooked on our first day together over a year ago. I sniffed.

"...Now what is it? Have I cooked the wrong things?"

"I guess I'm just really happy, that's all... Were you ok with the cows? They didn't kick you? Marilyn doesn't like it when you swear at her..."

"All done. Now stop worrying. Eat your breakfast!"

While I ate, we started talking about the television. He had wanted the engineer to show him how to adjust it. He said they'd had one for years back home at the Palace but it had never worked properly, even for the Queen's Coronation that his parents had actually attended in 1953. The rest of the household had to watch the flickering TV screen. Now he had been determined the men should get everything right this time before they drove away. That's why he'd been late getting breakfast. I looked at the alarm clock. It was almost twelve o'clock already.

"Is this what you'd call 'brunch' then?" I asked.

"Something like that. Now what do you want me to do today?"

"Come and sleep with me... please... and I want another massage."

"Well, I'll take these things downstairs, out of the way, anyway."

He put on his dressing gown again and returned to the kitchen with the tray.

I lay thinking. Was Simon getting bored? Was that why he thought we would need to watch a television set? But I was also getting excited. We'd never had one, only the radio. Every time you opened a newspaper these days there were adverts for TV sets with bigger 17–inch screens and the new ITV channels. We could watch current affairs programmes like 'Tonight with Cliff Michelmore' or BBC–TV News with Richard Baker. There were plays and comedies. I'd never seen 'Hancock's Half Hour', which the papers said had become a national institution after starting on the radio. The weather forecast would be useful, and my magazine 'Farmers Weekly' said the BBC had plans for more farming programmes. Now they would be worth watching. Perhaps it indicated the government intended to do something more to help small hill farmers like us in the Lake District. But it would be so nice to watch TV in the winter when it was too wet to walk down to the pub. I seemed to be dozing off to sleep again when Simon reappeared with two mugs of coffee and sat down on the bed.

"Take that off!" I insisted, pointing at the dressing gown.

He put it aside and once again knelt naked on the bed beside me. I rolled over on my front for another massage. This time, instead of giving a massage he tried to tickle me. I started to protest, when I felt a pang of pain.

"Ouch, my back!"

"I'll bring the television up here," he said, getting up again. "You can watch the sport this afternoon. The extension on the aerial lead is long enough to come up the stairs. I told them you were ill in bed. The driver said he knew your dad years ago and asked me where you'd got to. I pointed to this window. Nice man!"

"Is it a portable TV then?"

"What did you want?... The twenty–one inch console model?"

"The sound quality was good, anyway. I heard it through the floor."

"We were lucky," Simon said. "They told me this valley is neatly lined up with the transmitter. Other people with a mountain in the way of the signal can't get TV at all."

"I don't know what to say. You shouldn't spend all this money on me."

"Why not? Who else am I going to spend my money on?"

"You've still got some, then? Your father hasn't disinherited you?"

"I've got my own money. It was in trust for me until I was 21, thanks to my grandfather, bless him. Now I can do what I want with it."

"But if you spend it like this, buying TV sets, it won't last long, will it?"

"I'm spending interest not capital... don't worry."

"The cost of the new TV is interest, then?"

Simon nodded.

"All this year's probably…"

I didn't ask any more questions but did some sums at the back of my head in silence. Simon was obviously a wealthy young man in his own right. I wondered if my lover had any more secrets to hide.

"…Now lie back. I'll give you another massage…"

He climbed above me with one knee on the bed either side of my chest. It was extremely erotic and before long I complained he'd given me another hard–on.

"…Now turn over. I'm not wasting that," he insisted. "Relax, I want you to fuck me… please… and I'll do all the work. You mustn't strain your back again now it's stopped hurting."

"I do not know what I've done to deserve someone like you," I sniffed.

"Now you're going all soppy and sentimental… Age must be catching up with you!"

Simon happened to turn his back to me and leaned down to the floor for his new tube of Vaseline under the bed. I slapped his pert buttocks tenderly.

"Ouch!…Well, you must be feeling better already."

The lovemaking which followed was the most gentle and erotic I could ever remember. It was part massage and part sexual arousal. This was one birthday I would never forget. I was no longer only in my twenties. From now on I would be in my prime. I was thirty years old today but, at least, I'd found my other half. Unfortunately he was getting carried away and starting to bounce up and down on my pelvis.

"Huh... Oh, yes!" Simon muttered

"Not so fast," I complained. "Remember my backache!"

But both of us were too excited to stop.

"Huh!... Oh, fantastic!...Huh! ... Oh, yes!"

Simon was beyond the point of no return. But my back hurt again. I groaned. He started to tickle me. I just couldn't move and he knew it.

"Ouch!... Simon!... No!... Please."

"Huh!... Huh!... That's it, I am going to come!"

Suddenly we climaxed together. For a moment my backache disappeared. His cum spurted right over my head and landed on the pillow with a splat.

"Ouch!" I shrieked. "Now, you really will need to give me another massage. Pass those painkillers quickly!"

He realised what he had done and climbed off me again.

"Now you'll be in bed for days! I know it."

"Yes, and...you'll... be... sorry... Cheeky boy!"

But he started giggling. The awkward moment had passed. He kissed me gently. So this was the day I was finally convinced that Madame Claire Voyante had been right. My beautiful boyfriend and I really would stay together for the rest of our lives. Nothing would keep us apart – not the long arm of the law, not my responsibility for the farm or Simon's birth into the landed gentry, nor even illness or chronic backache, would ever separate us now. As he gently turned me over to massage my back again, I suddenly burst into floods of tears. He stopped and stared at me.

"What's wrong now? I couldn't have hurt you that much!"

I tugged a tissue out of the box and blew my nose.

"It's the relief... I don't mean that..." I insisted, as Simon climbed off me, giggling and wiping the massage lotion away with another paper tissue . "...It is just the relief of finding you... You have made my life worthwhile, after all those dreadful years with Elspeth..."

"You mean, the wicked witch we don't mention…"

"Well, it wasn't her fault it didn't work out," I insisted.

Simon giggled again. I knew he wanted to say something unkind about her.

"Why bring that topic up again?… I am the lucky winner and you've got me now. Anyway," he added. "You never know. I might become worse than two Elspeths!…"

I sighed, lay back on the pillows and smiled at him, but he hadn't finished yet.

"…You really must shut up and rest. I'll bring the TV upstairs. They've started 'Grandstand' now. You can watch the sport and see handsome young men in shorts running around the field, doing real man's stuff… It will help to take your mind off everything for the rest of the afternoon."

••••••••

Within a few days I felt better and we found ourselves once more sitting outside the pub, at the front this time. The autumn sunshine was still warm enough. The rooks circled noisily around the trees. Together we were looking out across the village square, towards the church where Fred's funeral was being held. For a moment I felt guilty. I'd been moaning in bed with backache but poor Fred had actually died. Perhaps we should have attended the service but I didn't want to intrude. Any connection between Fred's short illness and the fire at the Windscale atomic plant was still being officially denied. The local fire brigade had turned out in force to say goodbye to their colleague. He was only forty. It was so sad. The coffin was being carried out by firemen in smart black uniforms while the wind was carrying slow music from the organ inside the church. I remembered that sound. It had accompanied my wedding to Elspeth. But now I had Simon, thank goodness, and I turned to him again.

"Are you happy now you've quit the world of nuclear power?"

He smiled at me with those come–to–bed eyes and said nothing.

So we sat down to watch the new TV serial, about a hospital, called 'Emergency Ward 10'. But it reminded me too much of the time my mother went in and never came back. A few days later there was a brand new programme on the BBC called 'The Sky at Night'. Now that was interesting. On a clear dark night by the barn we could even see the Milky Way. It was a shame not to know more about it. I told Simon that Patrick Moore had got two more regular viewers already. So had 'Dixon of Dock Green', 'Panorama' and 'Zoo Quest'. But neither of us could stand 'The Billy Cotton Band Show' or endless song and dance acts. They were quickly switched off. The parade of the ladies in the chorus and the close–ups of other sweet young females did absolutely nothing for us. We both wanted programmes with more young men in them but I don't think they made programmes for people like us, not in 1958. But there was more excitement to come. The Queen would soon be giving her second Christmas speech on television. Now Simon would be able to tell his mother on the telephone that we had watched HMQ on a larger screen than the one they still made do with at the palace.

Bazz telephoned to say Bob had got leave from the Army to spend Christmas at home. Instead, they planned to spend it together. Could they come and stay with us if we wanted help with dinner on Christmas Day? He laughed when I suggested the Military Police might raid our farm on Christmas Eve.

Bob arrived on the back of Bazz's moped clutching a tin with the Christmas cake he'd made himself in the Army Catering Corps, which he'd just joined. When he opened it on the kitchen table, we were all surprised to see real marzipan and genuine glace cherries, which were still scarce and expensive at the shops in Coniston. He explained that they had been hijacked from the local NAAFI store and we shouldn't ask any questions. So Simon and I left Bazz and Bob in charge of the kitchen while the two of us retreated to the parlour to watch our television set. I sent Simon upstairs to put on his kilt again. I told him we'd never had kitchen staff before so it was time to dress for the occasion. Soon we lay on the floor in front of a roaring log fire and made love by the light of the flickering screen and the flames in the hearth. I locked the door to stop anyone coming in. Christmas dinner was wonderful and Bob's training in the art of Army catering paid off. Not since my mother died had the silverware and the best china been laid out. Bob and Bazz seemed to feel at home with us at last. It was a day to remember.

I will never forget that snowy Christmas of 1958. I'd got wind of something special from Simon for my Christmas present but he wouldn't give away the secret, no matter how much I tickled him in bed. I had no idea what to expect. It wasn't until a new ignition key fell out of the Christmas cracker I pulled with him after the brandy and cake that I had any idea. 'Land Rover' was stamped on the key fob. In the barn it stood, brand new and painted blue, which was much prettier than the choice of army green or grey you had before. This one also had a hard top, sprung seats and it even had a heater. I stood there gazing at it.

"Don't tell me this is only this month's interest," I said.

"Don't you like it, then?"

I put my arms around his waist and kissed him.

"Where's the old one?"

"I got them to part–exchange it. Well, they said it wasn't really worth doing up. The front suspension had gone, the piston rings had blown – there was no compression at all, the wheel bearings were leaking all the oil we poured in and as for the driver's seat… You know about the rusty chassis… Anyway it was just too cold in winter and I thought you deserved something better."

"Why not a second–hand one?"

"Because you are the best."

"The best what, exactly?" I asked, smiling.

"You know very well. If I had a gold medal, I'd award it right now. The Land Rover will just have to do!"

Simon blew a kiss at me like Miss Monroe did in her movies. He put down the bonnet over the engine and opened the side door for me to get in.

"The gear box is different," he said, getting in the driver's side. "I had to learn how to use it..."

There seemed to be two gear levers now. I had been used to only one.

"...High and low ratio," he said, starting the engine on the first turn of the key. "I'll take you on a demonstration up the hill to the lake."

Without all the clattering and grinding I had got used to from the old Land Rover, we glided smoothly up the track where Simon stopped briefly, slid the second gear lever into low ratio and we climbed up the steep slope the old one could no longer manage.

"You have a go now!" he said.

We swapped places. I had to adjust the seat. That was something new. The old seat had been welded to the floor and we just had to put up with the discomfort. I turned the ignition key. Wow! Heat started to clear the windscreen immediately. Progress indeed! Simon smiled at me with those come–to–bed eyes. I turned the Land Rover round and stopped, overlooking the valley and our farm down below. At their suggestion we left Bob and Bazz to finish the washing up. I think they just wanted some time alone together. Smoke from the kitchen was curling up from the chimney. It all looked so beautifully English, serene and picturesque.

"I don't know what to say," I said, gazing through the windscreen while snowflakes started to settle all around us.

"It is to say thank you for making this the happiest time of my life. I needed a real man who would give me all the happiness I could never find with a wife. I just walked into your farm yard... I had breakfast but stayed for over a year."

"You wanted milk and bread," I sighed. "I told you the store would open at nine... I nearly sent you away... Oh God, Simon... I nearly sent you away!"

For the second time, I started to cry. It was all too much.

"Now what's wrong?"

"Elspeth had money but she never bought me anything like this…"

I took hold of Simon's hand and kissed it. He switched on the car radio. I could hardly believe it. We were listening to 'Ding–Dong, Merrily on High' sung by the choir of King's College Chapel. I'd never felt so happy in my life. So we just sat there while the windscreen wipers silently cleared the snowflakes which were falling in front of us and piling up on the spare wheel bolted to the bonnet outside. Simon was singing the tenor part.

"I used to sing this at the Cathedral," Simon added.

"I love you so much," I sniffed. "You've given me too much already. You drive again now. I'm afraid of sliding the Land Rover off the track in all this deep snow."

We swapped places again and returned down the track in low ratio while a wonderful boy soprano sang 'Away in a Manger' over the airwaves from Cambridge.

The fire of apple logs was crackling in the grate. Then we switched on the television to watch the Queen. Simon sat on the floor at my feet and held the toasting fork in front of the flames. I had never been so happy. I leaned down to kiss him again. This would be a Christmas neither of us would ever forget. Our guests joined us and sat together on the settee while a black and white Queen Elizabeth smiled sedately at us through the television screen over the airwaves from London. Her clipped English made me smile. Nobody spoke like that up here, except Simon, perhaps. She wished all her loyal subjects a Merry Christmas. I wondered if she would include Simon and me if she knew the truth about us, especially when his parents had attended her coronation. We turned off the TV set again and finished the crumpets.

"Oh, I forgot," I said suddenly to Simon. "I've got something for you... It's not quite in the same league as a brand new Land Rover... but... I didn't know."

I squeezed past Simon and went out to the dairy to fetch the crate of bottled local beer, which we started to drink there and then. It was hot in the parlour and Bob and Bazz went off for a walk outside in the snow, so Simon slipped off his shirt and sat bare–chested in front of the fire. He looked truly magnificent in the flickering light of the fire. I told him to go and put on his kilt but no pants. He was about to get fucked in it for the third time. Then to the sounds of 'My Buddy' from a long–playing record played on Simon's portable gramophone, we climaxed together while Chet Baker crooned close up into his microphone and blew his soulful trumpet with the boys in his band.

Boxing Day was rather an anticlimax. Snow lay everywhere. We had to clear a path to the milking parlour. The cows were now housed in the large barn. It was too wintry for them in the fields. So Simon and I had to feed them every day with hay from the loft and high yield additive measured in a scoop from sacks. It took four of us to get the truck with the milk churns down the lane to the road for collection. In the snow everything seemed to take twice as long. We weren't finished until ten o'clock, when Simon said it was time for a special fry–up. There it was – exactly what he had cooked that very first morning, with mushrooms and fried bread.

"I am so lucky," I said putting out a hand to take hold of Simon's. "I often wonder what I've done to deserve someone like you."

"Well, I've got another surprise... You'll like this. My brother wants to come and stay for a few days. Now he's had a dreadful row with my father. He phoned while you were out."

"What's that row about?"

"He didn't say but you'll like him. He's like me but younger... and, well, he has a girlfriend... At least he's got that right. I think he just wants to come here and talk everything over at the New Year. Bob and Bazz will have gone by then. What do you say? I said we'd go and collect Harry at Windermere Station. He can stay in the spare room. I'll see to it."

"Does he know about you and me? I mean, we'll be sleeping in a double bed next door."

"He'll have to know some time. He's broadminded. You know I told him about my first lover, the Scottish gamekeeper. I know he will keep our secret. Well, what do you say? I think he wants to mend bridges... Well, after the pater's last visit with Mama... I think he wants to find out for himself."

"He's not bringing his girlfriend too?"

"No, no. I told him there just isn't the room."

So we said goodbye to Bazz and to Bob, who had to return to the freezing Army camp to resume his duties in the Catering Corps. Harry did indeed arrive at the railway station to come and stay with us over New Year. However, I was unprepared for the latest news he would bring.

"Simon," Harry said, as the three of us sat side by side on the bench seat of the Land Rover. "You've got to know some time. I've told my girlfriend and she still wants us to be friends but... you know, I've recently become a Roman Catholic. Well, I don't know how you're going to take this. I want to train for the priesthood… Yes, I know all about celibacy... That is what the big bust–up with father was all about."

I was shocked. Firstly, because I was a complete stranger to Harry and sat right next to him in the driver's seat. Secondly, Simon always assumed Harry would be able to provide the son and heir for the family estate, to get His Lordship off our backs. I decided to stop the Land Rover by the side of the road and pulled into a lay–by at the side of Lake Windermere. I suggested that we should get out and walk for a while. The snow lay crisp and inviting in the bright winter sun.

"I've always thought I might go abroad," Harry continued. "I want to work as a missionary somewhere... Africa, maybe – somewhere I can lose myself, out of touch with England... I guess, Simon, I feel just as you do... I don't want to be one of the landed gentry... I need to do other things with my life... Why can't I just be like you? Now I want to go off and do my own thing."

He turned to me with a warm smile. Simon was right. Harry was a younger version of him, but without those come–to–bed eyes I was so fond of staring into.

"...I'm really glad my brother has found the right man, at last. I suppose I'm envious in a way. From what mother told me, it sounded like real love – the two of you running the farm up here together, away from it all. The mater is a tough old cookie but very observant and she told me everything – how close you were and the things you'd achieved together like the hydroelectric plant. My God that sounds impressive! This I really must see..."

He turned to his brother.

"...But what is such a mystery is how the two of you actually met. Do tell!"

Simon explained how he'd arrived in the farmyard in the pouring rain, cooked breakfast, helped the sheepdog to have her puppies and then stayed for well over a year.

"The best thing that ever happened in my life!" I added.

"He's a really good fuck!" Simon chuckled, pointing at me. "A veritable stallion!"

"God!" Harry exclaimed. "I'm so envious of you, Simon... Everybody else is talking about sex after that Wolfenden Report. But you are actually doing it!"

"Life can get a bit boring out here in the winter!"

"What else is there to do?" I added, " Except to watch BBC television!"

His brother roared with laughter. The sun went in, the clouds came over and it started to snow again, so we all turned round and walked back to the Land Rover. I was beginning to like Harry already. He was the latest addition to my new, extended family. I thought he'd make an excellent parish priest or missionary. He was broadminded, sensitive and quite understanding, with exactly the sense of humour one would need in the confessional.

After the sun had melted some of the snow, which had then frozen over again, the roads were getting slippery. Suddenly we came across the milk lorry, which had slid sideways on the ice and ended up in a ditch. I didn't know about the winch on the front of this new Land Rover. Simon soon had it hauling the front end of the truck back onto the road so the driver could proceed to the next farm. His brother and I stood on the verge watching the operation. It was clear Simon had read the Land Rover instruction book and knew much more than I did already. Harry and I were very impressed. We also needed the four–wheel drive on the track up to the farm. Everyone agreed that the whole thing was now well and truly run in.

The problem of what Simon and Harry were going to do with the ancestral estate and their demanding parents was still unresolved. We retreated to the private bar at the village pub to discuss it further.

"I will never come back," Simon insisted.

"What never?" Harry sang, imitating a line from Gilbert and Sullivan, which his brother recognised instantly.

"Well... hardly ever!"

"Look, I don't want it either," his brother added, looking more serious again. "When the pater finally goes to the pulpit in the sky there will be lots of death duties to pay... We've got the socialists to thank for that!"

He turned to his brother as if he'd made a decision.

"...National Trust?"

"Yes, Harry, God bless the National Trust. A gift to the nation in lieu of death duties."

They held up their pint glasses as if a deal had been struck. I couldn't help smiling. So much for the noblesse oblige.

I decided to say nothing but let them sort it out for themselves. We waited while the landlord lit the log fire in the fireplace and left us in peace again. I introduced Harry to our landlord... I'd always been thankful to George, our postman, for not spreading gossip about Simon. I don't think the landlord would have been nearly so friendly towards the three of us if he knew there was an English noble heir and Harry, 'the spare', drinking in his private bar. He didn't like 'toffs' any more than newfangled atom power. Our landlord was a socialist at heart and he really hated Harold Macmillan, the First Earl of Stockton, as we approached the 1959 General Election. All the regulars had learned not to discuss this painful topic in the Public Bar next door, where politics and religion were already strictly taboo.

"The mater must go to the dower house," Simon insisted. "All the farms can be sold off, unless we get planning permission for housing estates on the outskirts of the village – council housing and all that sort of thing. Best get the lawyers onto that one."

"Well, I'll be in Africa. I'll have to leave that to you. Perhaps the Trust will want the estate as well. Best to ask first... unless you two come back to run the farms yourselves. If the Trust take 200 acres for the gardens and the deer park, that leaves one thousand acres of prime agricultural land – wheat fields and pasture for cattle and sheep. Well you're already in that business. If Britain joins the Common Market, agriculture might be the industry for the future – what with subsidies and so on. Well, we can't let the French have it all their own way, what?"

"No... never!" Simon added, singing again.

There was another chink of glasses. I was growing to like Harry immensely. If he ever became a Catholic priest, he might present a challenge for the Vatican one day.

2001

The Common Market, I thought, huh! Could we have foreseen the wine lake, the butter mountain, and all the petty squabbles in Brussels? Maybe the French President, Charles de Gaulle had been right, after all, to block our early application. Had it been a good idea for Britain to join the Common Market? Well, I was a farmer for over forty years and I still didn't know the answer to that one! I looked out of the side window again. No sign of Dominic or the spare fan belt. I was also getting thirsty again. Had Harry and Simon forgotten to bring my coffee–to–go? What on earth were they talking about in the cafeteria all this time? Life seemed to be so much more exciting in the old days before motorways and this boring service area. They could have made a fan belt by now! What on earth was taking so long? So much for England's scientific progress and the white heat of technology we'd all been promised in the 1950s!

Harry was wonderful – just like Simon but with a more cheeky sense of humour. He was so lucky to have found Dominic to share his life with. Dominic was the youngest of us and still kept his youthful beauty. After all these years he still retained a full head of hair, even if it was starting to turn grey now. Even today, he looked presentable in swimming trunks and still went jogging twice a week. He and Harry had always been inseparable and a perfect match. They played duets together on the piano and would still sing Noel Coward songs to cheer us up if there was nothing worth watching on the television. I sat there thinking about that. Such excitement there was back in the fifties when TV first arrived in the regions on tiny round screens... then colour TV...then big wide–screens. We'd seen all the developments over the decades but the programmes seemed to be disappointing today – too many repeats.' Dad's Army' wasn't really any better in wide–screen colour with stereo sound than it had been the first time round on a 17–inch screen in black and white. In 1999 we watched 'Queer as Folk' in which Stewart fucked under–age Nathan in Episode One. Well! It was like watching a porn movie. If I hadn't seen it with my own eyes I would have said no such thing would ever be shown on British public service television. Simon joked that Mary Whitehouse, late of the National Viewers and Listeners Association, must have been spinning in her grave. I really was shocked. But was I just becoming another grumpy old man, disillusioned with the modern age, out of touch with popular culture today? I could still remember watching David Jacobs on 'Juke Box Jury' playing songs we could tap our feet to. Today? Well, Simon and I had given up watching 'Top of the Pops'. It just sounded like mindless noise to us old–timers given to nostalgia about the good old days... However, from the days of squeaky clean stuff of the fifties like 'Sunday Night at the Palladium' to the challenging gay drama 'Queer as Folk', Simon and I had seen it all. But, of course, this was just something else we had always done together. Silently, I thanked Madame Claire Voyante for getting all her amazing prophecies correct so many years before.

1958

The following day we took Harry on a guided tour of the farm. I also wanted to have another go at driving the new Land Rover. Well, I'd never been given one for Christmas before. We drove up the valley to have a look at the lake which supplied our hydro–electricity. I was concerned that the streams which flowed into it would freeze over and cause the turbine to run out of water. But Simon pointed out that a lot of the water came from old mine workings from which the water was still flowing freely. Our area had been extensively mined for generations for copper and slate. Perhaps it wasn't freezing underground, where horizontal drift mines still drained water out of the side of the mountain. We got out of the Land Rover and walked round. The snow covered up the ugliness left by the miners and the valley below looked like a picture post card. Smoke curling up from the chimney of the Aga in the farmhouse added a final homely touch to the scene, which the three of us were admiring, leaning on the gate.

"I love your brother very much – much more than I can say," I said to Harry. "I'm telling you so you know. You are welcome here any time. You might think of it as a retreat, away from all that ... whenever you need to get away from His Lordship, the seminary or life in general. Are you really going to be a Catholic priest? Simon said you had a girlfriend. Won't you miss...?"

"I've made up my mind. Nothing will stop me, not even what my father said. We had the most dreadful row. That's why I had to get away."

"What was that?" Simon asked. "What's the pater said now?"

"That our family has always been C of E, since Henry the Eighth presented confiscated monastic land to our revered ancestor in 1538. Father pointed at that painting on the stairs – you know the pompous one we both used to laugh at... Well, I'm addressing the balance, I told him. Simon, you can imagine! I was afraid His Lordship might have a fit. My mother sent him to have a lie down. Believe me, what you two get up to in bed is nothing compared with the stain I have brought on the family escutcheon – a Catholic nurtured in the bosom of the family! The worst disgrace! You two are now back in favour because I am now beyond the pale..."

Simon and I started laughing while Simon patted his brother on the back.

"...Believe me that hydroelectric plant the two of you have built has got my father telling everyone all about it. He was really impressed. Applied science he calls it. He even mentioned it in a talk he gave from the pulpit at the cathedral – God's wonders harnessed for the good of mankind. Hydroelectricity even became a holy theme for the day... Simon, I think you have made him a proud father at last."

Much more cheerful now, we got back in the Land Rover and went back to the farm.

"Have you shown Harry your highland outfit?" I asked while we sat around the fire in the parlour.

Simon went upstairs to put it on. This gave me a while to talk to his brother in private.

"I'm concerned what your parents might think about us?" I

asked.

"Well, I think my mother has guessed but His Lordship... who can say? I don't really know him well enough. I think he's puzzled. He just doesn't understand why Simon wants nothing to do with his inheritance. He's also getting worried about money. The roof of the west wing – the oldest part of the palace – is leaking. Some of the rooms upstairs are uninhabitable. If Simon married a wealthy debutante like a Carnegie or a Rockefeller then money would come into the family. Oh, but don't think about all that. What matters is that my brother is really happy. I can see how much he loves it here with you..."

Simon came into the room and gave a swirl to show off his kilt, which I reached out and lifted up to reveal that he really was wearing nothing underneath.

"The pride of England dressed up in the garb of Scotland!" I joked.

"Yes," Harry added, "My brother has truly magnificent wedding tackle to continue the family tree but, sadly, not the inclination. Alas, poor England! ... Oh, decline and fall!"

We roared with laughter. Now here was a priest with a sense of humour.

"Look...this may sound dreadful..." Harry added.

"What is it, then?" Simon asked while his brother went red in the face.

"No, you'll say I'm dreadful."

"Oh, spit it out, Harry!" I insisted. "We're all family, now!"

I couldn't imagine what Harry wanted to say.

"Well..."

"You'll have to tell us now!" Simon giggled.

"Next time the two of you have sex... I'd like to watch, that's all... I've read about this sort of thing, of course. Well, the newspapers are full of the debate about Wolfenden. Now the Church has joined in – 'the beginning of the end' and all that sanctimonious rubbish about deviant sex... Opening the floodgates for the devil's work, etc... But now I want to know exactly how it's done!... What is it really all about?"

"Come here!" I said to Simon. "No time like the present."

He came to stand in front of me by the table. I pushed him down so he lay across it and grabbed hold of his kilt to tuck it around his shoulders out of the way.

"It's quite simple," I explained, undoing my zip. "Simon

breathes in …"

Simon turned his head to smile at his brother who moved round to watch at close hand exactly what was going on.

"See!... It turns me on so much..." Simon whispered. "Huh! ...Like that!... Yes every time... Oh fuck! ...Look out Harry!... I'm going to come!"

Simon's own semen spurted across the table, just missing his brother, while I climaxed deep inside him.

"Wow!..." muttered Harry. "I do see why you gave up everything... Now I know just what I've been missing!... It wasn't disgusting at all!... No matter what it says in the newspapers. Now I know, Simon, why you've given up your inheritance to stay here."

"It's real love, you see... not just sex!" I added. "But your brother is just fantastic. I am so lucky. That fortune–teller we consulted was right. She said some people never find anyone to make love with."

Harry was smiling at his brother as he got up off the table and adjusted his kilt.

"But it was wonderful, Simon... So moving... the two of you coupling together and becoming one... I want to do it myself one day... So is that what the Wolfenden Report is really all about, then?... But I can't see our father, His Lordship, voting in favour of it in the House of Lords, can you? He would probably bring back public flogging and transportation to the colonies."

"No, he'd hang us all if he could!" Simon giggled. "Such disgusting hanky–panky…The devil's work… Sin of the worst kind! I can hear him now. Death is too good for us… etc, etc."

"What about a good old–fashioned hanging, drawing and quartering like our poor ancestor imprisoned in the Tower of London?"

"So," I muttered, thinking back to the past. "That must have been what Madame saw in her crystal…"

Simon got up to answer the telephone while I continued to chat with Harry.

"I should thank you," Harry said quietly. "You've made my brother a happy man. I've never seen him enjoying himself so much. He hated living at home after Hamish, the gamekeeper, went off to war in Korea. He and my father just did not get on. I used to be my dad's favourite – until now!"

"How did he get on at that posh boarding school?"

"He was nearly expelled... We both were!...Best not to ask... You were married once, weren't you? Simon wrote to me in confidence."

"A mistake," I sighed. "But your brother has changed my life..."

Moments later Simon returned. The colour had gone from his face.

"What's the matter now?" I asked.

"That was Bazz's father at the farm in Keswick. They've just found poor Bazz out in the barn. He's blown his brains out with a shotgun."

"Oh God," I muttered, sitting down again. "I don't believe it."

"But he seemed to be ok when we saw him last."

"Poor Bazz – he just wanted somebody to love him..."

Gradually, the horror began to sink in. While Simon, Harry and I had been enjoying ourselves, Bazz must have been going through hell. I wondered if anyone had bothered to let Bob know at the army camp? Simon sat down and started shaking. Harry went to sit beside him. I explained the whole situation as best I could to Harry.

"Bazz was a friend of ours. Bob, his lover, has just gone back to the Army after Christmas leave. I guess Bazz just couldn't stand the thought of life without him until Easter. He found it hard enough before Christmas. They were here together just a day or so ago."

Simon just burst into tears and sobbed on his brother's shoulder.

"He was so pretty. Bob worshipped him. We told him to come and stay here with us whenever he felt depressed."

Harry grasped the tragedy at once.

"But now I'm here he probably didn't want to intrude. I guess that was it. Simon, you really should have told me about it."

"I told him you were my brother," Simon sobbed. "I tried to make him understand that there wouldn't be enough room."

"He could have slept on the settee," I added without thinking. "But maybe he thought he wouldn't be welcome. Anyway, perhaps we'll never know now."

We did not find out the truth until later. Poor Bazz had a history of depression. He had already tried to commit suicide two years before by hanging himself from a rope in his father's barn.

Fortunately on that occasion the rope broke and he survived. Medication was prescribed and he went off to agricultural college. His parents hoped this might help him to find a new direction in life.

They did not know he was homosexual and that this lay at the root of his personal problems. We learned all this from the coroner's enquiry at which Simon gave some evidence about Bazz's state of mind. The coroner was tactful, fortunately. No questions were asked about his sexual relationship with Bob, who was not even given leave from the Army to attend the coroner's court. Nor were any questions asked about Simon and myself or our relationship on the farm. The local paper simply noted that Bazz killed himself while his mind was unbalanced as the result of years of mental illness.

"That consultant," Simon commented later in the Land Rover. "How could he claim that homosexuality is a mental illness?... I'm just the same but am I mentally ill? You know me better than anyone else."

"You're the sanest person I know," I said confidently. "Without you, I am the one who would have ended up in a straightjacket. You know that, don't you?"

"But Bazz's death was so unnecessary," Simon insisted. "All he needed was a lover like Bob full–time...not just when Bob could get leave from the British Army. And what did that consultant psychologist think Bazz should have done with the rest of his life? Gone for aversion therapy or analysis to be made heterosexual and normal?... For God's sake! I suppose the consultant would have Bazz getting married and settling down with two point one kids and a dog...As if that would make him happy..."

"Marriage never worked for me," I added.

"And when that consultant was asked if he'd ever met a happy homosexual... Well!... As if that might, in some way, justify Bazz taking his own life. I nearly shouted out: Look at me! I'm living proof that Bazz might have been happy if he'd been left in peace with the right man!"

"I'm glad you didn't."

"Oh take me home for a really good fucking! I just can't think about it any more!"

More bad news arrived suddenly in the middle of the night a few days later. Harry was on the phone for Simon. His Lordship had just been rushed into hospital with a suspected coronary. The doctor was hopeful but his father would need to rest. Part of the roof in the west wing of the Palace had just collapsed under the weight of the snow. Now all the lights had fused. He was talking to us by the light of a candle because there was no electricity. His Lordship was shifting valuables away from another possible roof collapse when he was taken ill. Now Harry was helping his mother to remove family heirlooms to one of the stables out of danger. There was nobody else to do it. The housekeeper had just retired but they could not afford to replace her. Only the part–time staff were left and wouldn't be there until nine in the morning. Harry was in tears.

"You must go," I insisted to Simon. "Your family needs you."

"No! I'm staying here. Harry will have to deal with it. I told you. I will never go back."

I didn't argue. I would not know how to cope without him. We went back to bed.

The telephone rang again in the morning. Simon went downstairs to answer it. I could hear him crying down in the hall. His Lordship had suffered another heart attack in hospital. As I came down the stairs, he dropped the phone and sank down to the floor. I replaced the handset quietly and put my arm around his shoulder.

"I might have been too late. What if he had died this time?" I sat down on the stairs beside him. Simon lay his head on my lap and sobbed. I had no idea what to say.

"We'll get someone to look after the farm. I'll come with you."

He turned his face round to look at me.

"I need you so much! Don't ever leave me, will you."

"We need one another! But now your family needs you too."

"Will you really come with me?"

"Yes."

"Who would come and milk the cows?"

"One of my father's old farm hands still lives nearby. He knows how to use the machine. He might welcome some extra cash to supplement his pension."

"I'll pay! I promise."

"Ok. You're on! I'll phone him and ask today. Well, he can

only say no."

Simon sat up and seemed to recover himself.

"Curious thing, Harry said something on the phone about surveyors from the Department of Transport in trouble with His Lordship's gamekeeper for trespass. They wanted to route the new extension of the London to Leeds motorway down the valley right through the estate. He says this whole issue has been going on for months. Well, I've heard nothing about it. Now, a letter from the Department of Transport's solicitor has upset my father so much, it has caused his heart trouble. That's according to Harry."

The journey by road from Cumberland to Leeds was a slow one. Anyone familiar with the traffic jams on Britain's road network in the fifties could see the need for a system of motorways. Simon and I shared the driving along the A65 through Skipton and Ilkley, engaging our new four–wheel drive with low ratio on more than one occasion. Lorries stranded in the snow on one hill made it necessary for us to detour through a hedge and across farmland. We arrived at the Palace in the middle of another blizzard. I had mixed feelings about going to Simon's home territory after everything we'd talked about. So I was quite unprepared for the beauty of the scene which greeted us as he drove the Land Rover through the arched gatehouse. The snow presented a picture post card scene. On both sides of the valley, woodland and plantations stretched as far as the eye could see. In the centre, sheltered from the wind from the moors, stood the Palace, which Simon explained had been built in the baroque tradition some two hundred years before. Behind it, the so–called west wing was all that now remained of the original, much older, building dating back to the days Madame Claire Voyante had seen in her crystal. At this distance it looked splendid.

The day staff were shovelling snow away from the front steps when we crunched to a halt by a grand staircase. Harry came out to greet us, as friendly as ever. I banged the snow off my boots under the portico over the front door.

"Perhaps we should have gone round the back," Simon said to His Lordship's butler, who held the inner door open for us.

"But it hasn't been cleared of snow yet, My Lord."

I could see the grimace on Simon's face.

"I do wish he wouldn't call me that," he whispered aside to me. "Now do you understand?"

I nodded but said nothing.

"Tea, My Lord? It won't take me a moment to ring the kitchen. I expect the journey has been difficult over the hills."

"How is my father? I mean His Lordship?"

"As well as can be expected, My Lord. He's looking forward to your visit this afternoon. He has lots to discuss with you. Will you stay in your old apartment, Sir?"

"Yes, thank you. But first we'll visit the tented room."

The butler took our coats and disappeared down the side staircase. Simon put his hand on my shoulder.

"Now for Mama!" he muttered. "Prepare yourself!"

We made our way along a maze of freezing corridors to locate what Simon laughingly called her boudoir.

"At least she'll have a fire in here. There's no money to heat the rest of the house."

Mama's boudoir turned out to be a silk tent erected inside another room overlooking the courtyard. In one corner was a grate with a coal fire which spat sparks from time to time. His mother seemed alarmed in case all the silk fabric should catch fire around her. She sat beside a bowl of water with a jug at the ready to damp down any more sparks, which had already singed the hearthrug.

"Miss Havisham will go up in flames one day I swear it," he whispered.

I must have given Simon a doubtful glance

"Don't you remember Charles Dickens' story? Well, never mind."

The room was stuffy and smelled of smoke.

"Why can't they get me some decent coal?" she complained to Simon as he introduced me. She nodded but did not shake my hand. "The Coal Board have shut the local mine. Can you believe that? There's perfectly good coal left down there, so they say. Uneconomical, you see... And good local men are now unemployed."

I looked around the room. It was cluttered with family snapshots in frames on gilt tables, one of which had lost a leg and was propped up on a pile of 'Reader's Digests'. On another table was the last copy of 'Picture Post' Magazine, which had recently closed down. Simon chatted quietly with his mother until there was a knock on the door. The butler appeared with tea on a tray.

"My own maid had to go," Her Ladyship muttered to Simon.

"She said she could earn a lot more money working in a textile factory. Well!..."

Words failed her. Simon turned to me and smiled. Then his mother carried on.

"...I am so glad you've come home," she said to him, ignoring me completely. "Your father will need to be brought back from the hospital tomorrow. Could you manage that? Only the Rover saloon has got a flat tyre. Anyway, it's snowed in and we had to let the chauffeur go. We just couldn't afford to keep him on. You heard about the west wing. The tapestries are ruined. We couldn't salvage those. The roof came down under the weight of all this snow, do you see?"

"Yes, I heard, Mama. Harry phoned to tell us all about it."

She turned to look at me over her glasses.

"So," she said. "Us is it now? I do wish I knew who you really are."

Simon looked at me in despair. Her Ladyship turned to her son again.

"Don't you see the pickle we get into when you are away? Why can't you come back here where you belong?... Quick, get that spark!"

The fire had spat a smouldering lump on to the hearthrug. She hurled water at it out of the jug but missed. Simon picked it up with the fire tongs and put it safely on the bricks in front of the grate.

"Shall I pour the tea now, Mama?"

She nodded.

"Silly man has put it out of my reach. If only my maid was still here! Really, Simon, the trouble we have with staff these days... They all expect too much, you see. Your father says the socialists have a lot to answer for. I think Lloyd George gave the working classes too many privileges. Now they think they own this country. Girls just don't want to be servants any more."

Eventually we left her, still cursing the poor quality of nutty slack from the National Coal Board.

"She'll burn the place down, I swear it," Simon muttered. "Come, I'll show you the rooms where I grew up."

We climbed cold stone staircases, and walked along more corridors past ancient stone statues to the front of the building, where Simon's suite of rooms stood above the grand entrance. There was a magnificent low curved window overlooking the parkland outside. A table and two easy chairs were arranged in front of the view, where Simon and I sat down. The room was cold except for a small two–bar electric fire, which he moved as close as the lead would allow.

"Well, what do you think?" he asked. "My mother is such a snob...'The trouble we have with staff these days!' ... Do you see now why I wanted to live with you?"

"You weren't happy here, were you?!"

Someone had brought up our bags from the Land Rover and Simon rummaged in one to locate one of the bottles of beer I had given him for Christmas. He opened it and poured it out.

"We ought to go and look at the damage to the west wing. Can you help me shift some of the tapestries? When the snow melts, the water will ruin them. They've been in my family for generations."

So we picked our way carefully through the snow and some rubble into the ground floor of the oldest part of the building. It was clear that the weight of snow could bring down large sections of the roof over our heads at any time. It wasn't safe to go upstairs where the tapestries still hung from the wooden rails exposed to the elements. There was not much we could do. We did find the fuse board for the ancient electric wiring, where Simon removed all of the connections to protect the rest of the circuit. We retrieved an ormolu clock from its shattered glass dome but apart from that there was little we could do. Then we stumbled on the old inglenook fireplace. I nudged Simon.

"Look!... Just what Madame Claire Voyante saw in her crystal."

We stared at it in disbelief.

"Let's have a look under the hearthstone...You're right!"

I looked around for a lever to lift it.

"If we only had the Fergie tractor, we could lift it with the hydraulics."

So we found a torch and went rummaging down in the cellar where a few old wine bottles still lay on racks. Eventually we found an iron bar, which had once supported a shelf. Gradually we managed to shift the hearthstone. Once again we were doing something together as a partnership. Eventually, by using bricks and stones from the rubble to prop it up, we toppled the stone backwards out of the way.

"Look!" Simon muttered, trying to scoop the stones out of the way. He leant down into a cavity and lifted out the remains of a lead–lined box. He glanced up at me.

"Well?"

"Look!... It's empty! ...After all that ...nothing!"

He used a stick to scrape dust around the interior of the box.

"Don't tell me, Simon... Someone else got here first!"

"You see! You really are the only treasure I've got now."

But when we tried to replace the hearthstone we found a large old iron key. Had it been buried in the box? Or had it just fallen down the side of the hearth? What was this key for? Was that what Madame Claire Voyante had seen in her crystal? Was this key buried by Simon's ancestor to stop Oliver Cromwell's troops stealing some vast treasure? If so, where was it?

Simon and Harry took me on a tour of his ancestral estate. The Home Farm and the two other farms sat along the valley, stretching as far as the eye could see. We took the old track slowly, bumping over potholes and tree roots, where we could see them under the snow. The farm buildings had not been modernised and were mostly eighteenth century brick structures propped up here and there with timber to stop them collapsing into the lane. There was a collection of wooden huts, which Simon explained housed German prisoners of war years ago. These had been totally abandoned. I could not see how any farms could be profitable here. In one field was an abandoned horse plough, rusted and useless. It seemed to sum up the whole scene of neglect and decay but looked decorative in its shroud of snow. Finally we left the Land Rover and walked up a path through shallower snow to survey the scene.

"The motorway would be there," Harry said pointing down the valley, while we looked. "A surveyor told me there would be a cutting through the hill behind, so as to level the gradient; a flyover above the river; the Palace would be demolished for a service area; and the road would extend down there, back to Leeds, Nottingham, Leicester and finally to London. The M1 extension is what they intend to call this. His Lordship will have none of it, of course. But look! I ask you, is that worth restoring?..."

He pointed at the tumbledown barn with no roof which came into sight as we walked. On the top of one wall was a weather vane pointing north. It was decorated with the family coat of arms: two griffins rampant and a Latin motto I couldn't read. It seemed to defy the elements to do their worst.

"...My father sees himself as a valiant knight warding off the threat of progress. But he has a car. He knows how long it takes to drive to London by the old A–roads. The surveyor said, with the new M1 motorway, we could be there for lunch."

Simon turned to me.

"But His Lordship would ask: who wants to go to London for lunch, anyway? What? Anyway, he doesn't like the food at the House of Lords."

We laughed and I followed Simon and his brother back to the Land Rover.

Chapter 6

2001

I got out for a moment to take a closer look at this very same Land Rover. It was over forty years old now. If I remembered correctly, it had already had two replacement engines and at least one new gearbox over the years and probably as many replacement tyres as I'd had hot dinners. It was a bit like Trigger's broom in 'Only Fools and Horses', which was being repeated so often on television – the broom Trigger was so proud of but had been refitted with so many new brushes and handles. This wasn't the first time our Land Rover had let us down, like the time the roof blew off. But, as we always said, it was British and still going – well, most of the time. Perhaps we would buy a new one some time but money was in short supply these days. Hill farming just wasn't profitable any more. Now, in 2001, the foot–and–mouth epidemic was threatening everyone. We might be next. But I didn't want to think about that!

So I took another look around the car park. If Simon's family treasure actually ever existed, it was now buried under thousands of tons of asphalt and concrete beside the M1 motorway. Just supposing for one moment that we had found the treasure, could we have restored Simon's family fortune? But would he have still wanted me after becoming a multimillionaire? I sighed at the thought of all that. We would never know the truth after all this time.

I turned round to see Dominic returning and waving a new fan belt in the air. He lifted the bonnet and peered down into the engine. I went to see what he was doing.

"The garage mechanic found this," he said, holding up the

new one. "It's not really for a Land Rover but he said it might do for a while."

I looked at the engine, so rusty now, but it had done sterling work for a hundred thousand miles. I still remembered how it looked in 1958, freshly painted and still running in. It had been my Christmas present.

"Damn," Dominic muttered. "This one won't do. It is too small. I'll phone the AA."

He shut the bonnet again and walked back to the garage, leaving me to remember Simon's stately home as it was in the old days before the motorway arrived to cover it in concrete forever.

New Year 1959

The oldest part of the Palace was already collapsing under the weight of all the snow. So that evening we dined in a small Victorian parlour in the more modern section of the house. The table was clearly designed for intimate supper parties of no more than eight people. Simon promised to show me the grand dining hall another time. Apparently that could easily seat ninety people at one table but there was no heating and everything would be covered in dust cloths. We were now being directed where to sit as if it was a state occasion.

"I don't know how long I can take this!" Simon muttered.

"Will you carve?" Her Ladyship demanded, waving a hand at her eldest son. She sat down and unfolded a cheap paper napkin with the same elegance she would reserve for hand–pressed white linen.

"We only have day staff now," Harry added, aside to me. "Strictly do–it–yourself, tonight, I'm afraid. Austerity is here to stay if my elder brother will not marry into money. We need lots of US Dollars to get the old place out of hock, you see. Mama wants a transatlantic deal. She should have been a politician, don't you think?"

He winked at me and I was starting to enjoy his company. Her Ladyship graced one end of the table as if it was a state occasion and she insisted Simon should sit in the place of His Lordship at the other. Harry and I sat opposite one another. In view of the fact that none of us had dinner jackets, it was a fairly informal affair. Only Her Ladyship wore an evening dress with a tiara. We were eating late in order to see in the New Year at midnight and this tradition was as old as the house, apparently. But the soup was cold. The bread rolls were stale. The cold roast venison, which Simon attempted to carve with a blunt knife, turned out to be tough. It was quite inedible and as for the sherry trifle – well, the less said about that the better. The cream on top was decidedly 'off '. I whispered to Harry that Simon and I might take him to the local fish and chip shop tomorrow. Finally, after the final clang from the grandfather clock outside in the hall, we all joined hands to wish each other a Happy New Year. Suddenly it was 1959 but this had not been a joyous occasion. Now I knew the English landed gentry really were in decline.

As soon as we could, Simon and I made our excuses and retired to his rooms at the front. But I had not been prepared for Simon's four–poster bed. He laughed when he reminded me that it was called the Queen's Bed because Queen Victoria once slept in it on her way to Scotland when there was trouble on the railway line. Later on, apparently, she had her very own royal sleeping car, which the public could see in a museum. Unfortunately, after so many years, this bed now sagged in the middle but Simon said he'd just got used to it. So we sat for a while either side of the window in the easy chairs where the curtains now hung down to the floor to keep out the freezing cold. I smiled at him when he prodded the coal fire to bring some warmth into the room.

"Mama is right about this nutty slack. It hardly burns at all."

"Tell me more about the affair with your Scottish gamekeeper," I suggested.

"Oh, Hamish... the one who taught me to dance? Well! I was about 17 and home from school for the long vacation... it would be the summer of 1950. I went bathing in the lake over there in the nude. I noticed him watching me, climbed out and seduced him in the boat house."

"Disgusting!" I loved to tease him like this. "Such goings–on! What did Lady Chatterley have to say about that, then? Did she ever find out?"

"No, it was wonderful. He was like you – but not such an amazing fuck."

"So what happened to him?"

"Don't you remember? It was just as the fortune–teller saw

in her crystal. He got called up for National Service and ended up fighting the Communists in Korea. Hamish got killed in the second Inchon landings. What a dreadful farce that was!"

"I remember what Madame Claire Voyante said. ...Did you love him?"

"Yes for a while... But let's not talk about that. I've got you now – and you're twice the man he was. I brought him up here once when Ma and Pa were away and he fucked me while I was bending over the Queen's Bed... I was still wearing his kilt... It was wonderful."

"What would Queen Victoria have said about that?"

Simon and I were both starting to unwind after a difficult day and we laughed.

"We are not amused! Something like that?"

"I don't know... Let's do it again for old time's sake."

"What, now?"

"Yes," Simon sighed. "God, it's cold!... A really good fucking might warm me up! Now show me the lengths you will go to in order to give me a good time. Hamish was a bit challenged in that department. No contest!"

Somehow our lovemaking continued into the early morning. Simon had assumed that we were alone at the front of the house. Unfortunately, the canopy rail over the top of his old four–poster bed was banging against the wall but we were too involved to notice. He was now energetically bouncing up and down on top of me and we were both about to climax.

"Huh!… Oh yes!… That's it… Harder… F u c k!"

It must have been about three o'clock in the morning when we were interrupted by a loud knocking on the door.

"Simon!" shouted Her Ladyship, outside, waggling the door handle, fit to bust it. "Now open this door at once! I need to talk to you."

We froze.

"What on earth does she want?" Simon muttered and then called out: "It is so late, Mama. Can't it wait until tomorrow?"

"No, it most certainly will not! Now open this door at once!… At once! Do you hear me?"

He scrambled off me, pointed at the adjacent sitting room where we'd been earlier and put on his dressing gown. In this grand, period décor I felt like 'the lover discovered' on the stage of the restoration comedy they'd tried to do at our church hall.

"I'm sorry about this..." he whispered to me. "Go in there, will you, and lie down on the couch. Take this eiderdown. Pretend you are asleep in there."

I scurried out and shut the adjoining door behind me.

"Mama!" I heard Simon exclaim as he unlocked his door on to the landing. "What on earth is the matter with you now?"

I heard her push her way in. His door was closed again. I listened to the raised voices as she paraded around the room.

"I was awoken by an energetic banging on the wall by my bed," she complained bitterly. "What were you up to in here?"

"What banging, Mama?"

"Knocking and groaning so loud I couldn't sleep..."

"But, Mama, your bedroom used to be down the other corridor in the west wing – the one next to the tented room."

"I had to move out. It was the rain through the ceiling. The leaded roof leaks, you know, but your father has no money left to repair it."

Without Simon, I was getting so cold that I tried to plug in the two–bar electric fire by the easy chairs where we had been sitting earlier. I wrapped the eiderdown around myself as best I could because I was naked. Now there was stony silence outside. I knew he would be trying to think of an excuse for all our noise.

"Do you often hear this banging sound in your head, Mama? Perhaps you've got high blood pressure again. Have you talked to the doctor about this? Perhaps you should make an appointment."

I managed to hide a giggle. Mama clearly decided to ignore this insult and she dropped the subject. Her voice changed to a more motherly tone.

"Now, Simon, have you looked at those portraits of my friend's daughter in the United States? I think she's prettier than the one you saw before. You were quite right. She was rather plain. But I think Peggy–Sue would suit you very well. What do you think? They own the biggest department store in New York, you know, and they've just launched their own new look fashion range. It was featured in 'Vogue' last month. So I don't think money is a problem, if that is what you were worrying about."

I moved closer to the adjoining door. I had to hear as much as I could of this intriguing conversation. I heard Simon clear his throat. But then he suddenly opened the door where I was standing and almost banged my nose.

"Mama!" he said. "It is time you knew the truth. You won't like it, I know. But I can't help that."

Simon put his head around the door and beckoned to me.

"Come in here and talk to her, will you, please?"

He led me through the doorway by one hand while I was desperately attempting to hold the eiderdown up with the other.

"Oh, it's you," she exclaimed at me. "I thought you were sleeping in the guest wing."

"No, Mama, here is your son–in–law."

She took a step backwards in her old embroidered nightgown. What she made of me now I was half naked I did not know.

"What on earth do you mean by that, Simon? I have two sons. How could I ever find myself with a son–in–law?"

"You've got to know the truth, Mama. I can't stand this any longer. I love this man here with all my heart. Yes…Mama… I do mean!…"

She sat down on the side of the bed and stared at me, clearly lost for words.

"…I have loved this wonderful man for over a year, Mama. You must start to listen to me… I know you mean well by trying to find a wealthy daughter–in–law but I cannot and will not marry for the sake of US Dollars."

"I just can't believe this… This man must have corrupted you."

"No Mama! You are not listening to me. I am homosexual. I have always been a homosexual. I will never get married. I could never love a woman! I could only make Peggy–Sue unhappy. You've got to know the truth…"

She turned away from him but he grabbed her and turned her to face him again.

"…Listen to me, for once in your life. The noise you heard was the sound of me making love with this wonderful man here. I really love him… I cannot get enough of his cock…"

She sat still on the side of the bed, just staring at us. It seemed to me that Simon had been rehearsing his speech for such a momentous occasion as any he could have made in the House of Lords one day.

" …I'm sorry to disappoint you, Mama. I am not the son and heir you longed for… I like getting fucked. Yes, I am everything my father, His Lordship, loathes and detests. I am the personification of everything evil which he raves against from the pulpit. But I will never change, Mama. You just had to know the truth…"

Simon reached out to take both my hands and the eiderdown now slipped down and fell off on to the floor. Her Ladyship stared with her mouth open. I was completely naked and stooped down to try to retrieve it.

"No, you don't," he said aside to me. "You wanted Elspeth to see me. Now I want my mother to see just what I've got…"

So I stood up naked again. Simon turned round to face his mother and continued:

"…This wonderful man here has saved me from a life worse than death. You should say thank you to him. Without this man, I'd be lost in Hell on earth because a conventional marriage would become the death of me. Now if you have any love left for me at all, Mama, please, please will you go back to bed!"

"But Simon," she protested. "It might be a phase you'll grow out of soon…an infatuation which you'll learn to regret one day."

"No Mama! You've read the Wolfenden Report. I happen to know my father brought it home for you to look at. You already know about men like me and your older brother years ago – the one we don't mention. Did all his sessions with Sigmund Freud solve the problems with his love life years ago?…"

His mother made no reply but stared at her son and then at me again.

"…Now Wolfenden has confirmed that we don't just grow out of it. No, but some of us do find the man of our dreams. Here he is, Mama, and he really loves me. This wonderful man also allows me to love him… Now have you any idea of the odds against such a miracle in England today? But England should be proud of such a beautiful man. I know I am and you should be too."

Instead of feeling embarrassed at my nudity, I stood proudly and stared at Simon. He had never called me beautiful before. But his mother got up from the bed and turned towards the door.

"It is late," she said. "We will speak of this again some other time. I'm exhausted. If the two of you must fuck one another, please be so kind as to be a little more considerate for others. Don't make so much noise. I am trying to sleep on the other side of that wall… It is only a phase, my son. You will grow out of it soon enough."

She walked slowly towards the door but turned back for one second to look me up and down. For a moment, it seemed to me that she could be inspecting a handsome new footman or hired hand for the Home Farm. But perhaps she was just about to award First Prize to the pedigree pig at the next local agricultural show. She raised a condescending eyebrow and waved her hand in the air.

"...Well, my son, if you really are what Mr Wolfenden describes in his notorious report, I suppose I should feel sorry for you..."

She took another longer look at me from head to toe.

"...But, on second thoughts, I suppose you could do worse."

Simon went to hold the door open for her. Icy wind whistled in from the corridor outside.

"Good night to you, Mama!"

She cast one final glance at me and raised an eyebrow yet again.

"Well," she added. "If you really are my ersatz son–in–law, please will you be so good as to fetch Simon's father from hospital tomorrow in your new Land Rover. And don't be late for breakfast, either of you. Get some sleep now, Simon. I must trust you not to tell your father anything about this. A third heart attack might kill His Lordship..."

She even tried to smile at me and once again waved a hand in the air.

"...It will just have to remain our secret... Perhaps I will have to find a nice American, Roman Catholic girl for Harry. So, what do you think?... Anyway, ...Happy New Year for 1959! ...Now if you'll both excuse me..."

With that she left us, went out of the door with her head held high and my boyfriend quietly closed it behind her to stop the dreadful draught.

"That is what I call an exit!" Simon whispered. "Mama always was good at those!... Now, I'm so cold. Please come back to bed to warm me up... "

He put an arm around my shoulder.

"...And you must be freezing... Oh God, I hate this place! This old house is bloody cold! That's yet another reason why I want to live with you. But maybe I really fell in love with that lovely coal–fired Aga downstairs in your farmhouse kitchen back in '57."

"You said I was beautiful... You've never said anything like that before."

Simon dragged me across the room to stand in front of his full–length mirror.

"Look! What do you see?"

"A farmer," I sighed."...On the wrong side of thirty."

"No, you see yourself negatively, as Elspeth saw you... before she walked out."

"So what do you see then?"

"My dream come true! The gorgeous man I want to spend my life with and the best fucker in England."

I lifted his dressing gown and smacked Simon gently on the bottom.

"Oh, you cheeky boy!"

•••••••

His Lordship seemed genuinely pleased to see us when we walked into the hospital to collect him the following morning. He was sitting in his chair with his suitcase ready packed and his medication in a bag, waiting to go. Simon shook his hand stiffly.

"We brought the Land Rover, My Lord," I said. "The snow is melting but the lanes are still icy."

"Your saloon has got a flat tyre," Simon added.

"Four–wheel drive for extra British grip – what?"

I handed the old man his walking stick.

"Yes, My Lord. I hope you'll be comfortable. Simon will drive and I'll sit in the back."

"A petrol engined Land Rover, you say, what? Good, solid British engineering, like Army lorries during the war! I hope it is built to last!"

"It is brand new, My Lord."

His Lordship turned to me and smiled. I felt flattered.

"And the hydroelectric scheme... is that still working?"

"Yes, My Lord. Your son did an excellent job."

"Well, I do wish he'd come back here! ...High time... what?"

I exchanged a glance with Simon as I pulled down the step under the door to make it easier for His Lordship to climb in. He sat in the passenger seat beside his son, admiring the way Simon handled everything so confidently while I crouched on a fold–up seat in the back.

What was now left of the staff had turned out to greet His Lordship on the front steps of the Palace. I had no idea who all these people were as we helped the old man through the front entrance. Her Ladyship greeted him in the elegant entrance hall, where portraits of Simon's ancestors were arranged up the staircase. But I also noted the signs of peeling paint and damp patches on the ceiling as far as the eye could see.

"A new Land Rover, my dear," he repeated. "You should see how it handles all this snow... Time we had one for the estate."

"To be paid for how, exactly?" she asked sarcastically.

"Well Simon should marry some rich heiress. High time..."

His Lordship embraced his wife coldly and turned to look despairingly at his eldest son.

"Can't work out what's wrong with that boy! He can handle a Land Rover but not a woman. I don't understand, really, I don't! ... Is his wedding tackle actually working?"

Simon made our excuses and we went back upstairs to find another coal fire had been lit in the fireplace of Simon's sitting room. But he seemed too upset to notice.

"Now do you see?" he insisted, angrily, as we sat down by his window again. Outside, a stable hand was getting into the Land Rover to drive it round the back.

"Why don't you tell him the truth?"

"He'd murder me with his shotgun."

"Well, you'll just have to use some tact and diplomacy."

"So what do I say? ... Daddy I'm a poof! My Lord, I like to take it up the bum! ...I am everything that you and your sanctimonious church really hate..."

We sat quietly while Simon calmed down. Eventually he got up to put more coal on the fire and then sat down again, reaching out to take my hand.

"...Or do I say, 'My Lord, I want your blessing on my union with this wonderful man here... He has made me the happiest 24–year–old in England'? You have, you know…"

Simon leaned over to take my other hand as well and kissed it.

"…Should I say – 'Father, please can we borrow the private chapel to bless our union?' ...By the way, you must see it before we go. It is baroque and quite lovely – shame about the rain getting in... Fuck me again, please. Help me to forget everything. Only you can do that."

Simon got up, locked the door out onto the landing and started to strip off all his clothes. I followed him into the bedroom to find him bending over the Queen's Bed, looking back at me with his come–to–bed eyes. This time we completely exhausted one another and soon lay, naked, side by side, just staring up at the faded canopy decorated with the cross of Saint George and two emblazoned griffins rampant, lit by the two–bar electric fire perched beside us on a chair.

"What more can we do here?" he asked, placing one hand on mine. "I think we should go back to Cumberland soon. Take me away from all this. We don't belong here, do we? Besides, this dreadful old bed is giving me backache... You must be prepared to stop me striking my father if he makes comments like that again."

"You should talk to him," I insisted. "Tell him the truth..."

"I wouldn't dare! He's already had one heart attack too many."

The following morning His Lordship insisted on coming downstairs to preside over the breakfast where we sat in the sunlit morning room. The grand dining hall was still out of bounds because it was in the crumbling west wing. Outside the bay window there was another picture post card scene. Nobody seemed to look. Everyone had other things on their minds. Only Harry was missing. He had left very early to join the first classes at the Catholic seminary. Simon had warned me this topic was not to be raised over breakfast. His father seemed to be his old self again although he stared suspiciously at the letter from the Department of Transport, which his butler brought to him on a silver tray.

"You open it, my dear," he said, passing it down the table to Her Ladyship. "My reading glasses are upstairs."

While the butler poured out the Earl Grey, his wife slit open the envelope with a butter knife. She adjusted her spectacles.

"A compulsory purchase order, my dear. It is a compulsory purchase order for this house, the three farms along the valley... that's pretty much the whole estate... Signed, on behalf of the Minister, I can't read the signature... anyway he's in the Department of Transport. So this new road, the M1 extension, is being built through here after all..."

She looked more closely at the last paragraph.

"...You have one month to appeal."

The old man turned to Simon.

"Get my lawyer! Phone him now!"

"But, father, be reasonable! You can't hold out forever!..."

The old man stared at his son, saying nothing.

"...Listen, father, it is better for everyone if you sell out now before any more of the house falls down. You can't hold back the tide of progress like King Canute on the beach by sitting in the sea. Take the money and go to live abroad where the weather is warmer. You liked Venice. You and Mama could move out there. How about the South of France, perhaps?"

The old man was going red in the face.

"Never! Do you hear me? Never!"

"But be reasonable, My Lord! Are you going to sit down in front of the bulldozers? How are you going to stop this M1 motorway being built, now? Be practical for once! ... Well, King Canute thought he could hold back the tide of the ocean. Can you really prevent the march of progress like this?"

"I'll give a speech in the House of Lords. They'll listen to me!"

"But you're not well enough to go to London, father. The doctor told you to rest."

"Then you must go, my boy... Time to show them what you're made of... Your maiden speech. I'll tell them you are coming to speak for me. This pipsqueak Minister of Transport has got to be taught a lesson. The Tower is too good for him... What?"

"No, father, I will not. It would be quite ridiculous."

"Get out!"

I gestured to Simon that it was time to leave and I started to get up from the table. But Simon seemed determined to argue his case and leaned towards the old man.

"My Lord ...listen to me. You must instruct your lawyer to accept this compulsory purchase order before you waste any money on legal fees to fight it. The Department of Transport has public money to fight their case for the M1 motorway to London. You, however, do not. You just cannot win."

"Never! Do you hear me?... Never!"

Simon finally got up, folded his napkin and laid it neatly on the table while his father glared at him.

"Father, we must go. Sorry, Mama, I give up... I'll be in touch.

Give Harry our love."

I just looked away and followed Simon upstairs to fetch our things. We had to walk round the back to the stables to find the Land Rover and get the stable hand to open the doors.

"You drive," Simon said. "I'm just not in the mood!"

••••••••

"Perhaps you were right," I said. "I don't think it was a good idea for you to come back here."

But Simon made no comment. We drove sedately back along the road we came on. I let Simon take his time to calm down.

"If I ever say I'm going back there again, you must remind me how it was this time. I think if you hadn't been around, I would have drowned myself in the boating lake. Do you want me to take the wheel now? It is not easy driving up here on the hills..."

I pulled into a lay–by and we swapped places.

"...I can see His Lordship ending up in debt to fight this legal case. I'm so glad my grandfather put my legacy in trust where my father couldn't squander it. Did you see how he thought the family problems would be solved? ...By me marrying a debutante with a big dowry, preferably US Dollars. That's the currency my mother has so much faith in. Now do you understand? "

"Forget it!" I insisted, pointing at the signpost. "We're nearly there now. Try to be happy again. When we get in, I'm taking you straight upstairs for a fucking you'll never forget!"

"Do you like your Christmas present, then?..."

I looked at Simon blankly. Recent events had put Christmas out of my mind.

"...The Land Rover...!" he said, engaging four–wheel drive at the bottom of our lane.

I looked outside at the drifts of snow which had fallen since we left and then turned to him again.

"Just like you. I could no more go back to the old one any more than I could live with Elspeth again."

"That sounds like a compliment."

"Look," I said, as we pulled up outside the back door. "I want to get you something for your birthday. You must tell me what you want."

"But you know what I want... and you can't buy that at the

shops."

"Except at shady places in Soho, perhaps!"

He laughed and clutched my thigh.

"Why go all the way to Soho, when I've got the real thing right here?"

Simon took my hand, unlocked the door and led me inside. I grabbed hold of him and kissed him. He started to undo the buckle of my belt but I protested it was far too cold for sex. The fire in our Aga stove had long since gone out.

2001

I suddenly sat up in the Land Rover in amazement. A naked man had just streaked past the window. I was certain of it. He ran past the line of cars in the motorway service area wearing yellow leather boots and nothing else!

So I stared through the windscreen. But perhaps I'd imagined it. I'd become a dirty old man. Maybe, in my dotage, I was seeing naked young men. I would have to see a psychiatrist. I looked up and down the line of cars but he'd disappeared – that's if he'd been there at all. I'd seen streakers on television of course, either disrupting cricket or football matches. Now a security guard strolled by and disappeared around a parked van. So I waited, imagining myself explaining this vision to some grey haired psychiatrist while I lay on a couch. But, just as I was about to despair, suddenly the streaker reappeared from the opposite direction. Yes, there he was again! I had not imagined him. He was slim and very fast, followed by an overweight security guard in hot pursuit. This was fun – more exciting than the TV – but all too fast. I wanted a slow motion replay, only it didn't happen because this was real life when things all happen at the same time, or not at all. So I sat quietly while my fevered mind calmed down and I drifted back to memories of the old days of 1959.

January 1959

So we had to relight the Aga with coal from the shed in the yard outside.

"I do know what I'd like for my birthday," Simon said, shovelling cold clinker out of the ash tray. "A shower! Well, if the council won't give you planning permission for a bathroom, it is the next best thing. Look, if you buy it, I'll fit it... in that empty cupboard upstairs perhaps, where your wife used to have her dressing table. We'll take hot water from the stove to a heat exchanger on the landing. I'm good at plumbing and you don't need planning permission for an en suite shower."

"Is there anything you're not good at?"

"Yes, I'm no good at getting my way in an argument with His Lordship, my father... nor am I any good at producing grandchildren to continue the family tree. I told you ages ago. I never learned to handle women because I knew I could never love any of them."

"Forget it!"

Simon reassembled the fire basket of the Aga and came to sit at the table with me. He looked at me with his come–to–bed eyes.

"So what can we do about my parents now?"

"Why don't you talk to their lawyer on the phone? Tell him your father must sell out to the Department of Transport. Get the lawyer on your side! Surely any intelligent person can see it makes sense."

"Actually, that's a damned good idea. And if my father finds out, all he can do is to shout at me down the phone. I don't need to eat humble pie over breakfast in the morning. Look, I've got something special for you..."

Simon rummaged in the case we'd taken out of the Land Rover. He passed me a small box. Inside was a signet ring.

"...It was my grandfather's. He intended that I should have it to pass on to my nearest and dearest. So I'm giving it to you. It's gold!"

I slid it on my finger. It was rather too large.

"I'm afraid I might lose this in the field or in the fodder for the cows. Can I wear it on special occasions?"

"Yes, but not when my father's around. He still thinks it should have been left to him."

"What about Harry?"

"Oh it won't bother him."

So we made another appointment by phone to see Madame Claire Voyante. Once again I congratulated her over the accuracy of all her predictions. But we arrived in the middle of a thunderstorm.

"The ether is in turmoil," Madame complained, bitterly. "All this thunder and lightning upsets my crystal. I really can't work until the storm has gone away. But it is nice to see you two again. I knew you'd both come back."

"What if we wait a while?" Simon suggested. "If it blows over, your crystal might start working. Meanwhile, can I invite you out for afternoon tea in the town?"

Madame's eyes lit up. Perhaps it was a long time since a handsome young man had invited her out for afternoon tea.

"Two ticks," she said excitedly. "I'll fetch my hat."

The tea room was crowded. I suggested people might be taking shelter from the storm. We had to queue for a table. Meanwhile, a pianist was tinkling Cole Porter tunes on a piano. As we waited, I commented to Madame just how popular American music had become today.

"It must be American money," she said. "Big loans to get Britain out of the red and twelve million dollars from the Marshall Plan to rebuild Europe after the war. But, I ask you, how many decades will it take for Britain to repay all this money to the USA – twenty, thirty years or more? In the meantime, is Britain to become America's largest offshore aircraft carrier? Mark my words, my friend, England may not be independent much longer. Will we just become the fiftieth state of the USA, I wonder, like Alaska has just become number forty–nine on the 3rd January? But perhaps Hawaii will beat us to it…"

I was amazed by her insight into the state of world politics. We listened as the pianist played on. She turned to me again.

"…Unfortunately, with the money comes American culture and the music. He'll be playing Rogers and Hammerstein next. Just you wait."

She was right, too. Next, the pianist played the overture for 'South Pacific'. But perhaps she'd been here before and was familiar with the daily repertoire. Eventually, the waiter cleared a table for us by the window, apologised for the delay and brought cakes on a stand. Simon produced the rusty iron key which we'd found under the hearthstone and laid it on the table in front of her.

"I found the lead–lined box exactly where you predicted, Madame... See – we took photos."

I passed her the black and white snapshots I had made with my camera. She stared at them one by one through her reading glasses.

"The light wasn't good," Simon added. "But you may just make out – the box you saw in your crystal is empty."

"I was right, wasn't I?" she muttered.

"We found this key right by it...We are hoping you might be able to tell us what it is for. If it isn't important, why would anyone bury it under the fireplace?"

"And you think I will be able to tell you?"

The waiter brought the tea things and looked at Madame while she adjusted her reading glasses.

"Shall I pour?" she asked, looking from Simon to me over the top of the thick lenses.

The waiter set the teapot in front of her and went away again. She lifted the lid to look inside and stirred the tea with the spoon.

"I'll let it stand a while."

"Do you read tea leaves, Madame…?" Simon asked, smiling.

She stared at him with a horrified expression and said nothing.

"…Sorry ...I guess you don't."

So she turned to me, now pretending to ignore such impudence.

"You think I might be able to tell you where the treasure is?... If I had a pound every time someone asked me that question over the years, I'd be a rich woman, really I would..."

She picked up the key and looked at it closely through her glasses.

"...What was this key for?"

Simon leaned forward.

"Perhaps the treasure was moved to a new location, Madame... away from Oliver Cromwell's troops – the ones who used my ancestral home as a stable for their horses."

"I deal with auras," she explained. "People have auras... but things do not...Well, none I can ever focus on. Now your aura," she added, pointing at Simon, "that was amazing. By focussing on that with my crystal, I was able to go back in history, as you know. It enabled me to watch your ancestor burying the box under the hearth…"

"What if Simon was to hold this key, Madame?" I suggested excitedly. "Would his aura enable you to tell us where the treasure is now...while you go into a trance?"

"This happened in the war, you know," she explained, now pouring out the tea into the cups. "The wife of a serviceman missing in action would come to me with a scarf or a glove worn by the husband and ask where he was now... Well! I was tempted to take their money and concoct a story to make them happy. But I always told them the truth – Sorry, I cannot tell you. Anyway, some government department was trying to stop people like me and to put us all out of business after the 'HMS Barham' tragedy... I don't think that Winston Churchill believed in all this sort of thing... But that's boring... It's history... Anyway, I'm sorry to disappoint you... Well, I could play Madame Arcarti in 'Blithe Spirit' and recite poems and spells... 'Hickory rod and birch in bud'... all that sort of silly, theatrical nonsense! ... It wouldn't do any good!... I could charge you a fortune in fees... We could go on all night like Madame Arcarti did, standing on the top of her stepladder, but neither of you would be any the wiser... Noel Coward got it all wrong, I tell you. He should have asked me how a professional medium really works..."

She took a few sips of tea.

"What was the 'HMS Barham' tragedy?" I asked, trying to keep a straight face.

Madame put down the cup and leaned towards me to whisper.

"I saw it exploding in my crystal... Hundreds of British sailors died but everything was supposed to be most secret and hush–hush, you know... 'Bad for morale during the war' and all that!... I told everyone the truth – the pride of the British Navy has just gone bang. I've just seen it in my crystal and it has never been wrong! ...Well!... You can imagine... The police arrived and carted me off in a black van like some captured Nazi agent for interrogation. ...But that's history! ...I've never liked London coppers since... I don't want to talk about it!.... Why spoil such a lovely afternoon?"

She turned to Simon once again and smiled at him.

"Take my advice and forget the family treasure. Once you found it, all that wealth might just bring you bad luck. Anyway... young man, what if it was cursed? Who knows what demons you might unleash... Why don't you accept that the treasure has gone but you have found one another. Now this relationship will bring you a much happier life than trinkets or gold. I've seen it forty or fifty years into the future. I know …"

She took another sip of tea and prodded Simon on the arm.

"...Anyway I told you when I saw you last. So many people go through life finding nobody at all... Have faith in the wealth of human love and devotion instead. That's my advice. Suppose you found all that gold. Would it keep you warm at night? Would it get you so sexually excited? …Would it love you? Would it kiss you every morning and make you happy? I don't think so. Young man – just be happy about all the joy and happiness you've found with this wonderful man, here... Look after him for me, won't you… Believe me. He's worth his weight in gold."

Under the table Simon put a hand on my knee and squeezed it. Over the second cup of tea, we started talking about the Wolfenden Report and how it intended to legalise our unconventional but happy relationship. Madame proved to be remarkably well–informed and up to date with the news. I asked her if she knew why there was so much debate about it? After all, she had seen its implementation ten years away in her crystal. Why would it take so long, until 1967, to implement Wolfenden's recommendations?

"Religion," she protested over her reading glasses. "As Karl Marx said – 'the opiate of the masses'. It keeps people quiet and stops them thinking too much and asking such awkward questions. You know, I blame the doddering, old, conservative fuddy–duddies in the Church of England and the House of Lords ... But they and their kind will be less powerful by 1967... That's if they actually manage to live that long. Some of them will have simply died out..."

Simon suddenly choked on his cake.

"…Oh... have I touched a nerve?... So sorry."

I told her about His Lordship, Simon's father, and the trouble we'd had. She laughed.

"…I should have guessed, ...I'm sorry..."

Then she poured the hot water from the jug into the teapot and stirred it again. I decided to change the subject and asked if she'd foreseen any more momentous world events in her crystal recently. She put her teacup down and smiled at Simon again over the top of her glasses.

"…Well, I'll tell you both, I had a dream. I felt a bit like Nostradamus. In this dream I went down to London and banged on the door of the American Embassy. 'Hello,' I shouted.

Somewhere a window opened upstairs. 'Beware the Cuban Revolution and the rise of President Castro,' I yelled. 'Please give me two Dollars to help me pay my gas bill.'...I waited. The window opened again and someone threw down ten cents. 'Hello,' I called again. 'Beware the Bay of Pigs and Russian missiles on Cuba, yes, in Uncle Sam's back yard. Please give me three Dollars to help me pay my gas bill.' Well, I waited. The window opened again and someone threw down fifty cents. 'Hello,' I called once more. 'Those Twin Towers in Manhattan. I've seen them both tumble down like a house of cards in my crystal.' ...Please give me ten Dollars to help me pay my gas bill if I tell you more about it.' ...Well, I waited. The window opened again and someone shouted 'Go away you Mad Witch of Windermere, the World Trade Center hasn't even been built yet!'...I waited but the window closed again. Do you know what happened next in my dream?..."

I must have looked confused. I had no idea what on earth Madame was talking about, nor could I imagine what she meant by the World Trade Center. Simon just sat staring at her with his mouth open.

"...Well, I'll tell you. The doors of the US Embassy opened. Men with white coats came down to fit me with a straightjacket and they charged me seventy cents for their trouble. That's when I woke up... I have these nightmares sometimes. I feel a bit like the soothsayer in Julius Caesar – you know – 'Beware the Ides of March' and all that ...Well, did he take a blind bit of notice?..."

She looked at her watch.

"...I must be going... I've got another appointment. Some lady wants me to tell her where her cat is. She promised me five pounds. Well, you know, I've seen it – squashed in the road round the corner. Do I tell her the truth?... 'Your beloved Tiddles has gone to the heavenly cat basket in the sky' ...Tell me, what do you two think?"

Simon shrugged his shoulders and waved at the waiter to bring the bill.

Madame Claire Voyante disappeared out of our lives and I read in the local newspaper shortly after that she had died. How was the crystal ball in the sky, I wondered? Did she ever meet 'that old sinner' Oliver Cromwell in the afterlife? How about the spokeswoman from British Railways? But, without another séance, we would never know.

2001

I was awoken from my daydreams by a commotion outside in the motorway service area. Suddenly the athletic young streaker rushed by again but he paused and glanced towards the Land Rover. Now he looked very frightened and was followed by a group of rampaging yobs who were, in turn, followed by two younger and more agile security guards. But within a minute they had all disappeared from sight again. I climbed out of the door to take a look. This was too exciting to miss. From the distance came loud shouting and it seemed to me that they were coming back again. I didn't want to get involved when I was too old to run and climbed back into the safety of the Land Rover. This poor streaker now had a bloody nose, which looked painful. He was soon followed by three security guards plus even more shouting yobs than before. But they all disappeared again and my mind drifted back to 1959. How peaceful everything seemed to be in those days. While the Cold War loomed and the world teetered on the brink of nuclear obliteration, the Lake District seemed a haven of peace and tranquillity, troubled only by traffic jams of caravans on narrow lanes and the occasional sheep rustler out on the hills at night. Simon and I carried on our lives together just as before. Far away from the horrors of London, we lived as if blessed, just as the medium had predicted, and I silently wished her 'bon voyage' in the next world.

Spring 1959

We heard no more from Simon's family for several weeks. He had no telephone number for the Catholic seminary: that is if they actually had a telephone. We gathered it was on some remote island off the coast, somewhere which could only be reached at low tide. There was no news from the Palace either. Simon didn't phone them, nor did they telephone us. Life fell back into a routine of milking the cows, harvesting the hay and looking after the farm. Elspeth disappeared out of my life completely, thank goodness. I did eventually hear that she remarried, but if she was happy, I neither knew nor cared. Simon was the centre of my life. We relaxed back into the daily routine of running a dairy farm with sheep on the hills.

It was November when the telephone rang for Simon. His

brother Harry was at the station in Windermere. He seemed to be in a bit of a state but wouldn't explain over the phone so we packed up our work for the day and drove over to meet him. I spotted him sitting on a bench beside another young man. Simon left the engine of the Land Rover ticking over and went over to them. They both climbed in the back. Simon gave me a quizzical look but said nothing.

Once back at the farm I took a closer look at Harry's friend. He must have been about 17 and he was extraordinarily beautiful, in spite of the fact that his hair was cropped so short.

"This is Dominic," Harry explained. "He's a junior novice at the seminary."

Dominic smiled at us but said nothing. I left Harry whispering with his brother and went over to the Aga to make some tea. Now here was a turn–up for the books. Simon had said his brother had a girlfriend and was straight, but now I was starting to have my doubts. Right in front of his brother, Harry went over to Dominic and kissed him. Then Simon came to stand beside me.

"Harry has fallen in love," he whispered quietly aside to me. "They've just run away together but had nowhere else to go. My brother is upset. They want to stay here for a couple of days to sort things out. I told them it would be ok with you..."

I nodded.

"...They want to be able to sleep together and have sex where it is safe. Harry says that is impossible at the seminary. The abbot has put them under surveillance. It all sounds a bit drastic. Nobody knows where they are, apparently."

"But I thought you said Harry had a girlfriend..."

"Only to please His Lordship at the Palace. Now Harry says that was all a farce. He decided to enter the priesthood only to avoid all the pressure."

I couldn't help repeating Harry's own words.

"Alas poor England. Oh decline and fall!"

Simon smiled and we both turned to look at them still hugging one another.

"I don't know," I said. "How old is Dominic?"

"He's only eighteen – last month apparently."

We watched while Harry clutched Dominic closer and they kissed again.

"But do they really love one another?" I asked. "Or is it just an adolescent phase?"

"A phase? You sound just like our mother, Her Ladyship."

"Well, brotherly love, perhaps?"

I turned to take the boiling kettle off the hotplate. Simon picked up their bags and led them both up the stairs to the spare room where I heard the door close and Simon eventually returned to stand beside me.

"I've told them to get it out of their system. I don't think they've actually made love yet. Perhaps Harry will change his mind..."

"Why do you say that?"

Simon shrugged his shoulders and laughed.

"Well, we'll see. It all depends whether the actual deed lives up to all Harry's expectations... I mean the actual mechanics of the thing! ...getting the plumbing right... I gave them the Vaseline to make it easier."

Simon and I were sitting at the kitchen table listening to the noise of creaking bed springs through the ceiling. We glanced at one another and laughed.

"Young love!"

Then we smiled at one another. From the noise it was clear somebody was getting his bottom smacked.

"Do you remember our first time?"

"That wasn't so long ago!"

"But it was easy for us. We were older, less impulsive..."

Now the creaking above us was becoming more vigorous. The bed was banging against the wall. There was a sound of loud groaning and someone muttering 'Oh, oh yes!' ...and then 'Oh... I love you' ...and finally – 'Oh, yes! ...Huh! ...ff ...fuck!'.

We waited and just stared at one another, trying to hold back the giggles. Suddenly everything upstairs fell silent again. Only the occasional moo could be heard from the field outside. Simon laughed.

"Let's hope they think it was all worth it... now it's all over."

"The deed is done!"

"Dominic is a virgin no more! Deflowered but with a spanked bottom!"

"How do you know?" I giggled. "It might be the other way round! ... Think about it!"

We both laughed out loud.

"Shut up! They'll hear us!"

"Well," I whispered. "You never know!"

"My brother... lying on his back with his legs up in the air?"

I shrugged my shoulders.

"Well, you do! Perhaps youthful Dominic is the stallion!"

"I don't think so."

"Oh," I muttered between clenched teeth, "Alas poor England. Oh decline and fall!"

It was early the following morning. I got up as usual to milk the cows and discovered Harry sitting alone on the wall outside in the yard. He was staring at the first light of dawn in the distance.

"Hello!..." I said, startling him.

He looked at me sadly and I sat down beside him.

"Are you ok?"

"I don't know."

"What does that mean?... 'I don't know'.... Where's Dominic?"

"Still asleep. I've worn him out."

"Do you want to talk about it?"

Harry stared into the far distance as rooks fluttered over the trees in the churchyard.

"I've committed a mortal sin..."

"Do you really believe in all that stuff?"

"I've got to if I'm going to become a priest. But I have lain with another man. I have sampled forbidden fruit. I have defied the word of God."

"Look," I insisted. "It's only a sin if you think of it that way... Did Dominic enjoy what you did to him?"

"Oh yes. He couldn't get enough... but he's a bit sore now, that's all."

"Does Dominic think it was a sin?"

"I don't know. Perhaps he was the devil in disguise, here to tempt me, like Saint Ignatius warns us, the devil may appear in any form..."

"Perhaps you should ask Dominic," I said, thinking this might be a joke, but Harry looked at me seriously. "Dominic, a devil? Surely you don't think that about him!"

"It's too late now. The deed is done. If it was a venial sin we could get absolution."

"I don't understand," I interrupted. "You mean there are various kinds of sin?"

"Exactly. We are born into this world in a state of original sin.

Only the sacrament of penance can redeem the soul... Venial or minor sins can be made good with a Hail Mary or two but mortal sins... like we have committed... How may they be forgiven?"

"Does it really matter? Why worry about that sort of thing now?"

Harry turned to me with tears in his eyes.

"What do I say in the confessional next week?"

"You have to go to confession?"

"With the abbot. He will demand to know everything. I will have to name Dominic."

"You don't mean you are going back?"

"I must if I am to redeem my soul from eternal damnation."

"Surely you don't really believe all that stuff about fire and brimstone now?..."

Harry said nothing but stared into the far distance.

"...So what do you make of the Wolfenden Report now, then?" I asked, changing the subject. "After last night... it's proposed reforms matter to you as well."

"Oh that? It will never happen, will it? Imagine the law of England permitting buggery! How would the Church of England cope with that? Let alone, the Church of Rome!"

"Between consenting adults...over the age of 21."

"Precisely. Dominic is 18. Even with Wolfenden it would still be a crime in the eyes of the law... but it will always be a sin in the eyes of God."

"But how can you believe in such a wrathful, unforgiving God?"

"But I do. The whole concept is at the centre of Catholicism. How can I be a priest but only embrace what suits me? No, I must accept the whole gospel. I have sinned. Dominic has sinned. We must return to the seminary and humbly accept the penance declared by the abbot."

"Don't tell him... Tell him you had to get away to think – for a kind of retreat."

"What about Dominic?"

"Tell the abbot that Dominic also wanted to go and pray with you... for the good of his soul... well, something like that."

"Nobody would believe us."

"Have you talked to your brother?"

"He would only laugh. He thinks I'm mad anyway... to become a Catholic."

"Is Simon religious?"

"No, he's a pagan or at best an agnostic."

"But your brother really loves me," I insisted. "I'm a very lucky man, believe me."

"I know. He's lucky to have found you."

"But perhaps it is a good thing you have found Dominic – someone to love."

"No, I have committed his soul to eternal damnation."

"I don't understand you or your religion, I really don't. How can you embrace something as vengeful as this old-fashioned religion which can only make you unhappy?"

"What alternative is there?"

"Renounce it. Go back to the seminary. Tell the abbot you are sorry, you made a mistake. You don't want to be a priest."

"What about Dominic?"

"Persuade him to quit too. Wait until Wolfenden becomes law. By then Dominic will be over 21. You can live together..."

"In sin."

"Oh, I give up!"

I got up and left Harry, to go and attend to the cows. At least they didn't have morals to contend with. At least cattle didn't feel the need to worry about what was right or wrong. Perhaps it was just as well, considering how we abused them, taking their calves away so that we could drink their milk, and eating their kind for dinner. The cows did what came naturally, without reason or theology. These were things only mankind seemed to burden itself with, but why, if it only made him unhappy?

Simon was already in the milking parlour getting things ready. As I entered he opened the gate for the cows.

"Have you been talking to Harry?..."

I nodded.

"...Well, you've got further with him than I did. He wouldn't talk to me and I'm his brother."

"He says you are a pagan or at least an agnostic."

"Perhaps he's right but at least I'm happy!"

"He isn't," I insisted.

"I thought as much."

"He's talking about fire and brimstone... Now he says Dominic might have been a devil in disguise sent to tempt him from the straight and narrow... Who was Saint Ignatius, anyway?"

"A second century martyr who got thrown to the wild beasts

in Rome... something like that."

"Harry still believes in him."

"My brother is quite mad... Well, I ask you. Dominic is absolutely gorgeous and clearly loves him to bits... But now, I suppose, my brother will reject him because of a load of old religious doctrine. Why can't Harry just be happy?"

"He thinks too much."

Simon patted the cow in front of him as he fitted her to the milking machine.

"You don't need to think at all, do you, Mildred? Just so long as the grass is juicy and sweet. Why can't my brother be like you?"

"Perhaps you and I should talk to Dominic... I mean when Harry isn't around."

"Yes, good idea. I'll send Harry on some errand to get him out of the way...Anyway, I'll think of something."

So, we took Dominic for a walk while Harry washed the Land Rover and hoovered the interior. Simon had convinced him it might help to take his mind off things.

"Tell me, Dominic," Simon asked him later as we walked slowly. "Do you really love my brother?"

Dominic kicked a stone out of the path.

"Oh come on, young man," I insisted. "You can talk to us. We're not your father confessor. Simon and I have been having sex for ages."

Dominic kicked another stone, harder this time but still said nothing.

"Is Harry actually any good in bed?" Simon laughed..."Well he is my brother!"

Dominic didn't reply.

"You know," I said. "Harry feels guilty now... He thinks he has committed a mortal sin with you. He told me you might have been a devil to tempt him from the straight and narrow."

I wasn't prepared for Dominic bursting into tears. I put a fatherly arm around his shoulder. Simon passed him a tissue from his pocket.

"He's the only one who's been nice to me... They all hate me at the seminary..."

"Why's that then?"

"I'm too pretty... They all tease me... It never stops."

"Why don't you leave, then?"

"I'd miss Harry."

"Tell him to take you away with him."

"Would he take care of me?"

"You must ask him. We don't know."

Simon and I sat down on a fallen tree trunk with Dominic between us. Simon passed him another tissue.

"Harry loves you really."

"Does he? That's not what he said just now when he mentioned everlasting fire!"

"Of course he does," Simon sighed. "I know my brother. I've seen him look at you. He's never looked at anyone else like that before."

"This morning Harry said he doesn't want to see me any more..."

"He'll get over it. You must make him want to see you again!"

"Go back right now before he's finished the Land Rover... Grab hold of him and give him a big kiss... I mean like never before..."

"Yes, tell him you want to go straight back upstairs for a hard spanking and another good fucking. Say you want to try out a new position his brother has just told you about."

I looked despairingly at Dominic. I had no idea what Simon had in mind.

"But what if it really is a mortal sin?" Dominic sniffed.

"Well, if the two of you are going to spend eternity in Hell anyway," I added. "Why not have a bit of fun first?"

"You can only go to Hell once," Simon suggested. "Fucking you a second time won't make any difference, will it? ...Tell him that spanking you really hard might save both of you a couple of Hail Marys."

Suddenly Dominic turned on his heels and ran back to the farm. Simon and I walked on, giggling at one another.

"You've never given me a good spanking!" Simon laughed.

I turned to him with tears in my eyes. All this angst was proving too much for me.

"What's wrong now?"

"Surely... Simon... Surely you must know I could never really hit you hard, but only in fun... Never!"

"But it seems to work for my brother and Dominic..."

"They're different!"

Simon put his arm around my shoulder.

"Come on...you old softie!"

"Shut up now!" I insisted. "I'm only a few years older than you!"

"I love you more than you will ever know!"

I put my hand up to hold his arm.

"We were lucky to find each other ...not so long ago..."

"Do you remember the power cut?"

We wandered down the lane talking about that first rainy day back in '57.

....

So Harry and Dominic soon disappeared out of our lives again. They returned to the seminary with their tails between their legs. Simon's mother telephoned to say His Lordship had finally come to an agreement with the Department of Transport. They were now moving to Paris where an apartment was being refitted for them. The bulldozers would be arriving some time soon to start demolishing the outbuildings. She added that the cutting for the new M1 motorway extension was already changing the horizon at the head of the valley. Apparently His Lordship had finally taken the advice of his lawyer that the money would run out before they could defeat the Department of Transport in the High Court. Simon seemed relieved and was delighted by an invitation from Her Ladyship that the two of us might like to visit them in Paris one day.

"Does she really acknowledge me as part of your life now?" I asked.

"Apparently. By the way, they've got a new scandal to occupy their minds. She says Harry has run off with Dominic to live in Morocco."

"So she knows who Dominic is, then?"

"Apparently Harry took Dominic back with him to collect his belongings from the Palace. The oldest wing is being demolished next week so the foundations for the motorway service area can be started. She wanted Harry to empty his room."

"I think it is nice that Harry and Dominic are still together, don't you? In Morocco they could live together legally. Nobody will bother them there. They will just become part of the British expatriate community living overseas to get away from the Inland Revenue or the British police."

2001

The driver's door opened. I woke up from my snooze.

"The AA will be here soon, I hope," Dominic said, climbing in to sit in the driver's seat beside me.

"I've been thinking about the old days," I said. "Why did you and Harry leave the seminary and go off to live in Morocco? I never did hear about that."

Dominic laughed.

"You don't want me to tell you about that. It's ancient history!"

"Tell me... You returned to the seminary with Harry first. How long did that last?"

"About a month. We had to confess everything to the abbot. He was outraged. I had to scrub the latrines for a month as a penance."

"And Harry?"

"He wasn't allowed to see me at all. He had to wear a hair shirt."

"What? Even in 1959?"

"It was an ancient monastic order. He was given a lot of hard manual work on the monastery farm. The abbot thought Harry would forget about me that way."

"And did he?"

"No. He eventually threatened Harry with a public flogging... in front of all the monks... to set an example."

"So what happened next?"

"We met up in secret but the abbot found out... Harry couldn't sit down for two days after the public flogging with a birch... I had to hold him down while they were doing it. That was my penance."

"And this was in the name of Christian religion?"

"Yes, it almost became an exorcism. Between each stroke, the abbot demanded that Harry should tell me that he did not love me... Crack!... 'Tell him you were wrong!' ... 'Never'... Crack! ...over and over until I fainted on top of him."

"Harry endured all of this just for you?"

"But it just cemented our love, of course. You can still see his scars."

"How awful for you both!"

"Yes, they made Harry's buttocks bleed like Christ on the cross. I gave up religion after that. Our love proved to be more powerful than agonising pain or the Roman Catholic Church."

"Some test of true love!"

"It only made us need each other more. But the abbot eventually tried to convince Harry never to see me again on pain of excommunication and eternal damnation!"

"And did he?"

"Yes, that's why we ran away on the first tramp steamer we could find from Liverpool docks. It happened to be going to Morocco. So that is where we ended up."

"How did you make ends meet out there?"

"Harry got a job teaching English in a language school. I found work in a Catholic mission for destitute orphans."

"So why did you come back to England?"

"In 1967 the Sexual Offences Act made everything legal for adults over the age of 21 in the UK… I was by now 27. Harry was suffering from malaria, after being bitten by so many mosquitoes in Morocco... For some reason they never bit me. Anyway, he needed better medical treatment than we could get over there. So we came home again and lived in a tiny flat in Central London. I got a job working in Harrods while Harry recovered from his malaria. He wasn't really well enough to work for months. Then we moved to Paris to look after his mother, her Ladyship... Well, you remember, when she died, we found all the money had gone."

"You must have loved Harry very much."

Dominic just held up his hands, smiled but said nothing. Just then a yellow AA van drew up beside us and he got out to open the bonnet of the Land Rover again while I sat there, still thinking about the old days.

CHAPTER 7

1959

Harry brought Dominic to visit us on the farm again after they ran away from the seminary. They arrived at short notice and telephoned from Windermere Railway Station just as before. Simon drove over to collect them in the new Land Rover while I was out arguing with the bank manager after our first financial crisis. This involved the late compensation from the Ministry for the milk we'd poured down the drain after the Windscale disaster. On this occasion, the bank agreed an extended overdraft but we had not been able to settle it. This should have been a portent of things to come. When I returned to the farm I found everyone deep in conversation around the kitchen table but, fortunately, they were not talking about money.

"I'm not explaining my sex life to His Lordship," Harry insisted, turning to his brother. "Well, you didn't dare, because you were afraid of causing another heart attack..."

Simon didn't say anything.

"...Well, Mama told me she found out for herself when she walked into your bedroom on New Year's Eve and discovered you two at it......That's what she said..."

"It wasn't like that, at all," Simon interrupted. "Our bed was banging against the wall and woke her up! She banged on the door, which I'd locked incidentally. She came in to complain about the noise, that's all. Anyway, it was long past midnight. So, you see, she got that wrong."

Harry started laughing. I was glad he hadn't lost his sense of humour at the seminary. Dominic sat in silence with his mouth open. I put a hand on his shoulder and he turned to smile at me.

"I was brought out of the sitting room," I insisted, sitting down. "Simon decided it was time for us both to confront Her ladyship… I was completely naked, by the way… The eiderdown with which I was trying to cover myself fell off on the floor."

At this point Harry became hysterical and Dominic tried to get him to calm down by taking hold of his hand. Simon turned to me with a warm smile.

"If I remember, Mama looked you up and down like the prize pig at the agricultural fair," he added, pointing at me. "But, then she decided I could have done worse. I told her you were her son–in–law. She really did get an eyeful that night. But she couldn't offend you too much because there was nobody else to fetch Papa from the hospital. We got away with it…just!"

"That's not what she told me," Harry insisted, almost hysterical again. "She said your bedroom door was open and she just walked in… If I remember correctly, she said you two were at it like guinea pigs… …or was it donkeys."

"How did she know what donkeys get up to?" Simon asked, turning to me. "We never had any on the Home Farm, did we, Harry?"

"Perhaps she was jealous… Papa lost interest in her after I was born."

We all burst into hysterical laughter and Dominic leaned across to put his arms around Harry and kiss him.

2001

"You must have loved Harry very much all those years ago," I said, smiling at Dominic, who was leaning over the driver's seat.

He just held up his hands, smiled, but did not comment.

"I think I'll go and find Harry and Simon," he said. "I'll tell them the AA are on their way. I'll keep an eye open for the yellow AA van and come back. Anyway, you know how to open the bonnet. I'll bring you a takeaway coffee and some biscuits."

Dominic went off just as I looked out of the side window again. A big white van had just backed into the spare parking space beside us. The driver was walking away while some of the yobs reappeared. They seemed to be looking for someone. I watched and waited. They all went over to the fence where I had stood earlier and watched. None of them saw me because the sun was still shining on the windows of the Land Rover. Suddenly all hell broke out. Now there was shouting. They jumped over the fence. I slid the window open to listen to the mayhem from the other side of the hedge. The row was turning into fisticuffs. I was fascinated. Suddenly one of the boys jumped over the fence again and ran off, followed by the other young men. They disappeared. So I got out of the Land Rover to see what had been going on over the other side of the hedge. Now I could see the streaker lying on the grass but he wasn't moving. This looked serious. I felt concerned and squeezed through the gap in the fence.

"Are you ok…? …No, please don't worry. I'm going to help you…"

He looked up, afraid that I was another security guard. There was blood around one eye, which was already swelling up and he couldn't see properly. He was trying to cover himself with a bloody rag but I smiled at him.

"…I saw you running around naked earlier," I said and he gave up trying to cover his nudity. Instead he started to dab his face again.

"They're coming back to finish me off!" he muttered. "Oh God!"

I could hear shouting from the other side of the car park.

"Get in the back of the Land Rover, quick!" I said. "They'll never look for you in there."

He got up and followed me quickly through the gap in the hedge. I opened the rear door and he hopped inside. Just then, the yellow AA van appeared around the front of the large white van that had so conveniently hidden everything from sightseers. I went calmly to the front of the Land Rover and waved at the passing yellow van to draw the AA man's attention and he reversed again to stand in front. I just hoped he hadn't seen any of the action. How could I have explained the naked young man lying on the floor in the back? Instead, the smiling AA man leaned out of the window.

"Fan belt?"

I nodded and smiled. He got out and I lifted the bonnet. He looked inside.

"Oh yes, one of the old ones. I see. Well it shouldn't take long."

I got back inside the passenger's door and looked behind the seat. The boy was lying, shivering.

"Keep your head down! They're returning with some others," I said as a rowdy group of yobs appeared. "Cover yourself over with that black coat. We'll find you some clean jeans and a T–shirt in a moment."

The yobs clambered over the fence again, shouting at one another. I sat innocently looking out of the window while the mechanic fiddled under the bonnet. I was hoping any onlooker would be distracted by the activities of the AA man. Even the yobs seemed to be puzzled and spread out to search for their victim. I turned to look behind my seat.

"They're going away again," I muttered. "Don't worry. They have no idea you're in here."

"Thank you so much," the boy muttered. "I might have died."

"Just lie still. You'll be safe here. We'll take care of you."

Dominic reappeared with Simon to talk to the AA man and produced a membership card, followed by Harry, who got in the driver's side with my takeaway coffee and the biscuits. He passed them to me.

"We have a refugee in the back," I said. "I think he needs these more than I do."

I pointed behind me. Harry looked confused. "While you were at the cafe there was a fight behind the hedge here..."
I pointed at the fence outside.

"...One of them got beaten up. He's hiding in our Land Rover under the black coat!... Don't laugh, he hasn't got any clothes on."

Harry looked over his shoulder and then turned to me again.

"We heard about the streaker in the car park. Is that him?"
I nodded.

"Now there's a gang of yobs roaming the car park searching for him. His eye's all cut. I told him to get inside here. Give him the coffee, will you..."

I turned round in the seat to look for the streaker.

"...What's your name, then?"

"Guy," he muttered. "Have they gone now? I know you're

not going to believe this. I was doing a stunt to raise money for an AIDS charity. I had to streak once around the service area to earn a hundred pounds. But it all went wrong when the security guards confiscated my clothes while I was running around and then I found I'd got nothing to wear."

Harry reached over to pass him the coffee.

"Keep your head down!" I said. "I think they're coming back!"

The gang of yobs was shouting at one another as they clambered over the fence and then ran off again. Outside, the AA man was still talking to Dominic and Simon.

"Start the engine, Harry!" one of them shouted.

Harry turned the ignition key. The engine sprang into life and the AA man slammed the bonnet shut. With a wave he got back in his van and drove off. Simon and Dominic then came around my side of the Land Rover. I got out to talk to them.

"Those yobs you saw were about to murder the streaker," I explained, quietly, pointing in the side window. "He's hiding inside and he's badly cut up. They don't know where he is so they've run off again. I thought we might just drive out of here and drop him off somewhere safe. Simon, can you find your spare pair of jeans and that red T–shirt? It won't show up the blood from the cuts on his face."

As the yobs had now gone off to the other side of the car park, I went round to the back door with Simon and Dominic to show them.

"His name is Guy," I said. "Maybe we could pull in at the next service area and get his eye seen to. Perhaps they will have a nurse or medic on site."

I opened the door and we all looked inside. The boy sat up, now barely able to see through one swollen eye.

"We'll take you away from here," I said to him. "Try to relax now."

He tried to smile when I passed him the clean pair of jeans and the red T–shirt. Simon closed the door again.

So we stopped off at the next service area but there was no medical care available. I took the boy into the gents to bathe his eye in cold water.

"Could you drive me home, please?" he muttered. "It's not far off the motorway... only a mile or two. At least I'd feel safer there with my partner."

"What's the address?" I asked, passing him a paper towel and a ballpoint pen to write with.

"I can't see to write properly," he said.

"Well, tell me!"

He muttered the name of a house in a village not far away.

"So, if you sit in the front, can you see enough out of the window to show us the way?"

He nodded and I led him back to the Land Rover waiting outside.

"We're taking him home," I said to the others as I held the passenger's door open.

"You must all come in for tea," the boy said.

I turned to smile at the others and they nodded, so we went off again to the next motorway exit, where we took a minor road. Perhaps it was a side effect of my blood pressure medication. Maybe I was just starting to live in the past, I don't know. I had a flashback to the occasion we picked up a hitch–hiker in the Land Rover so many years ago. It must have been some time in the early sixties.

1960

There was a young man by the side of the road with a backpack. He was wearing short denim cut–offs and a vest but little else. He waved a thumb at us as we sailed by in the Land Rover.

"That's cute ...Look at that!"

Simon slammed the brakes on, nearly skidding into the ditch.

"He'll never thumb a lift up here from anyone else," I added. "There are so few cars up here."

We reversed and I slid the window open.

"Hop in!" Simon shouted. "Going far?"

"I'm trying to get home to Blackpool..."

We drove on. The hitch–hiker fell asleep on the back seat. Or so we thought.

"Woof woof!" Simon whispered across to me, readjusting the rear–view mirror to get a better look at him. I'd never seen Simon like this before.

"Really! ..." I laughed. "And I thought you were a decent

law–abiding citizen... Am I wrong after all these years?"

At this point the hitch–hiker sat up. Simon went red in the face. But instead of getting angry, the young man started chatting and smiling at us. We soon found ourselves driving along the main road linking with the side road to the farm. It was now getting dark outside.

"You won't pick up another hitch tonight," Simon advised him. "Who will see you now it's getting dark? ...Stay with us at the farm. You can get another ride tomorrow."

The young man seemed delighted.

As soon as we got inside, Simon suggested he might like to try out our new shower, which had just been completed. But instead of getting dressed again afterwards this young man came to sit with us in the kitchen for a cup of tea, clutching a towel around his waist. Well! This towel soon ended up on the floor. He was simply gorgeous and he knew it. Simon's eyes were nearly popping out. Fortunately, he liked us too and we quickly became friends. It turned out he was a dab hand in the kitchen and ended up cooking dinner for us that night. Well, to cut a long story short, he ended up sleeping naked between us and on several other occasions. He returned a couple of times to stay with us over the next few years and actually helped Simon to re–roof the barn when the corrugated iron blew off in a storm. Finally, however, he moved abroad to Australia to work on a sheep ranch, when we lost touch with him. I still wondered what became of that incredibly beautiful young man down under... Memories!

2001

This young man wasn't quite in the same league, however. Especially now his eye was starting to swell up so badly. He stared through the windscreen with his other undamaged eye. Finally he pointed at a prestigious gatehouse beside the road.

"It's up here."

We drove through a brick archway. Beyond, in the distance, was an enormous house surrounded by extensive parkland. I was suddenly reminded of the approach to the Palace years ago. But this looked much more grand and inviting – like something out of Brideshead Revisited, which we had recently bought on video. Behind the wire fence I could see the antlers of deer sticking out of the bushes beside the track. The boy turned round to look at us as best he could through the other uninjured eye.

"I'll need to trust you all, please... Have you heard of Bobbie, the pop star...?"

Harry said yes. I'd long since stopped watching 'Top of the Pops' on TV.

"...Well I'm his boyfriend. We live here away from the press reporters and the media in London. Can I trust you, please? I know he'd like to meet you, that's if he's here. Can you see the Rolls? I can't see much any more."

I peered through the windscreen into the distance. As we drove along the driveway, the front entrance came into sight. There, parked outside a magnificent stone staircase was a white Rolls Royce.

"A white one?" I asked.

He nodded. We pulled up beside it and got out. I held the door open for the boy, who was now holding both eyes shut. The daylight seemed to be too bright for him. I took hold of his hand and led him up the steps slowly to the front door and rang the bell.

"Master Guy!" muttered the butler.

"What is it?" someone called from inside the hall.

The butler turned round.

"Master Guy is here. Seems as if he's met with some accident, Sir."

The door opened further. A muscular young man in a vest appeared. I suddenly recognised him from the newspapers. He rushed out to put his arms around the boy, who burst into tears. He scooped him up as if he weighed nothing at all and carried him inside. Then our host reappeared and took a look outside while the butler held the door.

"Do, please, all of you, come in!"

I waved outside to the others, who were still sitting in the Land Rover. They got out and came up the steps. Guy was now sitting on a window seat in the hall, dabbing his eye with his partner's handkerchief.

"They rescued me," the boy said. "There was a fight at the motorway services and they hid me in the back of the Land Rover. My clothes were ruined and they found me some clean ones."

"We're very grateful," our host muttered and turned around to the butler standing behind us. "Tea, please, Smithers!

...Yes now!"

"Very good, Sir!"

The butler disappeared down the corridor and we were invited to take tea in the conservatory. I could see Harry and his brother looking around at everything. There were stone statues and paintings everywhere, just like they had at the Palace, years before. But these were all statues of classical male nudes, including a large copy of Michelangelo's David and others I'd never seen before. I paused briefly to look at a beautiful Eros of Praxiteles. Our host smiled at me and led us into the enormous Victorian conservatory, where palms drooped over an enclosed pond with goldfish swimming in circles around another statue of a beautiful boy with a fabulous winged horse. I stooped down to look. Pegasus and Bellerophon boasted the brass plaque below.

"My latest acquisition," muttered our host to me again. "Just a copy, for Guy's birthday."

We moved to some wicker chairs around an ornate table where everyone sat down. A woman in an apron appeared.

"Ah, Agnes, do we have something for Guy's eye? It's all swollen up."

"Right away, Sir!"

She led the boy off somewhere as the butler appeared pushing a tea trolley.

"Shall I serve, Sir?"

Our host said yes. The butler handed us all cups of tea in bone china cups.

"Shall I leave the cake here, Sir?"

He withdrew to leave us all together.

"I don't know what to say," our host muttered, passing us matching plates from the trolley. "Best if you come and help yourselves... scones, jam, cake?"

He gestured at it, sat down again and turned to me. I explained how we were waiting for the AA to come and fit a new fan belt on the Land Rover when there was a fight in the car park. So we brought the boy back with us to get him away from the gang.

"I really can't thank you enough," he said turning to the others and smiling again. "Would you care to stay for dinner, all of you?"

I looked at Simon, Harry and Dominic.

"We really ought to be moving on back to our farm in the Lake District," I said. "We are in the middle of this foot-and-mouth crisis you may have heard about on the news."

"Oh," said our host. "But come to dinner again, all of you, soon, when Guy's eye is better. No, come and stay for the weekend. We've got thirty rooms here... Then he can thank you properly, himself... Here's our card..."
He reached into his pocket.

'...I wish I knew how to thank you all. Guy is very important to me, as you can imagine, but can I ask you not to talk to the media or anyone from the papers, please? We do try to live quietly here, away from everything."

It really was a crisis, too. Within a few weeks, Ministry vets appeared to slaughter our entire herd. We had kept our fingers crossed but the latest samples had proved positive for foot–and–mouth disease. Thankfully, the carcasses of our animals were removed and not burned on our site. Suddenly the place fell quiet. There wasn't a single moo to be heard. We were placed in quarantine and confined to the boundaries of the farm, in an attempt to prevent the dread disease spreading any further. It was all in vain, however. Within a fortnight, the cattle from all our neighbours had also been destroyed. Everybody was depressed. We all felt helpless. The dairy business, which had taken generations to build up, was destroyed in a matter of hours. Our quarantine lasted for weeks and coincided with the final foreclosure notice from the finance company. In 1998, we'd been reduced to remortgaging the whole farm. Because of stock movement restrictions now imposed by the Ministry after the foot–and–mouth outbreak, we could not sell any animals to generate income. This really was the end. Thank goodness we were not alone on the farm. Both Simon and I would have been lonely and suicidal but for Harry and Dominic. Without the cows the place seemed deserted. Looking back now, this sad time united us together in an extended family. Why had Madame Claire Voyante not warned us of this?

Today, the only part of my life which had survived was my relationship with Simon. Everything else had fallen apart. In 2001 we were bankrupt but we were not alone. Hundreds of farmers like us were starting to sell up, quit the land or were diversifying into craft skills such as cheese production. But I was just too old to change now and even Simon would soon be collecting his old–age pension. However, some of the investments his grandfather put in trust for him when he was 21 would soon prove to be useful. Once again I silently thanked Madame Claire Voyante for her more cheerful prophecies so many years ago.

It was some weeks later when we locked up the empty farm and the four of us returned for a country house weekend with Bobbie and Guy. This holiday could not have come at a better time. They both came to greet us at the top of the steps by the front door. Guy, the boy, was looking much better now. His eye was still discoloured but it was now fully open so he could see us properly this time. Once again we were ushered into the conservatory for afternoon tea.

"I just want to thank all of you," the boy said, sitting down beside his partner and taking his hand. "We were expecting the telephone to start ringing with reporters from the press and media but thankfully..."

He turned to smile at us as the butler wheeled in the trolley again.

"We were watching the news about the foot–and–mouth epidemic," Bobbie added quietly. "We just couldn't believe it when the camera showed you talking at the gate of your farm. It must have been dreadful to see all the cows slaughtered."

"Simon is still upset about Marilyn," I said quietly. "She was his favourite, named after a similar cow he liked years ago in the 50s. I've never seen him cry so much when he heard the bang of the vet's gun. By the way, we've disinfected the Land Rover and our boots before we set out. People now say it might be a virus, anyway. Disinfectant is what everyone uses. That TV crew who came to film me got into hot water with the ministry vets. Their van had not been correctly treated. I sometimes wonder if it was the mud on the tyres of their van which carried the infection around the district."

"Thankfully foot–and–mouth hasn't reached us here," Bobbie sighed. "You saw the deer outside and we've got a herd of pedigree Aberdeen Angus longhorns as well. But they're out on the Home Farm behind us – so fingers crossed."

Guy tactfully changed the subject.

"We'll have a snack now. Dinner will be at eight. We've taken off all the dust covers, specially in your honour. It will be silver service tonight. I've made a special sherry trifle... Bobbie likes that... We've put you in two double rooms, overlooking the park outside. I hope you'll all be comfortable... Don't worry about dinner jackets – we don't – unless royalty is coming, or people like Elton or David ... as they do, from time to time... Just come to dinner as you are."

He waved the butler away and got up to serve us with tea and cake from the trolley himself.

"We watched your charity concert on the television," I said, now turning to Bobbie.

"What did you think?"

"Well, we thought the Queen was wearing ear plugs!"
He laughed.

"Not really her cup of tea!" Guy giggled. "Far too progressive for one's royal ears."

"She prefers classical stuff but we raised millions for AIDS research and famine relief," Bobbie said, getting up to pass round more cake.

"How's the eye, now?" I asked the boy as he handed me another cup of tea.

"The retina has been reattached by laser. They did it in Harley Street. Now I'm beginning to see things properly again."

"He's been poorly," Bobbie said, taking his hand. "But at least he's back here with me again, thanks to all of you."

"Who were they?" I asked.

"Queer bashers, that's all. We don't really know. Somebody said they'd arrived from a football match after drinking on the coach which pulled into the motorway service area. The police weren't called, by the way. That's how the press usually get hold of these things. We've managed to keep it quiet. Again, thank you."

I sat quietly for a while, just gazing at the goldfish swimming round in circles. I tried to remember if there was an indoor fish pond at the Palace years ago. I felt at peace here. Somehow I could see Simon and his brother felt the same. It must have looked just like their ancestral home in the old days, but without the leaky roofs and damp patches on the walls. Finally I turned to Guy once again.

"May I ask how the two of you met one another?"
Bobbie turned to his partner.

"Over the internet," the boy explained. "I sent him a picture by return of e–mail and the rest is history, as they say. I was living in a Brixton tower block with my mum. A month later I moved in here. That was eighteen months ago. Now mum lives here too."

"He's changed my life, after my divorce, the tabloid press

and all that stuff," Bobbie added, taking his hand and kissing it once more. "Now do you see why I was so grateful for what you all did? So how did all of you meet one another, then?"

I laughed, turning to Simon, who had been quiet until now.

"Well, it was 1957. Simon, here, was hiking in the Lake District in the rain. He came in the farmhouse kitchen for breakfast, which he had to cook himself... That's after he stripped off all his wet clothes in my kitchen...Yes, Y–fronts – the lot!"

"But I stayed forty–three years," Simon added while everyone laughed.

"That must have been some breakfast!" Bobbie laughed, nudging his partner.

"It was the coffee that did it!" I suggested, taking Simon's hand. "Best day of my life."

"It wasn't instant 'Nescafe' in those days," Simon giggled. "It was 'Camp Coffee'!"

Everyone laughed.

"...It really was called 'Camp Coffee' ...I even brought my own mushrooms!"

The boy now turned to Harry and Dominic.

"How did you two meet?"

"At a Roman Catholic seminary," Harry replied. "I was going to be a priest..."

"Hallelujah!"

"...Absolutely... Well, I didn't find God but I did find Dominic, thank goodness. We fell into disgrace with the Brothers, moved to Morocco, then to France and finally back here to England. Now we've been staying on the farm with them."

"What happened at the seminary?"

"I'd fallen in love with Dominic..."

"Ah, young love!" Bobbie nudged Guy again while Harry smiled at them.

"...The more the abbot insisted we should stay apart, the more we needed one another. Well it was true love forty years ago."

"When it was still illegal..."

"Yes, seven years before the Sexual Offences Act came into force July 1967 and made us legal at last."

The boy turned to his partner.

"What was that all about, then?"

Bobbie explained to him how the Wolfenden Report of 1957

was rejected by the government and took a further ten years to free gay men from the threat of prosecution. For a pop star, Bobbie was very well informed, I thought.

"We had a big party that night, 27th July 1967," I added. "Simon, ...do tell them all about it! ...the party of '67..."

He leaned forward with a glint in his eye.

"We'd been together for almost exactly ten years, so we decided to organise a party to celebrate that as well. People came to stay on the farm from all over the place. We even had to borrow a caravan to put them up. Several couples slept in the hayloft. Our house was too small to hold a big party, so we cleared out the big barn for a barn dance..."

"A gay barn dance?" Guy asked.

"Howdy partner," Bobby giggled, nudging Guy. "How about it, you sexy dude?"

"That's right, "Simon added. "Legal at last!"

"But we forgot to plan for gatecrashers, "I laughed. "Or how to get rid of them..."

"In the end half the village turned up," Simon continued. "Even the local vicar from the parish church got in and that somewhat dampened the occasion ...until he got drunk too!"

"Not a great success," I sighed.

Everyone was howling with laughter.

"He and I got drunk," Simon giggled.

"You and the vicar?" Bobby demanded.

"No," Simon insisted, pointing at me. "We did! So we were too far over–the–eight to throw out any gatecrashers... "

He looked at me to finish the story:

"Finally Simon and I went back to the farmhouse and locked ourselves in while everyone else got on with the party!" I added. "Remember this was the sixties. Somebody was smoking weed and started passing it round. We were afraid the local police would burst in and bust the joint!"

"But," Simon interrupted. "in the morning we found out that the local copper had turned up with the vicar to join the party as well!"

"Actually, they only called in to check that we were all right," I added. "I think they were concerned for our safety but maybe they joined in… We never found out. There was no sign of them the morning after."

By now Guy was rolling on the floor, getting hysterical, while Bobbie tickled him in the ribs with his foot.

•••••••

Dinner the next evening was a more sober affair. With the brandy I proposed a toast to Bobbie and Guy.

"It was so funny to learn about British gay history at first hand from you," Bobbie said to me.

"I wasn't much good at school and never learned anything useful," Guy added. "I've learned a lot more in the last eighteen months, of course. Bobbie's been the father I never had... Well, I mean as well as what went on in bed!"

"And," Bobbie added, "after marriage to my ex–wife, that was much more exciting!"

I reached out to take Simon's hand. Words just were not needed. Dominic took the opportunity to get down on the floor and sit between Harry's knees.

"Well," Bobbie said to his partner, looking around, "Before everyone falls asleep why don't we take them all on a tour of our place?"

So we followed them along corridors through the house to the back door and out to the stables, where there was a brand new long–wheelbase Land Rover Discovery waiting for us. I looked around at the luxury interior. It was far more comfortable than our poor old thing. Then Guy got in the driving seat beside his partner and everyone else piled in the back.

"I've passed my driving test," the boy said. "Bobbie paid for the lessons."

"He's a better driver than I am," his partner added, turning round and laughing. "I lost my licence after that bust–up with my wife. You probably read about it in the tabloids. Nobody got killed, thank God! But I've still got a chauffeur for the Rolls. He also looks after my collection of Bugattis. Now I have no licence, I can't drive any of them but Guy is learning on the remains of the old track at Brooklands, aren't you? "

"No synchromesh on a Bugatti...," Guy muttered. "Crash on all gears, but I'm learning to double de–clutch...!"

"Anyway, we'll show you the Bugattis tomorrow. The

photographer from Auto Sport has had them all out today for an advertising promotion."

Harry turned to his brother and smiled. I had no idea what to say. This was a whole new world.

We were taken on a conducted tour of the estate; which included a small village with its own parish church, a large lake, a deer park and several farms. Everything looked in far better repair than I could remember at the Palace. Memories! Would it be a good idea to tell our hosts how Simon and Harry were the last surviving members of a noble house going back to Henry the Eighth? I decided that it was their choice. They might think it was best to keep quiet about the decline and fall of the English landed gentry. Finally we were taken on a tour of Bobbie's own recording studio, which was in a converted barn in a quiet corner of the estate. Another pop group had rented it for the day but they had a break for cigarettes while he showed us around. Then we got back in the Land Rover.

"How did you come by all this?" I asked Bobbie eventually while we bounced over a cattle grid in the road.

"My accountant suggested that I should set up my own production and recording company ... This house is the company headquarters, which now occupies the west wing – about ten rooms for office space etc. Payment for my gigs gets paid to the company and not to me. I get paid a salary and expenses by the company, which owns the Rolls and pays for my chauffeur... A bit like Laurence Olivier Productions years ago, Guy says...You know – to avoid crippling tax... Poor Noel Coward eventually moved abroad... He was no friend of the Inland Revenue."

"To live with his boyfriend. That's what it said in that book you gave me last Christmas," Guy added, giggling, from the driving seat.

"Yes, well, anyway. I bought this place after it had stood empty and going damp for years ...together with the farms and the estate. The previous owners? ...I think the old family just died out... Anyway, Guy thinks they were probably crippled by tax demands, don't you?"

"Perhaps the last one turned out to be gay ...like Noel Coward!"

"Like the English landed gentry," I added, no longer caring what anyone would say.

"Alas poor England, Oh decline and fall!" muttered Harry

and we all laughed again.

Dinner was always held in the grand dining hall, not unlike the one I had seen under wraps at the Palace in the fifties. Once again the splendid gallery of pictures around the walls celebrated the beauty of the male form. I recognised Caravaggio's St John the Baptist but I had to go up to the fireplace to read the label under Marcantonio Pasqualini Crowned by Apollo because this Apollo reminded me of Simon years ago when we first met. However, I muttered to myself that he was more muscular when he was 23. This blond young man displayed no six–pack quite like the one I used to love so much.

"Only reproductions, I'm afraid," our host announced. "But now Guy is here, I've got the real thing! ...What need have I now for mere copies of images?"

Everyone laughed at this.

The dining table could have seated forty but we were placed up at one end with Guy's mother who, it seemed, now sat at the head of the table. How different from the tower block in Brixton, I wondered. But I never asked her. What would Simon's mother Her Ladyship have made of all this, I wondered. But this lady seemed relaxed and pleased to meet the men who had saved her son from the yobs at the motorway service area. Nor did I ask her how she felt about her gay son who had made such a remarkable change in her family's fortunes. I looked at Simon and his brother. I would have given anything to hear what they were thinking. Was this the life they could have had but rejected forty years ago? Memories! But our hosts were relaxed and friendly. Bobbie was telling us about his new CD album, which was being launched next month. He added that pirates on the internet were threatening the recording industry by illegally releasing songs to be downloaded free of charge, thus depriving the industry of revenue to encourage new singers and new bands.

"We're going to watch a movie this evening," Bobbie said. "What do you think? Guy likes 'The Wizard of Oz'. How about that then?"

"It's my favourite film," Guy told us. "We've just bought a television projector. We can watch it on the big screen."

I told them that our first TV had a 17–inch screen and how Simon bought it for me in 1958. They all laughed when I told them it would only receive two TV channels, in black and white. Soon we moved into the television room while the staff cleared the table.

This six foot television screen hung down from the ceiling. Around the room were several loudspeakers for stereophonic sound. We all sat in comfortable armchairs while the butler brought in coffee on a trolley. The movie began.

"All this technology and 'The Wizard of Oz' was made before the war with mono sound and it starts in black and white," Bobbie said, laughing.

"But I still love it," Simon agreed with Guy. "Because the Wicked Witch reminds me of Elspeth... his wife!" he added, pointing at me. "I always knew she used to fly around on a broomstick. I swear she spied on us in her magic crystal, just like the Wicked Witch does here! So she knew exactly what we got up to in the bedroom!"

"Yes – far more exciting sex than when she was around," I added while Leo, the MGM lion, roared at us from the screen.

We promised to tell them more about her when the film had finished. Finally, about eleven o'clock, Simon and I retreated to our room upstairs. It even had its own en suite bathroom. I gasped when Simon opened the door. The four–poster bed was almost exactly like the one we had slept in at the Palace forty years ago.

"Well?" I asked. "Does it remind you of the old days?"

"Only how lucky I was to find you."

"Forty years ago... Bobbie and the boy are only just starting out."

"It's easier now."

"Is it? I can't remember any gay bashing in 1957!"

"It probably went on but was kept quiet because of the law. What about the blackmail that went on in the fifties? You remember that movie 'Victim' starring Dirk Bogarde we saw on television. Perhaps that was the truth for some people in 1957."

"Well, I hope Bobbie and Guy will be as happy as I have been with you. Fancy Bobbie getting married..."

"Like you did with Elspeth."

"Don't remind me!"

Simon lay back on the bed and stared up at the canopy over the top.

"Forty years!"

"Do you remember the canopy over your bed?"

"Two griffins rampant and the cross of Saint George!"

"I forgot to tell you it was still on the barn outside the perimeter fence at the motorway service area. I meant to show you but that business with all the yobs fighting made me forget."

"Well show me next time."

I turned to look at Simon. The vigorous youth had faded but the sparkle in the eyes was still there. I hadn't been wrong. If I could have my time over again, I could not have wished for a more handsome companion or any other kind of love to share my life during the past forty–three years.

"Was it worth it?" I asked... "Giving up your career in nuclear engineering... to live with me all these years?"

"You worry too much."

"If you'd gone home as your parents wanted back in 1958, you might be living in the Palace still, surrounded by, God knows – a wife, children, grandchildren, to take over the old traditions and continue the family line, going back to Henry Eighth."

"We've talked about this so many times...You already know the answer. I've been happy with you...just like Harry has been happy with Dominic. Talk to him..."

"Yes. I will."

"He'll tell you the same... Go to sleep now."

I drifted off to sleep, curled up around Simon. Bobbie and his partner were so lucky now, accepted by the world, visited by royalty. How different it was for gay couples today. Even the newspapers were talking about equal rights and marriage for same–sex partners. But would I have wished for better if I could live life over again? My one regret was that I hadn't taken more photos of Simon years ago. Young men today seemed so weedy, never using their muscles for hard manual work. How many of them would be able to reduce a whole apple tree into a pile of logs with an axe? Guy was sweet but thin. At his age, Simon would have been a muscleman by comparison. Few photos now remained, only memories. I still thought about the time I'd sent him back to London. Why? But I was too tired to go over everything again.

About four in the morning I woke up after a nightmare. I nudged Simon to tell him all about it. He sat up and looked at me.

"A ghost!" I muttered. "Here in this room."

Simon looked around.

"Another of your dreams? You take too many of those blood

pressure pills. I told you."

"This was weird. It was as if I was looking down on the bed. A young man was asleep in it."

"This bed?"

I nodded.

"He was naked."

"How do you know, if he was actually in the bed?"

"Another young man came in and pulled off the covers. He jumped on the other one and they started making passionate love..."

I paused.

"Then what?"

"I don't know. I think that's when I woke up!"

"Go back to sleep."

But I couldn't go back to sleep. Instead I got up and went downstairs to find that Harry was also up early. While the servants were setting the breakfast table, the two of us sat together by the log fire in the morning room.

"Does it remind you of the old days at the Palace, then?…"

Harry smiled and said nothing while Smithers, the butler, brought us some coffee.

"…Dominic told me about your experience with the abbot years ago…"

Still Harry said nothing.

"...I'd no idea you went through such a harrowing experience."

Harry leaned towards me while Smithers walked away.

"The abbot couldn't break the bond between us, you see. The more threats he made, the more Dominic and I needed each other. Because it was illegal and strictly taboo, our love proved to be more final and lasting."

"Did the abbot really believe your love was evil?"

"Perhaps... Well I think he was just a bitter old man who'd never loved anyone and couldn't cope with real love between Dominic and myself... The stronger our love became, the more he resented it... I think he was just jealous, you see."

"But to have you beaten like that... while Dominic had to hold you down."

"It's history! ...But we've been together since 1959... over forty years."

"And you've been happy together..."

"We've had our ups and downs... You know I had malaria in Africa... That was enough to test any relationship. Then there was sickness and the diarrhoea... We won't go there... But Dominic looked after me... I mean unconditionally ...in sickness and in health... I owe him everything... But you found Simon first... Has it been like that for you?"

"I knew almost from the moment he walked into the kitchen... back in 1957."

"The famous breakfast...which he cooked himself for both of you."

"Don't forget about the power cut. But it was the most important day of my life…"

I looked around to check the servants had gone, leaned forward and then smiled at Harry.

"…Your brother was simply gorgeous. He just took all his clothes off and leaned back against the kitchen table...Yes, that very first morning back in '57!"

"Starkers – so he really did lose the Y–fronts? It wasn't just a joke? "

"Yes, really ... Because he said his clothes were all wet through from the rain."

"The shameless hussy... my brother!... But Dominic was just the same. We used to escape to the loft in the seminary... Once we even had sex in the confessional at the back of the chapel. He used to get really desperate. He left his pants hanging on the hook behind a door by mistake. His laundry name tag gave the game away!"

"Was that after you came to the farm that first time?"

"You still remember?"

"I was the one who suggested to Dominic that he should come back and kiss you while you were still cleaning the Land Rover."

"He wanted to make love again... Bless him. I was so lucky to have someone like that. He was not only gorgeous but also the best companion I could wish for."

I put down my coffee cup to share a laugh with Harry.

"Just like your brother was for me!"

Harry took the wallet out from his jacket pocket and passed me an old black and white photo of Dominic years ago. I gazed at the slim and elegant youth in a sepia tint.

"A work of art, like these in here," I whispered.

"Dominic just had to flutter his eyelids and I went weak at the knees."

"But it worked, I take it," I said. "Simon told me he used to go bathing in the nude..."

"The boating lake at the Palace... Did he tell you he seduced Hamish, His Lordship's gamekeeper? ...17 years old Simon was. And already he was at it... I knew! We had no secrets... We needed a united front against my father, His Lordship. It was like that, you see… contra mundum!"

"Simon told me he felt like a rebel in disguise... waiting for his moment to come. Until then, he bit the heads off jelly babies which the ladies of the church used to give him."

Harry poured out more coffee from the jug.

"He was lucky to find you... I mean in 1957 when it was still illegal. "

"Out in the countryside around the Lake District nobody bothered one little bit..."

"But you were still married then ...to...?"

"Elspeth, but we got a divorce soon after. Simon's name was never mentioned."

The butler reappeared and we stopped talking.

"Breakfast is served, gentlemen. My master, Bobbie and Guy will join you in a minute."

I watched Smithers go back into the breakfast room and turned to Harry again.

"Have you any regrets about life...looking back today?"

"Me?

"Yes."

"Only that I was made to feel so guilty about loving Dominic... The church can be a powerful persuader... convincing you about sin..."

"Mortal sin?"

"You remember... We talked, didn't we?"

"Forty years ago..."

"Has it really been forty years?"

"Have you been happy with Dominic?"

"When I look around me today I see divorced or single people everywhere... broken marriages, misery and bitterness. I've been really lucky with Dominic... That's how I look at it," he added, looking around. "He was such a wonderful fuck! But I couldn't stop him giggling. One time we were at it in a cupboard at the seminary. All his giggling gave us both away. But I don't regret anything at all. I wouldn't have missed it for anything."

"Let's get some breakfast, I suggested."

"Have you ever seen the photos we had done in Morocco?"

"Of Dominic?"

"Yes. Photographers out there only wanted trade. They weren't concerned with debates about pornography...or peculiarly English things like that."

"These were nude photos I take it?"

"He was so beautiful and so cute...I still look at them now and think gosh... Did I actually love someone who looked like that? Did he really love me? I'll show you some day."

We got up and went off to find the bacon, egg and sausage.

I was a bit bleary–eyed after breakfast. I told everyone that I'd been dreaming about ghosts in the four–poster bed. Simon denied having seen anything. But Bobbie seemed very interested.

"What period do you think it was? Georgian?"

"Could be. They both had long hair. The young man who jumped on the bed was wearing a gown."

"Who knows? The County Archive has only one or two documents covering that period. My solicitor said there wasn't much to go on."

"But," I said, "Simon, here, used to sleep in a four–poster like this one, known as the Queen's Bed. Queen Victoria was supposed to have slept in it."

"I got fucked in it," Simon giggled. "My first time was with the gamekeeper!"

"What would Lady Chatterley have said about that?"

"My mother was away visiting relatives. She never knew! Then he came along..."

Simon pointed at me while everyone laughed.

"...He was the best... He could fuck for England in 1957! ...If they'd given Olympic medals for that he would have won gold I tell you! ...And the rest, as they say, is history."

Everyone broke into fits of giggles.

"I was very, very lucky," I added. Simon gave up everything for me!"

I took hold of Simon's hand and kissed it but put it down quickly just as Smithers, the butler, walked in with the toast. Bobbie immediately took hold of Guy and started to smother him with kisses.

"Please..." muttered Smithers respectfully. "Don't mind me, gentlemen. I don't want to spoil all the fun."

We got on with the breakfast in silence. I was dying to talk about the old days back at the Palace but thought better of it.

"There's a Noel Coward song I must do for you," Guy said, changing the subject again, 'The Stately Homes of England'."

"He's good," Bobbie promised us. "Guy never had a piano in the flat at Brixton. He came here to play mine. That was the start of it all. I was still married, then. Now he even writes some of my songs... That's not for the tabloids!"

"Your secret is safe with us," I assured them. "But why doesn't Guy play the piano for you on stage in your sell–out concerts?"

"I'm strictly backstage," Guy assured us. "Life's quieter that way!"

"At least this relationship has lasted," Bobbie added. "After the paparazzi locked on to my former wife, they made her life a misery. But I tell you what we'll do. Just for you, Guy and I will sing some songs... only later tomorrow... in the evening, perhaps."

We hadn't been in the music room before. This overlooked an inner courtyard of the house where it was quiet. Clearly Bobbie also used it for recordings. There were microphones on stands lined up against the wall. We sat in easy chairs around the marble fireplace, where someone had lit a log fire. Guy lifted the lid of the Steinway.

"I bought it for his birthday," Bobbie assured me. "Mine is now at the recording studio in the stables. At least Guy looks after this one. One pop group who rented the studio tipped paint over the concert grand... Don't ask! Steinway charged us a fortune to clean it."

He raised his hands in despair and sat down on the stool beside his partner. They played a duet version of Noel Coward's song and then something from Bobbie's latest album, which Guy had written. It was about a lost love, to be sung by Bobbie right at the end of his stage show.

"Prince Charles was said to have tears in his eyes," Guy assured us as Bobbie got up to leave Guy to sing 'Mad Dogs and Englishmen' by himself.

He had perfected Noel Coward's voice, complete with the nasal articulation, after listening to old gramophone recordings. We were helpless with laughter. Then I knew immediately why

Bobbie and Guy's relationship had clicked so easily. They were both natural entertainers.

"I really love that young man," Bobbie said aside to me, quietly at the end. "I do know what you saw in your Simon forty years ago. I only hope Guy and I will last the next forty years. What do you think? Have we got what it takes?..."

I nodded and smiled.

"...Look," he added. "Guy supports an AIDS charity which does a lot of good work in Africa. You know how bad the epidemic is out there..."

I nodded. I still did not know if Guy had told Bobbie about his streak around the car park at the motorway service area to earn one hundred pounds for poor people with AIDS. I thought it best to say nothing.

"...Well, he's devised a new striptease routine... Yes, I do mean it. He does it himself with a friend... No, I'm not joking! They'd like to try it out on all of you, as it were, for a private party to invite your comments and any suggestions..."

I smiled.

"...Seriously! I kid you not! Guy says the need for funds is so great, the time for niceties is over. All gay men should be doing their bit. My agent is arranging a charity concert later this year where my band will play to raise money. We'll give you comps. You must come!"

I gasped.

"You don't mean Guy and his mate are going to do a striptease on stage. What would the tabloids make of that?"

"No, no, of course not... He means country house parties for a select audience."

"The discerning few...?"

Bobbie laughed.

"Yes, exactly. What do you think?"

"Well, I can ask the others..."

The outcome of all this was that Guy and his mate would do their striptease routine for us the following evening. We would be invited to donate cash to sponsor the event as it went along. I couldn't wait. We pledged the odd fiver or two. I'd never heard of men stripping off back in the fifties. Of course everyone had seen 'The Full Monty' at the cinema. How different things were today! Inhibitions about male nudity were clearly a thing of the past. But Bobbie was right. I had lost one or two gay friends to

AIDS back in the eighties. Everyone had. Now it was a disease of gays and straights. They had little money for AZT in Africa and combined drug therapy was out of the question until the international drug companies dropped their prices. It was a worthy cause.

As soon as I saw Guy's friend with whom he would do the striptease I knew I had seen him before. Was his photo in a newspaper? Had I passed him in the street? I sat there puzzled, watching him strut up and down to the music. Guy stood on a plinth where a classical statue had been removed. He was clearly wearing an enormous number of layers and started to shed one or two as the music started. This came from a CD player on the floor, behind an upturned bowler hat where we tossed our coins. It was great fun. As the layers came off, fifty pence and pound coins were thrown in. Eventually, now he was down to his T–shirt and Y–fronts, we started to throw in tenners and fivers. Well, it was fun but I'd seen better. My memories of Simon when he was 23 might have been gilded with the passing years. He had certainly been more muscular in 1957. Perhaps the shape of men had changed, I wasn't sure. But before he removed his pants, Guy's partner started to strip off, thus elongating the event. He was worth looking at and had spent a decent time in the gym. As his shirt came off I suddenly realised where I had seen him before. He was the one I had seen from the motorway car park covering another young man's chest with kisses. I decided to say nothing. Perhaps he was the one who had sponsored the streak.

Simon had walked everywhere and cut up apple trees with an axe – not something Guy did very often, apparently, judging by his physique. He was so slim – too thin for my liking but when he totted up the cash in the bowler hat, he'd raised over a hundred pounds – enough for several doses of AZT in Africa, he said.

"You should make it last longer," I suggested.

"Make the punters wait a while," Dominic added.

"Do more wriggling in time with the music," Harry proposed, getting up to waggle his hips.

"Make the music last by repeating it twice over," Simon said. "Record on tape and edit it..."

"How about changing the music to 'The Stripper'!" Bobbie was giggling. "You might raise even more cash that way."

....

I was surprised by an invitation from Bobbie to look at the private chapel attached to the house. He explained that it was still in a sorry state because it had not been restored. As we walked along corridors and down stone steps, he added that the house had at one time belonged to a family of Roman Catholics who actually retained their own priest. He pushed open a rather dusty door. There was that same musty smell of damp and dry rot which I always associated with my marriage to Elspeth back in the fifties. I told Bobbie all about it as we sat on dusty pews facing the altar. I just couldn't help thinking about Sebastian talking to Charles Ryder in 'Brideshead Revisited'. Only Aloysius, the teddy bear, seemed to be missing.

"Would it be worth restoring?" he asked, looking around. "What do you think?"

"It's baroque, isn't it?" I asked, trying to remember the scene in 'Brideshead Revisited'. "Why restore it if it would never be used?"

"But, that's my point. I do intend to use it...to get married!" I turned to him in disbelief.

"No, no," he insisted. "I don't mean to another woman... I mean to Guy... A gay wedding here in this chapel, away from the tabloids and all the paparazzi with a few selected guests who we know we can trust... like you!"

I didn't know what to say but looked up at the ceiling with the flaking painted angels.

"I owe Guy so much," he continued. "I met him when I was really down because I'd just got bad news from the STD clinic. Maybe I shouldn't tell you this, but you've got to know some time, now we are friends. I am HIV positive. Guy arrived just in time to save me from a drug overdose ...You don't mind me telling you?

I shook my head.

"I think Simon saved me from something like that back in '57."

"I haven't told anyone else any of this but I trust you. I don't think you'd dash off to the 'News of the World'. Anyway Guy came backstage at one of my concerts in London. I took him to a friend's apartment while he was abroad... Well, Guy gave himself to me... He lay down naked on the hearthrug and took me in his arms… I told him about my HIV status there and then… He said it didn't matter if we took all the right precautions… Was it like that with Simon and yourself?"

I sighed. The smell of the damp in the baroque interior reminded me of the parish church where I'd got married so many years before.

"My wife had just walked out," I said. "Simon arrived in the middle of a storm. The electricity went off but he cooked breakfast on our coal–fired Aga stove and, well, we fell in love. That was back in 1957, in the days long before HIV and AIDS, of course. We did everything bareback."

"Like real men?" Bobbie laughed.

"Yes, but perhaps we were lucky. Neither of us slept around, you see…"

I suddenly thought of the hiker who we'd picked up in 1960 and corrected myself.

"…Well, we once had a threesome with a drop–dead gorgeous hunk. That was the only time, I'm sure."

Bobbie smiled at me again and nodded.

"Guy was so cute... He still is," Bobbie added. "He knows how to really love a man... He really cares about me. I don't know what I'd do without him."

"My Simon was the same. How old is your Guy then?"

"Eighteen now... He was only 16 when we met...I was afraid the tabloids would find out but the law changed to 16 just in time... But it was the sex. That's what really sealed it..."

"My Simon was good at that too when he was 23."

"Well I tell you... Sometimes Guy wants fucking several times a day..."

"My Simon was insatiable forty years ago. He could not get enough!"

"Every time we always come together... He explodes in my hand... It's wonderful ...every time!... Wild, wild sex!... He has no inhibitions whatever... Unlike my ex–wife. She went all cold and frigid... Now do you understand?"

"Yes, I've been there. I know!"

He smiled and nodded at me again.

"And," I added, "as you might say these days, I bought the T–shirt!"

He put his hand on my shoulder and I laughed. There was so much the two of us had in common. I felt we had both experienced a new life after failed marriages.

"At first I thought Guy was after my money," he added. "Or worse...that he was a plant by a tabloid newspaper... Well!"

"But he wasn't?" I asked. "In my case, I never had any money – just the farm but I've lost that now. We've gone bankrupt and the finance company has repossessed it."

"Foot–and–mouth must have been the last straw… We followed the news on TV… I'm sorry. I wish there was something we could do. I owe you so much. Guy could have died if you hadn't stopped the gay bashing…"

We sat quietly for a moment while I looked around the chapel again. I decided to buy Simon a teddy bear for his birthday. I'd seen one in the local charity shop. Finally Bobbie put a hand on my shoulder.

"…For me, it was love, you see ...and it still is... unlike anything I have ever known before. Guy is my other half... Now do you see how glad I was that you saved him from the yobs?"

"I'm glad I was able to help."

"By the way, the specialist in Harley Street told me Guy nearly lost the sight in that eye ...another cut or blow ...and he would have been blind for life in one eye..."

He was now getting upset and I got up to have a closer look at some of the architectural details of the chapel. I was suddenly reminded of the baroque chapel in the Palace where Simon's family lived before the motorway was completed. It was also where the two of us had our first row.

1958

It was after discovering that the family treasure was missing from the lead–lined box under the hearthstone. So we were both in a rather emotional state. Simon took me to see their private family chapel. We had to walk across the courtyard to reach it. The chapel was locked up and he had to borrow the key from his mother. The door creaked when Simon unlocked it. There was a familiar musty smell inside. He locked it behind him again.

"Why did you do that?" I asked.

"Can't you guess?"

"Guess what?"

"Fuck me!"

"What ...in here?"

"Why not? Now I've locked the door, we cannot be disturbed!"

"But this is a holy place..."

"Not now, it's been deconsecrated...last year's economies, you know..."

"I'm not doing it in here!" I insisted.

"Please?"

"No! ...It's too spooky!"

I sat down on a dusty wooden bench and stared at Simon.

"But I've always wanted to do it in here!"

"No! ...I hate places like this... I think it's the smell of falling damp and the sound of deathwatch beetle in the roof... It reminds me too much of my marriage to Elspeth!"

"Why bring that subject up now?"

I sat quietly, not knowing what to say while he looked at me.

"Please?"

"No! Anyway, it's too cold in here!"

Simon sat down beside me with his head in his hands.

"You're getting tired of me! ...Perhaps we should never have come back here. Meeting my family has put you off."

"No... I'm not tired of you... Just because I don't want to do it in here... That doesn't mean I'm fed up with you, does it?"

"You don't love me any more!... I knew you'd get tired one day! ... Is it because I can't give you the children you might have had with that woman?"

The slanging match went downhill thereafter and doesn't bear thinking about today. But most relationships have stormy times. I am lucky that we got over this one and never spoke of it again.

CHAPTER 8

2001

I'd done everything I could to forget my occasional rows with Simon. Of course, there are ups and downs in all relationships of more than forty years, both gay and straight. Maybe, Simon and I had fewer disputes than other couples who ended up in the divorce courts. My own divorce from Elspeth, back in the straight-laced 1950s, was frowned on by some people who believed that a marriage was for life, for better or worse, for richer or poorer. But memories of my own marriage ceremony in our dark, damp and dismal parish church had spoilt religious faith for me. So had the church's opposition to the reforms in the law regarding gay relationships advocated by Wolfenden. But Simon changed all that for me when he walked into the farmhouse kitchen back in 1957. For it was he, and only that incredibly beautiful and erotic young man, who changed my life from a respectable one of quiet resignation to an illegal one of outrageous sexual excitement and passionate love. As I looked around Bobbie and Guy's crumbling baroque chapel nearly fifty years later, I had very mixed feelings and was lost in thought. Eventually, Bobbie got up and came across to stand by me. He tactfully changed the subject.

"Look, it must have been truly dreadful back at the farm... because of the foot–and–mouth disease. I don't know what to say."

"We knew all the cows by name, you see... Marilyn Monroe, Simon's favourite... she wiggled her back end. There was Hattie

Jacques, a fat one... but they're all gone now. The Ministry vet burned them all away from the site, thank goodness... Well you saw the news footage on TV."

I sniffed. He sat down and placed a hand upon my shoulder.

"Now what? Is there anything I can do?"

"The Ministry will provide compensation... in the fullness of time..."

Bobbie turned to me again with a glint in his eye.

"Tell you what?... Move here... One of our farms has been in a dreadful state. The tenant started another business and has neglected it... Now my estate manager has given him notice to quit. Guy and I intend to breed another rare breed of cattle... like longhorns, with a special grant to help to start a new herd... What do you think? We could do with your expertise... Talk to Simon and the others. Live here in the house if you like... Well, you've seen the size of the dining table..."

"Are you really serious?"

"Go on! Talk to them all...You can let us know."

I stared up at the ceiling above us. I had no idea what to say next. Bobbie was already talking to me as if I was an old friend. It was the common bond between openly gay men in the twenty–first century. I pointed at some flaking paint over a brown stain under an exquisite golden, but neglected, angel. Then I changed the subject.

"Is that water penetration?"

Now penetration was a subject I did know something about!

"We'd have to get a proper survey done first...to see if it is viable. I thought we might apply for a heritage grant."

"But then the public would get access..."

"Well, perhaps just a lick of new paint and a good clean."

"The roof would need seeing to, otherwise the water will spoil it."

"But my point is, is it worth restoring or shall we just start again from new? What do you think? Is it good art?"

Suddenly, I realised that in 'Brideshead', which we'd all watched together on TV, Bridey, Sebastian's brother, had asked Charles Ryder exactly the same question about Lady Marchmain's own private chapel. Was history repeating itself? But, unfortunately, unlike Charles, I was no qualified judge of classical architecture. Instead, I pointed at the organ with an impressive array of pipes above us. I'd heard enough dismal and depressing sounds from a similar instrument in our parish church to put anyone off sacred and classical music for life.

"Does that thing up there actually work?"

"The pipe organ? …No idea."

"But it might be useful if you ever needed a classical backing for a new recording. And the acoustics here might be good for choral music."

"I thought of that."

Bobbie snapped his fingers and we listened to the echo.

"Is that what you'd call a lively acoustic?"

"Probably, but it is no good for pop music."

I looked all the way around the ceiling. The damp patches and the peeling paint reminded me of Simon's ancestral home so many years ago. But its foundations now lay encased in concrete under the M1 motorway.

"It is beautiful in here," I insisted, pointing up at the cracked cornice over the window. "Craftsmen must have spent weeks on the artwork and all that ornate plaster. You must preserve it – if only for their sake."

"Well, if I do, will you give me away at the wedding ceremony?…"

I stared at him.

"…I can't ask my father. He died ages ago. So I'm asking you, as…well, an old pioneer of gay liberation... If I get married to Guy here, in this professionally restored chapel, with a gay priest in a proper ceremony... Will you give me away or be my best man? Yes, I suppose we could wait for Civil Partnerships, if that is what Tony Blair and New Labour intend to call them, but, you know I'm HIV positive… "

I was flattered. I'd never been called 'an old pioneer of gay lib' before. But younger gays had more serious concerns in the modern world. Bobbie was looking worried:

"…I do hope I don't give it to Guy so that he becomes HIV positive too. Anyway, I might not be here much longer if the combined drug therapy fails to work. You see, I want to give Guy a wedding to remember, before it is too late. I want to thank him for all the joy and happiness he has brought into my life after so many years of misery with my ex–wife. I want him, not my ex–wife, to inherit all this as my true partner, after I'm gone. And, yes, I do intend to write a new will because so many millions are at stake and the inheritance tax would ruin him. So, please, will you give me away?"

"I'd be delighted."

I looked around the chapel once more. What would Evelyn Waugh have thought about this, I wondered? If he were writing 'Brideshead Revisited' today, would Charles and Sebastian have celebrated their union in the baroque chapel which had been built for Lady Marchmain? Indeed, considering the new tradition set by 'Queer as Folk' on TV in 1999, might Evelyn Waugh have made Sebastian and Charles' obvious love affair less squeaky clean? An interesting twist, I thought. Bobbie scribbled a note in his diary and then looked up at me again.

"Good, that's settled. I'll phone the builders on Monday."

I hardly knew what to say. Bobbie was the idol of millions of teenage pop fans. His web site was blessed by thousands of hits per day. But I was seeing another, more human, side of this icon in the age of popular culture.

"Does he know?" I asked. "Guy, I mean... That you'd do all this for him...?"

"It would be his wedding present... A beautiful chapel for an incredibly beautiful young man – and he remains beautiful thanks to you, you know. I will never forget what you did… and so tactfully, without any press publicity at all… If he had died, I could not have gone on living any more, without him. Do you know that? We both owe you so much."

He appeared on the point of tears. I looked around again. I'd never been very keen on architecture until now. This enormous house, built in the classical baroque style by John Vanbrugh around 1700, had taught me to appreciate England's architectural heritage. I was on the point of telling Bobbie about Simon's ancestral home years ago but he turned to me again.

"Did you know Guy and his mum are both Roman Catholic? They go to mass every Sunday but they could have a private service of their own here one day!"

I gasped and sat quietly for a while. My life and 'Brideshead Revisited' seemed to be merging as if in a dream. Why hadn't Madame Claire Voyante foreseen this in her crystal? Bobbie and I both looked around. Dusty cobwebs festooned the pipes above the organ. A large spider was starting a new one. Now Bobbie turned to me again with a glint in his eye.

"Has your relationship with Simon ever been formally blessed by the church?"

"No, after my disastrous marriage to Elspeth, I'd had enough of church ceremonies. But it is something Harry and Dominic have been talking about. They are more into that kind of thing, having met in a seminary years ago. Religion is much more important to them, I guess."

"Why don't you think about it now?"

"You mean a blessing for all of us?"

"Why not? Your relationship with Simon has lasted since...?"

"Since 1957."

"I think that's something to celebrate, don't you? I'm sure the Reverend Abner McWitz – he's Guy's cousin, you know – from Los Angeles, would be delighted to honour a loving, gay relationship and one of forty years' standing at the same time."

"Is that the American guy you've signed up to do it?"
Bobbie nodded.

"Guy invited him backstage to meet me after one of my concerts in the United States last year."

I sat stunned, not knowing what to say. How times had changed. Forty–four years after Wolfenden, the church might embrace Simon and myself together in holy matrimony. Only this was not the Church of England but a breakaway clique from North America. They were starting a revolution – just like 'that old sinner' Oliver Cromwell who Madame had conjured up in her crystal all those years ago. But I didn't think that stuffy Cromwell would approve of such modernity! Now would an English parliament pass Civil Partnership before Tony Blair quit office? Perhaps he would need to resort to the Parliament Act if the House of Lords objected, just like the reduction in the age of male consent to 16. Bobbie got up.

"What do you think, then?"

"Sorry?"

He assumed I was going deaf in old age and spoke a bit louder, causing an echo from the end wall:

"A blessing here in this chapel."

"Oh, yes. I'd have to ask Simon first. His father was something important in the Church of England – I can't remember what exactly... They never got on... Yes, I'm sure Simon will agree, just to spite the old so–and–so."

"Shall I ask Harry and Dominic too?"
I nodded.

"How long will the Reverend McWitz be here?"

"A week... He's going to some important church congress in London – to do with the ordination of gay priests... anyway, something like that. I've invited him to stay here. You'll like him. He comes complete with a large retinue of altar boys and a small choir – he assures me they're all over 18 – sort of disciples, if you know what I mean... I've met them... Well, some of them are just gorgeous!"

"I can't wait!"

Bobbie sat down again.

"Can I ask you something?"

"Please... anything at all!"

"Is there some kind of secret... I mean to make a loving relationship last that long... for forty years?"

"You mean, how is it that Simon and I have lasted so long together?"

Bobbie smiled at me and I laughed. He raised his hands.

"Well, you must know what I mean."

"A secret for a happy relationship?"

"Guy and I are just starting out... I hope it will last a lifetime, well, combined drug therapy for my HIV permitting."

I thought for a moment.

"For what it's worth, I think a relationship needs strong contributions from both partners. In our case, Simon was always the planner, the guy with the Black and Decker who got things done, mended things, built things – like our hydroelectric plant. That's worked since 1958. We haven't paid an electricity bill for forty years."

"And what did you contribute?"
I smiled.

"You need to ask Simon that question... I hope he'll say good sex!"

"But that's very important."

"He actually quit London University to come back for more."

"There you are then. I'm sure Guy would say the same."
"I think Simon had been sex–starved for far too long."

2002

So the great day finally arrived. We'd all been sworn to secrecy. It was agreed that the tabloids were the greatest threat. Paparazzi had to be kept out at all costs. The private chapel was only accessible from the house but it was searched all the same. The organist for the newly restored organ was Bobbie's own brother, who'd flown in especially from Australia to play it. Apart from the Reverend Abner McWitz and his retinue of a dozen boys around the altar and in the choir, Guy's mother was the only witness, apart from ourselves. Everyone felt safe on the morning when the blessings would take place. Bobbie's wedding to Guy would take place after lunch on the same day to be followed by a banquet in the grand dining hall provided by contract caterers.

Neither Simon nor I got much sleep that night. We spent several hours reminiscing about the past forty years. We dissolved into fits of giggles over what Simon and Harry's father, His Lordship, would have had to say about all this. Perhaps it was just as well he died back in the 1960s before his little world collapsed around his ears. I had purchased a new suit, especially for the occasion. Simon, of course, brought his kilt. It was the same one. He'd kept it away from the moths all this time and it still looked magnificent. Harry and Dominic decided to wear matching white outfits. Nobody knew what Bobbie and Guy would wear – little did we know!

The chapel looked splendid. Bobbie had actually spent half a million on roof repairs, a new damp course and redecoration. The baroque interior had been cleaned by art restorers from London and the organ completely rebuilt by specialists who also added an electric blower to replace the hand operated bellows. Endless discussions had taken place to choose all the music. In the end, a compromise was drawn up. There would be everything from ABBA to Handel's 'Water Music', transcribed for a small organ with one keyboard.

For the blessings, I led Simon by the hand. Behind us walked Harry, who clutched Dominic's arm all the way down the aisle to the sound of the music of 'The Entry of the Queen of Sheba'. The choir occupied the stalls while the Reverend McWitz waited at the altar, surrounded by his gorgeous retinue, all dressed as pink angels, complete with wings.

"You might have to pass me a sick bucket," Simon whispered, giggling.

"Sh! ...Shut up! They'll hear you!" I muttered aside.

Then the four of us knelt on the cushions at the altar steps.

"Dearly beloved brethren," the Reverend began. "We are gathered here to honour two loving relationships of over forty years' standing..."

I turned round briefly to look at Harry and Dominic, who was now in tears. Of all of us, he was the most sentimental. Harry passed him the white handkerchief from his top pocket. But I didn't really know whether to laugh or cry. Instead, I grabbed hold of Simon's hand and kissed it. Why not? We'd waited forty–five years for this moment. In 2002, gay liberation had arrived from the United States with a loud bang – even if it was a pink one!

The choir then sang Parry's 'I Was Glad', from Psalm 122. The lead sopranos were so good that I had my doubts about whether they were actually over 18. It was all very moving. I turned to Simon. Now he was in tears too.

Each of us then got up to read a short piece of our own choosing. Harry and Simon both read from letters they had written years ago to Dominic and me. Well, I'd quite forgotten what Simon wrote to me from Glasgow while he was sorting out the supply of the hydroelectric equipment. I was soon in floods of tears. Memories ... or rather, what I had completely forgotten at my time of life! These days Simon blamed all the blood pressure medication for my lapses of memory.

The choir got up to sing Handel's 'In the Lord I put my trust!' and Simon came back to stand beside me while one of the altar boys swung a thurible of burning incense down the aisle. Finally, after a rather dry and lengthy sermon from the Reverend, which reminded me of the parish church back home, we walked out to the tune of 'Pomp and Circumstance March No 1', remarkably transcribed for the chamber organ and choir. What would pompous old Sir Edward Elgar have said about that, I wondered?

Luncheon was a buffet in the greenhouse around the fish pond, prepared by Guy's mum. It gave me the opportunity to take a closer look at the Reverend's altar boys and the choristers. I could see none who would have been capable of singing alto, let alone the soprano parts in Parry's 'I was glad!' So I picked up a sausage on a stick and I went over to ask the Reverend myself, how it was done?

"A confession, my dear friend," he chuckled. "It was all on a digital recording using loudspeakers hidden behind the choir stalls."

"So they were miming to playback."

He said nothing but just smiled at me.

"I was concerned in case they were castrati," I said.

"No, certainly not!" he laughed at me. "In the States we don't hold with such peculiarly continental mediaeval practices. I can assure you, my dear friend, they are all intacto!"

He winked but I wasn't quite sure what he meant by this; nor did I really want to know.

I wasn't prepared for the afternoon wedding of Bobbie and Guy. We were immediately struck by the heat inside the chapel where Simon and I now sat down in a pew at the front. The choirboys were still dressed in white gowns and sang some songs by ABBA while we waited. Suddenly the door by the altar screen was thrown open and the altar boys entered. I gasped. Except for leather thongs, they were now all completely naked. Each one held a tall flaming candle in front of him. Finally, the Reverend, still dressed in his regalia, closed the door behind him. I glanced at Simon. He was almost speechless too.

"Where's the sick bucket? Quick!" he muttered but I ignored him.

The wedding march was tinkled on the organ. The doors at the back opened. Now Bobbie entered, dressed in a pink suit. He came down to kneel on the altar steps. The doors at the back closed again. The wedding march began again on the organ. Why all the delay? I wondered.

Finally, we all turned to watch Guy appear through the doors accompanied by his mother. He too was naked, except for a bright white thong around his waist. He cast a nervous glance at his mum, who even wore a hat. She seemed to be on the point of hysteria. I don't think child care expert Benjamin Spock or Sigmund Freud's advice about the rearing of children could possibly have prepared her for anything quite as camp as this. Sedately, they made their way down the aisle to the altar.

We were both expecting some ornate Catholic affair. I was never prepared for the Anglican wedding service. Those words I remembered from my own wedding to Elspeth had come back to haunt me again. But this time they were being used to bless a truly loving relationship – everything Elspeth and I never had years ago. Bobbie looked truly magnificent in his pink suit. Guy looked rather thin and vulnerable in his white thong. I decided some brides would look better in a more traditional outfit. But I was being an old fogey, showing my age and much behind the times. In the twenty–first century we would all need to embrace the new spirit of liberalism and the inclusion of minorities, gay and otherwise. Mother Church had opened her doors to a new age and the proof was here in front of us. The gays had come out of the closet! Mr Wolfenden had started everything back in '57. Now what would he think, I wondered? I stood beside Bobbie and handed him the ring. He slid it on Guy's finger. They kissed. Soon it was all over.

Somehow I was relieved. This had all been too much. Real love didn't need ceremonies or rings, mumbo–jumbo or hymns. Simon and I had survived without all this 'til now. Our relationship had been based on other things, private and personal. I went back to the pew to sit with Simon for a while. We needed some quiet time together while an electrician came in to disconnect the rented speakers behind the choir stalls.

"Have you decided yet?" Simon asked me.

"About what?"

"Leaving the Lake District for good. "

"What do you think?"

"I say yes...Let's go for it! You know our soil is still contaminated with radioactivity from Chernobyl... That black rain cloud after the explosion in the USSR back in '86."

"Just like Windscale in '57..."

"And I wanted to be a nuclear scientist."

Tears came into my eyes.

"And I nearly sent you up the lane to the youth hostel... I nearly sent you on your way! I told you the village store would be open at nine. I nearly lost you for good!"

"Well, you didn't, you old softie!"

"No, I might have made the worst mistake of my life... You were so beautiful... I loved you so much!... Fucking you was so much fun!"

Simon ignored this but looked around the restored chapel while the final extension cable was being wound up by the electrician.

"Now we'll move here for good, then," Simon decided. "So we will leave the keys to the farm with the finance company...?"

"Yes, small scale dairy farming in the Lake District is finished... But you and I have lived through the lot...the world's first atomic disaster at Windscale..."

"Starting our own hydroelectric scheme."

"The snow in '59."

"The radioactive fallout again from Russia back in '86...worse than Windscale."

"Foot–and–mouth disease last year."

"But I wouldn't have missed it for anything...because you were there ...a gay marriage which actually worked!"

"So we're moving after forty years... That's settled then!"

"You know Bobbie and Guy want us to live here in this posh place...with them."

"Well, Simon," I sighed. "You and Harry were bred for such a stately lifestyle...at the Palace. You know how to live in a splendid place like this."

"The heir and a spare..."

I started laughing.

"Only both of you turned out to be gay! You two had the last laugh to spite His Lordship... The ancient dynasty going back to Henry the Eighth ended with the two of you..."

"Our ancestral family tree came to an end... two emblazoned griffins rampant over our Latin motto. I always knew they were two gay male griffins in anticipation…"

"In anticipation of what, then?"

"Me at it with you and Dominic with my brother... Bless him!"

I looked at Simon and we both recited Harry's words together.

"Alas poor England. Oh decline and fall!"

Simon looked around at the electrician, who was trying to wind up a cable jammed beneath the pew where we were sitting.

"I think we're in the way."

While the electrician stared, I took Simon's arm and we paraded, as if in a state occasion, down the aisle and out through the doors. After a lifetime together, two old men had finally been liberated from the closet. We would share our declining years together in a stately home and enjoy the life of the English landed gentry. But, sadly, it was not to last for long.

2003

So we finally moved out of the farmhouse in the Lake District. The finance company was about to send in the bailiffs anyway. They had already sold the site for an estate of holiday homes. The hillside pasture was absorbed by the National Park and one of the meadows would become an extension to the village recreation ground. We locked the front door and piled the last of our belongings into the removal van. I didn't even look back. We felt like the Joad family in John Ford's classic film 'The Grapes of Wrath', which had just been shown on TV, leaving poverty in the dustbowl to go fruit picking in California.

There were no tears, only relief. The financial crisis was over. The only asset left in my life was Simon but he wasn't feeling too well these days. He got out of breath quickly and he had lost that healthy glow we'd always taken for granted. I was starting to worry, especially since he had flatly refused to go and see the doctor. With a shudder, I remembered how Grandpa Joad soon died and had to be buried by the side of the state highway on the way to California. Perhaps this was an omen.

It was New Year's Eve 2003, while we were celebrating the New Year with Bobbie and Guy, that Simon suddenly collapsed. Paramedics arrived in an ambulance and he was rushed into hospital. Nobody had any idea what the problem could be. We waited for the results of his blood test. He had been a gay man for more than forty years. So could it be HIV? He had been vulnerable to infections for too long. But Leukaemia, a serious cancer of the blood, was diagnosed instead.

As Simon's closest living relative, the hospital immediately summoned Harry but he explained that I was the 'significant other' as gay partners were known these days. So I sat down in the specialist's consulting room. Bad memories of my mother's death came flooding back to my mind. But this charming young man was polite and considerate. I explained that Simon and I had lived together as a couple on a farm for over forty years. This interested him. Did we use strong industrial chemicals with a known cancer risk, he asked?

I couldn't think of any, apart from the gunge we added to our sheep dip. So, had Simon ever been exposed to nuclear radiation? I told the specialist the truth. We had lived a few miles from the Windscale nuclear plant for many years. Our farm had been washed in radioactive rain in 1957 and again in 1986 as the result of the radioactive cloud from Chernobyl in Russia. On both occasions our cows' milk had been tested and rejected by the dairy. But then I remembered the radioactive debris Simon picked up on the sole of his boot on the day we explored the beach beside the Windscale installation with the Geiger counter. Was it that, I asked? Could the disease have taken forty years to develop? The specialist didn't think so, but nobody could say for sure. In the meantime, Simon would need cytotoxic drugs or radiotherapy but, the specialist warned me, he was now probably too old for successful bone marrow transplantation, even if his brother Harry could be persuaded to provide it. I was devastated. I'd taken Simon for granted. The greatest love of my life was seriously ill. We would need to make the best of the limited time we had left together.

2004

I spent a good part of 2004 sitting at Simon's bedside in the hospital. Then an outbreak of MRSA, the notorious hospital bug, prompted Bobbie to pay for Simon to be moved to a private clinic specialising in cancer treatment and state of the art oncology. I could even stay in the guest room next door if he became seriously ill. This happened later in the year when a permanent drip was fitted to his arm. But Simon's mind was still active and boredom was the problem. He could watch TV but it gave him a headache after a while. So I started to take books to read aloud to him from the library. He got fed up with Agatha Christie's Miss Marple and Hercule Poirot. One day I carried in a large teddy bear I'd found in a window of the local charity shop. I sat him at the end of Simon's bed. His eyes lit up. He'd had a teddy just like this one in the nursery, upstairs with his nanny years ago at the Palace. She used to tuck them into bed together whenever Simon had bad toothache.

"So what shall we call him?" I asked. "How about Harry, in honour of your brother?"

Simon looked happier today. He was recovering from the nausea caused by the anti–cancer drugs and I was beginning to recognise a note of optimism in his voice. He was trying to remember something.

"What is it?"

"In 'Brideshead Revisited' we watched on TV together, Sebastian had a teddy bear. What on earth was it called? Didn't it begin with St...? ...Saint something or other? Wasn't he the patron saint of youth?"

I really couldn't remember.

"Saint Paul?" I suggested. "What about Saint Ignatius?"

"That was the name of the founder of the sacred order at Harry's seminary where he met Dominic."

"Do you know? I just cannot remember. Do you want me to watch the videotapes of 'Brideshead Revisited' and find out the name of Sebastian's teddy bear, then?"

"No, I tell you what... Bring the book in here next week to read to me."

"What?" I gasped "...You mean the whole novel? ...It must be a long one. It will take weeks to read all that."

"Yes, I want to know the name of Sebastian's teddy bear."

Simon smiled at me. The colour was coming back into his face. The long eyelashes that I had loved so much nearly fifty years ago had mostly fallen out, along with his beautiful hair, as the result of all the anti–cancer drugs.

But we had long since given up talking about this painful topic. I was about to buy him a new wig for Christmas. It would be a blond one, just like his floppy curls which once stuck around his face in the rain. So much of his masculine beauty had gone now and there was no way to turn back the clock. I had to accept the truth. My lover had only a few more months to live.

2005

So on the first of January 2005, I started reading the prologue of 'Brideshead Revisited' by the sickbed. I felt just like Julia reading aloud to the dying Lord Marchmain by the Queen's bed in the Chinese drawing room. But Evelyn Waugh's English prose was somewhat more difficult to read than Agatha Christie's paperbacks. However, I got into the habit of reading through the chapters the night before in order to avoid mistakes and became quite skilled in imitating different voices for Charles and Sebastian. But I had to consult Harry and Dominic about the correct pronunciation of 'Et In Arcadia Ego' and other Latin words to avoid annoying Simon. Anyway, we soon found that the teddy bear was called 'Aloysius' and at last Simon's old teddy bear now had a name. I particularly enjoyed imitating Anthony Blanche's affected voice and stuttering 'Real G–g–green Chartreuse'. At this point Simon became hysterical and the needle on the end of the drip came out of his arm. I pressed the emergency button by the bed and a nurse rushed in to replace it. Instead of resuming 'Brideshead', we started chatting about the old days once more.

"Do you remember that day the Ministry phoned up in '57 to say our milk was unfit for human consumption because it was radioactive?"

"And you pressed the red emergency stop button for the milking machine, just like that one."

"I thought..." Simon started laughing again but held the needle in his arm, this time... "I thought you'd switched it off because it was time for me to get another good fucking right there in the milking shed..."

"Sh!"

The nurse reappeared to check the drip–feed of the anti–cancer drug. She smiled and went away again. The pain had returned and Simon seemed to have tears in his eyes. I passed him a Kleenex from the bedside table.

"I wish we could do it now."

"You must be feeling better!"

"Why is youth wasted on the young?... Who said that?"

"Now you're really showing your age!"

Simon dozed off to sleep and I closed the book. So I left him cuddling Aloysius. At least I'd found a comforter to help him to sleep at night. But more than once the poor teddy bear had to be dry–cleaned when Simon vomited all over him. Anti–cancer drugs can have unpleasant side effects. Simon and Aloysius remained inseparable right up until the end.

When I returned to Simon's private room on another occasion, I found the drip had been removed and he was actually sitting out in a chair, reading a leaflet. He smiled and passed it to me. I put on my reading glasses. There was a small coat of arms and 'HM Government' at the top.

'Civil Partnership, Legal recognition for same–sex couples from December 2005'.

I gasped.

"Whatever would your sainted father, His Lordship, have said about this do you think?"

Simon puffed out his chest, sat up and rubbed his chin with

his hand.

"Ahem, My Lords, it is just as I said before!... All socialist nonsense.

I must beg Your Lordships not to vote in favour of it! ...Reform of the worst kind!... Lloyd George started it in 1908!... I blame him – undermining the power of the English establishment and the landed gentry... What? ...The result of sandal–wearing liberal idealism and the drive to get more votes... I tell you the Tower's too good for them... What?"

We both laughed. Simon could imitate his father so well and had added comic embellishments over the years. I remembered that my father had always admired David Lloyd George but I really didn't know what he would have said about Civil Partnership, either.

"Your Mama might have approved," I added. "Just to spite him, too."

Simon smiled and picked up the brochure from HM Government. It showed two men holding hands on the cover, just as the two of us had done for fifty years. To see such an image on an official publication from the Department of Trade and Industry was a big surprise. Why the DTI, I wondered?

"So how about it – you and I? Harry was here. He brought me this leaflet. He says Bobbie and Guy have booked a date for January 2007. Apparently Dominic wants a Civil Partnership with Harry. He said Dominic thinks it is time to make an honest man out of him after all these years. Bobbie told him Elton phoned. He and David are getting spliced at a registry office as soon as possible."

Simon put out his hand and I sat down on the edge of the bed to take hold of his with both of mine.

"You're feeling better today, then?"

"There's a new male nurse... Woof! ...He's changed my life, I tell you... I'm going to get better just for him."

"You sound like Barbara Windsor in 'Carry on Nurse.'"

"Did you see it on TV again last night?"

We sat quietly for a moment while a mature lady nurse came in to check Simon's temperature. She filled in the graph at the end of the bed and left without saying anything. I glanced at Simon.

"That didn't look like the dish of the day!" I muttered.

"More like Elspeth, your wife!"

"Don't remind me!"

"But she means well. At least they take care of me in here… and no MRSA, or any other hospital bugs to kill me off quickly."

I sniffed and turned to him.

"That just wasn't funny, Simon."

"I'm sorry… Listen. I had a dream. We were back in Cumbria, on the farm. I dreamed that we were up in the hills with the sheep, just you and I.

I was so happy. It was so quiet – just the wind, the birds and water in the stream – no mobile phones ringing, doors slamming or kids listening to pop music. What has happened to England? I must be getting old."

"You were telling me about your dream, Simon…"

"Yes, well, it was lambing time. We were putting those stray orphan lambs in the back of your old Land Rover and wrapping them in sackcloth to take them back to the farm. Do you remember? Then I sat in my kilt in front of the open fire to feed them milk from the bottle. You were toasting muffins on the end of your mother's brass toasting fork. It was heaven."

"I loved you so much! You were everything to me…"

"Now you're going all gooey–eyed again, you old softie! Look, there is something you really must know about that very first day back in 1957. For nearly fifty years I have never told you the whole truth…"

I stared at him. I had no idea what he had not told me after all this time.

"…If you remember, I shouted 'Hello' while you were up the ladder in the barn. Am I right?"

"I got that splinter in my hand," I said. "That was the one you got out by wrapping your lips around my thumb and chewing on it, as if it was a blowjob."

"Yes, that wet morning. You assumed I was looking for the youth hostel. What you don't know is that I'd been staying there for days. I could watch your farm out of the dormitory window. Yes, I had been spying on you. I've always been ashamed to tell you how it really was. You see, I saw you look at another young man in the village post office the day before. He had his back towards you because he was in front of you in the queue. You looked him up and down with that look on your face. My magic gaydar was always switched on when I was 23."

"What kind of look was that, then?"

"You looked him up and down with a look which said 'I could fuck that!'"

"Now you are ruining everything."

"No, you old softie, you've got to know the truth. That was the moment I realised if you liked him, you might love me – hence my famous strip in your kitchen that first day. I took a chance that you had no idea who I really was. I could have been anyone – a dustman, a rent boy, anybody. But you loved me because I was being myself – an incredibly randy 23–year–old. I already knew your wife had gone because I watched her put her suitcase in the back of her car and drive off in a huff. I already knew you'd be alone. I saw everything from the youth hostel window, you see."

"Why me then?"

"I fancied you, you idiot – your broad shoulders and your muscular arms. Woof! I said to myself from the back of the queue in the village post office. I imagined myself lying next to you in bed. You see, I was looking you up and down because I was standing behind you at the counter."

"And I thought it was all just by chance."

He could see I was upset so we sat quietly for a while. Simon picked up the leaflet about Civil Partnership once again and turned to the next page. He punched Aloysius and pulled his floppy ear to make me laugh.

"Do you know, you silly old bear? I'll forgive Tony Blair for Iraq, Afghanistan and everything else because of this. New Labour has made all of us old, gay, former social outcasts respectable at last!..."

Simon poked Aloysius once again and pointed at me.

"...I want to marry that man, just as Madame Claire Voyante predicted all those years ago. Do you think they'd do it at the hospital chapel, you silly old bear? You could be my best man... Well, best bear, perhaps... Now you've made me feel tired again. It's all your fault."

I left Simon to have a snooze with Aloysius in his arms just as he once fell asleep on that first day with an Old English puppy on his lap. History seemed to be repeating itself. But was Simon entering a second childhood? Maybe it was a side effect of the anti–cancer drugs. Surely they weren't already giving him the opium derivatives or morphine my mother had been prescribed.

2006

So I made an appointment at the local registry office. The registrar kindly offered to meet me by Simon's bedside in the hospital because he was still far too ill to come to her. Our Civil Partnership ceremony was booked as soon as possible and would be in the spring. We all assumed he would be much better in health by then. The hospital chapel had not been registered for Civil Partnerships so we would need to go to the registry office. So Simon would need to be strong enough to walk with me down the aisle. The thought of that boosted his determination to beat this leukaemia once and for all and it gave him everything to look forward to. The specialist seemed pleased with his progress and decided that the cancer would soon be in remission. Simon could come home for Christmas at last, but we would be by ourselves with Harry and Dominic. The confirmation of a new tour of pop concerts around the USA meant that Bobbie and Guy would be away. Except for the business wing, the garage for the Bugattis and the recording studio, we would have about twenty rooms all to ourselves. We would be 'house–sitting' as the wealthy and fashionable would say in the twenty–first century. Simon and I would have almost the whole stately home to choose a venue for our Christmas celebrations. Bobbie and Guy would return in time for our Civil Partnership. Anyway, that was the plan.

We found an old wheelchair up in the attic and I paraded Simon around the greenhouse and the indoor fish pond just like Charles pushed Sebastian around the hothouse in 'Brideshead Revisited'. Of course the teddy bear came too. He sat at the front on Simon's feet or sat squashed in the corner beside him. Just like them, we selected blooms for our buttonholes and drank wines brought up from the cellar, although we never did find anything really ancient celebrated by Evelyn Waugh. Our bottles came from Tesco or Waitrose and not a celebrated French Chateau in 1895. Over these last few weeks we passed together, both of us seemed to enjoy a second childhood, even if his was motivated by a prescription of happy pills. Bobbie e–mailed from the States that we could wear any of the posh clothes in his wardrobe and drink any wine in the cellar. His generosity knew no bounds. I remembered Waugh's own words in a beautiful passage I had read to Simon in the hospital:

"...it seemed as though I was being given a brief spell of what I had never known, a happy childhood, and though its toys were silk shirts and liqueurs and cigars and its naughtiness high in the catalogue of grave sins, there was something of nursery freshness about us that fell little short of the joy of innocence..."

So we sat by the fish pond drinking vodka and Coke. What was there to say? How could we make this precious time last? Simon wanted to talk about the past. It was as if the mind of a man who had been close to death was flashing through the past fifty years.

"It was before you sent me packing back to university in '57, I woke up early in the morning. Dawn was breaking through the curtains. I was naked in bed with you and your muscular body was curled around me. Our arms and legs were entwined around each other but your enormous erect penis was still inside me. I couldn't move because you were sound asleep. We stayed like that for over an hour and my life was never the same again. Then I knew for sure! ...You could not possibly expect to gain anything by way of pomp, circumstance, title, position in English society or tickets for HMQ's next garden party. You loved me for myself – my long eyelashes, my curly hair, my slim waist, my pert butt and all. The evidence was throbbing right inside me. That was the moment I knew I could never live without you any more... But one week later you put me on the train to carry me off to London."

I was starting to cry. These memories were just too much. Perhaps I'd tried hard to forget things after all these years. Suddenly Simon realised just how much he had just upset me.

"I'm sorry."

"Now cancer might carry you off for good, Simon."

"But I'm in remission now. The specialist told you. I'm a new man again."

"Yes... Pass the vodka bottle again."

"Do you remember Madame Claire Voyante and her bottles of Gordon's gin? No wonder she found it difficult to pay her gas bills when she was into mother's ruin. But it was so expensive in the fifties, what with purchase tax. But maybe Harold Macmillan didn't drink it when he was Chancellor of the Exchequer, before he became PM in 1957."

"Why is it you remember all this from years ago when you can't even remember the name of Blair's Chancellor today?"

I laughed but Simon's memory wasn't any better these days.

"Do you think Madame was always drunk?" I said.

"Probably," he muttered, pouring out more Tesco vodka for himself.

"But to be able to foresee the Twin Towers collapsing in Manhattan in her crystal so many years ago, just like we watched it happen on TV. She really was a modern Nostradamus."

"And she foresaw the rise of Castro and the Cuban missile crisis."

Simon and I smiled at one another, just as we had done in the old days. This really was turning into a trip down memory lane. How I was going to miss him when he'd gone!

"She confirmed my happy life with you... How did she see us fucking one another in her crystal, do you think? Was it magic? Were her spies out watching me on the farm? Well, you did! You told me all about it only the other day."

"I don't know, but I do know I wouldn't have missed sex with you for anything."

"Let's be happy again, just like that. Where's the tonic got to now?"

"Do you remember when the tube of Vaseline ran out?"

"We used margarine...'because there isn't anything else'. Oh, happy days! Now I need more vodka. Where have you hidden it, Aloysius, you silly old bear?"

And so, just like Sebastian in 'Brideshead Revisited', Simon started to drown his sorrows in alcohol from the cellar. Should I have intervened, just like Lady Marchmain, in an effort to put him back on the straight and narrow path to redemption? Her Ladyship, Simon's mother, had tried to change his mind with her glamorous photos of potential daughters–in–law from the USA. But I no longer believed in redemption, God, Heaven or Hell. I still believed in this sick old man who had once been my beautiful boyfriend. At least he was happy now. But it was not to last. The leukaemia returned with a vengeance at New Year and he was readmitted to the Oncology Department. The specialist warned me that preparations should be made because the end was near. The prescriptions of happy pills would be increased. There was nothing more medical science could do for Simon now. It would be a matter of when, not if, and some time in the next few days.

"You must prepare yourself for the worst," I warned Harry.

"Your brother won't be with us much longer."

"Thank God I've still got Dominic to fall back on," he added sadly. "You are going to miss him, aren't you?..."

I sniffed and didn't know what to say.

"...But you've got me and Dominic, Bobbie, Guy and Guy's mum. You have a new extended family now. Did you know that Bobbie has a daughter? She's nine years old apparently. Guy told me she's coming here to stay with her father soon – shared parental access as part of the divorce settlement, you know. She was very upset she wasn't invited to her father's gay wedding. She wanted to be Guy's bridesmaid! She wanted to carry his bouquet!"

"Bless!"

CHAPTER 9

2007

I returned from the Oncology Unit for what I thought would be the last time. I had given Simon one final kiss. He hardly seemed to know who I was now the happy pills had been replaced by all the sedatives. My mother had been exactly the same so many years ago, before Simon walked into my life.

This was just too much. I didn't want to talk to anybody but retreated to the quiet dignity of the baroque chapel, away from it all. Sunlight filtered in through the windows. It reminded me of that day I led Simon into our old parish church near the farm to show him where I had got married to Elspeth. Somehow this beautiful and sacred place refreshed me. I would have so many happy memories of Simon for my declining years but I was roused from my morbid thoughts by Bobbie's daughter, who sat down on the pew beside me. She was clutching Aloysius and propped him at my side. Her innocent cheerfulness was rather testing at times but I desperately needed some friendly words now.

"Uncle Simon might be going now, Grandpa," she said sadly. "Daddy told me all about it. I'm sorry… And my other gay dad, Guy – the one who still believes in Jesus – says Simon might be going off to spend a new life in Heaven. So you'll just have to put up with all of us now. We love you. You don't mind me calling you Grandpa, do you? You see, I've never had a grandpa… Well, I did, sort of,… only, they both died so long ago and now I've got two gay dads. So I might as well have one gay grandpa too..."

The profundity of what she had just said was lost on her, but I just smiled because I was happy already. She looked at the book that was on the seat beside me.

...What's that book then, Grandpa?"

"It's a story about a grand old house just like this, many years ago."

"Is it a nice story book? Does that one have a happy ending?"

"Simon loved it."

"Do you think Aloysius would like to hear you read something?"

"Well, I've nearly finished it. I was reading it to Uncle Simon in the hospital before he became too ill to listen. We never finished it."

"So, which page did you get to in the book? Aloysius wants to know, don't you, you tatty old bear..."

She lifted the teddy bear to her ear as if he was whispering to her.

"...Aloysius says he wants you to start reading where you left off last time."

So I picked up 'Brideshead Revisited', which I had left on the book–rest the previous day, and took out the bookmark from page 394 to find the passage I'd been reading before:

'The chapel showed no ill–effects of its long neglect; the art–nouveau paint was as fresh and bright as ever; the art–nouveau lamp burned once more before the altar. I said a prayer, an ancient, newly–learned form of words...'

I looked up and realised that Guy had followed us and sat down in the seat beside his boyfriend's daughter. He smiled and held out a book of organ music by Johann Sebastian Bach.

"It's lovely in here, isn't it? Mum and I like to come and sit here too, don't we, Natalie? Listen!... Bach wrote baroque music specially for a chamber organ just like the one up there. Harrisons of London did the restoration themselves, you know. The dry rot and the woodworm had eaten most of it away..."

He picked up Aloysius to balance him on his knee and put the other arm around Natalie.

"...Do you know? When I was living in that tower block in Brixton, I never thought anybody like your gorgeous father could love me. I never dreamed anyone would ever spend half a million pounds restoring a beautiful chapel with a classical organ just for me. So I have been learning to play it properly. Well, I can actually read music like this again, and that is very much thanks to this Good Samaritan here, you know…"

He turned to me with a beautiful smile.

"…There was a time I didn't think I would ever see anything at all…"

I raised my hand but could think of nothing to say. I had only done what I thought best at the time. Nobody had called me a Good Samaritan before. I had only acted as any kind person would do and I didn't think Natalie really understood what he was talking about.

"…Listen, I'll play something Bach wrote and it is especially for the two of you. This is called 'Komm nun Jesu vom Himmel herunter'…"

I looked blankly at him. The little girl took hold of Aloysius to cuddle him.

"…That means, I think, 'Now Come down from Heaven, Lord Jesus'. And I really believe he did, you know, that day in the motorway car park. He sent all of you to rescue me in the Land Rover…"

This was too much after saying goodbye to Simon. I turned away and sniffed while Guy climbed the spiral staircase to the organ loft. I had not heard this music before but in this baroque interior, so expertly restored, lit by candles and electric light over the music from which Guy played so beautifully, I stared at the altar, which Bobbie had arranged to be re–consecrated for his Catholic boyfriend and his mother. The sacred flame now burned brightly in the lamp once again. But I still felt I owed it to Simon to finish the novel and turned to the very last page while the little girl held up the teddy bear to watch when I read aloud by the light of the nearest candle:

'Something quite remote from anything the builders intended, has come out of their work, and out of the fierce little human tragedy in which I played; something none of us thought about at the time; a small red flame – a beaten copper lamp of deplorable design relit before the beaten–copper doors of a tabernacle; the flame which the old knights saw from their tombs, which they saw put out…'

It was all too much. I dropped the book on the floor and burst into floods of tears. The little girl put her arm around me and I sobbed on her shoulder. Guy stopped playing, climbed down the stairs and I found him sitting beside us once again. He picked up Aloysius to balance him on his knee and turned to me once more.

"Bach was only 19 years old when he became organist at Arnstadt. Well, I'm only a year or two older now, largely thanks to you, you know, and I thank God for it. Did you know Bach went blind, Natalie? Anna Magdelana Wulkens became his amanuensis and she had to write down his later work. That's why I love this sacred music so much. Before my operation in Harley Street, I was nearly blind myself… Wasn't I?"

Guy got up again and I reached for Aloysius. He looked at the teddy bear.

"…Did you know Saint Aloysius is the patron saint of youth? Bach had more than twenty children but a lot died young. That's sad, isn't it, Natalie."

I sniffed but tried to smile at him as he turned to climb back up into the organ loft to leave us quietly together.

"Listen, you'll like this next piece. It's called 'Wachet auf! Ruft uns die Stimme!' …That means 'Wake up! The voice is calling to us!'…"

So I sat crying quietly with Aloysius and the little girl. Nothing in my later life had prepared me for recent events. I had lost my father soon after the war. My mother died in hospital not long before Simon turned up in the farmyard, but now, after another fifty years together, to lose him as well was just too much. I was stunned and had no idea where life would lead me next. Guy finished the music and called out from his seat in front of the organ:

"I'll play you another piece. This is called 'Was Got tut ist wohl getan'… That means: 'Whatever God does, is done well'…"

Before he could begin, Harry suddenly burst in through the door at the back of the chapel. Natalie and I both looked up.

"The hospital has just phoned. They want me to go over there at once."

My heart sank. Simon must have passed away and Harry was the last surviving relative so I thought this meant the end had come.

"I'll drive you over there in the Land Rover," Dominic called out as he rushed down from the organ loft again. Harry came over to lean down close to my ear.

"The Professor of Oncology told me he'd arranged for a new batch of blood to be flown over from the United States. His colleague over there has just developed a new treatment involving a transfusion of genetically engineered white blood cells. They say this batch has Simon's blood group. They want permission to try it out on him but it must be this afternoon. Time is running out. What do you say? You must decide before it is too late."

I looked at him in amazement.

"What do you think, Harry?"

"It is our last chance to save my brother. The oncologist has tried everything else… I say go for it. But it is cutting edge, state of the art genetic engineering, tested on only a few patients in the USA. He says that it was still in the experimental stage of development."

I turned to Natalie. She looked fascinated.

"What do you think then? Shall we give Uncle Simon one last chance?"

She held Aloysius up to her ear again and smiled at me.

"Aloysius says yes. Jesus does not need another angel yet."

I nodded and Guy went away with Harry to find the Land Rover. Meanwhile Natalie, the teddy bear and I sat quietly together. The chapel was silent again except for the whirr of the electric fan blowing air into the wind chest under the organ above us. In his hurry, Guy had forgotten to switch it off. Then Natalie turned to me again.

"Guy has been teaching me about the Roman Catholic Church," she said. "He thinks I might become a nun one day, just like Julie Andrews in 'The Sound of Music'. Do you like that film, Grandpa?…"

I shook my head and frowned.

"…Anyway, I don't like it either because cutesy American kiddies make me so sick I want to strangle them! However, Guy says I've found the power of prayer just like Maria at the convent, before she became their governess."

I looked blankly at her.

"And what's that, then, Natalie?"

"My pussy cat was ill. We all thought that she was dying. Guy said he would drive me over to the vet's place with Bag Puss in a basket. He warned me the vet might say it would be the kindest thing for me to agree to have her put down, to save her from any more suffering. But do you know what I did first of all?…"

I looked blankly at her again.

"…Well, Grandpa, I came in here where it was quiet, like it is now. I knelt in front of the altar and I prayed, just the way Guy had taught me to."

"What did you say in your prayers, then?"

"I asked the Virgin Mary to save Bag Puss. I didn't want to have her put down before she had her kittens."

"What happened next?"

"When Guy took me to the vet's surgery with Bag Puss in the basket, we put her on the table in the surgery for the lady vet to examine her…"

"And?"

"The lady vet looked in Bag Puss's mouth, stuck her fingers down her throat and pulled out an enormous fluff ball. She'd just been licking off too much fur. Then Bag Puss sat up, jumped down off the table and ran out through the door into the waiting room. A lady sitting out there with her sick doggy said it was a bloody miracle. But Guy told me on the way home that the Virgin Mary must have been listening to my prayers. He said I should light another candle to say thank you for her grace and favour. It is that one over there."

She pointed but I had no idea what to say next. Instead, I got up to find the switch for the electricity supply to the organ and silenced the fan. Now it was completely quiet and serene, I sat down with Natalie once again.

"Grandpa, if Simon dies, you'll really miss him, won't you?"

"Of course, just as much as you would have missed your Bag Puss."

"That's why my daddy was so grateful when you saved Guy from those dreadful yobs in the motorway car park. He just could not live without him… I know, Grandpa. I've seen them together when they thought nobody was looking. I knew what they were up to because I watched Bag Puss do it with the tomcat from the gardener's cottage. That's how she got pregnant."

The sun from the window had moved round and was starting to strike the altar cloth and the crucifix. The bizarre contrast between this topic of conversation and the hallowed interior amazed me. Now Natalie went quiet.

We both watched in silence while a black cloud in the sky obscured the setting sun to darken the chapel interior once more. Clearly she was thinking deep thoughts today and she turned to me with a puzzled expression.

"My daddy won't make Guy pregnant, will he?"

"No, Natalie. That's one thing he cannot do."

I had no idea where this conversation was leading but she had not finished yet. I still felt shocked about what she had witnessed at such a tender age.

"Because my daddy is HIV positive. I don't want Guy to get it… Grandpa, if God loves us, why does he send bad things like HIV and AIDS?"

I was stumped and was grasping for straws but had a sudden flash of inspiration.

"Natalie, why do you think God allowed your Bag Puss to get ill with a fur ball jammed down her throat?"

"I asked Guy that one, too. He told me to pray to the Virgin Mary and ask her what it was all about. I love him but he gets a bit fed up with all my difficult questions, sometimes. That's why I need a grandpa just like you to talk to."

"And what did the Virgin Mary have to say to you, then?"

"Sometimes it is like getting through to British Gas, all her lines seem to be busy, especially when I have an awkward question which needs an urgent answer…"

I could not resist laughing but Natalie stared at me.

"…It was like that time Mummy's gas boiler went wrong two weeks after the men came to service it. Customer Services left her hanging on for too long, so she lost her temper, slammed down the phone and told me all men are pigs."

Visions of her unhappy home life came flashing through my mind. I wanted to give the little girl a more positive view of the world. I put my arm around her again.

"Perhaps, Natalie, your Lord God allows good people like the lady vet to put bad things right and cure sick animals. What do you think?"

She ignored this.

"My mummy was not easy to live with because of her bad temper. I was so young but I do remember the noise of them rowing all the time. Daddy had met Guy, you see. But Mummy didn't like Guy at all. She accused them of sleeping together and she was afraid of catching AIDS…"

I was shocked. Natalie seemed to know everything at far too young an age.

"...Mummy told me God had given HIV to my daddy as a punishment for going off and leaving her all alone. That was just one of many dreadful rows."

I still had memories of similar, bitter arguments with Elspeth.

"Perhaps she was angry with your daddy, Natalie. Ladies with short tempers tend to say things just like that. But they might not really mean it."

"Have you got HIV, Grandpa?"

"No, Natalie, I have not."

"Does Uncle Simon have HIV or AIDS, then?"

"No, he's got leukaemia."

"Then we will pray for him."

She got up from the pew and took my hand to lead me to the tabernacle. I felt numb and too old to protest about the Catholic religion. Natalie reached for a candle.

"Have you got a light, Grandpa?..."

I passed her a box of matches and she lit the candle to stand beside an old one, which had burned down and gone out.

"...That was the one I lit for Bag Puss. We will have to kneel down, Grandpa, can you manage that?"

I got down beside her. I had forgotten how to pray after all this time. Natalie put her hands together.

"Dear Mary, Blessed Virgin," she began. "I appeal to you. Please hear an innocent child's prayer... I kneel here today with Uncle Simon's lover. Somehow, I think they strayed from the straight and narrow a very long time ago... Do you think it is too late to save them?..."

She turned to me and I nodded my confirmation. I had no wish to become a Roman Catholic now but she ignored this and turned back to her prayers.

"...Dear Mary, Mother of God... please hear my prayer. You kindly stepped in to save my lovely Bag Puss..."

Immediately the sun reappeared through the window and lit up the tabernacle in front of us. I suddenly remembered the way the sun shone across Simon's naked body in the farmhouse kitchen fifty years ago. Now an old man was being blessed with one last glorious epiphany. But Natalie closed her eyes together tightly and pressed her hands together.

"Dear Mary, Mother of God, please intercede once again to help strengthen the blood cells in Uncle Simon's transfusion today. I don't really understand what genetic engineering is but I am sure it is a good thing if God has allowed the Americans to develop it... to treat poor patients in the Oncology Ward...like Uncle Simon, even if he is an old sinner like my daddy. But I love him too, just like my Bag Puss. We have lit this candle to invite your blessing..."

She thought for a moment.

"...Well, I can't remember exactly what it is for because Daddy's sexy boyfriend, Guy, is still teaching me about the Catholic faith... But I hope you like it, anyway... Amen."

We got up slowly and she led me outside by the hand. One more old sinner had been blessed in the chapel today.

It was just a few weeks later when I walked into Simon's private room in the Oncology Ward and was astounded to find him sitting out in the chair once again. A shaft of sunlight from the window lit up his face. Here was a beautiful sight. He turned towards me.

"Hello, where have you put Aloysius, my teddy bear? I can't find it."

"I gave him to Natalie, Bobbie's daughter... Well I thought you'd finished with him now."

I sat down on the side of the bed. The drip, the heart monitor and the oxygen cylinder had all been taken away. There were fresh flowers on the table.

"You might have shut the door!"

I turned to look behind me and sure enough, in my surprise at seeing Simon again, I had forgotten to close it. But before I could reach out to grab hold of the doorknob, Simon got up out of his chair and went to look in the hallway. I just could not believe my eyes. Only a few weeks ago we'd all been drawing up plans for his funeral in the private chapel. In the corridor outside he met the cleaning lady mopping the floor with her disinfectant.

"Good Lord!" she muttered, staring at him. "You must be feeling better today, mate. We thought you was a goner! ...A miracle of modern science I calls it! ...God bless America!"

She shouted to her colleague down the hallway and Simon shut the door to sit down beside me quietly again. I put my hands on his.

"She's right, you know," I insisted. "Natalie said a special prayer for you in her father's chapel. I think the Virgin Mary was listening."

"I'm sure that's more than I deserve. I thought you'd given up religion."

"Well sometimes I get things wrong…"

We stared at each other, just like that very first day in the kitchen fifty years ago. Simon's eyes, which had been so dull and lifeless only a few weeks before, were now shining brightly once again.

"…Madame Claire Voyante was right, you know. She told me that you and I were blessed."

"So how about it, you old softie. Is our Civil Partnership still on?"

"If you will still have me."

"Well, if you don't know the answer to that after all these years…"

I laughed. Somehow Simon hadn't changed.

"…Natalie insists on being our bridesmaid," he said. "She came to tell me about my brother's Civil Partnership with Dominic. So they're married now. But why could you all not have waited for me a bit longer?"

At this point I burst into tears. Simon put his arm around my shoulder.

"Dominic just couldn't wait," I sobbed. "Nobody thought you'd still be here today. Now Natalie insists she will carry your bouquet down the aisle behind your wheelchair in the registry office. She's good at things like that."

"Who said anything about a wheelchair…?"

Simon got up from his seat again and looked back at me over his shoulder just as he used to in the old days. After being ill so long he'd lost weight and regained his youthful profile.

"…Well? Do you think I will need a wheelchair?"

"No… Do you remember what Celia Johnson's husband said to her at the end of 'Brief Encounter'?"

"Yes, he said: 'Thank you for coming back to me'. "

"Well, Simon, now I know exactly what he meant."

"But in the cinema all those years ago you just burst out laughing… We had to leave the cinema early by the side door. You must be going soft in your old age."

"Now I know I cannot live without you after fifty years.

Listen, I forgot to cancel our Civil Partnership at the registry office."

"When is it?"

"Next week. Could you manage that?"

"You try and stop me. I've already invited the ward sister, the professor of Oncology and this dishy male nurse…"

A beautiful young man in a uniform came in, pushing the trolley with all the patients' medication for the whole Oncology Ward.

"…You've never been introduced properly, have you? This is my partner of the last fifty years – since 1957…"

I'd met him several times when Simon seemed to be unconscious but we shook hands.

"…John is gay too, that's right, isn't it? I invited his partner as well because they haven't been to a Civil Partnership yet."

I smiled at the pretty young man and he pushed his trolley outside into the corridor once again.

••••••••

So our big day arrived. True to his word, Simon was determined to walk down the aisle beside me without a wheelchair. We arrived at the registry office in Bobbie's chauffeur–driven white Rolls Royce. Guy had brought his portable keyboard to play songs from Will Young's first CD and was playing it as we walked inside where the registrar was waiting.

Now, fifty years after the Wolfenden Report was published in 1957, the relationship between Simon and myself was about to be registered with the blessing of Her Majesty's Government and the local council. Only the Church of England was missing. I smiled. Maybe Simon's father, His Lordship, was looking down on us disapprovingly from his stately cloud up in Heaven today.

But, perhaps, thanks to Natalie and her prayers to the Virgin Mary in the baroque private chapel, the Roman Catholic Church was really responsible for our joy today and not His Lordship's stuffy Church of England. On this occasion, Bobbie acted as my witness to sign the book with me, and Guy left his keyboard to act as a witness for Simon.

The registrar had suggested that we might choose a short text to be read at the front, so Bobbie read from one of Shakespeare's sonnets I had selected. But I was quite unprepared for the reading Harry got up to read. He looked around our guests in the registry office, cleared his throat and unfolded his reading glasses:

"My brother wrote two versions of this piece – one to be read at a funeral and one at a wedding. I am delighted to be able to read you the second version. It is headed 'To my most civil partner'... My brother adds here that he hopes everyone has already seen 'Four Weddings and a Funeral' on the TV. So here it is:

"'Never stop all the clocks! They are chiming the happy hours I can still spend with you. If you thought I might have lost my way, relax. You really are my beautiful South, my North, my East, my West, and you always will be.'"

He turned to me and smiled. I heard someone say: "Isn't that nice?"

Then Harry carried on:

"'So, where might I have gone, if I'd gone over... to the other side?... Would I have flown up to Heaven? I don't think so. That's where His Lordship, my blessed father, must have gone to spend eternity with the great and the good. For he was both of those, even though, alas, I cannot say I ever knew him well.

"'So, would I have gone 'down there' with our fortune–teller Madame Claire Voyante, Oliver Cromwell and all the other old sinners?... I might also have met that snooty spokeswoman from British Railways who told Madame it was impossible to predict railway disasters in 1957. Madame took great pride in telling her where to go!'"

There were one or two titters around the room. Somebody muttered, "Come back British Railways – after Hatfield and Potters Bar, all is forgiven!"

I laughed. Harry waited a moment and then carried on reading again:

"'Well, I still do not know where I might have gone, because I am still standing here with you today.'"

Someone at the back started crying but Harry carried on:

'When we next watch 'The Wizard of Oz', 'Brief Encounter' or 'A Night to Remember' on TV, we will remember how we watched them first, fifty years ago. For it is fifty years that you and I have been together – and a most civil partnership it turned out to be! ...I will still be there to watch those old movies again with you… plus all the repeats of the repeats of the other old TV programmes we have watched so many times before…'"

Harry looked around the room while disgruntled viewers laughed. There were one or two claps and someone muttered, "Hear, hear!"

"'…we have watched so many times over the years – first in black and white on a tiny 17–inch screen, then in colour and now six feet wide with stereophonic sound. Well, I'll still be sitting down beside you to hold your hand in the dark, just like we used to do at 'The Regal' fifty years ago. We might even watch 'Four Weddings and a Funeral' and shed a tear or two…'"

Harry looked over his reading glasses while several people sighed.

" '…But I want you to remember me in my prime, fifty years ago, sitting naked in your arms…'"

Now there were one or two titters and a gasp. "'…Think of me standing naked by your bed with early morning breakfast back in 1957, so excited because you have just smiled lovingly at me…'"

Harry smiled and looked over his glasses when someone at the back muttered, "Ah, bless! How sweet."

He cleared his throat and continued: " '…Never think of me leaving Windermere Station in tears to return to the University of London, before your wife got back.'"

Somewhere somebody muttered "Naughty, naughty!" but Harry carried on:

" '… Instead, remember me as I was, waiting for your old Land Rover to take me back home to the farm to stay with you for the rest of my life. For then, and only then, was I ever really happy.'"

Like several people in the room, I was fumbling for a handkerchief to dry my eyes. Even Harry's voice sounded emotional. He cleared his throat.

" '…Remember, us together discovered flagrante delicto on New Year's Eve, yes, that memorable night… when my mother, Her Ladyship (God bless her!) walked in and …she got an eyeful…'"

Harry seemed to be about to break into hysterics but he stared at the page in front while the gasps around me subsided.

"'…Yes, an eyeful of… all your many and… varied… naked charms…!'"

Now he had to stop until several people stopped giggling. Somebody at the back was still spluttering into a handkerchief. I just could not believe what we were listening to. How different from my dreary marriage ceremony to Elspeth so many years ago! Harry looked down through his lenses at his brother's notes once again while several of our friends smiled at me.

"'…I told Her Ladyship straight. I said I never thought anyone as beautiful as you would ever love me… for fifty years! That's almost a lifetime!'"

Now he smiled and looked at us over his glasses when someone at the side suggested: "Hallelujah!… Simon, that's longer than my all my three straight marriages put together!"

"'…So… let's give three cheers to Tony Blair, New Labour and the Civil Partnership legislation which made this day possible… in spite of what my father, His Lordship, might have had to say about it in the House of Lords! 'The Tower's too good for them', probably… Well, something like that, anyway.'"

The registrar was amazed when Dominic stood up, put his hand in the air and shouted "Hip, hip, hurrah!" Everyone joined in and the stately occasion was interrupted by guffaws all around. Finally, Simon and I exchanged rings and in front of everybody we kissed, without fear of persecution, freely and publicly. British legal history had been made. As somebody said on the TV recently, radical English legislation seldom brings happiness into the world. So I swore then and there to forgive Her Majesty's Government for the wars in Afghanistan and Iraq because they had made two old men so happy on this day. All too quickly our ceremony ended and we went outside for digital photos around the white Rolls, which would drive us back to join the motorway. Guy's mother had prepared a special luncheon for us in the Grand Dining Hall. But a few miles up the M1 all the traffic came to a standstill. We should have taken the side roads. The chauffeur phoned up the traffic control centre on his mobile and slid the glass window behind him aside to talk to us.

"The carriageway is closed. A lorry has jack–knifed. We must wait for the heavy lifting gear to clear it. I'm sorry, we'll just have to wait."

Madame Claire Voyante had been right about this as well. The M1 motorway had been cursed right from the start. So Simon and I sat in the luxury of Bobbie's tax–deductible Rolls Royce and reminisced about the past as old men like to do. We arrived very late for our ceremonial luncheon.

"Where did you get to, Grandpa?" Natalie asked, standing on the stone steps at the front of the house and holding the toy Spider–Man her father had given her for her birthday. "We came by the scenic route."

Beside me, Harry was helping his brother up the steps to the door while Bobbie took hold of the bouquets.

"Traffic congestion," I explained. "There are just too many cars on the motorway these days."

"Well, Guy's mum says lunch has gone cold. She'll have to reheat yours in the microwave…"

I passed Aloysius to her from the back of the car.

"…Does Aloysius want some dinner too, Grandpa? He can sit and eat cold boeuf bourguignon with my Spider–Man and Bag Puss, can't he?"

Guy climbed down the steps, swept up his boyfriend's daughter in his arms and the four of us, clutching the teddy bear and the Spider–Man, followed the butler to find the others once again.

THE END

THE END